revival

revival

AN ANTHOLOGY OF BLACK CANADIAN WRITING

edited by
DONNA BAILEY NURSE

McCLELLAND & STEWART

Library and Archives Canada Cataloguing in Publication

Revival : an anthology of Black Canadian writing /
Donna Bailey Nurse, editor.

ISBN 13: 978-0-7710-6763-1
ISBN 10: 0-7710-6763-1

1. Canadian literature (English) – Black-Canadian authors. 2. Canadian literature (English) – 20th century. 3. Canadian literature (English) – 21st century.
I. Bailey Nurse, Donna, 1961-

PS8235.B53R49 2006 C810.8'0896071 C2005-906884-1

We acknowledge the financial support of the Government of Canada through the Book Publishing Industry Development Program and that of the Government of Ontario through the Ontario Media Development Corporation's Ontario Book Initiative. We further acknowledge the support of the Canada Council for the Arts and the Ontario Arts Council for our publishing program.

The acknowledgements on pages 380-385 constitute an extension of this copyright page.

Typeset in Bembo by M&S, Toronto
Printed and bound in Canada

This book is printed on acid-free paper that is 100% recycled, ancient-forest friendly (100% post-consumer recycled).

McClelland & Stewart Ltd.
75 Sherbourne Street
Toronto, Ontario
M5A 2P9
www.mcclelland.com

1 2 3 4 5 10 09 08 07 06

For the bookshelves of my children, Alex and Noëlle
And for my mother, Sylvia Bailey

Contents

Introduction

I grew up on the elbow of land between Lake Ontario and Frenchman's Bay, surrounded by Pickering's towering blue spruce and pungent wetlands. We played in fields of ruined farmhouses during summers as green and perpetual as the Caribbean Sea. In winter, the sky was white and still, like the land itself. The schoolyard was a snowy desert, and bundled thick as snowmen, my sister and I sank through to our knees. At home, Miss Iris, our Jamaican grandma, fixed us Ovaltine, then sat with her sisters in the back room, mending clothes and talking "big people business," while a pot of pigs' tail sputtered on the stove. I curled up on the sofa with Lucy Maud and Laura Ingalls and wondered, What did Katy do? But outside, brown skin was harder to negotiate than snowdrifts. You had to play dumb. A little girl asked: "Are you a ghost?" But she was the one who was white. I was a little girl too, but I knew that much. Skin colour was no big deal, until suddenly, without warning, it was. The ambush comment or question, the backhanded compliment, the acts of emotional violence meant to remind me of what I was not, which was not white and not from here. They were right and wrong. I'm not white but I am from here. Black and Canadian: equal parts race and place.

Literature has been the means through which I have learned to understand who I am and who I might be – as a human being, as a woman, and as a person of African descent. Over the years, my experience reading, studying, and writing about black Canadian letters, most recently as a literary critic, has served to reaffirm my identity as a Canadian. I became a critic of black Canadian literature largely because I wanted to engage others in a dialogue about black writing in this country, and it was important to me that the dialogue be led by somebody who was black. This literature is at the forefront of public and artistic spaces grappling with what it means to be of this race and of this place, and as such, it represents a crucial voice in the necessary conversation about the black experience in Canada.

Revival constitutes a conversation about the relevance of black Canadian writing like no other, and celebrates the coming of age of a black Canadian literature. It builds proudly upon previous anthologies that confirmed the existence of a growing body of black Canadian writing, including Lorris Elliott's *Other Voices: Writings by Blacks in Canada* (1985), Cyril Dabydeen's *A Shapely Fire: Changing the Literary Landscape* (1987), Ayanna Black's *Voices: Canadian Writers of African Descent* (1992), and George Elliott Clarke's *Eyeing the North Star: Directions in African-Canadian Literature* (1997).

Eyeing the North Star marked a pivotal moment in the development of a black Canadian literature. It reaffirmed the importance of such established figures as Austin Clarke, M. NourbeSe Philip, and Claire Harris, while showcasing newer voices, including Lawrence Hill, André Alexis, and David N. Odhiambo. In his introduction, George Elliott Clarke addressed the characteristics of a black Canadian aesthetic; he defined it as "international" in its "concern for African people everywhere," in its "solidarity with third world peoples," and in its "utilization of a diverse range of rhetorical styles." Agreeing with writer Liz Cromwell, Clarke describes the literature as concerned with a history of forced relocation, coerced labour, and the struggle against discrimination.

The publication of Clarke's anthology in 1997 was also significant for its timing and as an indication of the growing interest in black Canadian writing. Beginning in the mid-nineties, the literature began to accumulate critical mass. The ensuing decade would see the publication of award-winning works of fiction (including André Alexis's *Childhood*, Austin Clarke's *The Polished Hoe*, and Nalo Hopkinson's *Brown Girl in the Ring*), memoir (Rachel Manley's *Drumblair* and Ken Wiwa's *In the Shadow of a Saint*); drama (Djanet Sears's *Harlem Duet*), and poetry (Dionne Brand's *Land to Light On*).

Black Canadian writing has come of age over the last decade, and the time now seems right for a reconsideration of this increasingly influential literature. With twenty-nine contributors and over fifty pieces drawn from works of fiction, poetry, and memoir, *Revival* provides a varied overview of contemporary black Canadian literature. Previous anthologies have confirmed the diversity of black Canada's literary voices, and *Revival* acknowledges this multiplicity, with contributors originally from Africa and the Caribbean, as well as several born in Canada.

The astonishing gifts of the newer voices in the anthology merit extra mention. Poets Wayde Compton and Shane Book and novelists Esi Edugyan and Kim Barry Brunhuber assimilate and alchemize a wealth of literary influences to produce original and distinct individual styles. In addition, *Revival* is the first Canadian anthology to feature Okey Chigbo, whose work has appeared in Chinua Achebe and Lynn Innes's influential *Contemporary African Short Stories*.

For me, the seeds of contemporary black Canadian literature were sown in the mid-sixties with the novels of Austin Clarke. Clarke's early success had partly to do with the time and place in which he launched his career. Beginning in the mid-fifties, when Clarke arrived in Canada to attend the University of Toronto, the Canadian government began opening the doors to Caribbean immigrants through student visas and through programs such as the Caribbean Domestic Scheme, which saw thousands of women enter the country to work as nannies and maids. At the same time, the civil rights movement in the United States, with its attendant turmoil, attuned

Canadians to issues of race and racism. Just as important was Toronto's burgeoning creative scene. Clarke belonged to a number of artistic circles, among them a group of Toronto writers that included Barry Callaghan and Margaret Atwood, who were nurturing a vision of a homegrown literature. The proximity of major publishing houses also meant he had access to people who might publish his work.

Austin Clarke's early novels – *The Survivors of the Crossing* (1964), *Amongst Thistles and Thorns* (1965), and the three books that comprise his Toronto Trilogy, *The Meeting Point* (1967), *Storm of Fortune* (1973), and *The Bigger Light* (1975) – described the condition of the West Indian at home and in Canada, and in so doing brought colonialism and post-colonialism into the larger Canadian literary context. Through such characters as Rufus, the poor plantation worker in *The Survivors of the Crossing*, and Milton, the child of a black washerwoman in *Amongst Thistles and Thorns*, Clarke delineates the rigid, colour-coded class system fostered by the Caribbean's colonial culture. The obstacles these characters face are not just social and economic, but also psychological. Indoctrinated by church and school and life to revere the colonizer's customs and white skin, they are encouraged to view their own darkness – their African heritage – with suspicion and disdain. Clarke's characters immigrate to Canada in search of new opportunities, but once they arrive, they confront a lack of acceptance, economic exploitation, and cultural dislocation.

A number of other black Canadian writers, among them Althea Prince, H. Nigel Thomas, and Olive Senior, have perused the tensions of the colonial context. In Senior's "Do Angels Wear Brassieres?" for instance, the anxiety produces a comic air of insecurity and self-doubt. In the story, a young girl's relatives are undone by her irreverent comments to the visiting archdeacon. Much more disturbing is the way in which some characters inherit and pass down the colonizer's brutal power structures. In H. Nigel Thomas's "How Loud Can the Village Cock Crow?" the cruelty of slavery is re-enacted by Ataviso, the abusive patriarch of a poor family. As the narrator's father explains: "Ataviso comes from a people who treat their children exactly the way white people used to treat their slaves." Okey Chigbo's story, "The Housegirl," in which the mistress of a Nigerian household misuses her young servants, offers a variation on the same theme.

Some black characters are so enamoured with the idea of "foreign" (i.e. Canada) or "the motherland" that they perceive this other place as the only one capable of facilitating their aspirations. As a result, the land they inhabit fades around them. In Makeda Silvera's *The Heart Does Not Bend*, the entire Galloway family eventually emigrates from Jamaica to Canada, leaving behind their beloved, hard-earned property. Likewise, the protagonist of Althea Prince's *Loving This Man* excitedly departs Antigua for Toronto, with the most nebulous dreams of "bettering herself."

This ongoing concern with the immigrant story, a story that remains central to the larger Canadian narrative, makes this body of writing a quintessentially Canadian literature. But if, as British novelist Caryl Phillips has said, home is where you feel welcome, it is the absence of welcome that often characterizes the experiences of black immigrants in Canada. The lack of welcome is frequently expressed by the lack of opportunity. In David N. Odhiambo's *Kipligat's Chance*, John's well-educated Kenyan parents cannot find suitable work. His mother, a teacher, settles for a position nursing a disabled child, while his father gives up on finding work altogether. Novels like Althea Prince's *Loving This Man* describe how awareness of racial differences is constantly thrust upon black immigrants. Sayshelle complains of the baleful stares she and her friends endure as they ride public transit. Racial hostility is the main reason Sayshelle never adjusts to life in Toronto. She feels her life has been "divided into two halves: 'before I left Antigua' and 'after I came to Toronto.'" Says Sayshelle: "No love, no hatred . . . nothing could fill the space that leaving Antigua had made . . . nothing."

In W.E.B. Du Bois's *The Souls of Black Folks*, the eminent African American thinker conceives of "double consciousness" as the paradox at the heart of black American experience:

> One ever feels his twoness – an American, a Negro; two souls, two thoughts, two unreconciled strivings; two warring ideals in one dark body, whose dogged strength alone keeps it from being torn asunder.

In *The Black Atlantic: Modernity and Double Consciousness,* British cultural critic Paul Gilroy incorporates elements of Du Bois's philosophy to develop his theory of Black Atlantic identity. The Black Atlantic comprises the nations and territories involved in the Atlantic slave trade and later in black immigration routes, primarily Britain, Africa, the Caribbean, and the United States. As the slave ships travelled back and forth across the Atlantic, Gilroy argues that the exchange of cultural influences culminated in a hybrid culture characterized by an "in-between" identity that transcends national borders and fixed ideas about identity.

Black Canadians are likewise sometimes said to occupy an in-between space in that they are from neither here nor there, and belong fully to neither this nor that culture. But in fact, black Canadians are both this *and* that: two things (at least) at once. To be black and Canadian is to engage in the ongoing interaction between primarily African and European elements. In the poetry of Wayde Compton, this interaction manifests itself in the urge to integrate two peoples and two histories, whereas in the work of Lawrence Hill it prompts an inquiry into the nature of racial identification. The relative ease with which the two cultures commingle within an individual can be influenced by his or her response to such external societal forces as racism. This tension finds a metaphoric equivalent in the dilemma faced by mixed race individuals, as articulated in a passage from Kim Barry Brunhuber's *Kameleon Man*, in which Stacey Schmidt, the mixed race protagonist, describes the imperative to identify with either one race or the other:

> There was no black or white in my world until that day at camp when David Wiener asked me why I looked like poo. Since then I've realized the world isn't shot in colour film, where everyone's a different hue. It's shot in black-and-white. There are only different degrees of one or the other. We're black, or we're white. Or, like me, we're shades. Insubstantial images of something real. Reduced almost to nothing. The only thing worse than living in that black-and-white world is living in a grey one, in which race doesn't matter except to everyone else. In which nothing's black or white, and everything's both. The problem with living in grey is that one grows no natural defences. Growing up grey is like growing up weightless on the moon. To return to earth is to be crushed by the weight of one's own skin.

In black Canadian writing, mixed race identity can operate as a metaphor for the larger black Canadian experience. Just as Kim Barry Brunhuber's hero attempts to wrest a black identity from a Canadian landscape, the black protagonists in George Elliott Clarke's *George & Rue* likewise endeavour to fashion meaningful lives as black men in rural Nova Scotia. Clarke goes so far as to craft a language that might encapsulate his characters' dual experiences of blackness and Canadianness.

In addition to the thematic significance of mixed race, the world of black Canadian letters includes many writers of mixed descent, such as Shane Book, Kim Barry Brunhuber, Honor Ford-Smith, Suzette Mayr, Wayde Compton, and Lawrence Hill, among others.

Interracial relationships are as prevalent in the work of black writers as they are in black life. Marriages between black women and white men occur in Suzette Mayr's *The Widows* and Lorna Goodison's

From Harvey River, while relationships between black men and white women appear in Lawrence Hill's *Any Known Blood* and Dany Laferrière's *How to Make Love to a Negro.* Black Canadian writing is one of the few literatures prepared to engage in a sophisticated discussion about interracial relationships, and whether or not such relationships are an expression or a disavowal of the significance of race.

Interracial relationships, like mixed race identity, also operate on a metaphoric level. In Brunhuber's *Kameleon Man*, for example, Stacey's on-again, off-again affair with his white girlfriend may be seen to symbolize the bewildering combination of intimacy and alienation that frequently characterizes interracial relations in Canada.

Paul Gilroy characterizes the hybrid culture of the Black Atlantic as one that transcends fixed notions of identity and national borders. As a hybrid literature, black Canadian writing fits into the Black Atlantic model, except that very few black Canadian writers wish to transcend borders. Rather, they use their dual consciousness to explore the limits and the possibilities of multicultural citizenship, a hallmark of Canadian life. Black Canadian literature ponders exactly who is enjoying the benefits and opportunities of full citizenship, as well as the extent to which black Canadians and other Canadians of colour are perceived as full citizens. But just as significant, the literature investigates and reveals the aspirations of those of us who would like multiculturalism to succeed. In so doing, it both questions and affirms what it means to be Canadian.

The story of the Underground Railroad is one of the few black stories incorporated into Canadian history, and yet slavery itself has thus far not been a major theme in black Canadian writing. The literature does have a handful of slave narratives, most famously Josiah Henson's life story, which inspired Harriet Beecher Stowe's *Uncle Tom's Cabin*. For the most part, slavery in contemporary black Canadian literature has occupied corners or operated as backdrop. George Elliott Clarke's libretto for *Beatrice Chancy* is one of the few works to devote full space to the topic. This is in sharp contrast to

African-American literature, where books about slavery practically constitute a separate genre, one that includes such lasting works as Toni Morrison's *Beloved*, Charles Johnson's *Middle Passage,* and Edward P. Jones's *The Known World*. The peculiar absence of the "peculiar institution" may stem from black Canadian literature's colonial context. The story of slavery has been repressed in Canada as well as in the Caribbean, where British colonizers have long obscured it behind a history of half-truths.

Where the subject of slavery, along with that of conquest, has had a presence in black Canadian writing is in its poetry – exquisite artillery in the battle to decolonize the mind, a distinguishing feature of post-colonial literatures. Accepted myths come under attack and occasionally so does the reader. In "Christopher Columbus," Afua Cooper questions our compliance with the colonizer's nefarious account, while Olive Senior looks forward to the end of five hundred years of servitude in "Meditation on Yellow." A number of the poets appropriate and interrogate well-known figures and literary works, adapting them to their own purposes. In "To Poitier," Wayde Compton reconsiders the significance of the iconic actor from the perspective of a black man. In "Thirteen Ways of Looking at Blackbird," Olive Senior borrows Wallace Stevens's imagistic phrasing to distill the bleak essence of the passage to slavery. In M. NourbeSe Philip's "Meditations on the Declension of Beauty by the Girl with the Flying Cheek-bones," Philip worries the oppressor's language – aggravates and teases it – until it reluctantly releases her. For Philip, language is a prison from which she struggles to get free, whereas for dub poets like Jemeni and Motion, language constitutes a bold challenge to the status quo.

Women writers are strongly represented in the anthology. A number of the contributors, including Afua Cooper, Honor Ford-Smith, Pamela Mordecai, Althea Prince, and Makeda Silvera, were first published by Sister Vision Press, a small publishing house founded in 1985 by Silvera and Stephanie Martin that has done much to encourage Canada's women writers of colour. Black women's writing offers a perspective unusual in Canadian literature: it highlights the point at which sexism and racism intersect and at the same time draws parallels between these two forms of discrimination. This is brilliantly and succinctly communicated in M. NourbeSe Philip's poem "The Catechist," which features a young woman preparing to enter an adult world shaped by men, white people, and the Christian church. In "Girl," Motion subtly alludes to the racial impediments that inevitably come between black girls and their white friends.

In many examples of black women's writing, women are frequently without male protection, and danger lurks everywhere. Pamela Mordecai's unequivocal "Convent Girl" tells of a young woman who is raped by a group of men who are threatened by her confidence. The excerpt from Nalo Hopkinson's *Midnight Robber* vividly conveys the alien world of a girl emotionally abandoned by her father. The effects of male absence and abandonment is sometimes eased by the presence of strong maternal figures who act as fonts of love and guidance. Afua Cooper's "Memories Have Tongue" honours her grandmother and also the act of remembering, just as Molly's story in Makeda Silvera's *The Heart Does Not Bend* is a tribute to the spirit of her wise and difficult grandmother. In Althea Prince's *Loving This Man*, it is the black literature, recipes, and superstitions passed along by Aunt Helen that help Sayshelle survive an uneasy existence in Toronto.

In spite of the reality of sexism and racism, the poems and stories of black Canadian women are overwhelmingly sensuous, celebratory, and illuminating. Claire Harris's poem "Travelling to Find a Remedy" is a delicious expression of a romantic love that cannot be made to serve antiquated patriarchal customs. M. NourbeSe Philip's erotic "Cashew #4" compares the sexual maturation of young women with the seductive ripening of a cashew nut. Among other things, the writings of women of African descent, both in Canada and elsewhere, articulate a vision for how to love oneself and foregrounds the need to have respect for your history – for the people and place you come from. For Lorna Goodison, Harvey River, the Jamaican village founded by her great-grandfather, becomes a source of self-knowledge and inspiration, just as Rachel Manley's family homes, Drumblair and Nomdmi, come to embody and represent the character of her grandparents' lives.

Black women's writing also testifies to the power of art – especially the making of art – to enable female characters not only to survive, but to thrive. Pamela Mordecai's "Poems Grow" catalogues the unlikely spaces and situations from which creativity can bloom. The mother in Honor Ford-Smith's memoir, *My Mother's Last Dance*, refuses to die until her daughter accepts the legacy of her creative history. The story concludes like this: "And I am crossing the Rio Nuevo swinging bridge alone, heavy with my bag of poems, my medical words, my colours, my scraps and herbs and the songs of the revival women to sing me home."

Since Olaudah Equiano became the first slave to publish his life story in 1789, which chronicled his kidnapping in Africa and his bondage in Carolina and beyond, autobiography has held a position of honour in the literatures of the African diaspora. Its importance is rooted in the ability to assert the freedom and the power to tell your own story in your own voice, which remains a central concern for black writers. In the eighteenth and nineteenth centuries, these autobiographical narratives were largely African-American "up from slavery" accounts. Like their forebears, contemporary black memoirists continue to weave together an intricate tapestry of social, historical, and political struggle to convey their personal histories. In Ken Wiwa's *In the Shadow of a Saint*, his memoir of coming to terms with the legacy of his father, famed Nigerian writer and political activist Ken Saro-Wiwa, the personal and political are inextricably linked. Likewise, Rachel Manley's *Drumblair* is an intimate account of her own childhood in Jamaica, set against the rise of her family's political dynasty. In Lorna Goodison's *From Harvey River*, scheduled for publication by McClelland & Stewart in early 2007, she writes, "over time I have come to see that my parents' story is really a story about rising up to a new life."

An anthology can serve only as an introduction to a literature, and *Revival* is no exception. I had originally planned to include drama, criticism, and race writing, but space was an issue. Instead I have included a suggested reading list and hope readers will be moved to use it as a starting point to deepen their familiarity with the breadth and richness of black Canadian literature.

There are writers I would have liked to include in the anthology but could not for reasons of space, budget, and permissions. I regret the absence of Austin Clarke. There are many equally talented writers in *Revival* whose work deserves recognition, and I hope this anthology will reveal the true wealth of black talent that exists in this country.

Revival is a celebration of the vibrant, vigorous, and flourishing literature that is black Canadian writing. It contains works of startling power, works I consider classics, and works that will become classics in the years to come. It is bound to invigorate, enrich, and make bolder the discussion of black Canadian literature and black Canadian culture – and it brings us all a little closer to what it means to be Canadian.

Donna Bailey Nurse
Toronto
November 2005

revival

CLAIRE HARRIS

UNTITLED

in the prairie dawn
a pheasant calls to its mate
love   go hide   go hide

TRAVELLING TO FIND A REMEDY

I cannot be sure

        perhaps it was your stillness
perhaps the directness of your touch   I cannot
even remember whether we talked   only that it
seemed   common sense
the night dark and airless   the field wet
the hostel windows blank yellow squares
still the next morning I came awake
thinking of you
how your shadow breached my wall   reached
for roof and stars   how the room was torn
but there were no stars   only globes
of light strung two by two across the campus

I cannot be sure
        I   remember hovering

You offered me
a gift
wrapped in red
and hooped with gold
with reverence I
unfold the paper
boxes
ancient   inlaid
with bronze
each one
prisoned in the other
magic boxes
growing
smaller and smaller

We have loved when the moon washed our bodies of
darkness to glow in each secret place   we have loved

in sunlight sharp as a sword   the wheels of our
car sang like the wings of humming-birds feeding

we have loved in the late afternoon even in the market
place   though your eyes were red with the dust of

evening and the smell of rotten beef clogged my throat
why then did we unravel the snare of safety to slip

from glittering encounter to the moment of contract
is it because we did not think to encounter ourselves

violent
unabashed

The car is blue   very cool in the heat   and sterile
burnished black you lean back against cushions
take my hand and say   "well . . ."
eyes straight ahead negotiating the contract   careful
there should be no misunderstanding
you say slowly
      "you must bear me a son"
sudden thunder   Orisa* three hundred years later
chuckling
I say nothing
drawn by my silence   "you have a choice
few women do"
Rain spilling over the hood   streaming down
the windshield   seen through sealed windows Lagos
under water   distorted   a face
pressed against the window tapping   holding up
newspapers under tarpaulin
you shake your head   "remember it's different here"
rain searching its way   nosing a path down fine
blue upholstery
      "then I can take care of you"
a glance like mirror lenses on dark glasses
"we can be married quite quickly   but first . . ."
the grip on my hand tightens
I translate
lightning shocking the gloom   rain trickling
beneath my feet circles into a puddle
I ask   I say the unimaginable
"And if there is no child . . ."
Silence roars with the waves of the Middle
Passage crashing on African shores

---

* minor gods

How can I taste the difference between you
what you are
and what I have invested you with
and this is not to deny
your particular brand
of beauty
but this burden of glory
I have laid on you
you must lay down
I know   inevitably the glow of party
light fades   in the harsh sunlight
water lilies flower from
dark leaves in murky pools

There must be a parting

    I cannot stand on the edge
of your life   giving way to club and custom
forever oyibo*
so I give you back   your heart   your piece of
mind   your safe ritualized living
I had thought to jeer at history
that here knowing what it meant I could throw
my heart across alien centuries
and slavery   to follow safely

but I dream in another tongue
I cannot

Still your absence thins the surface of things
when you said "I love you"
I thought to infest your days
to swarm in your mind like bees in cloud
and you could rejoice in the colour of my murmuring

There are advantages
    to your ebon calm
your reason   but I was not born to it

---

* foreigner (Yoruba)

dim moroccan day
sahara sand swaddles the sun
still leaf tips gleam

TOWARDS THE COLOUR OF SUMMER

That is the colour of hunger
sliding off gull wings
hanging from nothing
before it slips
into ocean   drowns
in excess
the colour of exploration
of search
sometimes frantic
sometimes lazy   drifting
dark
it hides behind faces
conceives
old age   winter
light
it surfaces in dreams
stranger stories
deep laughter
not the colour of rivers
or stones   perhaps
the colour of caves
or wombs
in deed   of   future
immanent   blurred

Before a clear summer afternoon we wait
where tarmac wavers in unusual heat

through portholes far off Calgary drifting
into sky   I close dark eyes against this plane

its subterranean rustle   the ebb and flow
of excitement   where atavistic fear pools

feathers and melting wax become sheared trees
the fateful earth leaping upwards   curious

I wait for the engines' sensual crescendo
for power to enter and lift   Far away

in my shuttered house everything dims
its breathing   books   ferns   drapes close

to their long communion   I go out as one
would who gathers in handfuls summer's early

peas intending to pore over them in a winter
kitchen   to remember then their first flush

and sweet green   Engines roar   surge   a minute
darkness   clouds   we watch the toy city slip away

I become blue   meaning by this a measure
of release   what I imagine the soul feels

as it escapes drained bone   or pained
medieval angels suspect who long to escape

strictures wooden wings/simple plane/gold leaf
into rosy form   and the fair loose-draped airy

ease the renaissance frames (those angels
whose skins would run blue-black eyes slant

whose dusky pink soles would flash   and deep palms
lifted to sky draw the moon   are framed

in some distant future grace) blue as in
the tail feathers of tropical birds I knew

as a child or heart petals seen in tall shade trees
on long july roamings among the cocoa   bird/orchid

too far above ground for traps   in such blue
I float suspended   disguised in my favourite self

which blooms from my mouth unexpectedly
in the narrow formal ease that is the people's airline

KAY IN SUMMER

Someone waiting in the lobby of a Hotel Imperial amid
    the spaciousness tourists and peeling gold leaf
    might see it all as too hesitant for truth
Might think for a moment   about the art in scattering
    too solidly carved tables   crowding too many dreams
    before dim Victorian sofas
Might remember certain high-backed chairs or a woman
    that could lend a touch of veracity to this place
From this might wonder if truth is possible   if always
    and everywhere there is the notion   stage
    as true of a bed as of a lobby

Imagine now Kay   as she steps through glass doors   and
    someone who glancing up   sees her suggest everything
    is possible   no   is probable in this place
Someone who can tell from the easy music of her walk
    how decades and sophistication have slipped from her
    without a rustle
How she has stepped into these brighter softer eyes
    into this clear joyous laughter   with out memory
Such a man now iron-grey and ramrod may welcome years

hovering about her bare feet   scent of prairies
songs of experience and struggle
May insist only on allegory: glitter and glass slippers
smile on a killer toy

From the roof garden   opposite our old old man ungentle
in this summer night gestures furiously   slashes
at his wheelchair   a daughter burdened with wet sheets
hurries to hang them
Then kneels before the old one to rub his hands between
her own until he smiles
I turn away from this worrying its meaning   its small
beauties   tiny hungers and comforts   how like
an electric charge the attentions of One

They step together into the leafy romantic air   and
Las Ramblas   Kay jaunty as hell   her summer affairs
the slow burning flame that makes autumn bearable
That perfumes her air as she moves towards the grave
its slow   inexorable stages
Jane flat in her deck chair calls to me . . . she didn't
come to Barcelona for love   love is hard   one wants
something softer   only a little pain   a little grace
and limited fallout . . .

On our last evening I search for the world that is resolution
to her story but she dances down stone streets
shimmies in tavernas spins in the dim light
and that spurious lobby
Perhaps more allegory perhaps someone watching closely
will see her catch her lower lip between bruising teeth
on the stroke of midnight

Now high above the city we stand on that terrace
    I am saying   Look look where we are   the rotting stone
    the ragged haze from a thousand years of intention
    the avenue   those trees
Listen   she says   listen to bells carve the hours

ÉMILE OLLIVIER

from Mother Solitude

In Which 1979 Becomes an Important Date in the History of Human Paleontology

The question of my paternal origins was settled once and for all by my late mother. I was seven years old. Like a good little devil, I had disrupted the arithmetic lesson of old Father Anselme, who flew into a rage, as only a white man knows how to do, and banished me from the classroom, charging me not to return without my father. My father? This request left me dumbfounded. I knew nothing of a father, I had never set eyes on such a creature. There was no father in the Morelli household. Of course, there was Grandfather Astrel, whose photograph occupied the place of honour in the living room, but he had been dead for a long time. And there was Uncle Gabriel. Every evening, in my prayers, Aunt Hortense made me ask the Baby Jesus to intercede with the blue dragons for his imminent return. And there was Sylvain, my mother's youngest brother. But there had never been a father. I flew into the house that afternoon, oblivious of the fact that my presence there at that hour of the day might be a cause for alarm. Only my mother could help me resolve this enigma – though, needless to say, I didn't use that word at the time.

Ignoring Absalon, who called to me from the garden where he was hard at work amongst the flowers, I raced through the vestibule, not even stopping to kiss Eva Maria, sped up the stairs on all fours and, without pausing to knock, burst into my mother's bedroom, where I promptly acquainted her with the cause of my confusion.

"Ah, little monster!" she exclaimed, breaking into laughter. "You want to know how I got you, eh?" She ruffled my hair. My bewilderment was now complete. Then she took me in her arms and explained in a gentle tone: "It's like this: you take an egg laid by a hen, preferably a healthy hen, preferably on a Good Friday, and you hold it under your arm for nine days and nine nights, until it hatches. What pops out in most cases isn't a chick but a shapeless little creature that cackles and screeches. When it starts to make a fuss, you take it in your arms and feed it from little jars of creamed vegetables and fruits. If you should happen to forget the dinner hour, it will cry and cry without a pause for breath, then you must hurry and give it something to eat. When it goes back to sleep, you lay it in its nest, and the next thing you know, it's well on its way to dreamland . . ." The next day, at the sharp, clear hour of dawn, feeling completely refreshed, I was awakened by a cat fight in the eaves above my balcony, which was caressed year in and year out by the ancient Caribbean wind.

Today, what remains of my mother? It has been so many years. An aroma, a smile, an oval photo I carry in my pocket, trifles that obsess me to the point that I have no eyes for the young girls who cross my path. For the moment, they do not exist: I was not born of them nor they of me. I have not yet awakened to their presence, I have not been inspired to give them names, I have not learned from them the alphabet of wordless languages, the geometry of bodies, the trembling theorems of desire. I am eighteen years old and I have not yet encountered you, lamb or gazelle. But in the hollow of my bed I lick the salt from your plum-coloured body, I clasp your loins like an offertory urn, I search with my lips along the edge of your own, and like Oedipus at the gates of Thebes, I penetrate the mystery of the long passage that leads to the shores of incomparable delight. I am eighteen years old and I have not yet met you. What must I do to exorcise this obsession with my mother? Must I force the bolts and plunder my past, like a burglar breaking into his own home? Must I rummage in the dresser drawers, ransack the cupboards, plunge into the deepest chests, displace photos, read the pages of diaries grown stiff and yellow with age? And who is to say that, having turned the house upside down in search of clues, ribbons, relics of the dead woman, having inspected everything that might once have made contact with her body, sunbonnets hanging in the closet, nests woven of the straw of dreams in which lurks the odour of her hair and that might once have contained the birds of her bird-filled head – who is to say that, having done all that, I shall find myself in possession of the truth, the whole truth? My mother, Noémie Morelli, my unhealthy obsession! The black waters of my daydreams are nourished by that woman, the foam-froth of my days tastes of the salty kisses she once gave me. In January, she transformed each day into New Year's. In April, we went strolling amongst the bougainvillea. In May – oh, the lovely songs of the month of May! In June, I was a Midsummer Eve's butterfly, come to light up the world. In August, I was immobile, and again in November, on All Hallows' Day in sticky November. I never liked November, the cruellest month of the year. Everything began on a Sunday in sticky November. I had a rendezvous that day in the lower town with my schoolmates, faithful disciples like myself of Edmond Bernissart, who was giving a talk that day. For us, Edmond Bernissart was a real oddball. The singularity of his subject was bound to draw a large crowd of people hard up for amusement, eternal idlers in quest of diversion in boring Trou-Bordet.

Fifty-three years of age, Edmond Bernissart was as thin as a broomstick. A renowned autodidact, Doctor Bernissart, as we called him, had dedicated his life to the study of the apparition, evolution, and extinction of the race of iguanodons on the planet Earth. He cared nothing for social distinctions, those cherished abstractions of demagogues. Apolitical by persuasion, he lived somewhere outside the parameters of polite society. The economic, social, political, ideological and epidermic concerns of his fellow citizens slid off him like water off the back of a duck.

Impervious to public opinion, Edmond Bernissart was convinced that only the close study of fossilized vertebrates would permit one to penetrate the secret of that page of life devoted to the gradual supplantation of the reptiles by the mammals in the age-old struggle for supremacy. As for the birds, their oviparous cousins, they had taken possession of the air, where they competed in their acrobatic virtuosity with the insects, the pollen and the wind.

Edmond Bernissart had been a confirmed bachelor since that April morning (the story was recounted by Bernissart himself), when, summoning up all his courage, he had succeeded for a moment in controlling his clumsiness, the corporeal symptoms of a legendary timidity, and had boldly crossed the threshold of one of the more distinguished dwellings in Trou-Bordet. He even described the owner to us: a strange bird with a long neck, on top of which perched a bony skull, with a rough, furrowed brow, jet-black eyes, a beak-like nose and lips pinched into a permanent pout of disdain. To complete the picture, the man was endowed with an uncommonly acerbic tongue, from which the words dropped like vitriol. On that day, he hadn't even deigned to lift his nose from his newspaper until he was certain that Bernissart had finished articulating his intentions. What was one to do with such a nincompoop? How could one presume that the daughter of such an illustrious family would be allowed to marry a Bernissart, even if she *was* carrying his child? The social opprobrium added to the moral stain would be equivalent to draining the cup to the dregs – worse, to swallowing the cup itself.

Edmond Bernissart was one of those men to whom life had not taught the assimilation of minor setbacks. At the least catastrophe, he resorted to dire measures. Emerging from this incident, he had once and for all discounted the possibility of union with a member of the opposite sex, taking refuge in his books, convinced that the passage of aquatic life to the terrestrial plane, an evolutionary development that had been accomplished through the acquisition of four legs and a respiratory system, represented an important, indeed a crucial, date in the history of the human race. He even went so far as to affirm that we were still to a large degree descendants of that larval form of life, possessing traces in our organism of the first morning of the world, the dawn's early dew, the crack in the ice age, the seam dividing light and shadow. For Master Bernissart, he was ready to stake his life on this, the human race still had a long row to hoe before attaining the age of maturity. All these things explained his decision to live on the fringes of society, ignoring the main currents of thought that had guided men for the previous two decades. He had never travelled; the other island, faintly visible in the distance, constituted his sole horizon. His eyes weakened from the perusal of ancient texts and yellowed documents, his spine curved from countless nights spent poring over old maps, he had tirelessly tracked the movements and migratory habits of the dinosaurs. Now, approaching the autumn of his life, he had the feeling he was nearing the end of his quest, having finally penetrated the mystery of the dinosaurs' extinction. In the symphonic production of Beethoven, the ultimate stage had come with the introduction of the voice of Man. Edmond Bernissart was obsessed with another worry: what if, in this case, there had been no ultimate stage? Wasn't the belief that Man represented the final step in the evolution of a species the proof of a narrow, insular outlook? The planet, after all, was no more than a huge island. How was it possible to attribute a universal value to something as paltry as human destiny?

A scrupulous investigator as thin as a nail, Edmond Bernissart contended that, without going so far as to credit the hypothesis of a first cause (a theory that would seem to be confirmed by the universality of the principles of modern science), it was conceivable to him that life might have appeared at different moments on various other planets in the universe – and who knows what strides toward consciousness it might not already have taken in the unexplored regions of space? This was a very serious problem. "It will be for future generations to raise the veil on this mystery," he might have declared on the eve of his talk. Meanwhile, faced with the impossibility of bending time to his will, he could assert that in the course of this abominable life he had found ample reason to rejoice. He nurtured no dreams of fame or wealth; at the very most, he hoped that his name might figure in the *Great Illustrated Directory of the Universe*. In this way, he might survive in the memories of certain men and women of goodwill. This, he believed, would be just recompense for all his efforts, the legitimate reward for a life of extraordinary discipline and self-denial. Hadn't he recently succeeded in exhuming, in the south of the country, a few specimens of iguanodons dating from the pre-Columbian age? Didn't the strange forms assumed by life in the past bear sufficient witness to an astonishing number of possibilities?

Considering the vast period of time in which they had reigned, to say nothing of their significance to our present existence, these giant lizards with whom paleontologists had made us familiar merited more than our indifference, did they not, more than just a fleeting glance? Indeed, wasn't there a distinct link between their existence and our own? Might the iguanodons not be said to serve as a sort of refracting mirror? Wasn't it to be hoped that something might be learned in the vicissitudes of their evolution about our own nature: the mechanical urge to walk, to talk, to defecate; to say nothing of the determination, even when reduced to the lowest degree of misery, to cling to life, as witnessed in our own time by the Khmer refugees, the abandoned boat people, the millions of children suffering from malnutrition, diphtheria and poliomyelitis. If his talk could contribute to awakening, in those who did not suspect that it was in their own interest to work for a better world, a determination to dissociate themselves from the mad race for material comforts and to lift themselves wilfully back onto the road of life (and perhaps, in the process, to learn to respect life's principles, even as they discovered its grandeur), then he, Edmond Bernissart, could die happy, content to turn the little page of his life, aware that he was no more than a mere fart in the bowels of

Eternity, aware that nothing justifies a life, not even if one's remains should be laid to rest for all eternity in a tomb that surpasses in magnificence the sepulchres of the Pharaohs.

It was thoughts such as these that occupied Edmond Bernissart on that November Sunday as he was about to enter the hall that had been placed at his disposal by the Salesian fathers so that he might deliver his first (and, who knows, perhaps his last) talk on "The Extinction of the Dinosaurs." He rubbed his hands vigorously together. This notion of the kinship of the evolution of the human race and the destiny of a certain people, a notion that the clarity of his exposé would be sure to kindle in the minds of his audience, left him in a state of anticipated jubilation.

Sticky November had succeeded October, a prostrate October laid waste by the sun. In that cramped hall, designed to hold no more than three hundred people, upwards of a thousand humans – schoolboys, students, unemployed men in search of a platform, nubile young women, dignified mothers, greying fathers with constipated looks on their faces – found themselves pressed, compressed, squeezed mercilessly together. The heat was suffocating.

It was exactly five o'clock when, with the punctuality of a clock, Master Bernissart stepped into the Salesian Fathers' Parish Hall. It was a sticky Sunday in November at five o'clock in the afternoon. He was greeted by a round of applause, amused and skeptical smiles, wagging heads, admiring and mocking whistles. When he had taken his place on the platform, a woman in a long flowered dress, decked out like a statue in a shrine, primped, powdered, heavily perfumed, emerged from the wings and pompously announced her title: President of the Association of Research Scientists. She reminded the audience of the great difficulties faced by researchers in "these damned algebraic times," in a world where their activities were perceived as, at best, anachronistic. She gave a succinct resumé of the principal events in the life of Doctor Bernissart, then, raising her fluty voice a half-tone, she solemnly declared: "Master Bernissart, the floor is yours!" But this celebrated formula did not seem to please her and she corrected herself: "What am I saying, Master, it is all yours, floor, ceiling, walls!"

At the back of the hall, a few schoolboys began timidly to applaud. Amongst them, myself, Narcès Morelli. Not for a moment did I suspect that, prior to my birth, Edmond Bernissart and the Morelli family had almost come to blows over me, thrown into a frenzy by the ancient taboos of blood.

Ignoring custom, the speaker did not thank the president for her introductory remarks, nor did he welcome the public. Instead, he launched straight into his subject:

"When, at the beginning of the last century, Georges Cuvier published his memorable findings on fossil bones, paleontology was born as a science worthy of the name. Until then an empirical study, it entered, along with comparative anatomy (another creation of this brilliant naturalist), a new phase and became a rational discipline – despite the fact that it was to remain for some time in the realm of pure morphology. It was only later that evolution entered the picture, prompting paleontologists to search for the links connecting the various forms they had identified – in other words, to engage in the study of phylogeny. Systematics was to find itself considerably enriched as a result of these developments. It is one of paleontology's claims to glory that it opened the way to such advances."

Edmond Bernissart went on to give a brief resumé of the contributions made to the study of paleontology by individuals working in a number of parallel disciplines. He pointed out that it was men like Moseley and Dollo who had resurrected "the lost world," to borrow an expression from Conan Doyle, and he suggested that the study of dinosaurs might eventually prove to be one of the more promising pursuits in the fertile field of modern paleontology. At this point, he paused to acquaint his listeners with some of the vocabulary associated with the discipline:

"The word *dinosaur* or *dinosaurian* is used to refer to an order of terrestrial reptiles, now extinct, that lived on the Earth during the secondary era. These creatures came in many sizes, varying in length from a few decimetres to thirty metres. Though they often bore little resemblance to one another, they all shared certain traits: a massive body terminating in a long tail; an elongated neck; a small head with a narrow brain pan; a firm, flexible spinal column; a sacrum containing numerous vertebrae; posterior limbs more highly developed than their anterior counterparts; bones with large medullary cavities; a pelvis not unlike that of a bird, with which the dinosaur moreover shared a number of characteristics . . ."

This was followed by a description of the four principal groups of dinosaurs: the carnivores, armed with teeth and claws; the herbivores, which grew to a gigantic size; the bipeds, with their corneous beaks; and the large, horned beasts. A round of applause greeted each of these descriptions.

It should be pointed out that the audience did not fail to recognize, in these laconic portraits, certain state officials, ministers who had held their posts for upwards of two decades, as well as members of the security forces who were getting on in age but who were renowned for their guile, their *savoir faire* in the shady domain of corruption, torture and assassination. First names, last names, nicknames circulated in whispers about the room. Some members of the audience began to wonder about the real motive of this so-called "scientific" discourse. Was Bernissart really the apolitical creature he claimed to be, living somewhere outside the margins of society, or was this merely a front?

Meanwhile, Edmond Bernissart continued to speak serenely of forms of life that had been extinct on Earth for millions of years. But the deeper he delved into the subject, the more decidedly his words brought his listeners back to the immediate present. Was it possible that this man who seemed, in the strictest sense of the word, deaf to public rumour – was it possible that he had decided that his talk on an extinct species might serve as a "dinosaurian" device for the identification of certain thugs in the employment of a government that had been in power for nearly a quarter-century, a government whose perpetuity these very thugs were engaged to ensure, an assignment that obliged them periodically to dip their hands in blood, to resort to brutality and to engage in the most barbaric behaviour?

At Tête-Boeuf, on that All Hallows' Day, on that Sunday afternoon in sticky November, the auditorium of the Salesian fathers was bursting at the seams. The convulsive rays of the afternoon sun tinted the austere stained-glass windows a deep violet hue and ignited the flowered skirts and pastel-tinted *guayabelles* scattered about the hall. All the social classes were represented on this occasion. Even Lamy Jambat had come, like a cormorant, to exhibit his ex-ministerial disgrace on the arm of his stiff, pinch-lipped wife, Man Jambat, who spent the afternoon desperately trying to make herself comfortable in the rigid confines of a corset she had recently bought on credit. Hadn't she been seen, only the previous evening, emerging from *La Belle Créole* Department Store, wearing a look of delirious optimism? Three days prior to the great event, all the merchants of the seashore had exhausted their entire stock of scent. Even the newly arrived, rawboned country bumpkins had come to proudly exhibit their country bumpkin wives, frizzy-haired creatures, their faces smeared with paint and Parami powder. The hall was bursting at the seams. It was even possible to make out a few unlikely presences: Mr. John Gleen, the U.S. ambassador, and his wife, Mrs. Gleen; François Martin, cultural attaché and director of the Institut Français; Moshé Dachwig, Israeli consul; André LaSource, Canadian chargé d'affaires for the Francophone Antilles, which had a branch office in Trou-Bordet; and a number of other members of society and authorities of greater and lesser weight. It was five o'clock in the afternoon. The speaker, whose voice had reached a passionate, exalted pitch, proceeded with his exposition, oblivious of the fact that the entire hall was holding its breath, a sure sign of mounting tension. Edmond Bernissart, for whom words held no secret (in that, the president had been correct), found expressions that were more and more judicious in his attempt to elucidate the problematics governing the phenomena underlying the size and shape of all the known species of dinosaurs. From the audience there rose sporadic bursts of applause, underscored by a dull rumble, like that of the sea heard from a distance. It had been many years since such eloquence had been encountered in the city, ebbing and flowing in such waves of irrepressible grandeur. According to the old people, you would have had to go back to the fifties to discover an orator capable of surpassing Master Bernissart. Then, a certain populist from the outlying regions had used his oratorical gifts to get himself named president after having clawed his way to the top of the power structure. His mandate hadn't lasted long, however, no more than twenty days – nineteen, to be precise. But that was another story. A crossroads orator, an incomparable rhetorician, he had mastered the spoken word to the point that, once elected to Parliament, he had become the terror of the interpellated ministers in the House. It was even said that a woman who was nine months pregnant had been so carried away by the magic of his words at a public assembly that she had given birth between two gasps and a cry of admiration. Whatever had become of that man with the golden tongue? Apparently he was wasting away in a suburb of New York. But that was another story.

Suddenly, a firecracker exploded and someone cried: "Death to the dinosaurs!" Chairs were raised over heads and bullets whistled through the air. Two or three diplomats were jostled; pregnant women were trampled underfoot. Though the incredible was a daily occurrence in Trou-Bordet, the old people were frightened on this occasion, no longer sporting the disillusioned smiles of players who have lived through several wars and several defeats and who expect to live to see several more. Death was on the prowl. Let's get the hell out of here, let's make tracks! Alas, it was too late. All the exits were blocked by strange men wielding machine guns. At first in whispers, then in a roar, the news circulated through the auditorium: "The dinosaurs are here!" Heads turned toward the stage. Edmond Bernissart lay sprawled on his back, a knife in his chest. On that bad-luck Sunday in sticky November, Tête-Boeuf had ceased to breathe.

Ah, the strange destiny of a land! Exactly 60,145 days prior to this event, on 17 October 1806 (all the history texts will confirm the fact), some six hundred metres from Tête-Boeuf – at Pont-Rouge, to be precise – Jean-Jacques Dessalines had met his untimely end, the same Jean-Jacques Dessalines who occupies such an important place in the revolutionary annals of this country. On that day, he had summoned to his side a certain Charlotin Marcadieu, a valiant colonel of his regiment, a man of exemplary fidelity. Upon receiving the call, Marcadieu leapt onto his horse and galloped off to lend support to his leader. The two men were to perish in a hail of conspiratorial gunfire. Though the accounts of the historians Thomas Madiou and Beaubrun Ardouin differed on certain details and on the interpretation of this event, they concur on one point: the corpse of the proud, intrepid Dessalines was treated in a most abominable fashion by the officers in whose company he had fought for independence. They cut off the fingers to get at the expensive rings, they stripped the body of its fine raiment, and they treated the man's arms, his pistols and sabre and dagger, as so much booty. The corpse was then transported to the city, under orders of General Yayou, where it was to be displayed on the Place d'Armes before the governmental palace. In the course of the half-league trajectory, it was exposed to the insults and abuse of Dessalines's enemies, who came running up on all sides, some slashing at it with sabres, some hurling stones. Torn to shreds, the mutilated corpse remained exposed on the Place d'Armes throughout the day, at its side, a black woman, Défilée la Folle, moaning softly. When the body was transported to the inner cemetery to await burial, Défilée accompanied it. Long afterwards, she would continue to haunt the cemetery to toss flowers on that anonymous grave. A few years later, a certain Madame Inginac, a woman of means, had a modest stone erected on the spot, no one knew why, on which the following inscription may still be read: HERE LIES DESSALINES, DEAD AT THE AGE OF 48. Ah, the strange destiny of a land! Only recently, a gang of ruffians had brought back from the southern peninsula the corpse of Alain Laraque, one of twelve guerrillas cut down in the flower of their youth. For three days, his body had lain beneath a sign that read WELCOME TO THE SUN, exposed to the flies and the ants. A tear of pain for the emperor! A tear of admiration for Défilée la Folle! A tear of recognition for Madame Inginac! A tear of bitterness for Alain Laraque! A tear of rage for Edmond Bernissart!

Disastrous November! Wretched Tête-Boeuf! Tyranny is sombre, monotonous, sad. Following a brief period of respite, during which the more optimistic spoke of "liberalization," tyranny had once again descended upon the city. The hand that struck Tête-Boeuf that afternoon was even more terrible than the iron fist of Tony Brizo, the former commander of Fort-Touron, who had built his reputation on a systematic campaign of torture, sadism and blood. Was it possible that this country had been permanently launched into the orbit of violence? Was it possible that human life in this country was fated never again to be respected, appreciated, esteemed? On that sticky November afternoon, Narcès Morelli found himself submerged in a sea of anguish. Eventually, he succeeded in breaking a way through the panic-stricken mob and arrived, out of breath, at the large gateway leading out of the yard.

Outside, the street was blocked to traffic. Everywhere he looked, there were enormous army trucks and hundreds of militiamen armed with rifles and machine guns. An old lady, on the verge of hysteria, collapsed in his arms: "We mustn't stay here, my boy! They're going to take everyone away!" Narcès Morelli saw all those closed trucks descending the street, moving in a westerly direction, and he broke into a run. He ran for his home, the secular cell of his ancestors, the Morellis. There at least he would be safe, amongst his aunts, in the company of Absalon. The images that had unfolded before his eyes that afternoon evoked other, more intimate images. That sticky November afternoon reminded him of another afternoon in sticky November: Place des Héros de l'Indépendance, a gallows, the body of a woman swaying slowly in the wind, obscene insults, cries of hatred, gobs of spittle . . . and the firm fist of Absalon restraining the frantic efforts of a little boy in short pants to flee. Noémie Morelli had departed this world in front of the packed gallery on Champ de Mars, with its scattering of flowered skirts and pastel-tinted *guayabelles*. Absalon had insisted that these images be permanently engraved on his memory. Now, the hazy recollection floated back to the surface of his mind. The death of Bernissart had evoked another death. He raced for home. A tear of mercy for Noémie Morelli!

What can I say about that country? What can I say about that city? I was born and raised in that city. A city that was vomited up by the sea at the foot of a rocky mountain. What do I know of that mountain, beyond its hairless, mangy, rat's hump, its ravaged face? Today, like a beggar seated in the shade of a dying palm tree, at the side of a road that leads nowhere, my hand held before me, I implore the passersby, uttering an ancient refrain drawn from the depths of my fading memory: *May I be repaid for the charitable acts of my past, may you be repaid one day for your own!* Lost in the labyrinth of my inner landscapes, I have applied myself to the mute exploration of my past, as well as that of my country. I hold out my empty hands. The only reward: silence. A silence peopled with signs, which I tirelessly examine, grinding them to a powder, in the futile hope of finding the original text that I know to be buried somewhere in the machicolations of my memory. The death of Bernissart had opened a way for me into the forest. Forms took shape. I began to see, to know. I crossed the city under the November sun. I prepared myself to confront the terrors of the night, the gypsum night, the November night with its teeth of gypsum. I knew now that this country would take an eternity to rise out of the night, its veins laid bare to the four points of the compass. I ran through the city, passing men and women who would go to bed again that night with uneasy consciences. Men and women who would lie in their beds, their eyes open wide upon the horrors of the night. Men and women who remained silent in the face of despotism, the terrorist tactics of blind commandos, the unofficial police and their hired assassins. I raced across the city, the kingdom of the mad. Landscape of mountain and sea, horizon of pine trees and plains. There is no way to describe it. City with its single basilica, its gallows and its mud. City oozing into the sea like an abscess. Incandescent city, flaming like a spruce tree in a high wind, with its everlasting paroxysms of marvels and terrors. Trou-Bordet, they called you, but they might as well have called you Trou-aux-Vices, Trou-aux-Assassins, Trou-aux-Crimes. City of blood and filth! City constantly on the alert! City of asphalt and gaping holes! No, there is no way to describe it. On one side, acacia and bougainvillea; on the other, parched, skeletal trees blackened by the smoke of the sugar-cane trains. Ah! There is no way to describe this city. Especially this side of the city, with its heaped-up shacks and shanties, its conglomeration of wood, sheet metal and woven reeds, its tangle of haphazardly-erected shelters crouched in the ravines, climbing the steep slopes. Here, they sit over the fetid waters of a sewer; here, they straddle a ditch. Ah! This side of the city, with its foul-smelling alleys, its tortuous alleys teeming with life, its populous families, its opulent Mamas and its stray dogs, its stone-pickers and its alley cats, its little old women in rags, its blackened coconut palms, its whimpering brats and its bedraggled turkeycocks and its guinea hens and its roosters and its pigs and cows and goats and sheep, all God's creatures swarming like maggots on a November Sunday at sunset, a sticky November with its teeth of gypsum and misery.

OLIVE SENIOR

DO ANGELS WEAR BRASSIERES?

Beccka down on her knees ending her goodnight prayers and Cherry telling her softly, "And Ask God to bless Auntie Mary." Beccka vex that anybody could interrupt her private conversation with God so, say loud loud, "No. Not praying for nobody that tek weh mi best glassy eye marble."

"Beccka!" Cherry almost crying in shame, "Shhhhh! She wi hear you. Anyway she did tell you not to roll them on the floor when she have her headache."

"A hear her already" – this is the righteous voice of Auntie Mary in the next room – "But I am sure that God is not listening to the like of she. Blasphemous little wretch."

She add the last part under her breath and with much lifting of her eyes to heaven she turn back to her nightly reading of the Imitation of Christ.

"Oooh Beccka, Rebecca, see what yu do," Cherry whispering crying in her voice.

Beccka just stick out her tongue at the world, wink at God who she know right now in the shape of a big fat anansi in a corner of the roof, kiss her mother, and get into bed.

As soon as her mother gone into Auntie Mary room to try make it up and the whole night come down with whispering, Beccka whip the flashlight from off the dressing table and settle down under the blanket to read. Beccka reading the Bible in secret from cover to cover not from any conviction the little wretch but because everybody round her always quoting that book and Beccka want to try and find flaw and question she can best them with.

Next morning Auntie Mary still vex. Auntie Mary out by the tank washing clothes and slapping them hard on the big rock. Fat sly-eye Katie from the next yard visiting and consoling her. Everybody visiting Auntie Mary these days and consoling her for the crosses she have to bear (that is Beccka they talking about). Fat Katie have a lot of time to walk bout consoling because ever since hard time catch her son and him wife a town they come country to cotch with Katie. And from the girl walk through the door so braps! Katie claim she too sickly to do any washing or housework. So while the daughter-in-law beating suds at her yard she over by Auntie Mary washpan say she keeping her company. Right now she consoling about Beccka who (as she telling Auntie Mary) every decent-living upright Christian soul who is everybody round here except that Dorcas Waite about whom one should not dirty one's mouth to talk yes every clean living person heart go out to Auntie Mary for with all due respect to a sweet mannersable child like Cherry her daughter is the devil own pickney. Not that anybody saying a word about Cherry God know she have enough trouble on her head from she meet up that big hard back man though young little gal like that never shoulda have business with no married man. Katie take a breath long enough to ask question:

"But see here Miss Mary you no think Cherry buck up the devil own self when she carrying her? Plenty time that happen you know. Remember that woman over Allside that born the pickney with two head praise Jesus it did born dead. But see here you did know one day she was going down river to wash clothes and is the devil own self she meet. Yes'm. Standing right there in her way. She pop one big bawling before she faint weh and when everybody run come not a soul see him. Is gone he gone. But you no know where he did gone?

No right inside that gal. Right inna her belly. And Miss Mary I telling you the living truth, just as the baby borning the midwife no see a shadow fly out of the mother and go right cross the room. She frighten so till she close her two eye tight and is so the devil escape."

"Well I dont know about that. Beccka certainly dont born with no two head or nothing wrong with her. Is just hard ears she hard ears."

"Den no so me saying?"

"The trouble is, Cherry is too soft to manage her. As you look hard at Cherry herself she start cry. She was never a strong child and she not a strong woman, her heart just too soft."

"All the same right is right and there is only one right way to bring up a child and that is by bus' ass pardon my French Miss Mary but hard things call for hard words. That child should be getting blows from the day she born. Then she wouldnt be so force-ripe now. Who cant hear must feel for the rod and reproof bring wisdom but a child left to himself bringeth his mother to shame. Shame, Miss Mary."

"Is true. And you know I wouldn't mind if she did only get into mischief Miss Katie but what really hurt me is how the child know so much and show off. Little children have no right to have so many things in their brain. Guess what she ask me the other day nuh? – if me know how worms reproduce."

"Say what, maam?"

"As Jesus is me judge. Me big woman she come and ask that. Reproduce I say. Yes Auntie Mary she say as if I stupid. When the man worm and the lady worm come together and they have baby. You know how it happen? – is so she ask me."

"What you saying maam? Jesus of Nazareth!"

"Yes, please. That is what the child ask me. Lightning come strike me dead if is lie I lie. In my own house. My own sister pickney. So help me I was so frighten that pickney could so impertinent that right away a headache strike me like autoclaps. But before I go lie down you see Miss Katie, I give her some licks so hot there she forget bout worm and reproduction."

"In Jesus name!"

"Yes. Is all those books her father pack her up with. Book is all him ever good for. Rather than buy food put in the pickney mouth or help Cherry find shelter his only contribution is book. Nuh his character stamp on her. No responsibility that man ever have. Look how him just take off for foreign without a word even to his lawful wife and children much less Cherry and hers. God knows where it going to end."

"Den Miss M. They really come to live with you for all time?"

"I dont know my dear. What are they to do? You know Cherry cant keep a job from one day to the next. From she was a little girl she so nervous she could never settle down long enough to anything. And you know since Papa and Mama pass away is me one she have to turn to. I tell you even if they eat me out of house and home and the child drive me to Bellevue I accept that this is the crosses that I put on this earth to bear ya Miss Katie."

"Amen. Anyway dont forget what I was saying to you about the devil. The child could have a devil inside her. No pickney suppose to come facety and force-ripe so. You better ask the Archdeacon to check it out next time he come here."

"Well. All the same Miss Katie she not all bad you know. Sometime at night when she ready to sing and dance and make up play and perform for us we laugh so till! And those times when I watch her I say to myself, this is really a gifted child."

"Well my dear is your crosses. If is so you see it then is your sister child."

"Aie. I have one hope in God and that is the child take scholarship exam and God know she so bright she bound to pass. And you know what, Miss Katie, I put her name down for the three boarding school them that furthest from here. Make them teacher deal with her. That is what they get paid for."

Beccka hiding behind the tank listening to the conversation as usual. She think about stringing a wire across the track to trip fat Katie but she feeling too lazy today. Fat Katie will get her comeuppance on Judgment Day for she wont able to run quick enough to join the heavenly hosts. Beccka there thinking of fat Katie huffing and puffing arriving at the pasture just as the company of the faithful in their white robes are rising as one body on a shaft of light. She see Katie a-clutch at the hem of the gown of one of the faithful and miraculously, slowly, slowly, Katie start to rise. But her weight really too much and with a tearing sound that spoil the solemn moment the hem tear way from the garment and Katie fall back to earth with a big buff, shouting and wailing for them to wait on her. Beccka snickering so hard at the sight she have to scoot way quick before Auntie Mary and Katie hear her. They think the crashing about in the cocoa walk is mongoose.

Beccka in Auntie Mary room – which is forbidden – dress up in Auntie Mary bead, Auntie Mary high heel shoes, Auntie Mary shawl, and Auntie Mary big floppy hat which she only wear to wedding – all forbidden. Beccka mincing and prancing prancing and mincing in front of the three-way adjustable mirror in Auntie Mary vanity she brought all the way from Cuba with her hard-earned money. Beccka seeing herself as a beautiful lady on the arms of a handsome gentleman who look just like her father. They about to enter a nightclub neon sign flashing for Beccka know this is the second wickedest thing a woman can do. At a corner table lit by Chinese lantern soft music playing Beccka do the wickedest thing a woman can do – she take a drink. Not rum. One day Beccka went to wedding with Auntie Mary and sneak a drink of rum and stay sick for two days. Beccka thinking of all the bright-colour drink she see advertise in the magazine Cherry get from a lady she use to work for in town a nice yellow drink in a tall frosted glass . . .

"Beccka, Rebecca O My God!" That is Cherry rushing into the room and wailing. "You know she wi mad like hell if she see you with her things you know you not to touch her things."

Cherry grab Auntie Mary things from off Beccka and fling them back into where she hope is the right place, adjust the mirror to what she hope is the right angle, and pray just pray that Auntie Mary wont find out that Beccka was messing with her things. Again. Though Auntie Mary so absolutely neat she always know if a pin out of place. "O God Beccka," Cherry moaning.

Beccka stripped of her fancy clothes dont pay no mind to her mother fluttering about her. She take the story in her head to the room next door though here the mirror much too high for Beccka to see the sweep of her gown as she does the third wickedest thing a woman can do which is dance all night.

Auntie Mary is a nervous wreck and Cherry weeping daily in excitement. The Archdeacon is coming. Auntie Mary so excited she cant sit cant stand cant do her embroidery cant eat she forgetting things the house going to the dog she dont even notice that Beccka been using her lipstick. Again. The Archdeacon coming Wednesday to the churches in the area and afterwards – as usual – Archdeacon sure to stop outside Auntie Mary gate even for one second – as usual – to get two dozen of Auntie Mary best roses and a bottle of pimento dram save from Christmas. And maybe just this one time Archdeacon will give in to Auntie Mary pleading and step inside her humble abode for tea. Just this one time.

Auntie Mary is due this honour at least once because she is head of Mothers' Union and though a lot of them jealous and backbiting her because Archdeacon never stop outside their gate even once let them say anything to her face.

For Archdeacon's certain stop outside her gate Auntie Mary scrub the house from top to bottom put back up the freshly laundered Christmas curtains and the lace tablecloth and the newly starch doilies and the antimacassars clean all the windows in the house get the thick hibiscus hedge trim so you can skate across the top wash the dog whitewash every rock in the garden and the trunk of every tree paint the gate polish the silver and bring out the crystal cake plate and glasses she bring from Cuba twenty-five years ago and is saving for her old age. Just in case Archdeacon can stop for tea Auntie Mary bake a fruitcake a upside-down cake a three-layer cake a chocolate cake for she dont know which he prefer also some coconut cookies for although the Archdeacon is an Englishman dont say he dont like his little Jamaican dainties. Everything will be pretty and nice for the Archdeacon just like the American lady she did work for in Cuba taught her to make them.

The only thing that now bothering Auntie Mary as she give a last look over her clean and well-ordered household is Beccka, dirty Beccka right now sitting on the kitchen steps licking out the mixing bowls. The thought of Beccka in the same house with Archdeacon bring on one of Auntie Mary headache. She think of asking Cherry to take Beccka somewhere else for the afternoon when Archdeacon coming but poor Cherry work so hard and is just as excited. Auntie Mary dont have the courage to send Beccka to stay with anyone for nobody know what that child is going to come out with next and a lot of people not so broadmind as Auntie Mary. She pray that Beccka will get sick enough to have to stay in bed she – O God forgive her but is for a worthy cause – she even consider drugging the child for the afternoon. But she dont have the heart. And anyway she dont know how. So Auntie Mary take two Aspirin and a small glass of tonic wine and pray hard that Beccka will vanish like magic on the afternoon that Archdeacon visit.

Now Archdeacon here and Beccka and everybody in their very best clothes. Beccka thank God also on her best behaviour which can be very good so far in fact she really look like a little angel she so clean and behaving.

Archdeacon is quite taken with Beccka and more and more please that this is the afternoon he decide to consent to come inside Auntie

Mary parlour for one little cup of tea. Beccka behaving so well and talking so nice to the Archdeacon Auntie Mary feel her heart swell with pride and joy over everything. Beccka behaving so beautiful in fact that Auntie Mary and Cherry dont even think twice about leaving her to talk to Archdeacon in the parlour while they out in the kitchen preparing tea.

By now Beccka and the Archdeacon exchanging Bible knowledge. Beccka asking him question and he trying his best to answer but they never really tell him any of these things in theological college. First he go ask Beccka if she is a good little girl. Beccka say yes she read her Bible every day. Do you now say the Archdeacon, splendid. Beccka smile and look shy.

"Tell me, my little girl, is there anything in the Bible you would like to ask me about?"

"Yes sir. Who in the Bible wrote big?"

"Who in the Bible wrote big. My dear child!"

This wasnt the kind of question Archdeacon expecting but him always telling himself how he have rapport with children so he decide to confess his ignorance.

"Tell me, who?"

"Paul!" Beccka shout.

"Paul?"

"Galations six-eleven 'See with how large letters I write onto you with mine own hands.'"

"Ho Ho Ho Ho," Archdeacon laugh. "Well done. Try me with another one."

Beccka decide to ease him up this time.

"What animal saw an angel?"

"What animal saw an angel? My word. What animal . . . of course. Balaam's ass."

"Yes you got it."

Beccka jumping up and down she so excited. She decide to ask the Archdeacon a trick question her father did teach her.

"What did Adam and Eve do when they were driven out of the garden?"

"Hmm," the Archdeacon sputtered but could not think of a suitable answer.

"Raise Cain ha ha ha ha ha."

"They raised Cain Ho Ho Ho Ho Ho."

The Archdeacon promise himself to remember that one to tell the Deacon. All the same he not feeling strictly comfortable. It really dont seem dignified for an Archdeacon to be having this type of conversation with an eleven-year-old girl. But Beccka already in high gear with the next question and Archdeacon tense himself.

"Who is the shortest man in the Bible?"

Archdeacon groan.

"Peter. Because him sleep on his watch. Ha Ha Ha."

"Ho Ho Ho Ho Ho."

"What is the smallest insect in the Bible?"

"The widow's mite," Archdeacon shout.

"The wicked flee," Beccka cry.

"Ho Ho Ho Ho Ho Ho."

Archdeacon laughing so hard now he starting to cough. He cough and cough till the coughing bring him to his senses. He there looking down the passage where Auntie Mary gone and wish she would hurry come back. He sputter a few time into his handkerchief, wipe his eye, sit up straight, and assume his most religious expression. Even Beccka impress.

"Now Rebecca. Hmm. You are a very clever very entertaining little girl. Very. But what I had in mind were questions that are a bit more serious. Your aunt tells me you are being prepared for confirmation. Surely you must have some questions about doctrine hmm, religion, that puzzle you. No serious questions?"

Beccka look at Archdeacon long and hard. "Yes," she say at long last in a small voice. Right away Archdeacon sit up straighter.

"What is it, my little one?"

Beccka screwing up her face in concentration.

"Sir, what I want to know is this for I cant find it in the Bible. Please sir, do angels wear brassieres?"

Auntie Mary just that minute coming through the doorway with a full tea tray with Cherry carrying another big tray right behind her. Enough food and drink for ten Archdeacon. Auntie Mary stop braps in the doorway with fright when she hear Beccka question. She stop so sudden that Cherry bounce into her and spill a whole pitcher of cold drink all down Auntie Mary back. As the coldness hit her Auntie Mary jump and half her tray throw way on the floor milk and sugar and sandwiches a rain down on Archdeacon. Archdeacon jump up with his handkerchief and start mop himself and Auntie Mary at the same time he trying to take the tray from her. Auntie Mary at the same time trying to mop up the Archdeacon with a napkin in her mortification not even noticing how Archdeacon relieve that so much confusion come at this time. Poor soft-hearted Cherry only see that her sister whole life ruin now she dont yet know the cause run and sit on the kitchen stool and throw kitchen cloth over her head and sit there bawling and bawling in sympathy.

Beccka win the scholarship to high school. She pass so high she getting to go to the school of Auntie Mary choice which is the one that is farthest away. Beccka vex because she dont want go no boarding school with no heap of girl. Beccka dont want to go to no school at all.

Everyone so please with Beccka. Auntie Mary even more please when she get letter from the headmistress setting out Rules and Regulation. She only sorry that the list not longer for she could think of many things she could add. She get another letter setting out uniform and right away Auntie Mary start sewing. Cherry take the bus to town one day with money coming from God know where for the poor child dont have no father to speak of and she buy shoes and socks and underwear and hair ribbon and towels and toothbrush and a suitcase for Beccka. Beccka normally please like puss with every new thing vain like peacock in ribbons and clothes. Now she hardly look at them. Beccka thinking. She dont want to go to no school. But how to get out of it. When Beccka think done she decide to run away and find her father who like a miracle have job now in a circus. And as Beccka find him so she get job in the circus as a tightrope walker and in spangles and tights lipstick and powder (her own) Beccka perform every night before a cheering crowd in a blaze of light. Beccka and the circus go right round the world. Every now and then, dress up in furs and hats like Auntie Mary wedding hat Beccka come home to visit Cherry and Auntie Mary. She arrive in a chauffeur-driven limousine pile high with luggage. Beccka shower them with presents. The whole village. For fat Katie Beccka bring a year's supply of diet pill and a exercise machine just like the one she see advertise in the magazine the lady did give to Cherry.

Now Beccka ready to run away. In the books, the picture always show children running away with their things tied in a bundle on a stick. The stick easy. Beccka take one of the walking stick that did belong to Auntie Mary's dear departed. Out of spite she take Auntie Mary silk scarf to wrap her things in for Auntie Mary is to blame for her going to school at all. She pack in the bundle Auntie Mary lipstick Auntie Mary face powder and a pair of Auntie Mary stockings for she need these for her first appearance as a tightrope walker. She take a slice of cake, her shiny eye marble, and a yellow nicol which is her best taa in case she get a chance to play in the marble championship of the world. She also take the Bible. She want to find some real hard question for the Archdeacon next time he come to Auntie Mary house for tea.

When Auntie Mary and Cherry busy sewing her school clothes Beccka take off with her bundle and cut across the road into the field. Mr. O'Connor is her best friend and she know he wont mind if she walk across his pasture. Mr. O'Connor is her best friend because he is the only person Beccka can hold a real conversation with. Beccka start to walk toward the mountain that hazy in the distance. She plan to climb the mountain and when she is high enough she will look for a sign that will lead her to her father. Beccka walk and walk through the pasture divided by stone wall and wooden gates which she climb. Sometime a few trees tell her where a pond is. But it is very lonely. All Beccka see is john crow and cow and cattle egret blackbird and parrotlets that scream at her from the trees. But Beccka dont notice them. Her mind busy on how Auntie Mary and Cherry going to be sad now she gone and she composing letter she will write to tell them she safe and she forgive them everything. But the sun getting too high in the sky and Beccka thirsty. She eat the cake but she dont have water. Far in the distance she see a bamboo clump and hope is round a spring with water. But when she get to the bamboo all it offer is shade. In fact the dry bamboo leaves on the ground so soft and inviting that Beccka decide to sit and rest for awhile. Is sleep Beccka sleep. When she wake she see a stand above her four horse leg and when she raise up and look, stirrups, boots, and sitting atop the horse her best friend, Mr. O'Connor.

"Well Beccka, taking a long walk?"

"Yes sir."

"Far from home eh?"

"Yes sir."

"Running away?"

"Yes sir."

"Hmm. What are you taking with you?"

Beccka tell him what she have in the bundle. Mr. O'Connor shock.

"What, no money?"

"Oooh!"

Beccka shame like anything for she never remember anything about money.

"Well you need money for running away you know. How else you going to pay for trains and planes and taxis and buy ice cream and pindar cake?"

Beccka didn't think about any of these things before she run away. But now she see that is sense Mr. O'Connor talking but she dont know what to do. So the two of them just stand there for a while. They thinking hard.

"You know Beccka if I was you I wouldnt bother with the running away today. Maybe they dont find out you gone yet. So I would go back home and wait until I save enough money to finance my journey."

Beccka love how that sound. To finance my journey. She think about that a long time. Mr. O'Connor say, "Tell you what. Why dont you let me give you a ride back and you can pretend this was just a practice and you can start saving your money to run away properly next time."

Beccka look at Mr. O'Connor. He looking off into the distance and she follow where he gazing and when she see the mountain she decide to leave it for another day. All the way back riding with Mr. O'Connor Beccka thinking and thinking and her smile getting bigger and bigger. Beccka cant wait to get home to dream up all the tricky question she could put to a whole school full of girl. Not to mention the teachers. Beccka laughing for half the way home. Suddenly she say –

"Mr. Connor, you know the Bible?"

"Well Beccka I read my Bible every day so I should think so."

"Promise you will answer a question."

"Promise."

"Mr. Connor, do angels wear brassieres?"

"Well Beccka, as far as I know only the lady angels need to."

Beccka laugh cant done. Wasnt that the answer she was waiting for?

MEDITATION ON YELLOW

"The yellow of the Caribbean seen from Jamaica at three in the afternoon."
– Gabriel García Márquez

I

At three in the afternoon
you landed here at El Dorado
(for heat engenders gold and
fires the brain)
Had I known I would have
brewed you up some yellow fever-grass
and arsenic

but we were peaceful then
child-like in the yellow dawn of our innocence

so in exchange for a string of islands
and two continents

you gave us a string of beads
and some hawk's bells

which was fine by me personally
for I have never wanted to possess things
I prefer copper anyway
the smell pleases our lord Yucahuna
our mother Attabeira
It's just that copper and gold hammered into guanin
worn in the solar pendants favoured by our holy men
fooled you into thinking we possessed the real thing
(you were not the last to be fooled by our
patina)

As for silver
I find that metal a bit cold
The contents of our mines
I would have let you take for one small mirror
to catch and hold the sun

I like to feel alive
to the possibilities
of yellow

lightning striking

perhaps as you sip tea
at three in the afternoon
a bit incontinent
despite your vast holdings
(though I was gratified to note
that despite the difference in our skins
our piss was exactly the same shade of yellow)

I wished for you
a sudden enlightenment that

we were not the Indies
nor Cathay
No Yellow Peril here
though after you came
plenty of bananas
oranges
sugar cane
You gave us these for our
maize
pineapples
guavas
– in that respect
there was fair exchange

But it was gold
on your mind
gold the light
in your eyes
gold the crown
of the Queen of Spain
(who had a daughter)
gold the prize
of your life
the crowning glory
the gateway to heaven
the golden altar
(which I saw in Seville
five hundred years after)

Though I couldn't help noticing
(this filled me with dread):

silver was your armour
silver the cross of your Lord
silver the steel in your countenance
silver the glint of your sword
silver the bullet I bite

Golden the macca
the weeds
which mark our passing
the only survivors
on yellow-streaked soil

We were The Good Indians
The Red Indians
The Dead Indians

We were not golden
We were a shade too brown.

II

At some hotel
overlooking the sea
you can take tea
at three in the afternoon
served by me
skin burnt black as toast
(for which management apologizes)

but I've been travelling long
cross the sea in the sun-hot
I've been slaving in the cane rows
for your sugar

I've been ripening coffee beans
for your morning break
I've been dallying on the docks
loading your bananas
I've been toiling in orange groves
for your marmalade
I've been peeling ginger
for your relish
I've been chopping cocoa pods
for your chocolate bars
I've been mining aluminum
for your foil

And just when I thought
I could rest
pour my own
– something soothing
like fever-grass and lemon –
cut my ten
in the kitchen
take five
a new set of people
arrive
to lie bare-assed in the sun
wanting gold on their bodies
cane-rows in their hair
with beads – even bells

So I serving them
coffee
tea
cock-soup
rum

Red Stripe beer
sinsemilla
I cane-rowing their hair
with my beads

But still they want more
want it strong
want it long
want it black
want it green
want it dread

Though I not quarrelsome
I have to say: look
I tired now

I give you the gold
I give you the land
I give you the breeze
I give you the beaches
I give you the yellow sand
I give you the golden crystals

And I reach to the stage where
(though I not impolite)
I have to say: lump it
or leave it
I can't give anymore

For one day before I die
from five hundred years of servitude
I due to move
from kitchen to front verandah

overlooking the Caribbean Sea
drinking real tea
with honey and lemon
eating bread (lightly toasted, well buttered)
with Seville orange marmalade

I want to feel mellow
in that three o'clock yellow

I want to feel
though you own
the silver tea service
the communion plate
you don't own
the tropics anymore

I want to feel
you cannot take away

the sun dropping by every day
for a chat

I want to feel
you cannot stop
Yellow Macca bursting through
the soil reminding us
of what's buried there

You cannot stop
those street gals
those streggehs
Allamanda
Cassia

Poui
Golden Shower
flaunting themselves everywhere

I want to feel:

you cannot tear my song
from my throat

you cannot erase the memory
of my story

you cannot catch
my rhythm

(for you have to born
with that)

you cannot comprehend
the magic

of anacondas changing into rivers
like the Amazon
boas dancing in my garden
arcing into rainbows
(and I haven't had a drop
to drink – yet)

You cannot reverse
Bob Marley wailing

making me feel
so mellow

in that Caribbean yellow
at three o'clock

any day now.

THE PULL OF BIRDS

Colón, son and grand-son of weavers
rejected that calling but did not
neglect craft (keeping two sets of books).
On his first voyage, landfall receding
(where was Japan?) he sailed on

praying for a miracle to centre him
in that unmarked immensity, as warp to woof.
And suddenly from the north a density
of birds flying south, their autumn migration
intersecting his westward passage.

At such an auspicious conjunction, his charts
he threw out, the flocks drew him south
across the blue fabric of the Atlantic.
Weary mariners buoyed by the miracle
of land soon, of birds flying across the moon.

Birds seeking to outdistance three raptors skimming
the surface of the sea and sending skyward
their doomsday utterance of hawks' bells
tinkling endlessly. Birds speeding
to make landfall at Guanahaní.

THIRTEEN WAYS OF LOOKING AT BLACKBIRD

(after Wallace Stevens)

I

The ship
    trips
into sight of land. Blackbird
is all eyes. Vows nothing but sunlight
will ever hold him now.

II

Survivor of the crossing, Blackbird
the lucky one in three, moves
his eyes and weary
limbs. Finds his wings clipped.
Palm trees gaze and swoon.

III

Swept like the leaves on autumn wind,
Blackbird is bought and sold and bought
again, whirled into waving fields
of sugar cane.

IV

Blackbird no longer knows
if he is man or woman or bird or simply is.
Or if among the sugar cane he is
sprouting.

V

Blackbird's voice has turned rusty
The voice of the field mice
is thin and squeaky
I do not know which to prefer.

VI

Blackbird traces in the shadow not cast
the indecipherable past.

VII

Blackbird finds thrilling
      the drumbeats drilling
            the feet of
men of women into
      utterance.

VIII

To Blackbird rhythm
      is inescapable
Fired to heights alchemical
the immortal bird consumed

Charlie Parker

wired.

IX

Blackbird once again
attempts flight. Crashes into
the circle's contracting edge.

X

Even the sight of the whip makes
Blackbird cry out sharply.
No euphony.

XI

Pierced by fear, Massa and all his generation
mistake Blackbird for the long shadow.

XII

Blackbird strips to reduce gravity's pull
readying for flight again. Fate hauls him in
to another impetus.

XIII

In the dark
    out of the sun
Blackbird sits
    among the shavings
from the cedar coffins.

PAMELA MORDECAI

POEMS GROW

on window ledges or especial corners
of slightly dirty kitchens where rats hide

or offices where men above the street
desert their cyphers of the market place

to track the clouds for rain or ride the wind
guileless as gulls oblivious of the girl

upon the desk who proffers wilting breasts
for a fast lunch.   Ah which of us wants

anything but love? And first upon the hillside where bare feet in a goat's wake

avoiding small brown pebbles
know earth as it was made

and women working fields
releasing cotton from the mother tree

milking teats heavy with white
wholesomeness or riding wave

on wave of green cane till
the swell abates and the warm

winds find only calm brown surfaces
thick with the juicy flotsam of the storm

make poems

and men who speak the drum bembe
dundun conga dudups cutter

or blow the brass or play the rhumba box
or lick croix-croix marimba or tack-tack

and women who record all this
to make the tribe for start in blood

send it to school to factory to sea
to office university   to death

make poems

and we who write them down
make pictures intermittently

(sweet silhouettes fine profiles
a marked face) but the bright light

that makes these darknesses
moves always always beyond mastery

Griot older than time on Zion Hill
weaving a song into eternity.

CONVENT GIRL

She was a convent girl, that's all.
Granted, arrayed against a wall
tummy tucked in tail under and
a saucy cigarette in hand,
the average self-respecting wand
inside the average room of men
would always stand and wave.
A minor talent, that, it gave
her little comfort once she knew

men liked her. Liked her. One or two
knew why. The common-herdy rest
made it a case of clump and curve
of winey waist and bubbly breast.

But sooth the girl had winkled out
the thing that made them tick.
She saw it wasn't any sexy trick
of lingering, no style of rock-
your-body, swing-your-tit,
or heave-your-ass. What she
could screw so it would fit
a man was her mind's eye.

It was a dangerous oversight.

They said she was a boasie bitch
they said it really wasn't right
that such a slutty little tease
should soak up sun and feel cool breeze.
They catch her in the road one night
fuck out her life and fling her in a ditch.

She was a convent girl, that's all –
a little girl that five men fall
because she see over their head
beyond their footsole to their dread
of having passed and not been there.

She died for having felt their fear.

THE ANGEL IN THE HOUSE

First January find me here
considering this writer
who glad that she inherit
five hundred pound a year
so she could choke a Angel
in her House. No sooner than
the Spirit dead, she feel
she can inscribe exactly
what she please at any time
she please, being as how
she now decide she safe
inside this room for just
she-one.

Well, to start with,
I feel this sister mean.
Whole world of somebody
pile up on top them one
another and she out
looking wider berth for
she alone? Nobody
tell her all o' we cramp

up out here struggling for
abbreviated air?

You say she mad? You say
is mad she say *she* mad?
So tell me where to find
any sane body these
dread days when every soul
outside them skull walking
and talking to themself
a raving recitation.

As for the Cherub
I feel it for this Spirit who
ten chance to one just
never had no choice
but had to put sheself
into a house accept
the job to jook and cook
to clean and care for man
and pikni pot and pan.

This Miss Woolf take a simple
view of pum-pum politics,
she make a crass construction
of the sweet domestic life.
She don't know Wife is just
another way to make it
through?

    I feel this getty-getty
attitude passing obscene.
I feel this own-room business

smack of Mistress Queen.
I feel this graceful space
for croquet and the season's
change wide hats and flailing
arms and cool white beauty
and Leonard let's arrange
for Vita to be here
till spring hijack disgrace
and take it pretty far.

And say for argument
she feel that she must go
another way, she have no
cause to wring the Spirit neck!
Don't that must summon serried
ranks of the angelic hosts?
Set them upon the path
to war? Don't that must be
a clarion call to all the ghosts
of women wearied into
time by tendering?

Is who she think she be?

Gloom get her in the end.
At home we'd say selfish –
so Angel Duppy come
claim she.

I say House Angel
make her play – baking
babies and fine embroidery.
She plant her one small

talent and it bear.
Miss Woolf she make a
follow-fashion move behind
a bird manoeuvring
in circles never noticing
the circles narrowing
with each fly past.

The end, old people say,
of such a route is
penetration of your
own lugubrious ass.

ALTHEA PRINCE

from Loving This Man

II

My great-aunt Helen was Papa Emmanuel's oldest surviving relative. She was someone I had never seen before; for she left Antigua in the 1920s to marry her childhood sweetheart. He had worked on a ship that sailed to Canada. One year he "jumped ship" and stayed in Montreal. Later, when he obtained immigrant status, he sent for his fiancée and married her. He had died several years before my arrival, and he and Aunt Helen had not had any children. I wondered if they had chosen to be childless, but could not ask Aunt Helen the question. It would have been considered rude to ask about such a private part of her life.

In the first months in Toronto, my head whirled with the books that Aunt Helen pressed on me. She found my knowledge lacking in the area of black writers and things about black people. She introduced me to all of her dog-eared copies of books by Frantz Fanon, W.E.B. Du Bois, Zora Neale Hurston, Langston Hughes, and C.L.R. James. Aunt Helen read everything that she could put her hands on by and about black people, and she made sure that I did the same. In the evenings, we would curl up with books, or watch a show on television. It was not the same as my evenings with Mama Reevah, but it was close, and I enjoyed them.

During the week, I worked at a bank, having secured a job as a clerk, where I took down details of applications for loans. On weekends, I danced to calypso and ska and soul and funk music with the new friends I met in nightclubs and at parties.

The first friendship I made in Toronto was with the granddaughter of one of Aunt Helen's friends. She was my age, and was a schoolteacher and a very nice person. She told me a lot about the university system and the kinds of courses that I could take. And she introduced me to the nightclubs that she and her friends went to on weekends.

Although she was not from the Caribbean, she liked going to Caribbean nightclubs, as they were among the few places where she could meet groups of young black people. We would dance until the wee hours of the morning and then make our way home to tumble into bed and sleep until late-late the next day.

We became a tightly knit group of friends and talked on the telephone in the evenings. I figured I was living like people lived in the movies, for I was talking to people on the phone instead of walking about. It was not as fascinating as I had thought it would be; in fact, it felt rather alienating and lonely. I missed my family and friends and glad noises and sun and twilight and the smell of the sea.

I tried to find the smell and sounds I longed for in the music of the voices, in the words and in the faces of the people from the Caribbean whom I met. A lot of women from the Caribbean had come to Toronto as domestic workers and had sent for their families later on. There were also many Caribbean nurses who had come from England. And there were others, like me, who had left high school and come to Canada as immigrants.

Their presence, like Aunt Helen's, eased my feelings of being ungrounded and dislocated from my centre. But I could not duplicate all that my heart longed to hear, all that my eyes yearned to see. I did have memories *longer than who*, and I called back as much as I could from the corners where I stored them for safekeeping. It was a way to manage newness, loneliness, the cold, and the blues that had begun to seep into my life and take up residence deep inside of me.

Some days, I felt as if my head was turned to Antigua at the same time that I had my eyes focused on Toronto. It was a kind of anguish I lived in: being in one place, with my heart in another. Sometimes I felt as if I was marking time, just hovering around in my life, not really present in it. I wondered if that was how Seleena had felt, living life away from those she loved and who loved her.

During the evenings when I went out with my friends, joy would grudgingly come to the top, pulling itself from among the ruins, the ashes of all of the feelings that were not bright and beautiful.

A few months after I arrived in Toronto, Aunt Helen became ill with a heart condition and complications of high blood pressure. She asked me if I would continue to live in her house and pay the same small rent that she had been charging me. She would move into an apartment in a fully serviced senior citizens' building, for she could no longer manage to look after herself in a three-storey house.

She asked only that I not bring anyone to live in her house, as she had never considered having tenants. That was what she said, but underneath it I heard a warning not to take a boyfriend to live with me. Aunt Helen was very prim and proper, and it would have been against her principles to have that kind of living arrangement going on in her house, whether she was living in it or not.

I tried to convince her that we could manage by finding someone who would take care of her during the day while I was at work. Aunt Helen would not hear of it. She did not want to deal with a person in her home all day, she said; that was too risky.

"And besides," she said, "there are activities at the seniors' apartment building; and there are other people my age to talk with and play cards. There are trips here and there, and to tell you the truth, I would enjoy those trips. They go to lunchtime plays and sometimes to hear a speaker and so on. It sounds good; I checked it out a few years ago. It is a very well-run apartment building."

I had thought that she was putting herself into a "home," but the building she described was not a "home." She would have her own apartment, with a kitchen and bathroom, and she would have the choice of eating meals in a common dining room. This arrangement sounded more acceptable than a "home." It had been a shock to me to discover that people in Canada did not always look after their elderly relatives. Some of them shunted them off to a "home" as soon as they became old.

I gave up trying to talk Aunt Helen out of her decision to move to a senior citizens' building. I believe that she worried about being a burden to me, and I tried to make her understand that I did not see her that way. Finally, I accepted the offer she made and thanked her from the bottom of my heart for her generosity. My salary barely allowed me to pay the rent she charged me and provide my other very simple needs, since I was also trying to save money to go to school. It would have been a great hardship to suddenly be confronted with regular apartment rent.

Aunt Helen in turn thanked me for being in Toronto at the right time to be a companion to her. I loved her company. Sometimes we talked for hours and hours, or rather, Aunt Helen talked and I listened, for she was full of stories about how things had been for her when she first came to live in Canada.

She and her husband had lived first in Montreal and then moved to Toronto after they retired. He had been a builder and Aunt Helen had been a schoolteacher. She had gone to school and received her teaching certificate soon after she came to Canada. At first she had worked as a scullery maid in a big mansion for a rich white family in Montreal. Then she had saved for the fees to go to school.

She told me that she had not realized that people still engaged scullery maids. She had thought that it was only in the novels she read that such a job existed. "And 'scullery' it was too, child. I worked in the pantry."

At my surprised look she said: "Oh yes, my dear, there was a pantry and that is where I worked, day in and day out. I polished the silver and I set the table and I made sure that the trays of food were filled . . . and . . . you know, took a damp cloth and kept the gravy spills from the edges."

There was a thoughtful look on her face. "You know, I would never hire people to look after my whole life like that. I would feel so babyish. Those people could not even boil water to save their life." She laughed a deep, infectious belly laugh that made me laugh too.

They had had friends in Toronto then, Aunt Helen and her husband. She told me in a sad little voice: "Most of them are all gone now." Some had gone home to the Caribbean, others, like Aunt Helen, had stayed and experienced a great loneliness. Most of their relatives were in the Caribbean, in other North American cities, or in England.

When I first arrived, Aunt Helen told me that she had two black women friends who were born and bred in Toronto. I thought that she meant that they were black-*skinned*. I was surprised, when I met her friends, to see that one of them was brown-brown, and the other was light-skinned. I was reminded that in Canada, *black* was the word that was used to refer to all who looked like me, regardless of the shade of their skin.

In Antigua, there had been white people and there had been all of us. I never knew that I was black. This realization was what had prompted Aunt Helen to assail me with books about who I was, so that I would see myself as a member of a group larger than just my family. My head and heart had to stretch to accommodate this new group identification and membership.

Aunt Helen and her two friends got together once a week for breakfast at Fran's Restaurant at St. Clair and Yonge. "We talk over old times and laugh and cry in our coffee," Aunt Helen laughingly told me. She invited me to join them each week, but I felt that I would have been intruding to go every time. I went once soon after I arrived, just so Aunt Helen could show me off to her friends.

It felt like a kind of old ladies' show and tell. Her friends showed me pictures of their grandchildren and their great-grandchildren, and they asked me questions about my goals. Those were tricky questions to answer, but I repeated some of the things that Mama Reevah and my aunts had said about going to school and finding a good job, and bettering myself. It must have been the right thing to say, because Aunt Helen's friends nodded approvingly, and Aunt Helen looked pleased and proud. After Aunt Helen moved into the seniors' apartment building, I visited her one evening during the week and every Sunday. And Saturday was a permanent, well-rehearsed arrangement with us. We went to Kensington Market and sought out the ingredients to make Antiguan pepperpot and foongie. Then we cooked the pepperpot and foongie in the tiny kitchen in Aunt Helen's new apartment or at her house, and we ate, seated on the couch in the living room, while we watched television.

The first time she came back to her house, I watched Aunt Helen walk around the living room, touching everything, as if she was greeting her things. I suggested to her that she take more of the figurines and pictures off the wall, even if they cluttered her new apartment. "You can put them in a cupboard and then sometimes change the ones you keep out," I suggested. She welcomed the idea, and I realized just how hard it was for her to be away from all of her memories.

After that, I made sure that we spent more Saturdays at her house than we did at her apartment. Sometimes Aunt Helen would stay with me for the entire weekend.

Whether we spent Saturdays at Aunt Helen's apartment or at her house, we followed the same routine. We ate our dinner sitting on the couch with trays perched precariously on our laps. While we ate, we watched *Soul Train* on the old television set that looked like a piece of antique furniture. It was encased in an oak cabinet with elegantly carved legs. Its black-and-white picture was clear as day and Aunt Helen took pride in it, saying that she had no intention of getting a colour television set.

When the dance segment of the show began, Aunt Helen would say in a voice filled with consternation: "But these people don't have no bones in they body!" She said it every time with the same degree of incredulity. And I laughed every time.

The Saturday pepperpot and foongie ritual was something Aunt Helen had always done, ever since she came to Canada in the 1920s. She had roped me into doing it with her as soon as I arrived in Toronto, saying that I made her feel connected to Antigua.

Aunt Helen told me that when she was growing up, she and her mother used to go to the market every Saturday morning and buy the ingredients for pepperpot and foongie. Then they would return home, cook the pepperpot and foongie, and serve it to the whole family. It was the same kind of Saturday that I was accustomed to having with Mama Reevah, and so I found it comforting to have it recreated, without fail, every single week.

I used to wish that Aunt Helen's memory of my Papa Emmanuel had not been so fleeting. She had *some* memory of him, but more than forty years had passed and she had never returned to Antigua for a visit. When I told Aunt Helen that I wished there had been more of my Papa Emmanuel in her memory, she patted my hand and said: "I wish so too, child. I wish so too."

Were it not for Aunt Helen, those first immigrant-months in Canada would have been like living Seleena's life, a life lived away from love. I was a shy-shy girl and spent more than a healthy amount of my spare time pining for my family. While I had made quite a few friends, friends could not replace a person from my family who knew me and loved me for me.

When Aunt Helen died, I felt a sense of desolation that I could not explain to anyone. Friends asked how it was that I felt so connected, so close to someone whom I had only known for a short time. I shook my head, unable to explain the enormity of my sense of loss.

Aunt Helen left me all of her life's savings, as well as the house and all its contents. I was so overwhelmed at the reading of the will that I stumbled out of the lawyer's office onto the sidewalk, my eyes filled with tears.

I thanked Aunt Helen in my heart, but I would rather have had her with me. I wished that she had told me about the contents of her will, so that I could have thanked her properly for being so good to me. I knew, however, that given what I had seen of her generous spirit, she would not have wanted to hear my thanks.

I buried Aunt Helen in a gravesite in Mount Pleasant Cemetery with a headstone that carried her particulars. I asked for the lettering to be the same as that which Mama Reevah had chosen for Papa Emmanuel. I wished for a snow-on-the-mountain tree that I could plant, but there were none in Canada. Aunt Helen would have liked that reminder of Antigua. She would have to be satisfied with my second choice: a beautiful silver birch tree.

It had intrigued me to learn from Aunt Helen that the silver birch tree, which looked so serene, could wreak havoc with its roots. She told me of a neighbour who had to repair the foundation of her house when a silver birch tree damaged the concrete structures in its path, deep underneath the soil. Aunt Helen said that she had always wanted a silver birch in her front yard, but her friend's experience had stopped her in good time. Now she would have one with her throughout eternity.

I chose a gravesite that faced the traffic, because I thought that Aunt Helen would have liked that; she enjoyed activity and action. She liked peaceful nights too, and each evening, when the traffic eased, there would be peace and quiet. But her days would be filled with the hustle and bustle of the crosstown traffic on Mount Pleasant Road.

As I left the cemetery, I remembered how I had delighted in watching Aunt Helen as she danced a few halting steps with me. She had often played calypsos on her decrepit record player. Its needle was so old that it sounded like a nail scratching on the vinyl, but Aunt Helen did not care. So long as she heard the words of Sparrow and Kitchener and Melody, that was sufficient for her. They were the three calypsonians she remembered from her young days, and she had quite a few of their albums. She would sing along lustily as we danced: "The creature from the black lagoon is your father!"

Lord Melody was the calypsonian she liked best of all, "because his voice is raucous and he tells it like it is," she said. She believed that the way he told it was exactly how black people felt about their own colour and their big noses and thick lips.

Whenever we danced to Lord Melody's last chorus of "The Creature From the Black Lagoon Is Your Father," Aunt Helen would drop into a chair, saying, "That is for you young people." I would smile as I continued dancing, for I understood that it was her invitation to me to entertain her with my dancing. I knew that she liked to watch me dance, and it was easy to oblige her, because I loved to dance. I enjoyed hearing the music that used to ring in my ears and my heart day in and day out in Antigua.

I had danced a lot in Antigua. Mama Reevah was not partial to dancing; Papa Emmanuel used to try and drag her up whenever there was a calypso on the radio, but she would pull away from him, saying, "Emmanuel, you know I don't like to dance. Teach Sayshelle to dance." He would pull me up then, and teach me the intricate steps that he used to do when he went to dance halls. I would dance with him, happily watching as he twirled and twisted and swung his waist.

I missed Aunt Helen very badly and thought that it would help me to continue our Saturday pepperpot and foongie ritual. The trip to Kensington Market without her was wrenching. However, I returned home and resolutely recreated the pepperpot and foongie, but the food tasted bad in my mouth. It had lost its joy without Aunt Helen's company.

I turned on the television set and tried to watch the *Soul Train* dancers. They looked ordinary now; without Aunt Helen's voice commenting, all the magic of their contortions was gone. I said her words out loud: "But these people don't have no bones in they body!" And I laughed for the first time since the funeral. I got to my feet and danced with the *Soul Train* dancers. I could almost hear Aunt Helen say: "But you don't have no bones in your body!"

III

Months passed into years, and still there were moments when a great longing for Aunt Helen would take me over. It would suck my breath away, leaving me gasping for air. A longing for her essence and her presence would arrive with a sound, or a memory, or the smell of something that she had liked. Florida Water; or Lavender Water; or English pork sausages sizzling in a frying pan; eggs waiting on the side. It would come too with the sight of large slivers of rind in orange marmalade, and on days when the rain came "non-stop," as the weatherman said.

One such rainy day, I went outside, just to smell the air and look at the clean-clean plants and the leaves that had been washed off of the trees. I said goodbye to Aunt Helen in a more final way than I had ever done, for the rain had stopped . . . and everything was new . . . and fresh . . . and washed clean.

There was no gutter overflowing into the street in which to dabble my feet after the rain, so I satisfied myself with walking through the Humewood neighbourhood that was my home. All around me, I saw other people who looked as if they were having some version of my experience. They had said goodbye until eternity and were as far away from their families as I was.

They too sought ways to live without their Mama Reevahs; their Papa Emmanuels; their aunts, cousins, families; their navel-strings buried under a backyard tree without so much as a by-your-leave. Like Aunt Helen, they faced being buried here, far away from the land and the sea and the sounds that they held close in their hearts . . . still, after so much time.

The snow falling in the middle of winter gave me that same feeling that everything was being cleansed. The sun made little highlights on the top of the waist-high snowbanks along both sides of St. Clair Avenue. It was a pretty picture, and reminded me of the Christmas cards that Mama Reevah used to hang on a string across the bookshelf in our drawing room. When the time came, I too hung Christmas cards across a bookshelf in the drawing room of Aunt Helen's house. It was one of the things I did to keep my Mama Reevah's essence close. It took some effort to remember that in Toronto, there was a "living room" and not a "drawing room."

Mama Reevah's essence came in letters every week. I loved receiving her letters. She wrote joyfully of familiar things, and of political events that saddened me. "There are accusations of corruption in government, accusations of corruption in the elections. Things are worse than your Papa Emmanuel could have ever imagined. I am so glad that you are over there in Canada, away from it all. Your father would have been happy to know that you are making a good life for yourself somewhere else, instead of being trapped here and prevented from advancing in your life." I did not want her to worry about me. She had had enough worry in her life, I figured. I turned my eyes to Toronto and looked toward trying to make a life for myself.

The Toronto of my dreams was sweet-sweet and soft-soft: feeding squirrels in the park, resting easy in my mind, working hard by day and at peace at night, welcomed in society and offered equality. The Toronto of my immigrant-life was a different reality. In this-here space, in this-here place, and in this-here time, I struggled to breathe, and I walked my own ground with my head held down, my chin on my chest.

I felt a relentless fear taking hold inside me that I would never catch my breath if I let it out. For white people would snap it up and prevent me from *being*. I could see their intent lurking in their eyes, especially when the headlines screamed of black people in the U.S. demanding equality in all areas of life. I could feel them breathing in and out, wondering: "When will they do it here?"

It was present, too, in the way they sidled away from me in the subway trains, on streetcars, on buses, in supermarkets. I joked with friends that it was great that no one sat next to us on the subway; we got two whole seats to ourselves.

Toronto moved through my life, drying and hardening into my bones. I felt crisp and petrified, like moths and mosquitoes stuck on a kitchen door screen.

I thought of how women like me were still running home from the attack of men who were not like me. I thought of "sailor-pickneys" in Antigua, doomed for life to bear the mark of the scandal of their mothers. And I winced at the numerous men like me whom I saw in Toronto rushing headlong, seeking women who were not like me. There would soon be many "pickneys" of another hue. I wondered what Canada would look like in a hundred years.

When night came, I hurried home, away from the Toronto streets, for none of my friends had cars. We were too newly arrived, my friends and I, to do more than submit to the discomfort of stares on public transportation.

The rain came as I walked and dreamed Toronto. My feet were damp at the ankles, despite two pairs of thick socks and lined knee-high boots. In the wetness of the streets, the lamplight shone brightly on the puddles, so I could avoid them. But instead of walking around their ragged circle, I stepped over them, consciously breaking my Mama Reevah's taboo:

"Don't step over water at a crossroads. Evil people throw out their sickness at the crossroads. It could be somebody's dead-water; or worse yet, their sore-foot water; or even worse still: their throw-way-pickney water. Then for sure, your insides going need to be cleaned from all their sickness."

In the shimmering water I saw grotesque images of the silenced candle-flies and mosquitoes, smashed against mesh screens. All life was dead and gone from them, except for the fear. The fear was preserved forever.

Wanting to prove to myself that I had evolved from the prohibitions of my growing-up, I pretended that I did not know that in big-city life people do not go to the crossroads to throw their sickness onto the street. I pushed away the knowledge that no one looks after their sickness at home in this new place. I let myself act as if I had forgotten that everyone has running water in their homes, so that bath-pans filled with sickness are things of the past.

I did not miss the closeness of sickness that I had experienced in Antigua. It had filled up my nostrils and my senses in childhood. Besides Papa Emmanuel's time of sickness, I still held a disturbing memory from when I was very small, of the scent of the antiseptic in Granny's dead-water. Despite myself, I had listened for the drip-drip sound of the drops of dead-water falling into aluminum buckets placed strategically around the dead-board. The ice was an attempt to preserve her body. I would walk past her room with my head averted at least twice each day: once in the morning to leave my bedroom, and once at night to go to sleep.

Her body waited for people to arrive to see it before the minister would sing hymns and make a sermon and speak of our loved one. I had made sure that I did not see her body laid out in the coffin in church. And I resented those who walked past the coffin and made comments under their hands, as if they thought that we really could not hear them.

"But she look good-ee? Like say she just sleeping. Is how old she is? They write her age on the program? Is how come she look so *likkle* an' shrivel-up? They shrink her, or she shrink by herself? Her shroud look good-ee? I wonder if is Mistress Hughes make it, or if she did give it out?"

These people who viewed Granny, all beautiful in her silk-lined casket, had not seen life through her eyes: cold, with a pinpoint of blue at the centre of the blackness. They could afford to enjoy the tableau of the white shroud on white saint, the arranged smile, the silken, blue-black hair, serene, not a strand out of place. And all was dry.

In Granny's day, unlike in Papa Emmanuel's, there were no funeral homes to prepare loved ones for burial. Working silently, women removed bucketfuls of dead-water . . . reeking of antiseptic. They were careful not to spill the dead-water on the inside of the house, for that would have required scrubbing the floor even more carefully afterwards. And there was still the bedding to be burned.

The women did not take Granny's dead-water out to the crossroads. They simply tipped it over into the trench leading out of the yard, and the water ran to meet the green slime in the gutter-water in the street. Then Mama Reevah threw bucket after bucket of fresh water behind Granny's dead-water. She stood on the back step and looked behind it as it was washed away from our lives.

As I stepped over a puddle in a Toronto street, I felt a little tug of fear, a moment of unease at what I had done. Shaking off years of memory, I boldly loosened the hold of Mama Reevah's words. I felt as if I lost something precious as I broke the sacred taboo. For I liked the mystical nature of it; liked knowing that I had been handed something. It had been passed on with as much seriousness as the ritual of my Anglican confirmation.

Life in Toronto did not exactly smack me in the face in the way moths and mosquitoes slammed into a screen door, but it did not exactly embrace me either. I felt that it was more correct to say that life had taken me over, chewed me up, and spat me out in small pieces. All of my pieces felt as if they were being stuck back together in the wrong places.

I did not write that in my letters to Mama Reevah for fear that she would think me crazy. And maybe she would be disappointed that I was not full of glowing reports of a life being well lived with enjoyment and peace. I wrote long-long letters that said in small emotions: "I miss you."

I still desperately missed Aunt Helen, and I still excluded that fact from my letters to Mama Reevah, and from my letters to Aunt Juniper Berry and Aunt Sage. I wrote lovely little letters to my three cousins. And at night I cried, missing them all so much that my belly hurt, right where my navel-string would have connected me with them. I remembered that I had left my navel-string buried under a tree in the yard and had not even said goodbye.

I worked at my job; I did household chores; I spoke to people who spoke to me; I did things that seemed necessary to enable the rest of my day and my life. I lived uneventfully from day to day, taking up space, marking time, like the bark of some weathered tree. At the end of each season, I was like the aged tree: still standing, no taller, and yet much more come-of-age in the space and time that I occupied. It was a narrow existence.

I did not notice just when it was that the sound of the song of my family moved itself to a more distant place inside me. When I reached to embrace it, there were only faint strains playing in the distance. I feared that eventually the song would leave my heart altogether. I also knew that I would need to hear it again; when things changed; when time passed; and when my ears were clear of the clutter that I had allowed to take over.

All things moved through me in a slow, jangling kind of passage. It seemed sometimes that the descant of my life was heard through grooves that were etched long-long ago. Although joy was a constant hum in the foreground, there were many yesterdays in the background marked by tears and sorrow.

I dared not make prognostications for the future, but I knew that there was a cool-cool spot awaiting me. In that place, flames would take me breathless by the hand and clear the way through my heart's badlands. I asked myself if it was worth the promise of treasure waiting under the covers of the cool-cool forest and the rushes.

The answer was clear: through streams of pure heart's desire, tempered by truth, I would find that cool-cool spot, untouched by human hand, caressed only by soft breezes. The promise of the taste of the joy that would come made me breathless.

Days slipped into nights as gently as the spinach leaves showed themselves in the mornings in Antigua. Nighttime would close with just a few leaves curled on the vine. Then morningtime would arrive and reveal four leaves unfurled, fresh as the new day; a drop of dew nesting here and there, testimony to freshness.

As my Toronto-days drifted into months, then into years, tears became the hallmark of the quality of my life. I cried rivers of tears; they fell on me and around me. There was no gutter to catch them; they overflowed and washed the street.

I consoled myself with the thought that time was a material construct. Observed, it offered only limitations, frustrations, and even hopelessness. Spirit, on the other hand, was ethereal. Acknowledged, it brought freedom, liberation, celebration of moments that appeared temporal. In essence, Spirit's markings were far more permanent than the limitations that time sought to impose.

I came to see that Toronto made my Spirit poor. I did not want to be who I used to be. I found myself struggling to remember the girl I was, the girl who was hurtled into Toronto-life; chilled to the bone in winter; overheated in summer; unable to fully embrace springtime; devastated by the fall.

I searched in the people around me for all that I knew as normal from my growing-up in Antigua. My Mama Reevah's song, my family's song; both grew more and more elusive. Not even memories of Saturdays spent with Aunt Helen's pepperpot and *Soul Train* eased my heart. The essence of my life had been inexorably changed; it was forever divided into two halves: "before I left Antigua" and "after I came to Toronto." It was as simple as that.

My life had other defining moments, but none could compare to the hollow in my heart that had been made by immigration. I told myself that that was what it was: a big hole that nothing would ever fill up again; no love, no hatred . . . nothing could fill the space that leaving Antigua had made . . . nothing.

LORNA GOODISON

WHAT WE CARRIED THAT CARRIED US

I

Song and Story

In ship's belly, song and story dispensed as medicine,
story and song, bay rum and camphor for faint way.

Song propelled you to fly through hidden other eye,
between seen eyes and out of structure, hover.

In barks of destruction, story functioned as talisman
against give-up death, cramped paralyzed darkness.

Remaining remnant tasting all of life, blood, salt,
bitter wet sugar. Ball of light, balance power,

pellucid spirit wafer without weight, ingested,
taken in as nourishment, leaven within the system.

Remnant remaining rise now.

II

Dance Rocksteady

You danced upon the deck of the slaver *Antonia*
named for the cherubic daughter of sea captain Fraser.
Aye kumina.

You moved just so, in and out between wild notes
sounded by the suicide followers, staying well within
rock steady rhythm,

range of Kilimanjaro, length of river Limpopo.
Respond again to higher rimshot and one drop
ride rocksteady.

NEVER EXPECT

Burchell the Baptist
handed you the landpapers.
You were not in a position
to read them, so you call
the name of your place
into the responding wind

by so doing recreating
your ancestral ceremony
of naming. "Never Expect"
you name your place,
your own spot to cultivate
a small start-over Eden.

Plot for fruit and flowering trees
for your children.
Burying ground for family tombs
and navel strings.
Your strict drawn boundary line
against intruder,

prickle dildo-makka fence
militant as living barbwire.
Begin with one room, piecen it,
fling open your door
or turn your key
when you private.

Build your firewall high.
Raise up your wide barbecue.
Pop loud laugh for pea soup.
Remark openly upon
your ceiling of the sky
and its shifting shade of blue.

Hosanna you build your house.
Yes, Alleluia, you never expect it.

QUESTIONS FOR MARCUS MOSIAH GARVEY

And did prophets ascended come swift
to attend you at the end
in your small cold water room in London?

Was it William Blake now seraph and ferryman
who rowed you across the Thames to where Africans
took you by longboat home?

And did the Nazarene walking upon water
come alongside to bless and assure you that he
of all prophets understood and knew

just how they had betrayed and ill-used you?
And did you wonder again what manner of people
sell out prophets for silver and food?

from From Harvey River

A Memoir

Throughout her life my mother lived in two places at the same time: Kingston, Jamaica, where she raised a family of nine children; and Harvey River, where she was born and grew up. Harvey River had been settled by her grandfather William Harvey, who gave his name to the river, and the river in turn gave its name to the village. I do not think that there was ever a day in my childhood when the river or the village was not mentioned in our house. Over the years Harvey River came to function as an enchanted place in my imagination, an Eden from which we fell to the city of Kingston. But over time I have come to see that my parents' story is really a story about rising up to a new life. As a child I constantly asked my mother about her life before, as she put it, "things changed." I listened carefully to her stories, and repeated them to myself. I also took to asking urgent questions of my father. I have an image of me standing outside the bathroom door calling in to him over the noise of the shower, "So what was your mother's name and what was her mother's name?" But my father's people do not live long, and he died when I was fifteen years old. So I never did get to ask him all my questions. After my mother's death nearly thirty-five years later, I began to "dream" her, as Jamaicans say; and in those dreams I continued to ask her questions about her life before and after she came to Kingston. And then there was this one very vivid visitation when I dreamt that I went to see her in her new residence, a really palatial and splendid sewing room with high stained-glass windows where she was now in charge of sewing gorgeous garments for top-ranking angels. She said they were paying her a lot for her sewing in this place, and that all her friends came to talk angelic, big woman business with her there as she sewed. She said she could not tell me more as she did not want me to stay with her too long, because the living should not mix up too much with the dead. But as I was leaving the celestial workroom she handed me a book. This is that book.

Part II
How Harvey River Became Harvey River

For all we know, the village of Harvey River used to have another name, but when my mother's grandfather and his brother founded it in 1840 the old name was lost forever. The Harvey River was the source of life to everyone in the village. It was named by David's father, William, and his brother John, two of five brothers named Harvey who had come from England sometime during the early half of the nineteenth century. They may have been related to one Thomas Harvey, a Quaker who had come to Jamaica in 1837, along with Joseph Sturge; together they had written a powerful and moving account of slavery in the British West Indies. The other Harvey brothers split up and went to live in different parishes in Jamaica after their arrival; only William and John stayed together. At first, they took up jobs as bookkeepers on the San Flebyn sugar estate, but one day soon after their arrival they witnessed something that made them decide to abandon all ideas about joining the plantocracy.

The estate overseer had hired two new Africans fresh off the boat in Lucea Harbour. Although slavery was officially abolished in 1838, some Africans were now being brought to Jamaica, along with East Indians and Chinese, to work as indentured labourers on sugar plantations where production was severely affected by the loss of slave labour.

Among the new Africans was a pair of twins from Liberia, the great-grandchildren of fighting Maroons who had been transported from Jamaica after the Maroon War in 1795. These fierce fighters had been banished to Nova Scotia in Canada, and later settled in Liberia. The twin boys had grown up hearing many tales of Jamaica and of the courage of their ancestors, runaway Africans who refused to accept the yoke of slavery. The twins even claimed to be related to the supreme warrior woman, Nanny of the Maroons. Grandy Nanny, as I have heard some Maroons call her, had led her people in a protracted guerrilla war against the British until they were forced to make peace with her, on her terms.

These two young men had chosen to come from Liberia on a one-year contract as indentured labourers, mainly to see for themselves the green and mountainous land to which their foreparents always longed to return. The Land of Look Behind, of Cockpit Country, Nanny Town, and Accompong, Bush Country, Maroon Country, where places had sinister and coded names like "Me No Send, You No Come."

They stood like twin panthers on the docks at Lucea, with such a fierce, mesmerizing presence that the overseer of the San Flebyn estate, one Grant Elbridge, felt compelled to hire them as a matching pair. He did this partly with his own amusement in mind, for he and his wife often indulged in elaborate sex games with the Africans on the property. One week after he hired them, Elbridge announced that the twins had to be whipped, abolition of slavery or not, for who the hell were these goddamned twin savages to disobey and disrespect him? Last night, when he had summoned them to his overseer's quarters, and he and his wife had indicated to them that they wanted them to take off their clothes, the two, acting as one, had spit in his face and stalked out into the dark night.

So Elbridge ordered the twins to take off their shirts again, this time in the middle of the cane field, and this time the twins obeyed at once. They tore off their shirts and bared their chests to him before the other labourers, who now worked under conditions that were hardly better than before their emancipation. The huge, dark eyes of the twins locked on to Elbridge. The Harvey brothers, who had been ordered by Elbridge to leave their bookkeeping and come down into the cane piece to watch him, in his words, "tan the hide of these heathen savages," stood close to each other and watched, sick to their stomachs, as the long, thick strip of cowhide lashed across the backs of the Maroons, raising raw, bloody welts. But they became truly terrified when they saw that it was Elbridge who bawled and bellowed in pain. The whip dropped from his hand and coiled loosely like a harmless yellow snake when he fell, face down in the cane field. The Maroon twins seemed to have mastered the "bounce back" techniques of Nanny, who was able to make bullets ricochet off her body back at the British soldiers. Just as the bullets had bounced off Nanny's body into the flesh of the soldiers, so too did the twins redirect Elbridge's chastisement onto him. As Elbridge screamed and writhed in pain, the Harveys watched as the Liberian twins walked out of the cane piece and turned their faces toward the Cockpit Country, knowing that no one would ever find them once they disappeared into Maroon territory. After witnessing this, the Harveys resigned from their jobs as bookkeeping clerks on the San Flebyn estate and decided to find some land to make a life for themselves.

In the spirit of true conquistadors, my mother's paternal grandfather and his brother had come across a small clearing up in the Hanover Hills on a Sunday as they combed the area outside the estate in search of a place to settle themselves. It was not far from a place named Jericho, and the entire area was cool and scented by pimento or "allspice" bushes. They did not know it then, but in years to come, almost all the world's allspice would come from the island of Jamaica.

Tall bamboo trees bowed and bumped feathery heads together to create flexible, swaying arches, and here and there solid dark blocks of shale jutted up from the ground in strange Stonehenge-like formations. On close examination, they saw that the rocks had bits of seashells embedded in them, so it is fair to say that at some point that area must have been under the sea. The clearing was verdant and watered by a strong, coursing river. They had reached it by following one of the paths leading away from the estate. These paths had been created by the feet of men and women fleeing from the beatings and torture that was their only payment for making absentee landlords some of the richest men in the world. "Rich as a West Indian planter" was a common saying when sugar was king during the eighteenth and nineteenth centuries.

Some of those paths led to small food plots, often set on stony hillsides, that were cultivated by the enslaved Africans to feed themselves. At the end of fourteen working days cultivating cane, and on Sundays, their one day off, they had planted vegetables like pumpkins, okras, dasheens, plantains, and yams, the food of their native Africa. For some reason, the soil of the parish of Hanover produced the best yams known to the palate. The moon-white Lucea yam, surely the monarch of all yams, was first cultivated in the parish of Hanover.

Every time she cooked and served Lucea yam, my mother would tell us the same story, that Jamaica's first prime minister, Sir Alexander Bustamante, who was himself a native of Hanover and a man who claimed to have been descended from Arawak Indians, would say that "Lucea yam is such a perfect food that it can be eaten alone, with no fish nor meat." She too subscribed to the belief that the Lucea yam needed nothing, no accompanying "salt ting," as the Africans referred to pickled pig or beef parts, dried, salted codfish, shad, and mackerel that was imported by estate owners as protein for their diet.

The clearing that was later to become the village of Harvey River was near the hillside plots farmed by some of the freed Africans, many of whom now worked as hired labourers on nearby estates. The Harveys decided to "settle" the land, and giddy at the prospect of imitating men like Christopher Columbus, Walter Raleigh, and Francis Drake, they named the river after themselves. They had spent the night sleeping on its banks, having come upon the place toward evening.

"I wonder if this river has a name," said William.

"Aye, it has one now," said John.

"And what might that be?"

"Harvey River."

They had bathed in it, and caught fat river mullets and quick, dark eels, which they roasted on stones. Then they had fallen asleep to the sound of the rush of the waters they now called by their name.

The Harvey brothers built their first small house of wattles and daub. Later they built a larger house of mahogany, cedar, and stone. Then William sent for his wife, Lily, and his children, Edward John, and Fanny, whom he had left behind in London when he and his brother had come to Jamaica. Nobody knows where their money came from, but they were able to acquire considerable property in the area and to live comfortably for the rest of their days.

In time the village grew. Grocery shops were established; there were at least two rum bars, churches, and a school. But no matter who came to live there, the Harveys were considered to be the first family of the village. And when the government built a bridge over a section of the Harvey River and tried to name it after some minor colonial flunky, William Harvey himself went and took down the government's sign and erected a sign of his own saying Harvey Bridge.

He was a tall, big-boned man
The earth shuddered under his steps
but the caught-quiet at his centre
pulled peace to him like a magnet.

Whenever she spoke of her paternal grandfather, my mother would say that he was one of the biggest, tallest, quietest men that anybody had ever met. Actually, because she had a love for imagery, she would say something like "When he walked, the ground would shake, but he was silent as a lamb, a giant of a man with a still spirit." True or not, there was something remarkable about the character of William Harvey, who became one of the few Englishmen in his time to legally marry an African woman. By all accounts he was a very moral man who would not have countenanced living in sin with Frances Duhaney. He took her as his legal wife in the Lucea Parish Church, and none of his English neighbours attended the wedding. Some of them even cautioned him that black women were only fit to be concubines. William's response to that particular piece of advice was that any woman who was good enough to share his bed was good enough for him to marry.

RACHEL MANLEY

from Drumblair

Memories of a Jamaican Childhood

11. Nomdmi

Let me tell you about my grandfather.

Pardi was a handsome man. As far as I was concerned he was the most handsome man in all the world. His father, Thomas Albert Manley, was the son of a travelling English tradesman and a black Jamaican woman. Looking at the only picture that exists of him, I believe he must have had some East Indian blood. His mother, Margaret, was a mulatto who appeared more white than black. The mixtures produced an uncommon harmony in Pardi. He had comparatively aquiline features, with deep-set communicative eyes, a "noble Roman nose" that made his face strong and distinguished, and a slight mouth which actually seemed unintrusive rather than mean. His face expressed all of the good qualities in life: intelligence, kindness, generosity, strength and courage, humour, gentleness, compassion and love. He was five feet ten inches tall, with long, slim limbs and slender feet which Mardi claimed were aristocratic. His being was one of quiet thoughtfulness. He was the colour of mahogany, warm and glowing.

Pardi was, as I have said, a Rhodes Scholar. Pardi was a war hero with a medal in a box in his top drawer which he didn't like to wear, and two letters *M* at the end of his name which he didn't like to use either. Pardi once held the world schoolboy record of ten seconds flat for the hundred-yard dash, and there is no point arguing that it was only the island schoolboy record, for that's not how I got the story in my head.

He was the brightest and best barrister in all the world. He was the only person I knew who played a mouth organ, and by the time I came on the scene he had become what Miss Boyd called a "nation builder." This last pursuit had apparently begun in 1938 with what was generally described as "national unrest," which always made me think that everyone on the island of Jamaica had been unable to sleep one night.

In 1938 there had been an important strike in Jamaica. The strike had started with sugar workers on plantations and had spread to the dock workers in the capital city, Kingston. The strike had been called by Pardi's famous elder cousin, Alexander Bustamante, fondly called Busta by most people. My family said this was his last attempt at being radical in his life. His fervour for the working class cause got him thrown into jail. Pardi negotiated with the British governor on his behalf. When Bustamante was released from prison, there was a big crowd that cheered him; he got all the praise and according to Mardi, who always defended Pardi, even when he didn't seem to need defending, Pardi got pushed to one side and Bustamante never even mentioned who had got him out of jail. Mardi would always finish the story sadly: "and we just left that massive crowd who were in love with Busta, and in the darkness made our way to the car unnoticed, and drove quietly home."

And that was really the start of the first big mass-based union in Jamaica, though there were smaller ones for more specific groups of workers before. It was named after Bustamante, the Bustamante Industrial Trade Union. By September 1938, the first Jamaican political party to survive in modern Jamaica was launched, at the Ward

Theatre. People said it was for the cause of freedom. They called it the People's National Party and Pardi was its unopposed leader. Bustamante was on the platform too that day, as a founding member. So was Sir Stafford Cripps, a lofty Englishman who represented the British Labour Party.

Two years later, according to family legend, Busta got jealous of Pardi. Pardi had not only kept Busta's namesake union alive while Busta was in jail, but had got them an increase of a penny in the shilling. People said that Busta thought Pardi was trying to take over his union.

"Imagine Norman Manley thinks you're only worth a penny," Busta told the workers. He was the most canny and street-smart politician.

"The antennae of a cat and the ethics of the alley," remarked Aunt Vera, Pardi's sometimes acerbic sister.

And away Busta went and formed his own party, the Jamaica Labour Party, of which he was president. The JLP supporters said it was because the PNP had just declared itself for socialism, which in fact it had. Whatever the reason, there was a big eruption and Busta went his own way.

That, as far as I knew, was the start of our two-party system. These were the facts I knew, the facts I was brought up on, though clearly they were biased by my family's point of view.

We didn't then have "universal adult suffrage." I relished reciting this term to my friends, who were as bewildered by it as I pretended not to be; I had a vague notion of a world where grown-ups were somehow entitled to their pain. That advance didn't come until 1944. Pardi fought for it without, he said, any particular help from his cousin Busta. And when we did get it, it was ironic that it proved to be the very factor that soundly defeated Pardi at the polls. His party lost again in 1949, but this time, I was told, he at least kept his own seat. I assumed this was a type of chair, as he had become an "Emaychar" –

my interpretation of the initials MHR, which stood for "Member of the House of Representatives," the House still being fully answerable to His Majesty the King of England.

At first I thought "nation building" was a job in construction. I imagined that Pardi built all the big buildings I saw going up in the city. Since he had a workroom with a carpenter's table and saws and planes and sandpaper and spirit levels, and he made big, stable pieces of furniture that we all had to try for size and assist in varnishing afterwards, I imagined he was a sort of head carpenter who would sit astride a roof under construction and finish the building. I was sure that finishing anything was the most important thing one could do.

Then I was reminded that houses were only a small part of development, and that the roads and dams and markets had to be built too, and then there were all the schools that had to be not only built but made to work. Money had to be somehow extracted from rich people and shared out to poor people so they didn't starve, and robbers and madmen had to have special places to go, and natural disasters like hurricanes had to be coped with – no, not during the rain and wind, never during the rain and wind – you just have to sit that out. I could never understand the point of coping with a hurricane after it was over and done with, but grown-ups were like that.

And before one could do any of this, one had to own one's own country. And the first step toward this was something Pardi was struggling for all the time, which he called "internal self-government."

It was clear to me that nation building was a very big responsibility, and now I adjusted my sights and placed Pardi on some not clearly defined roof over the whole island, where he was finishing the job. But I could never get anyone to answer the simplest questions: when would the nation be built, when would we own it, and would Pardi then have to find a new job? Mardi said that first he would have to get a good rest.

If I believed it was Pardi who wrote the script of our country's story, then I believed equally that Mardi somehow illustrated the text. Her sculptures seemed to coincide with these watersheds that redefined us. *The Prophet*, *Strike*, *Negro Aroused*. If anyone suggested that Mardi's illustrations came first, Miss Boyd would close her eyes to dismiss such heresy, and say, "Sshh," as though to soothe such a thought to sleep. Mardi's name might be there under "illustrations by," but as far as either Mardi or Miss Boyd was concerned, Pardi was the great "written by" author in the sky.

But I had my very own relationship with Pardi, which had nothing to do with history.

I got to know Pardi best up in the hills, "in the middle of nowhere," as Mardi called it, where he was also a builder of sorts, and where, by the time I arrived, they had a small wooden house which they called "Nomdmi." We spent many weekends and holidays there.

A long, long time ago, Mardi had ridden off the bridle track on one of her freedom trails, and ended up high in the Blue Mountains, where the skies met the clouds and the altitude made her ears pop, and where the sturdy mountain population was not even registered at birth.

"So much for adult suffrage!" He would shake his head at the irony.

"Pack of Labourites," Mardi would say. "Good thing they don't register!"

Labourites were supporters of the JLP, Busta's party, which was then in power, though that just meant they had more seats in the elected legislature through which, as I said, we were ruled by the British. Supporters of the People's National Party were called comrades.

Pardi swore Mardi was mad, but he accompanied her on her adventure as she had so often accompanied him on his. The mounds of shale from the landslides, the patches of torn hillside and brutal black burns on the bodies of his mountains were more than Pardi could bear to see, and resurrected the "bush man" he had been in his youth, when he had grown up on his mother's farm in the country, cleaning pastures and chipping logwood for pocket money.

"They must learn to terrace. They burn the land to get a quick crop next season, but in the long run they will diminish these hills, and the very earth will die!"

So by the time he got to the top of the mountain, where she had already purchased her site of refuge at little cost, he had committed himself, on his own terms, to her new cosmos.

The view from those hills was startling, and threw back an unforgiving image of the island's gnarled and sporadic survival. Kingston, a city created to serve a great natural harbour, nestled in a side pocket of a distant plain, where it looked oddly practical beneath the virgin mountains. In the distance the encircling sea stretched like the island's imagination.

Most of the land in the mountains belonged legally to no one, and those who laid claim to it expected little for this arid hilltop that had no agricultural value; the valleys collected the fertile soil, and a view was not a priority for these farmers. A small payment usually ensured that one's squatter's rights would go unmolested. But Mardi discovered that this piece of land was actually the edge of a property that was accounted for, and bought it for a modest price.

It was Mardi's idea to build a house. She planned two rooms, one on top of the other, a small kitchen at the back and at the front a veranda.

"Why not side by side? It would be easier to build."

"No, dear, I must have a dormer window upstairs where I can peep through the trees in the morning and look across at the mountains."

Pardi soon appropriated her dream house, deciding on a carpenter he knew from nearby Mavis Bank who could help him to build it. He would return to his first love, the land, and his agricultural exploits would, he felt sure, set an example for the hill farmers.

The dormer window became the focal point around which the house was built. The tree that Pardi decided she should peep through was identified; it was a juniper and became the marker for the window, and the two rooms followed, stacked one on top of the other to accommodate the view. But the rooms were built beneath the brow of the hill, facing its descent. The mountains, including Blue Mountain and Lady Peak, actually climbed up behind them and out of view. This was never mentioned. Instead of trying to rectify the problem by asking that the window be put in another wall, Mardi made a point of exclaiming about the view of the sky, clouded or cloudless, so as never to alert Pardi to the awkward fact that he had chosen the wrong tree and therefore the wrong view.

They then discovered that they had forgotten a staircase, so it had to be tacked on, and for many years it ran up the outside of the cottage as a cheerful afterthought.

The house became known as Nomdmi through a misadventure. Mike Smith, who in his youth had lived with the family like a son, was then spending a weekend at the cottage. Mike was a poet – at least until shortly after the Second World War, when, from a vantage point in the English countryside, he gazed over an industrial valley and decided in a fit of pique that poetry was useless in the faceless world of modern progress. He claimed that he never wrote another line of verse, proceeding instead to arm himself with anthropology, becoming a professor and writing through the course of his life many highly acclaimed books on the Hausa – books with which those who loved him persevered, and none of which any of our family members ever claimed to fully understand.

Pardi and my father had painstakingly constructed a small bridge over a waterway that crossed the entrance, erecting gateposts which would wait a long time for an actual gate. Mike was asked to paint a "No Admittance" sign on the new gatepost. While he painted, Pardi and Mike and my father were deep in some philosophical meandering. Whether distracted by this conversation or by his earlier longings, or maybe by a rum too many, or just victim to the absent-mindedness of his new-found profession, he got as far as "No Mdmi" and realized his mistake: the *M* should have been an *A*. Mike, greatly irritated with himself, would have corrected the mistake if Mardi had not ventured along the path and been delighted with the semantic consequence of his error. On discovering this, he packed in the project. So the letters remained in orange paint over the years, and people started trying to pronounce them, which bestowed on it the full authority of a name.

To journey through the house meant weaving in and out of the elements, for you had to cross a muddy path to get to the kitchen built separately at the back. On their first weekend there they discovered that the chimmey, an enamelled chamber pot, was not adequate for their needs, so a pit toilet was constructed at quite some distance, which was a constant reminder to Mardi of the evolution of the artist. She was haunted by the story of a fierce and tender writer she knew who, as a child, had accidentally dropped a roll of toilet paper down the subterranean belly of a pit toilet; his father, as punishment, had made him retrieve it.

"He could have become a murderer. He might simply have become a civil servant and tried to forget it. Instead he became a writer."

"I'm not sure I follow your reasoning on that one, my dear."

The thoughtful lawyer in Pardi was perpetually challenged by the intuitive shorthand of his wife's conclusions. He had learned to follow her trail and not to dismiss what he could not logically recognize. Within the turbulence of her being, insights flashed with the whimsy of sheet lightning. This made her a shrewd politician.

"After an experience like that, one is never a nice person," she reasoned.

"But who says he was a nice person in the first place? I believe the Freudians blame a lot of genetic traits on the retrieval of toilet rolls from pit lavatories!"

"So you believe he was just born a very difficult man? You think it's congenital?"

He could always lure her into the labyrinth of his mind, where she tiptoed through a million traps. She felt silly entering at all, but had long since learnt that on these expeditions her company delighted and amused him.

"I did not say congenital. I said genetic."

"Oh, don't be so tiresome! What difference does it make whether it's congenital or genetic?"

"There is a lot of difference. Congenital is from birth. But genetic comes from one's chromosomes, and so is handed down through heredity. If the Freudians are right, and they may be, partially, then I suppose one could argue that it is possible that personality traits develop after birth, as a response to a child's stimuli and environment."

"So you are saying that he was conceived a difficult man, and no matter what happens in his life, that's what he is. And nothing can change that."

"I did not say that," he countered. "Of course he can behave differently if he chooses to. But however he may alter his behaviour, it will be a reaction to what he ultimately knows himself to be, and in this case you described that as not a nice person!"

"I can't believe you could be so ungenerous," she said petulantly, beginning to feel trapped. In court, the cool of his logic unravelled even the most conscientious witnesses.

"Generosity has nothing to do with it." He was getting an ox-blood tinge in his cheeks from repressing a smile as his mind sprinted from one marker to the next, down the trail that his reasoning prepared for him. Her frustration reminded him of the moment when a witness discovered the inevitability of his own destruction.

"You are genetically ungenerous, then," she said triumphantly.

"Has it occurred to you" – and now he was trying to tame the words that arrived in spurts on his laughter – "that the father was not himself a nice person, judging from what he did to his son over the toilet-paper roll? So it would be logical to assume that his son inherited his chromosomes and therefore was genetically predisposed to being not a nice person too. Now, you could argue that if the father hadn't sent the son into that hellhole of a pit, maybe the son would have done more to temper his natural inclinations!"

She didn't sulk. Sulking was too negative and persistent for her mercurial nature. She might pretend to sulk if it suited her, but only as a ploy. He would always beat her at the minutiae.

"Maybe so," she sighed, "but that still brings me back to my point. Having to endure such an unjust act of cruelty, he was faced with options. He could have felt enough outrage to become a murderer. He might have hidden his outrage by submerging the memory in his subconscious and filling his life with the day-to-dayness of the civil service. Or he could do what he did, which was to face the horror of evil headlong, and commit himself to his demons. He harnessed all that pain, damned to hell the loss of his innocence and became a writer! Amen."

She might very well be right. Maybe you couldn't be an artist worth a damn and be a nice person too. Being a nice person was a sort of refuge from the darker side of life. To be an artist one had to be able to make the extremes of human experience speak and be real. Maybe to be good at anything you had to be able to understand evil in a visceral way, as he did in his courtroom. Once again she had flashed illumination on a horizon that would have passed him unseen, had he not been travelling with her.

And when the young writer, lit by liquor or memory, stood on the table at Drumblair urinating at Mardi's alarmed guests, as he once did at a party, or uncharacteristically goaded her by defending the painting of daffodils, or writing about daffodils, in a land where daffodils were only a colonial rumour, she forgave him for being provocative and contradictory, remembering his dark journey into the fouled earth, and his father's evil.

"And he never once wrote of daffodils or of anything that didn't belong to his beloved Jamaica! He hated his father, but he forgave the earth!" she announced with satisfaction.

And Pardi understood. He understood because he had watched her battle over the daffodil syndrome as she struggled against the neatly but firmly imposed images of snowy Christmas cards in a land without winter, blond Christs in a country of black congregations, daffodils and tulips in a land of ram-goat roses and poinciana trees.

A quarter of a century earlier she had found her land legs after a grim passage from England on a banana boat, crossing from one limb of her ancestry to the other, her pale grey eyes adjusting to the brilliance of colour under a sun that few clouds dared to challenge. She was coming to Jamaica for the first time, with her husband and their infant son, Douglas. Mardi was born in England, but although her father was a Yorkshireman, her mother was a Jamaican, the sister of Pardi's mother, Margaret. Although she had grown up abroad, she always claimed to have a deep sense of being Jamaican and – what seemed incongruous, as she was very fair – a deep sense of being coloured, as she was of mixed blood.

"We are not a mixed marriage," she'd insist, "but a marriage of mixtures!"

In Jamaica she found a people who were more massive than the English, and yet who moved with ebullience through their lives, though the majority had little to share among themselves. The English had managed to subdue only a small fringe of this island's leaves; the rest of the tree, biding its time, swayed above its own deepening roots.

So she began her work: goats instead of the basic British lion; buxom bodies and Caribbean life with pain and rum and laughter, the local revivalist cult of pocomania; women whose heavy loads swayed for balance and not, as the British expatriates neatly patronized, because while they worked their bodies were happy dancing to some imaginary music that kept them besotted and unsuspicious of the ravages taking place.

She taught young artists, and then writers as well started to wander into Drumblair, with their poems and short stories. It was here that the young writer would have brooded over the incongruity of daffodils, irritated by a growing enthusiasm that was collecting itself into anthologies of Jamaican literature. These early publications were called *Focus*, and by the time Mardi had edited two issues, he had contributed

Jamaican white-wings, Jamaican dumplings and Jamaicans talking Jamaican, his short stories picking their way through the human seasons and the contradictions of the island's landscape.

Both Pardi and Mardi relished the rustic deprivation of their modest mountain cabin with a cussed determination. They kept life arduous even after the addition to Nomdmi, one at a time, of a dining room and living room and more bedrooms, which all squatted on the ground floor, leaving the upstairs dormer window as the visionary eye of the house.

A bench was built where Mardi would sit to face the procession of peaks which she could not see from her bed, and their ruling gods as they triumphed across the sky from Catherine's Peak to Blue Mountain Peak. Mardi named the mountains, met the gods who were there and made up some more. They had their very own names, I suppose, but also names Mardi gave them, like Kablan and Hooman. Catherine's Peak we always called Dillmoon because Mardi said she was a mystic mountain and passed through the dawn as only a memory.

She discovered her very own cosmos. It all began very early when she sat on that very same bench at the edge of this world, facing the reopening sky to watch the dawn. There, incredibly, as if in slow motion, she saw the ascension of a single, golden, majestic horse, its mane coming up first behind the mountains, flooding the sky with light; then the forelock beneath which the lidless wide-open orbs charged the world to life; and then a single lifted foreleg. She recognized it. It was the Horse of the Morning.

"I've seen the Horse of the Morning," she announced to Pardi.

"That's good," he said, but she always felt he didn't believe her.

She never was sure that Blue Mountain Peak was really the highest point in Jamaica. From certain directions Lady Peak beside him looked higher, and there were days when they both looked the same, so she didn't see why he should be known as the major peak of the Blue Mountain Range. She decided to call them the August Pair. When Pardi said that they had found ice on the Peak, or that he had seen Cuba from the Peak because it was a clear day, she would always ask, "Blue Mountain or Lady Peak, dear? It could have been either!"

Then there was the tiny, unmarked grave in the pines behind the house. It looked like a child's. No, Mardi said, it was not a child's. She said the grave belonged to the little old lady who had built Bellevue, the great house which stood on the adjacent hill, and of whose property the Nomdmi land had once been a part. In her youth she had fallen in love with a visiting sailor. She sat in the upstairs window, also a dormer, and waited for the rest of her life for his return. He never came, and she lost first her youth, then her weight, and finally even her height, as she never stood up to stretch or exercise, but just sat gazing out at Kingston harbour, where she thought his ship would come in. Who this was I do not know, as the original owners were in fact Governor James Swettenham and his wife, Lady Swettenham. Lady Swettenham brought tree tomatoes from England, tasting more of fruit than of vegetable, along with lupins and lavender and hydrangeas, cottage flowers that could grow in the mountain cool all year round. There was even a nearby path to a spring called the Lady Swettenham walk.

After that another English couple came to Bellevue. She was loved by her husband and loved by her friends, and loved by the women in the village, whom she taught to plait the dry leaves of the watsonia Easter lily into long tresses which they wound tightly and sewed into mats and sold in Kingston. And then the husband died and it is said that she went quite mad, and had to be taken from her Bellevue on the hilltop to its namesake in Kingston, which was an asylum for lunatics. It was rumoured that finally, in a gross act of frustration, she set herself alight, leaving her mountain home and its ghosts as a gift in perpetuity to the newly created West Indian university.

Mardi built a studio in which to carve the mythical gods of her cosmos, a shingle shack with a concrete floor among the pine trees on the way to the gate. She called it Mini, short for Minimus.

Lurking behind every summer of weekends that he spent in the hills was Pardi's hurricane vigil. Nomdmi had no electricity, no running water except from the old oil-drums used to collect rainwater, no postal service and no telephone, and no driving road above the bottom of the hill. Any news came slowly up the hill by bearer in a letter or telegram, or by radio with the advent of the battery-powered transistor. The latter carried the meteorological bulletins which supplied Pardi with information to plot the course of each storm. He used a large blue and white map of the region, which he would spread out over his homemade dining table. The map was already well worn from the leanings of anticipatory elbows and the pencilled journeys of each storm when, in those hottest of months, the weather could no longer keep its temper.

It would be unfair to say that he wished for a hurricane, for he was conscious of the devastation it would wreak on the island. But if a hurricane should come, an arbitrary act of God beyond any man's control, he would be able to prove the worth of Nomdmi's construction; insofar as he had supervised it with a pencil over his ear each weekend, he felt himself in large part responsible for it.

The map became a family tree. He would show me the sporadic progression of islands that formed the Caribbean like footprints across the sea. His stories swept the map. There was British Guiana, on the South American continent, where Cheddi Jagan struggled to achieve a perpetually noble but often illusive socialist dream; his activist wife, Janet, sent logs of purple-heart wood like lovers for Mardi's desires. We travelled through Williams's Trinidad (and don't forget Tobago), where I heard of pitch lakes, steel drums and hearing aids; through the mountains and patois of St. Lucia, and Dominica, and Marryshow's Grenada. We lingered in Adams's Barbados, where I heard of the superb batting styles of the three great *W*s of West Indies cricket – Worrell, Walcott and Weeks – 97 per cent literacy and a society unofficially divided by the colour of people's skin. On to Muñoz Marín's Puerto Rico, shaking its fist at the mighty States while toe to toe in a cha-cha-cha; across Bird's flat Antigua and the donkeys of Barbuda, past Dutch and Spanish and French possessions and Haiti, the betrayed land of Toussaint L'Ouverture, till beneath Cuba we came to rest at our heartland, Jamaica.

It seemed to me that our English-speaking brothers and sisters on the family tree were comparatively very small; I was, however, mesmerized by our fat foreign cousins, huge islands with exotic names and bloody revolutions from which emerged wicked "desk-pots," as I thought they were called, whose balletic names – Machado, Trujillo, Batista, Duvalier – curled with difficulty off my grandfather's lips and spun around in my head.

M. NOURBESE PHILIP

SALMON COURAGE

Here at Woodlands, Moriah,
these thirty-five years later,
still I could smell her fear.
Then, the huddled hills would not have
calmed her, now as they do me.
Then, the view did not snatch
the panting breath, now, as it does
these thirty-five years later, to the day,
I relive the journey of my salmon mother.

This salmon woman of Woodlands, Moriah
took the sharp hook of death
in her mouth, broke free and beat
her way upstream, uphill; spurned
all but the challenge of gravity,
answered the silver call of the moon,
danced to the drag and pull of the
tides, fate a silver thorn in her side,
brought her back here to spawn with
the hunchbacked hills humping the horizon,
under a careless blue sky.

My salmon father now talks of how
he could walk over there, to those same hills,
and think and walk some more with his dreams,
then that he had,
now lost and replaced.
His father (was he salmon?)
weighted him with the millstones of
a teacher's certificate, a plot of land
(believed them milestones to where he hadn't been),
that dragged him downstream to the ocean.

Now, he and his salmon daughter
face those same huddled, hunchbacked hills.
She a millstoned lawyer, his milestone
to where he hadn't been.
He pulls her out, a blood rusted weapon,
to wield against his friends
"This, my daughter, the lawyer!"
She takes her pound of dreams neat,
no blood under that careless blue sky,
suggests he wear a sign around his neck,
"My Daughter IS a Lawyer,"
and drives the point home,
quod erat demonstrandum.

But I will be salmon.
Wasn't it for this he made the journey
downstream, my salmon father?
Why then do I insist on swimming
against the tide, upstream,
leaping, jumping, flying floating,
hurling myself at under, over,
around all obstacles, backwards

in time to the spawning
grounds of knotted dreams?
My scales shed, I am Admiral red,
but he, my salmon father, will not
accept that I too am salmon,
whose fate it is to swim against the time,
whose lodestar is to be salmon.

This is called salmon courage my dear father,
salmon courage,
and when I am all spawned out
like the salmon, I too must die –
but this child will be born,
must be born salmon.

MEDITATIONS ON THE DECLENSION OF BEAUTY BY THE GIRL WITH THE FLYING CHEEK-BONES

If not   If not   If

Not

If not in yours

                    In whose

In whose language

Am I

If not in yours

                    In whose

In whose language

Am I   I am

                If not in yours

In whose

Am I

(if not in yours)

I am yours

In whose language

Am I not

Am I not I am yours

If not in yours

If not in yours

In whose

In whose language

Am I . . .

Girl with the flying cheek-bones:
She is
I am
Woman with the behind that drives men mad
And if not in yours
Where is the woman with a nose broad
As her strength
If not in yours
In whose language

Is the man with the full-moon lips
Carrying the midnight of colour
Split by the stars – a smile
If not in yours

In whose

In whose language

Am I

Am I not

Am I   I am yours

Am I not   I am yours

Am I   I am

If not in yours

In whose

In whose language

Am I

If not in yours

Beautiful

THE CATECHIST

Early-blooming brown legs
satin-cotton
(was all the rage those days)
in their sheen and skinny;
around them
the confirmation dress crinolines stiff –
black girl white dress
– photograph circa 1960 –
a stiff-petalled cyclamen
hot-housed
on green stalks of ignorance.
The finger now traces the negative
outline of the white dress
– or is it the positive form of the girl
where sudden edges meet?
Images blur – bleed into each other
as if the fixer didn't quite work,
or maybe it was the heat that caused the leak;
in those days nothing could be counted on –
least of all cyclamen girls
early bloomers in the heat of it all
with the lurking smell of early pregnancy.

So there, circa 1960, she stands –
black and white in frozen fluidity
                                        aging
photograph of the cyclamen girl
                                    caught between
blurred images of
                                massa and master.

CASHEW #4

firm-fleshed
red pendulous breast
nipple
hardened into promise
in seed
curled green fetus
the cashew
hangs
longs for the sharp white teeth of girls
their tiny perfect tongues
licking its juice that
stains the white gowns
marks them with desire
as racing
nightdress sails
masted with slender sinewy
mahogany of limbs
lengthening into a future
perfect
they hurtle
toward the unfurl
in girl

H. NIGEL THOMAS

HOW LOUD CAN THE VILLAGE COCK CROW?

The straight road that curved exactly where the village began was now paved; the dirt road that powdered everyone golden during dry spells was now trapped under tar. As he looked at the new stream of black tar – for that was how the road appeared – and the telephone poles and high-tension wires, he knew that there had been dramatic change. The old wooden houses had for the most part been torn down and replaced with larger concrete structures. He gasped. "Sorry for poor" – that huge breadfruit tree that his grandmother said had been there when she had been an infant, which had got its name because during a terrible drought when every green thing turned brown and died, the breadfruit tree that had been a pelican and had adopted the villagers as its young had kept on wrenching fruit from its entrails – had been cut down; and to David, that was sacrilege.

And so it was that he was surprised to hear a woman, her head tied, as he remembered his grandmother's, in a plaid rag, saying, "If you do good, good going follow you. Take care; if you plant dumb cane, you will never reap tannia." She said it much as his grandmother, he was sure, had said it to his mother, as his mother had said it to him; and David wondered whether he too would say it to his children. At least that had not changed. The little boy she spoke to was about four and clothed only in a shirt, leaving his mud-marked extremities and genitalia unprotected. He eyed the pea switch in the woman's hand.

She pleaded with him to advance but the youngster stood rooted, his gaze fixed on the pea switch that moved ever so slightly in the woman's fleshy arms.

David moved on, trying to remember who had lived in the wooden shacks where these spacious cement houses now stood, too spacious for the little land whose soul they were crushing. But one spot had not changed. There, marring the symmetry of generous porches encircled by potted palms, flowering gerberas, and geraniums, was Ataviso's shack, listing heavily toward the valley decline. Huge beams were angled at the side – massive stilts transversely rooted in the earth came to the aid of the shack, hindering it from gaining whatever it hankered after down the valley slope. Not unlike the clothing of Ataviso's wife, which had placed a barrier between him and her tormenting spirit. David wondered whether Ataviso was still alive. If he were, he would have to be in his sixties. He had been Ataviso's neighbour.

In his heyday Ataviso was called the Village Cock. He boasted five mistresses and fifteen children. In fact, one night when one mistress sent for Ataviso at his wife's home to go fetch the midwife, who lived three villages away, he had met another of his sons bearing a similar message. So he had fetched the midwife, who delivered him two more sons that night.

The following Wednesday when Ataviso stopped off at the rum shop, where every impoverished rum drinker was habitually waiting, they had another detail to add to the repertory of his fine feathers, his castle-like comb, and his ever-flowing sperm jug; now his hens had had simultaneous hatchings. A marvellous rooster was Ataviso, and Ataviso was pleased, and the fat wad of dollar bills the hundreds of bunches of bananas had been exchanged for earlier that day was in turn exchanged for the rum that kept the compliments coming. And Ataviso was pleased. Later that night he got home staggering and saw only the blurred outline of the expectant faces of his wife and the three children, who fearfully wondered whether they'd manage to sleep there that night or have to run – at first it had been in their pyjamas, their mother in her nightgown; now they kept their street clothes handy, to grab whenever they had to run – for Ataviso knew that on banana-selling day his wife expected money, and with none to give, he would beat her, and the children too, should they cry over their mother's pain.

At that time, Ataviso's oldest son was fourteen, and David remembered – the words had a way of gripping his intestines – "Big man like you still pissing yo' bed!" And Ataviso would throw the barfleur mattress out in the yard; there would be explosive sounds against the roadside wall of the house; and the lanky youngster, who looked more like ten, would emerge, his right hand cupping the side of his head that Ataviso had used to resonate the walls, smiling broadly no doubt as he did so. That smile always accompanied Ataviso's infliction of pain. Derivo (his real name was Alfred; Ataviso's was Percy; they were renamed by David's brother, who had a passion for foreign languages; eventually the names gained currency in Hillsdale) would drag the mattress to the back of the house, more out of sight, while Ataviso looked on, chuckling.

"Yo' want yo' bladder sew up! And I will sew it up fo' yo'! Be Christ, I will!"

He would then look around him, at his wife and the other children, for signs of defiance. (He always boasted that he was not like other men, who had lost their pants. For if a man did not beat his wife and women, it meant that he was wearing their bloomers and they his trousers. "Go from me!" he would tell his drinking buddies; "I bet yo' wife got on yo' trousers and you wearing her bloomers.") Derivo would remain behind the house and would slip his forefinger and its neighbour into his mouth; the habit had bleached the lower half of those fingers white and the sucking left a constant flow of saliva down his chin and neck. The blows did not cure the bladder weakness, and so Ataviso found a novel idea, borrowed no doubt from the tar-and-feather practices of earlier times. He got a twenty-five-pound empty

Palm Tree butter tin, still coloured in saffron yellow, and two drumsticks. He attached a string to the tin. He stuck some feathers to an old sheet. The children and neighbours looked on at the activities in the open yard.

Around 4 P.M., the following Sunday, when all the Methodists who attended church had already returned and dined and the children who attended Sunday school were emerging from the church, they heard a few unwilling drum sounds and saw a strange apparition followed by a small procession descending the hill. The villagers came onto the side of the road, and children on their way home stopped. It was Derivo, draped in his pee-stained sheets, the feathered sheet thrown on top of these. Ataviso walked behind him, from time to time hitting him with a piece of rope. Derivo knocked the drum (the butter tin) languidly, a little faster each time he was hit by the rope. At times he staggered. A procession of gazing children followed. Some parents ran toward the procession, pulled their children away, and took them home.

When Derivo passed the church, those at the front of the procession smelled feces and saw it falling in liquid drops from beneath the feathers and the sheets. Ataviso laughed. The children looked on, frightened.

About three houses below the church, Beulah Abbot stood up watching the procession. When it got to her gate she approached Derivo and shook her head. She pulled off the feathered sheet and pee-stained rags and threw them on Ataviso. Her right hand firmly clasped around Derivo, she said to Ataviso, "You're not fit to take care o' jackasses, let alone children. I hope you die without anybody there to give you a drink of water. Watch out, 'What you sow is what you going reap.' " She pulled Derivo into her yard, where, away from his father, Derivo spurted a blood-streaked, sour-smelling vomit.

Ataviso's children always trembled. And if a teacher asked them a question, it increased the trembling to the point where it resembled an ague. Therefore, the following Tuesday, when Derivo was seen trembling, no one paid any attention. The trembling increased, and Derivo blacked out. A message was sent home and his mother came. He was taken to the hospital in the capital, where it was found that he had a bleeding intestinal ulcer. From his father, David learned that the next night the rum drinkers changed their tune about Ataviso.

"Phoo, man! What smell like that!"

"Did you see the blood in the vomit?"

"Some men love their children to beat them, all the way in the gut, until they shit theyselves."

Ataviso had remained quiet through all this but had continued to pay for the rum just the same.

Derivo was released from the hospital on a Thursday. David had gone to see him and was still standing at the gate when Ataviso arrived from his lands.

He entered the yard and screamed at his wife, "Yo' ain't finish cooking yet? What the fuck you been doing home all day?" This was followed by the sounds of iron crashing on stones and his wife's "Lord Jesus, hear my cry!" The neighbours gathered to watch the steam rising from the food and the pieces of broken cast-iron pot on the bleaching stones. Gradually the fowls began to gather, waiting for the heat to subside. Mrs. Jones (Jones was her maiden name – they called her that in defiance of Ataviso, whose surname was Sweet – long changed to Sinistro by David's brother) had run to sit squat in the middle of the yard. With her eyes turned to the sky and her body shrouded by the rays of the setting sun, she clutched her two-year-old quite tightly. The child had begun to wail.

At home David told his mother what he had seen. His father too had witnessed it and instructed his mother to prepare enough food so that there would be a meal for Mrs. Jones and her children. She made oatmeal with milk for Derivo. She sent David to sit on the porch to watch for Ataviso's departure. Around six-thirty she and David took the food. There were a few neighbours there. Each of them had brought some of what they had cooked. Mrs. Jones was sitting on the floor of the living room, wearing a dress that had been bleached colourless from countless washings. The infant was asleep on her lap. Some of the women sat on the floor with her. They coaxed her to eat, telling her she had to keep her strength to defend her children against Ataviso. One of the women pushed back the loose strands of her hair and started to hum, "What a friend we have in Jesus, all our sins and grief to bear . . ."

Worst of all was the evening when Ataviso arrived home, walked into the house, and dragged Maurice (Egado) into the open yard. His hand tightened Egado's shirt collar, choking him, and he shook him so violently that sometimes he lifted him completely off the ground.

"Yo' is a man?" he asked Egado. Egado did not answer (he could not answer).

With his free hand Ataviso slapped him. "Answer me! How you could order Lisa off the land?" (Lisa was one of Ataviso's mistresses.) He choked Egado some more. The neighbours looked on. The shirt collar deeply indented Egado's neck and his eyes bulged. Finally Ataviso let him go long enough to give him a knock-down blow. "Yo' is a man, yo' must take man blows." Egado fell to the ground. Ataviso placed his right foot on his neck. From the pocket of his overalls he produced a coil of mahoe, which he unravelled and began raining down blows on Egado. It seemed as if he had lost all awareness of what he was doing. David's father and another neighbour, Mr. Burch, had had to restrain Ataviso and literally box him back into reality. Mrs. Jones had collapsed at the sight of her husband's actions. The women came with buckets of water and revived Egado. Ataviso remained long enough to see Egado revived and then walked away. For a long time the neighbours debated what to do with Ataviso. Some said he should be sent to the insane asylum. Some said he needed a dose of his own medicine. Some said it was because the law never did anything to people like Ataviso that they went on as they did.

That night David asked his father why Ataviso treated Mrs. Jones and his children like that.

"He's an estate nigger, that's why. He's not from this village. Ataviso is the crudest estate nigger I know of. They're not much different from animals.

"You see, son, Ataviso comes from people who treat their children exactly the way white people used to treat their slaves. They use whips and their fists to get obedience. It's as if that is how they were trained to bring up children. I bet you Ataviso doesn't know the difference between how to treat his jackass and his children."

"But why did Mrs. Jones marry him?"

"That's a difficult question. I could easier tell you why he married her."

Mrs. Jones was a mulatto woman, the daughter of a white father and a black mother. She was ten years older than Ataviso and was in her mid-thirties when she married him. Her mother had already been dead, but her father opposed the marriage, even though Mrs. Jones was pregnant. "Anything," he told her, "but an estate nigger."

But she married Ataviso. At the beginning he was a model husband. So Mr. Jones let him have the use of most of his unrented land. He also gave his daughter the money that bought the plot and built the house they lived in. For three years Ataviso lived like this. Eventually Mr. Jones made him manager over his entire two-hundred-acre farm. A year after this Mr. Jones suffered a stroke and died. Gradually Ataviso became involved with other women and began having outside children, and when his wife protested he began to beat her. She saw less and less of the money that came from rents, from nutmegs, cocoa, coconuts – all of which had been planted before Ataviso had married her. It got to the point where Ataviso forbade her from going to the farm on the pain of being beaten. When the last child was born and Mrs. Jones complained that she was destitute, Ataviso suggested that she consider whoring. David remembered hearing his parents and the neighbours discussing this. This was hard for them to accept, considering that Mr. Jones had been a university graduate and his wife an elementary school principal. They could not understand why she remained with him. Except maybe it was because Ataviso was a handsome man – very slim with glistening black skin, strong jaws, an angular face, and dancing eyes that blazed when he was bestial.

The years passed and the situation in Ataviso's family remained much the same, except when Robert, the youngest child, was five, one of Mrs. Jones's sisters, who was a university lecturer in Jamaica, came home to Isabella Island for a visit. She could not persuade her sister to leave Ataviso, but she convinced Mrs. Jones to let her take Robert to Jamaica with her. Mrs. Jones consented.

Four nights after her departure it occurred to Ataviso that he had not seen Robert. He inquired but got no answer from his wife. He began to beat her and vowed he would not stop until she told him what had become of his son. Egado rushed outside and returned with a machete, with which he proceeded to chop his father as if his intention were to retail him by the pound. His mother screamed. Derivo screamed. The neighbours came and took the blood-effusing Ataviso to the hospital. The doctors saved his life with transfusions of Derivo's and Egado's blood.

The community was divided in its feelings. There was the belief that a child who hit his parents would be cursed for life and that the curse would devolve on his offspring. But some, mostly women, thought it was a token righting of wrongs. They also noted that Ataviso did not seek revenge. The left arm never completely stretched out after the wound on it had healed. It remained at an angle of 110 degrees; and scars, a shade lighter than the rest of his skin, on his neck, both of his upper arms, his back, and even on his left buttock, formed ridges of proud flesh rising from the skin's surface like termite tunnels. After that day he never beat his wife or her children. Some people remarked that the cutting up should have come sooner. But Ataviso turned to beating his mistresses and their children.

During the dry season a year later, Mrs. Jones grew paler and more gaunt. Her jaws were now sunken and the skin on them lay in parallel folds; her bluish grey eyes had less blue in them and sank deeper into their sockets, and her shinbones were blade-edged. She had a wracking cough that was obviously getting worse. When evening chills and fever and a damp brow began to accompany it, everyone knew. By the time the rainy season arrived, she had to be taken to the TB sanitarium. Within a month she died.

When Ataviso heard the news he got drunk. But even in his drunken stupor, he was able to purchase the lumber for the village carpenters, who built the coffin cost-free. The village grocer, out of kindness to the memory of Ataviso's father-in-law, brought the body back to the village in his grocery van. She was interred in the Jones's burial plot.

The Third Night arrived, the night when his wife's spirit was deemed to visit. A huge tarpaulin tent was set up in the yard, for it had been raining constantly. The Spiritual Baptists came to sing the eulogy to the dead and to pray for the living and whatever it was that they did as part of their secret code, until midnight, when the spirit arrived.

As the magic hour drew near, Ataviso began to tremble. At midnight everyone jumped when he shouted, "There she is!" and fainted (of course, no one saw her). The women applied ammonia salts to his nostrils and rubbed his neck muscles with Limacol. When he recovered, he began to run and shout and later sob, "Tell her to leave me alone. Tell – her – to – leave – me – a – lone." His head bobbed up and down uncontrollably. "She is cha-cha-cha-s-ing me." His teeth chattered. With his arms held out before him and his palms upheld in a defensive gesture, as if fending off something, and without once turning his head to see the road, he backed into it, tripped on something, fell, got up, and continued down the road. He did not sleep in his house that night, nor did he ever return there. A few days later, he moved into the shack at which David was now looking, and in which he still lived when David left the village for England eighteen years before.

Ataviso had frequent and prolonged visits from his wife. When he was lucid he told how she hugged him and pressed her lips onto his, while the flames leaped from her eyes. And perhaps it was true, for everyone had at one time or other heard his shouting.

One night he moved through the street, his arms stiffly stretched out before him, his shoulders hunched forward, his head thrown back, and his feet dragging as though someone were pulling him. People shouted at him, but it was clear that he heard nothing; he merely moved along, like a calf roped for the first time refuses to walk and is pulled along. The people followed at a distance. Eventually someone had the insight to dash a bucket of cold water on him, the impact of which shocked him into reality. After a few minutes he spoke: "My wife was leading me – leave me alone! – have mercy, leave me alone – she had a rope around my neck – leave me alone! . . ."

The villagers led him back to his house, and two men watched over him that night.

The next day the villagers exchanged ideas about what needed to be done. The Spiritual Baptist leader rounded up his flock and they assembled in the yard of Ataviso's shack that evening. They sang and prayed, invoked the ancestral spirits, performed ecstatic rites, and with long, flaying brooms and branches they flogged the ground and the sides of the shack inside and outside. Then they marched around the shack seven times, uttering an incomprehensible chant.

For two weeks following this Ataviso had no visitations. He believed the cure had worked and so decided to pay a visit to one of his mistresses. But he never quite got to her house. A month after that Ataviso was reduced to two-thirds his former size. He exhaled an odour of apples in their earliest phase of rot. His eyes rolled constantly in their deepening sockets. It was as if some string beneath the skin was tying back his facial muscles. His blue dungarees, which now he did not change, looked as if they were hung on a six-foot mobile cross to form an animate scarecrow. The mud that splotched the dungarees brown in some places mixed with his sweat and fermented and dried, coating him with an odour that the wind blowing by his shack took away in varying amounts. The smell became known as Ataviso's cologne. At this stage Egado trudged to the estate ten miles away where his grandmother squatted and still worked as a day labourer, to ask her to come and look after Ataviso. Mrs. Sweet came, an overpowering, strapping woman with thick braids, a commanding voice, and a penetrating stare. She remained watching him at nights for about three weeks.

David liked her and thought that what his father had told him about "estate niggers" did not apply to Mrs. Sweet. He had heard her talking and giving advice on various occasions.

"How your son doing?" a woman asked her.

"As best he can."

"But I hear you good at medicine yourself; how's it you can't help him?"

Mrs. Sweet looked at the woman intensely and then away before saying, "They got some people medicine can't help. Some people can only cure theyselves. If you know any bush that good for a bad conscience you must let me know."

"What you mean, a bad conscience?"

"I mean it ain't nothing but his conscience creating them things he seeing. You know how he treat his wife."

David heard his father reporting another story about her. "That woman is special," his father said to David's mother. "I heard she met Clarissa on the road taking her baby to the doctor, and she asked Clarissa what wrong. Clarissa told her the baby pining away because her milk dry up. She told Clarissa to forget about the doctor and find somebody with a goat that giving milk or else a cow, but better a goat. 'Buy at least three cups for the child. Instead of giving the child plain water to drink, give it a mixture of three leaves of cudjoe root, two leaves of man peaba, two leaves of woman peaba, and two leaves of grannyhaulback boiled in two cups of water. Squeeze the juice of a' orange and give that to the child. No doctor medicine better than that.' Sure enough the child's eyes not turning inwards anymore."

His mother had been standing at the sink drying dishes while David washed them.

"How can an 'estate nigger' know such things?"

For a while she seemed lost in her thoughts, and David, who had had many arguments with her on her class views, knew that she was searching for some platitude to disparage Mrs. Sweet. Finally she said, "Well I guess there are exceptions. She's the exception."

Eventually Mrs. Sweet returned to her village. Her husband was bedridden and she depended on neighbours to look after him while she was taking care of Ataviso. She told the villagers that how a person made up his bed was exactly how he would have to lie on it. This was not how she had brought up Ataviso. She went on to say that her husband had never hit her and she had rarely ever beaten her children, so Ataviso did not learn his behaviour from her. The dead would have to bury their dead. After she left, people began suggesting all sorts of solutions to Ataviso. Someone suggested he roll on his wife's grave at midnight for forty nights; he rejected that. One woman brought him a pail of dirt from his wife's grave and told him to mix a little of it in the water he drank. This brought him a little relief.

One night he appeared on the street naked and completely incoherent. The men carried him to the shack and had to tie him up to get him to stay still. One of the rum drinkers whom Ataviso used to entertain remembered the "bloomers" story and told his buddies of a little trick they might play on Ataviso. Eventually they told Ataviso that one of them had had a dream in which Ataviso's wife told him that if Ataviso wore one of her dresses and a pair of her bloomers, she would no longer torture him. Ataviso balked at first. Later he sent a message to Egado and arranged to have his wife's clothes brought to his shack. He later told anyone wanting to hear how his knees had buckled at the thought of putting on his wife's clothing. He said she had waved a forefinger at him and ordered him to put them on.

Within a few days the entire village knew of the joke the men had planned. They intended to have him appear in public dressed in his wife's clothing.

For the four days he wore her clothes, her ghost did not trouble him. He would wait until around 3 A.M., when everyone was asleep, to empty his chamber pot and to bring water from the standpipe. Now that he was free from torture his appetite had returned. He had eaten up all the crackers his mother had left and finished the sugar, too, drinking sweet water. How would he go to the shop?

The villagers intervened. "Ataviso, it's days we ain't see yo'; answer us if yo' still living."

He said he looked down at the skirt he was wearing and clamped his teeth. He made an attempt to change it, but his wife's ghost appeared and his hands froze.

"Ataviso, we's coming in."

The men entered and began laughing. And the crowd outside began laughing too. Without realizing it, he got up and walked out into the yard. First came the chuckles of children, then scattered guffaws, followed by laughter like a convectional downpour. When one of the men lifted up the skirt and showed the panties, some of the crowd embraced the nearest partner. The laughter kept dying down and rekindling for some ten minutes as more and more people came to see what was going on.

Later that day, when the crowd had left, Ataviso went to the shop and bought what he needed, and people lined the street to look at him. He later said that it was the first time in years that he had felt at peace with himself.

He reported seeing his wife's ghost twice after that. Once after Derivo's death. He died two days before the second anniversary of his mother's death. His health had declined considerably. Egado and the neighbours had helped care for him. Egado even provided his father with money to look after his needs. Derivo developed a fever one night and his abdomen became as hard as stone. He died just before daybreak, in the ambulance transporting him to the hospital. Mrs. Jones returned to tell Ataviso he could wear a suit to the funeral. The second occasion was a month later. Ataviso's in-laws had come home to settle their father's estate. Forty acres had been willed to Mrs. Jones. Legally it now belonged to Ataviso. When he attempted to visit it, she appeared in front of him in her vengeful form. So he never went back or attempted to claim ownership.

It was obvious that Ataviso as well as the villagers became accustomed to his dress. His major concern was what would happen after the clothes were worn out. One of the Spiritual Baptists returning from a two-week sojourn in the spirit world reported, among her other encounters, one with Ataviso's wife, who she said looked happy and well, and who wished to inform Ataviso that he could have new female garments made, only he had to have a piece of her original garments sewn into the new ones. She promised to release him after fifteen years.

David's thoughts returned to the present. He wondered why the villagers had never thought of Ataviso's suffering while he was abusing his wife. He beat them to make himself feel important; those he couldn't beat he bribed. Was he so different from kings and politicians? For the villagers, Ataviso had represented the bottom, where the dregs sank and stayed, what they conveniently called "estate nigger," where the distinctions between man and beast were blurred, where the "better class" – for so they considered themselves – dared not descend. Only when those dregs that would not sink floated on the surface with disturbing visibility did they become bothered. And if they had heard of Jack the Ripper and his sons and grandsons – not to mention his ancestors – their need to feel superior made them forget. Ataviso's problems probably would not have occurred had he let his wife wear his trousers, even if he had not worn her "bloomers." Even that, too. Oh, David, what does mankind know?

He got up from the stone he had been sitting on and resumed his walk through the village. All his school friends had emigrated. His own parents and brother lived in New York. But there were still a few people he'd remember and who'd remember him. They would tell him what had become of Ataviso.

HONOR FORD-SMITH

from My Mother's Last Dance

History's Posse

The first I knew myself was in a white house on a hill. It looked out on a bright aqua sea and a smooth palm-lined road below. Orchids bloomed and there were rare birds in the yard. One day I saw a man chopped to death outside the gate. The killers were uniformed. From every finger on their hands a knife blade bloomed. Silver bullets and shark's teeth lined their throats. There were diamond knuckle-dusters on their fingers.

"Who's that?" I asked my mother as the body twitched to silence in the dirt.

"Sshhh," she said. "That's History's posse come back again. What a crosses come down on me! Don't ask no more. Do, mi baby keep quiet. Get inside and close the door."

Some children were playing in the mud walking barefoot, eating guinep, and singing, "What canya do Punchinella little fella? What canya do Punchinella little gal?"

"Let me go and play," I said to Mama. "Hmmph," she said. "Not today. History's posse might be passing by."

"Who is this History?" I asked. "I want to see his face."

"Sshh! Child, nobody looks in History's face. His people are everywhere. He's all around like the air," she whispered. "Do, mi baby, keep quiet. Let's go inside."

"No," I stamped. "If I can't play at least I can watch."

"Come down from there. Is not safe. There are rules, yuh know. Try to make things different and you'll lose everything. That's rule number one."

"Are you my real mother?" I asked her the next day.

"What a crosses this," she said. I asked again, but she shut her mouth and looked far away.

"Where's my real mother then?" and I jooked her hard in her side.

"All right. Since yuh so fast and so womanish I will tell yuh. Your mother is dead for going gainst History. Come. Close the door and stay inside."

"Where's my father?"

"Don't ask me no more question child. He left yuh this big house to live in. He sends money every month. What more yuh want than that? What a trial, what a cross this child is to bear."

"Where's my father?"

"All right. Since yuh so inquisitive, since yuh so forceripe, I will tell yuh. Your father is History, himself."

A woman was passing on the road below. She sang:

Peel head John crow sit up a treetop
Pick off di blossom.
Let me hold yuh hand gal.
Let me hold yuh hand.

I thought if I could sing like that, the world would be safe and Mama would laugh and everything would be all right.

Well, I stayed in that house for a time. Every day I practised till I could sing my songs with a voice clear like river water. Mama would smile and rock to the beat. People passing would hear and stand still as ghosts on the road below. But my mind had already gone from that house. Its emptiness cramped me then like a cell. It pressed on my throat like a chain. Only the gardens felt safe to me. I prowled the paths like a cat, tearing out the weeds and chopping back the vines. Night-blooming jasmine scented the air. There was desert flower and there was a cactus that bloomed at midnight. There were bohinia and surprise bougainvillea.

One night in the rainy season I ran away from the yard, dressed up just like a boy. I hid out my first night in a bus shell, near to a tourist town. My teeth chattered from fear, but I was proud to hell of myself. All night I perched up watching, but in the morning I was fine. I must have got a little too boasty though, for the next night some men stopped me on the road.

"Where yuh going?" they said. "This road not yours to walk. Go home to yuh big yard. That's where yuh belong."

"Tell History for me," I said, "I not playing his game."

They pulled off my disguise then, laughing so hard they could hardly stand up. But they only scratched my throat with the ratchet blade. Blood dulled the knife's silver-edged glint.

"History say yuh can take yuh chances, but yuh can't hide," one said. "Your skin glitters bright in the dark. We can sight yuh anyweh yuh go."

"I'll zip out of it," I said. "There's an opening between my legs." They only laughed more.

Well I did. Unzipped, I rose up flapping, high and cool as a kite. But I had no form. Unnamed, nameless, invisible, I floated over the landscape of burnt cane, over the all-inclusives and their swimming pools, over the markets and the stalls of jerk chicken. I looked down on everything. I was hungry but I couldn't eat. I was tired but I couldn't sleep. I was vulgar abstract. No context at all. It was like being trapped in a dream. "History," I thought, "you win this first round."

A woman was there sweeping the street. She had a cast eye, but her body was wiry and hard. I knew she had courage if that means nothing to lose. "Catch me in a bottle and I'll come down," I entered her vision. "What yuh going gimme?" she said and hissed her teeth like a snake.

"I'll give yuh my dreams."

"Dream?" she steuptsed again. "Dream can build house?"

I said, "Yes."

"Yuh too lie," she laughed, "but yuh funny and I like to laugh."

She brought me down and hid me and I lived in her board house near the train tracks. On her dresser she kept the Bible, a big pink comb, and a leaf of aloes. We didn't eat much. I taught her my songs and she showed me tricks I could use in a fight. At night we slept in a bed of rags scented with khus khus, her arm around me like a shield. I called her Vida for she was the first life I knew.

One day, there was money on the counter and fancy linen on the bed. She said, "Yuh mean all this time yuh have yuh big house and yuh don't say not one word. Imagine. I never know is so yuh stay and I struggling to keep body and soul together."

I thought, "Time to go."

"Yuh can't just walk out like that," she said. I figured she was History's woman now and we would have to fight. I slipped her through the back, but History's posse was in the yard.

"Dutty gal. Sodomite gal," a red-eye one said. "Yuh notten more than a mule. Get back inside. I'm the Don Gorgan, here. This is my territory. Yuh can't negotiate."

"Slip him like I did show yuh, idiot," Vida shouted.

"Shut up yuh two-mouthed bitch," I screamed, but I was scared to rass. I froze to the spot and the pee-pee ran down my legs. The red-eye one laughed. He pulled out his teeth and scattered them on the ground. They bloomed like the sweet jasmine I'd left behind. I wanted my old house and Mama. I wanted to close the door. I longed for a glimpse of the sea and the white road below.

"Yuh can't even go back to your risto yard. Yuh too soiled with the sex of ole neaga. Yuh can't do notten. Yuh don't have no use to us, wandering like a crazy red cockroach."

I wanted to clothe myself in my songs, wrap myself in a sheath of pure sound. I opened my mouth, but not a single note came out. Not a sound. Silence.

Then a man they said was History himself came in. He was a greyish man in a greyish suit, but I couldn't get a look at his face. I wouldn't know him if I saw him again. The thing is, I couldn't make myself struggle at all. My spirit was nearly gone, yuh hear?

I remember that he said a lesson is a lesson and if I'd learn mine and do mine I'd be all right. He said, "Yuh pass your place, gal."

When I came to I was somewhere dark and stink like a jail. My body was twisted and swollen and it felt hot and cold, hot and cold. "I'll die now," I supposed, "for I'm all alone and I don't even know how to fight. Mama was right. I shouldn't have tried to escape."

I lay there at the curve of a white darkness – in the middle of that hot and cold bleeding. A woman like someone in a dream came in. Maybe I made her up; maybe she was real. I have no memory of how she looked. I only remember the swish of her skirts and that she brought sinkle bible and a cup of something cool to drink.

I said, "Tell History I'll do whatever he wants."

"What yuh want with him again. Yuh don't learn nothing yet?"

"He take away my songs," I muttered hoarse. "I want them back."

She whispered, "Stop sorry for yuhself. If yuh want get out of here, make the sounds like how yuh feel. It won't sound lovely but it will ease yuh heart." And then she left and closed the heavy door.

I cried then, softly at first and then loud and horrible, tearing the night in half. I bawled for my mother who had left me, for my father trapped in his cruelty. I bawled for my fraidy-puss Mama. I bawled for the garden swallowed up with bush and weeds. I cried for the blood and the death I had seen. I bawled for my lost songs and for Vida. But most of all I cried for myself. I drank eyewater for breakfast, lunch, and dinner. I cussed everything and hit myself against the wall. Sometimes I just stared into the darkness and let the water run down my face. Day followed night while I cried. My tongue stuck to my dry mouth, and my eyes were swollen shut. My heart was locked in an iron grid but it beat slow and stubborn like a repeater drum.

Then one day I saw the sky grow bright, like a pastel pallet outside the bars on the window. It was magenta and grey and blue over the mountains. The crescent moon was watching in the pale sunrise. Mawga dogs barked at the daylight. Between some old newspaper and a rusty tin can, two grass quits did little dances on the ground. There were women selling at the corner and people going up and down. Minibuses were at the bus stop and the ductors in the doorways fought over the fares. The door seemed to open then and a thin bright ledge stretched out. "Go on quick," said the woman's voice. I stepped outside then and stood up straight in the morning dew. I brushed off my old dirty clothes, wiped my face, and headed out for the open road.

My Mother's Last Dance

First, the humming drum and then the solo violin.

My mother is beginning her last dance, deep in the valley of the Rio Nuevo, her first home is now her last. Reaching up up up to where the kites are trapped in the wires: high high she goes walking on wires, loosening the children's kites, and bright colours rain down to open hands, like all the words she thought but never spoke.

Then the Don, Death, arrives in a big old Benz. He unfolds his huge height like a long ribbon from the car. His legs are sharp stilts, and in his white gloved hand is a silver capped walking stick. His dark glasses are one-way mirrors. Guns bulge beneath his pin-striped long-tailed coat. He looks at the old watch at the end of a long gold chain on his belly and he flashes his gold-teeth smile, crooks his finger at my Ma, and waits. He stands at one end of the swinging bridge. I am at the other. He doesn't have to say stop tapping my wires. The last duel has begun.

My brown mother, the colonized, is doing ballet in the tops of the bamboo clumps, on the edges of the remains of her father's pimento and banana ground. A boy shouts "Get flat" and people get down in the bush, ready for the shots to start. She turns to me where I am standing shrunken into the old board of the bridge and she shows me how long she has been there, loving deep in the black black soil between the rocks, where Mammy Eva took her to bathe, at Oracabessa at the river mouth where they raced on muleback before there were hotels on the bright sands. And Death has manners, for he backs off and leans up gainst a tree. She shows me again the place where the bones of the ancestors are buried under the old guango tree.

Then she comes back to me at the swinging bridge and says, "Now you must learn to cross." But the height makes my eyes turn and there is nothing to hold onto for the rope rails are rotten and the old board slats are rotten from rain and chi chi. There are holes where you should walk and through the holes I see the foaming white water and the slippery green stones like knives beneath the surface.

My mother says, "It is the only road left. We must cross." Across the bridge Death is pacing, crushing the leaf of life and the baby's breath fern with his pointed feet. Old friends leave one by one. They not staying for this. The sun grows hard and gold.

My mother takes my hand and *abracadabra* I am little again and we are hopscotching across the bridge one foot at a time. I see she has picked up her old black medicine bag, the one like a grip with a hundred tiny drawers. It's big and bufuto and it weighs so heavy now, she cannot manage it at all. I know it will drop and pull her down into the river water. I know she wants me to take the bag, with its medicines and injections, its rusting stethoscopes and the old silver boxes for sterilized things. "Again?" I say, for I know the bag. It is an old argument we have. "It don't have no use to me," I say. "And is you cause it."

She leans on the worn rope at the edge of the swaying bridge, her black eyes shrouded with sadness. Death is bored with this. He wants to done this contract and go home for his dinner. He cleans his gun. I hear the catch go "click click." I see the sparks from his eyes as he loads the lead.

"Take the bag, man," she says. I look at Death, his brazen brass-face self all exposed now coming with his twisted gold-teeth smile down the other end of the swinging bridge. I look at the goddamn bag. I know it's all she has. The fool-fool thing is dragging her into the river and she is still struggling to hold onto it. And so I kiss my teeth and take the whatsitnotsit bag. "Open it," she says.

I open the cracked leather and I open the drawers. In each of the drawers there are delicate old green and blue glass bottles with poems neatly folded inside. And between the bottles there are round card-board pillboxes with words like *intravenous*, *arterial*, and *subcutaneous* packed in them. In the silver boxes are all the colours of the Rio Nuevo valley and the Blue Mountains and the scraps from my grand-mother's sewing and the recipes for the natural remedies my great-great-grandfather sold at Apothecary Hall in Savanna la Mar.

My mother and I dance a duet on the swinging bridge and the old man from the mento band cross the river raises his battered violin and the guitar men come in and the tempo of the rhumba box is triumphant and the women from the Church of Zion come with their drummer to dance too – dressed in white, yellow pencils in their red headties and their wide skirts spin out like shelters for the homeless. And my mother smiles because she has given me what I need and I can cross the bridge alone at last. I hold her close and feel her tears on my neck. She who never cries. And the women are singing *Rock O/Rock Holy/Mount Zion children/Rock Holy.*

Then Death taps his walking stick and the gun salute begins. *Bye bye bye bye bye* – fireworks in the daylight. He puts his cloak on her as she falls and lifts her high in his stiltman's arms and they go through the field of red ginger, through the red mud of the mountain between the ackee and the macafat palm up up up into the blue hilltops where the mist covers them.

And I am crossing the Rio Nuevo swinging bridge alone, heavy with my bag of poems, my medical words, my colours, my scraps and herbs and the songs of the revival women to sing me home.

DANY LAFERRIÈRE

from How to Make Love to a Negro

The Great Mandala of the Western World

Things are going terribly wrong these days for the conscientious, professional black pickup artist. The black period is over, has-been, kaput, finito, whited out. Nigger, go home. *Va-t-en, Nègre.* The Black Bottom's off the Top 20. *Hasta la vista, Negro.* Last call, coloured man. Go back to the bush, man. Do yourself a hara-kiri you-know-where. Look, Mamma, says the Young White Girl, look at the Cut Negro. A good Negro, her father answers, is a Negro with no balls. In a nutshell, that's the situation in the 1980s, a dark day for Negro Civilization. On the stock market of the Western World, ebony has taken another spectacular fall. If only the Negro ejaculated oil. Black gold. Oh sadness, the Negro's sperm is ivory. Meanwhile, Yellow is coming on strong. The Japanese are clean, they don't take up much space, and they know the *Kama Sutra* like the back of their Nikons. The sight of one of those yellow dolls (four feet ten, 110 pounds), as portable as a makeup case, on the arm of a long, tall girl (a model or salesgirl in a department store) is enough to make you cry the blues. I hear the Japs are as good at disco as Negroes are at jazz. It wasn't always that way. God didn't used to be yellow – the traitor! During the seventies, America got off on Red. White girls practically moved onto Indian reservations to earn their sexual B.A.s. The coeds who stayed behind had to settle for the handful of Indian students still left on the campuses. Naturally, a great number of Redskins came running from a great number of tribes, attracted by the scent of young, white squaw. A young Iroquois had his pride, but a free fuck is better than a bottle of rotgut. White girls were doing it Huron-style. A Cheyenne screw was the hottest thing around. Don't underestimate the effect of fucking a guy whose real name is Roaring Bull. At night in the dormitories, each cry, according to its modulation, told of a Huron or an Iroquois or a Cheyenne inseminating a young white girl with his red jism. It lasted until each and every Indian had come down with chronic syphilis. With the survival of the white Anglo-Saxon race in danger, the Establishment halted the massacre. WASP girls received drastic doses of penicillin, and the Indian students were sent back to their respective reservations to finish the genocide begun with the discovery of the Americas. The universities reverted to their daily routine, grey, washed out, going nowhere, and just as girls were about to succumb to boredom with the pallid, pale, faded Ivy League boys, the violent, potent, incendiary Black Panthers burst upon the campus scene. "Finally, some real blood!" came a choir of exultations from the Joyces, Phyllises, Marys, and Kays driven desperate by the medicine-dropper sex of conventional unions and a grey life of frustration with the Johns, Harrys, Walters, and Company. Fucking black was fucking exotic. And America loves to fuck exotic. Put black vengeance and white guilt together in the same bed and you had a night to remember! Those blond-haired, pink-cheeked girls practically had to be dragged out of the black dormitories. The Big Nigger from Harlem fucked the stuffing out of the girlfriend of the Razor Blade King, the whitest, most arrogant racist on campus. The Big Nigger from Harlem's head spun at the prospect of sodomizing the daughter of the slumlord of 125th Street, fucking her for all the repairs her bastard father never made, fornicating for the horrible winter last year when his younger brother died of TB. The Young White Girl gets off too.

It's the first time anyone's manifested such high-quality hatred toward her. In the sexual act, hatred is more effective than love. But it's all over now. The second war fought on American soil. Compared to the war of the coloured sexes, Korea was a skirmish. And Vietnam a mere afterthought in the flow of Judeo-Christian civilization. If you want to know what nuclear war is all about, put a black man and a white woman in the same bed. But it's all over now. We came close to total annihilation without knowing it. The black was the last sexual bomb that could have blown up this planet. And now he's dead. Sputtered out between the thighs of a white girl. When you come down to it, the black was just a wet firecracker, but that's not for me to say. Make way for the Yellows. The Japanese are going to take us dancing on the volcano. It's their turn. The great roulette wheel of the flesh. That's how it turns. Red, Black, Yellow. Black, Yellow, Red. Yellow, Red, Black. The Great Mandala of the Western World.

Beelzebub, Lord of the Flies, Lives Upstairs

Hemingway should be read standing up, Basho walking, Proust in the bath, Cervantes in a hospital, Simenon in a train (Canadian Pacific, anyone?), Dante in paradise, Dosto in the underground, Miller in a smoky bar with hot dogs, fries, and a Coke . . . I was reading Mishima with a cheap bottle of wine by the bed, totally exhausted, and a girl in the shower.

She stuck her dripping head through the half-open bathroom door and issued two or three rapid requests: a towel to cover her breasts, another to go around her hips (I love Gauguin!), a third for her wet hair, and a fourth so she wouldn't have to set foot on the filthy floor.

She came out of the bathroom with a smile. It cost me four towels to see her teeth. I resumed my position, opening Mishima to page 78, and disappeared into pre-war Japan for eighty-eight seconds, good for three and two-thirds pages, before falling into a Fuji bonze Negro sleep.

Sleep is practically impossible in this muggy heat. I left the window open and the hot air completely knocked me out. I'm as groggy as one of those small-time boxers who turn up in Hemingway stories. I don't even have the strength to drag myself to the shower. An ocean of cotton closes around me.

I don't know how long I spent in that state. A distant buzzing awoke me. Airborne above the sink, an enormous green fly with bloodshot eyes is crashing into things. The fly looks blind. Totally drunk on the heat. Frenzied beating of wings. A fly high on codeine. A final collision with the wall and it does a kamikaze dive into the dishwater.

From the horizontal position I consider the cardboard boxes and green garbage bags stuffed with dirty laundry, books, used records, and spice bottles that have been cluttering the floor for two days now.

The old fly is inert. It floats on its back. Its pollen-yellow belly swells with water. I pick up Mishima, page 81. The words run like fly streaks. The letters tremble and shimmer. Sentences jump like living things and move before my eyes.

The fly is a stiff corpse drifting among the glasses. I alone am responsible in the eyes of the Lord of the Flies. Bouba maintains that Beelzebub lives upstairs.

The bottle slumps sadly at the foot of the bed. I take a good pull and drift off into sweet somnolence. The wine trickles down my throat, smooth and warm. Not bad for the cheap stuff. I feel soft and sated.

The Negro Is of the Vegetable Kingdom

1 2 3 4 5 6 7 8 9 10 I get up, steer clear of the shower, and give myself a brisk face-wash in the sink. The cold water finishes the slow process

of my awakening. Bouba must be on the Mountain, checking out the girls getting a tan. The couch resembles an abandoned wife. Bouba will be back later; today is his weekly day out. Bouba is a true hermit. He can spend whole days without even turning on the light. The day passes; Bouba meditates and prays. He wishes to become the purest among pure men. He intends to accept the challenge issued to Muhammad: "You cannot make the deaf hear, nor can you guide the blind or those who are in gross error." (Sura XLIII, 39.)

Miz Literature left me a note, folded in four and stuck in the corner of the mirror. She had almost slipped my mind. She's the McGill girl, the one Bouba nicknamed Miz Literature. That's Bouba's method. The girl we met the other day at a sidewalk café on St. Denis eating ice cream – he called her Miz Sundae. So as not to get Gloria Steinem on our case we say "Miz."

Miz Literature used two long paragraphs to tell me she had gone to a "delicious Greek bakery on Park Avenue." She's some kind of girl. I met her at McGill, at a typically McGill literary soiree. I let on that Virginia Woolf was as good as Yeats or some kind of nonsense like that. Maybe she thought that was baroque coming from a Negro.

The room is awash in dark sweat. The fly has long since joined his comrades in the great beyond. Above, Beelzebub has been appeased. Green garbage bags litter the middle of the room, their mouths agape. In a box (Steinberg cardboard special), with no semblance of order: a pair of shoes, a box of Sifto iodized salt, turned-up winter boots, a toothbrush, a tube of toothpaste, books, rolled-up Van Gogh reproductions, pens, a pair of sunglasses, a new ribbon for my old Remington, and an alarm clock. Idly, I stow it away in a corner, by the fridge. The sun comes slanting through the window in blades of light.

I pile the old newspapers into two stacks. It takes a while to bundle them up, then I stack them at the end of the table. I move silently through the darkness. I've sweated enough for a shower. The bathroom is tiny but at least there's a tub, a sink, and a shower – a miracle for this part of town. The old buildings in the barrio, if they're lucky enough to have a bathtub, never have a shower.

Miz Literature left her scent in the bathroom. In his journal (*Retour de Tchad*), Gide writes that what struck him most in Africa was the smell. A smell of strong spices. A smell of leaves. The Negro is of the vegetable kingdom. Whites forget that they have a smell too. Most McGill girls smell like Johnson's Baby Powder. I don't know what making love to a girl (over twenty-one, duly vaccinated) who stinks of baby powder does for you. I can never resist going kitchie-kitchie-koo under her chin.

Miz Literature brought her bag of toiletries. *Danger.* What is she after? Is she intent on subletting the single room Bouba and I share? She must have a spacious Outremont apartment, full of light and fresh air and sweet smells, and now she wants to come down here to live! In the heart of the Third World. These infidels are so perverse!

Miz Literature's open bag reveals a toothbrush (there's already a constellation of toothbrushes above my sink) and a tube of Ultra Brite toothpaste (does she think the Negro's sparkling white teeth are pure myth? Well, think again, WASP. No kidding, it's the real thing. Ivory jewels on an ebony ring!). Special soap for dry skin, two tubes of lipstick, an eyebrow pencil, some tampons, and a little bottle of Tylenol.

I never go anywhere without my photo of Carole Laure. Hungry mouth and wide eyes next to the long, soft, refined adolescent face of Lewis Furey. The rich boy, intelligent, sophisticated, gentle, clever as they come – shit! Everything I'd like to be. Starring Carole Laure. Carole Laure starring in my bed. Carole Laure fixing me a tribal dish (spicy chicken and rice). Carole Laure listening to jazz with me in this lousy, filthy room. Carole Laure, slave to a Negro. Why not?

Through a microscope, this room would look like a camembert cheese. A forest of odours. The teeming (like the tearing noise of silk paper) of shiny creatures. In summer everything spoils so quickly. A fuckfest of a million germs. I picture the planet that way and among those millions of yellow seeds, I dream of the five hundred out of the 500 million Chinawomen who would take me for their black Mao.

Cannibalism with a Human Face

A discreet knock-knock-knock at the door. I open. Miz Literature comes in, arms loaded with pâté, croissants, cheese (brie, oka, camembert), smoked sausages, French bread, Greek desserts, and a bottle of wine. I make a summary stab at housekeeping, all aglow at the prospect of eating something besides Zorbaburgers or spaghetti à la DaGiovanni.

I throw open the window: dry, burning air pours into the room in waves. I clear the sink of dirty plates and glasses and drain the soapy water. The fly is sucked downward into a better world. "I swear, by the moon!" (Sura LXXIV, 35.) Farewell, Fly.

Miz Literature finishes cleaning the table. She puts water on to boil for tea. I get comfortable. She fills my glass with wine. I close my eyes. To be waited on by an English girl (Allah is great). Fulfillment is mine. The world is opening to my desires.

I begin to look at Miz Literature with new eyes, though she hasn't changed. She's a tall girl, a little hunched over, with albatross arms, her eyes are a little too bright (too trusting), she has pianist's fingers and a face with astonishingly regular features. Apparently she never had to wear braces, incredible for an Outremont girl. She has small breasts and wears a size ten shoe.

"Aren't you eating?" I ask her.

"No."

She answers with a smile. The smile is a British invention. Actually, the British brought it back from one of their Japanese campaigns.

"Don't you want to eat?"

"I'll just watch you," she breathes.

Just like that, with her eyes on mine.

"I see. You'll just watch me."

"I'll watch you."

"You like watching me eat?"

"You have such a good appetite . . ."

"You're making fun of me."

"Watching you eat fascinates me. You eat with such passion. I've never seen anyone do it like you do."

"Is it funny to watch?"

"I don't know. I don't think so. I find it moving, that's all."

Watching me eat moves her. Miz Literature is incredible. She was brought up to believe everything she's told. Her cultural heritage. I can tell her the most outlandish stories and she'll nod her head and stare with those believing eyes. She'll be moved. I can tell her I consume human flesh, that somewhere in my genetic code the desire to eat white flesh is inscribed, that my nights are haunted by her breasts, her hips, her thighs, I swear it, I can tell her all that and more and she'll understand. She'll believe me. Imagine: she's studying at McGill (venerable institution to which the bourgeoisie sends its children to learn clarity, analysis, and scientific doubt) and the first Negro who tells her some kind of fancy tale takes her to bed. Why? Because she can afford that luxury. I surrender to the least bit of naïveté, even for a second, and I'm one dead nigger. Literally. I have to be a moving target, otherwise, at the first emotion, my ass would be grass. Miz Literature can afford a clean, clear conscience. She has the means. I gave up on that luxury a long time ago. No conscience. No paradise lost. No promised land. You tell me: what good can a conscience possibly do me? It can only cause problems for a Negro brimming over with unappeased fantasies, desires, and dreams. Put it this way: *I want America.* Not one iota less. With her Radio City girls, her buildings, her automobiles, her enormous waste – even her bureaucracy. I want it all: good and bad, what you throw away and what you keep, the ugly and beautiful alike. America is a totality. What do you expect me to do with a conscience? I can't afford one anyway. The way things are going, it would be down at the pawnshop in a flash.

I have to make sure not to bug Miz Literature about being so nice. She's still the best thing a Negro can afford in these hard times of ours.

from An Aroma of Coffee

1. The Gallery

The Summer of 1963

I grew up in Petit-Goâve, a town a few kilometres from Port-au-Prince. If you take the National Highway south, Petit-Goâve is just after the great Tapion mountain. Let your truck (because you will be travelling by truck) coast down to the barracks (painted canary yellow), bear to the left, go up the hill, and see if you can stop at number 88 on the rue Lamarre.

There, you may very well discover, sitting on the gallery, a smiling, peaceful old woman and a ten-year-old boy. The old woman is my grandmother. Call her Da. Just Da. The boy is me. It's the summer of 1963.

Bouts of Fever

When I think about it, nothing much happened that summer, besides my tenth birthday. True, I was sick, I had bouts of high fever, which is why you would have found me sitting quietly at my grandmother's feet. According to Dr. Cayemitte (whose wonderful name is that of a tropical fruit), I was to stay in bed over summer vacation. But Da let me sit out on the gallery and listen to my friends shouting and yelling as they played soccer, next door, in the animal pen. The smell of manure made my head spin.

The Landscape

Like the canvas of a naive painter: in the distance, the great bald, smoking mountains. On their slopes, peasants gather dry wood for burning. I can see the shapes of a man, a woman, and three children on the side of the old mountain. The man is building a fire only steps from his house, a little thatched hut with a door and two windows. The woman goes into the house, then comes out immediately and stands in front of the man. She is talking to him, waving her arms in the air. Thick black smoke rises into the clear blue sky. The man picks up a bundle of twigs and throws them onto the fire. The flames rise higher. The children run around the house. The woman chases them inside, then walks back to the man. The fire stands between them.

I told Da all about it. It's true. I tell Da everything. Da says I have an eagle eye.

The Sea

All I do is turn around, and I can see the red sun sinking slowly into a turquoise sea. The Caribbean Sea is at the end of my street. I see it sparkling beyond the coconut trees, behind the barracks.

The Wind

Sometimes, late in the afternoon, I feel the breath of the trade winds on my neck. A soft breeze that scarcely stirs the dust in the street and, sometimes, the black dresses of the peasant women coming down from the mountains with sacks of coal balanced on their heads.

A Yellow Liquid

Once, a peasant woman stopped just in front of our gallery. She spread her thin legs under her black dress, and a strong stream of yellow liquid followed. She lifted her dress ever so slightly and stared straight ahead. The sack of coal did not even move.

I couldn't help giggling.

Dog

We have a dog, but he's so skinny and ugly I pretend I don't know him. He had an accident, and ever since, he has a funny way of walking. As if he were wearing high-heeled shoes, as if he had adopted the careful, elegant walk of old ladies coming back from church. We call him Marquis, but my friends nicknamed him Madame the Marquise.

The Red Bicycle

Another summer, and I still won't get the bicycle I've always wanted. The red bicycle I was promised. Of course, I wouldn't have been able to ride it because of my dizzy spells, but there's nothing more alive than a bicycle leaning against a wall. A red bicycle.

Flight

Last summer, I stole a bicycle, Montilas the blacksmith's bicycle, from right in front of his house. The bicycle was leaning against a tree, by the town library. In the shade. The bicycle was just waiting for someone to jump on it and ride south. I climbed on quietly and rode behind the church, all the way to Petite Guinée. There's a little hill you go down. Montilas's bicycle was well oiled. The wind on my chest, my shirt off (I had tied it around my waist), I lost track of time. I had never gone so far in that direction. By the time I returned, the sun was halfway in the sea. Da was waiting for me, standing on the gallery.

Yellow Dress

I didn't see her coming. She came up behind me, the way she always does. She was returning from afternoon Mass with her mother. Vava lives at the top of the hill. She was wearing a yellow dress. Like the fever of the same name.

Kite

I watched her for a long time. Her mother was holding her hand tightly. I counted the number of steps it takes her to reach her house. Sometimes she reminds me of a kite flying above the trees. You can't see the string.

The Street

Our street isn't straight. It twists like a cobra blinded by the sun. It begins at the barracks and stops suddenly at the foot of the Croix de la

Jubilée. A street of speculators who buy coffee and sisal from the peasants. Saturday is market day. A regular hive of activity. People come from the twelve neighbouring rural sections that form the district of Petit-Goâve. They walk barefoot, wide-brimmed straw hats on their heads. The mules go before them, heavy with sacks of coffee. Long before sun-up, you can hear the racket from the street. The animals paw the ground. The men shout. The women cry. Da gets up early on Saturday to make them coffee. Strong black coffee.

Fishing

The women sell eggs, vegetables, fruit, and milk to buy salt, sugar, soap, and oil. My dog Marquis loves to push through the crowd and bring me back a piece of soap or a fish in his mouth. He puts it down next to me, looks up with his soft eyes, then runs off to go fishing again.

The Coffee of Les Palmes

According to Da, the best coffee comes from Les Palmes. In any case, that's what she always drinks. Da can't buy large amounts of coffee, like before. We went bankrupt ten years ago, long before my grandfather died. But the peasants go on offering to sell Da coffee. When they see she doesn't have the money, they leave a half-bag of coffee beans on the gallery. Da looks the other way, and they disappear without being paid. The coffee lasts a week because Da is always pouring a cup for everyone.

Paradise

One day, I asked Da to tell me about paradise. She showed me her coffee pot. In it was the coffee from Les Palmes that she prefers, mostly because of its aroma. The aroma of Les Palmes coffee. Da closed her eyes. As for me, the smell makes my head spin.

Tobacco

Every peasant woman smokes a pipe, a short cutty made of baked red clay. They rub big leaves of dried tobacco between their palms to make powder. They smoke their pipes under their wide-brimmed straw hats.

The Blue Cup

Da is sitting in a big chair with a coffee pot at her feet. I'm close by, lying on my stomach, watching the ants.

From time to time, people stop to talk to Da.

"How are you, Da?"

"Very well, Absalom."

"And your health, Da?"

"Just fine, thanks to God . . . A cup of coffee, Absalom?"

"I won't say no, Da."

Absalom's face as he concentrates, inhaling the coffee. He drinks slowly, clicks his tongue from time to time. The little blue cup that Da keeps for the inner circle. The last sip. Absalom sighs; Da smiles. He gives her back the cup and thanks her with a tip of his hat.

Ants

The gallery is paved with yellow bricks. Colonies of ants live in the interstices between them. There are little black ants, heedless and gay. Red ants, cruel and carnivorous. And the worst kind of all: the flying ants.

On my left: a dragonfly covered with ants.

No Bones

My body is elastic. I can stretch it out and shrink it, swell it up or flatten it down, in any way I wish. But, usually, I have a long, boneless body, like an eel. When they try to catch me, I slip through their fingers.

"Why are you fidgeting like that?" Da asks me.

"I want to go."

"You know you're sick."

"Just to watch."

"Only for an hour, then."

I dash off to the park.

The Park

It's really an empty lot where the peasants tie up their horses when they come down for the market. Actually, they leave them with old Oginé, whose job is to find them a good spot in the park. He brings them plenty of hay and gives them water to drink when the sun is at its zenith. Most of the horses have sores all over their backs. Oginé rubs down their backs with a brush, then puts big leaves over their open sores. Without flinching, the animals let him tend to them. Oginé is in charge of the park. We give him a little something (money or fruit), and he lets us play soccer next to the animals. The smell of manure turns my stomach every time. I hold onto a horse's neck. The horse's left eye is full of flies, little green flies. I won't leave my spot. I wait for the end of the game.

Animals

Animals are dangerous. You have to be especially careful with those that pretend to be sleeping. Last year, Auguste got kicked in the stomach. It happened at the beginning of vacation. He spent the whole month of July in bed. His mother put dozens of little leeches on his stomach to suck out the bad blood. As soon as she turned her back, Auguste swallowed the leeches, one after the other. Never stand behind an animal. Da tells me that every time I go to the park.

The Game

It's almost dark but they're still playing in the park. They won't stop until it's completely dark and no one can see the ball. One time, we kept on playing through the darkness. That's the way it always is at the beginning of summer. You want to see how far you can go.

Night

Da likes to stay up late. Once, she saw Gideon, with his white dog following behind, on his way to the river. That was a month after he died. Da isn't afraid of anything. She even called out to Gideon, who was hiding behind his big straw hat. He murmured something that Da didn't catch.

It had to be Gideon, because his dog was following him.

Night Owls

Da went inside to make fresh coffee. I think we'll be night owls, this evening. Da will tell me all kinds of stories about zombies, werewolves, and she-devils until I fall asleep. When I awake, I'm always amazed to be back in my own bed. I love falling asleep that way, with my head on Da's lap, and she telling me scary stories. One evening, Da asked me to go inside and go to bed a little earlier than usual. She wanted to be alone. I always know when she wants to be alone. But I wanted to be with her, so I pretended to go inside, then I slipped back onto the gallery. I lay down in a dark spot, near the old coffee scale. Da didn't see me. I watched her in the darkness. Her eyes were shining and she was looking up at the sky. As if she were trying to count the stars. Finally, I fell asleep. When I awoke, I was alone on the gallery. All the doors were locked and there was no one in the street. It was the middle of the night. I thought I was in bed, having a nightmare. I stood up; my eyes were open. But that can happen to you in a dream. So I banged my head against the scale to see if it would hurt. But I banged myself too hard. The pain was terrible. I screamed, and that woke up Da. She opened the door for me. Scarcely had we closed the front door when a horse came galloping past at full speed.

In Petit-Goâve, everyone knows that Passilus changes into a horse after midnight.

The Gallery

Around two o'clock on any summer afternoon, Da washes down the gallery. She places a big white tub full of water on one of the trays of the scale, and with a small plastic bucket, she throws the water onto the gallery with a flick of her wrist. She cleans the corners carefully with her rag. The bricks turn as shiny as new pennies. I love lying on the cool gallery and looking at the drowned ant colonies in the spaces between the bricks. With a blade of grass, I try to save some of them. The ants can't swim. They let themselves be washed away by the current until they can grab onto something. I watch them for hours.

Da drinks her coffee. I observe the ants. Time has no meaning.

OKEY CHIGBO

THE HOUSEGIRL

Look, I don't want what I am going to tell you repeated anywhere. The last time I told anyone anything, that terrible gossip Nkechi Obiago got to hear it through God knows who, and now the whole world knows my life history. First of all, did I tell you that Madam has returned from Lagos? You should see the things she brought back. *Chineke!* Lagos na so so enjoyment! All kinds of beautiful trinkets that shone as if the sun and moon had come down to adorn Madam's portmanteau; all kinds of dazzling things from that wonderful heaven on earth where everyone wears the latest fashions and discards them in a week. She gave Obiageli a beautiful gown with enough wonderful colours to shame all the pretty flowers in our village of Aniugwu. Obiageli was ordered to give one of her old gowns to that witch Selina.

As usual, there was nothing for me. You know how it goes. Selina gets everything just because she is from Madam's hometown. My seniority as number one housegirl does not mean anything to Madam. The world knows how competent I am in cooking: Master is often asking for my delicious *egusi* soup, but does Madam care? The world knows how well I do the household chores, but does Madam care? Have you ever seen Selina sweep a room? It is as if her mother never taught her anything. I sometimes ask her who she is leaving the dust in the corners for. But that is another story.

Anyhow, you remember when Madam's son Callistus returned? It was about three months ago, I think. He was doing poorly in school at Enugu, so Master either pulled him out, or he got expelled for failing his exams. It is not that he does not have a head for books; it is just that he is such a wild boy, he never reads. Did you know he was running about with a harlot woman instead of reading his books? This harlot woman was also Chief M.A. Nwachukwu's girlfriend, the very same chief who fired a double-barrelled shotgun at a man he caught leaving his fifth wife's bedroom. You know the very chief I am talking about. Cally is lucky he did not get caught by Chief Nwachukwu. Obiageli says Cally must have been giving the harlot woman money because he was always broke. What a silly boy, eh? Can you imagine us sixteen-year-old housegirls giving our little wages to boys? Ha! We will make them give us money first.

Oby-girl says that he used to write Madam every week begging for money, telling all kinds of lies about new school uniforms and new books. She would send it because he is her favourite son. She is also making a lot of money as an Army contractor, but when I ask about my pay, she either ignores me or tries to bite my head off. Oh hard cruel world! Just because I ask for what is mine, she snaps at me. Do you know that since my father died, she has not paid me a penny? Oh hard cruel world! I have no one to defend my interests. Don't mind me, please. I will continue with the story as soon as I have wiped my tears.

Cally stayed home while his father decided what to do with him. I used to listen to him boast about the harlot woman when his friends came visiting. I would pretend to sweep the room next to his, and you know me, I would open my ears wide. You can trust me in these matters. If there is anything worth hearing in that house, I will hear it. The things those boys used to talk about. *Chineke!* Those boys are more rotten than overripe fruit with maggots in it.

One morning I found him sitting at the dining table resting his elbows on the table, and carrying his face in his palms. He looked like he alone had been given the task of shouldering all the world's troubles. When I asked what was wrong he did not reply. He just rose and walked away. I did not think too much about it, but went on to complete my morning duties by sweeping his room. Well, who did I find there but the headmistress of witches herself, Selina Okorie, doing the job. Or rather, she had stopped work by his table and was looking at something on it. I have to tell you that ever since Cally returned from Enugu, she had been trying to get into his good graces, running all kinds of errands for him, arranging his room for him whenever he messed it up, and always hanging around him to ask in her sweetest voice, "Cally, is there anything you want? Can I wash your clothes? Can I prepare some *ugba* for you?" That kind of behaviour might have bothered some people, but it did not bother me because I am too big to be bothered by such things. But I am not surprised that Cally took no notice of her because her protruding teeth – which make her look like Agaba the dread spirit mask – are enough to frighten the stoutest heart.

I stood for some time at Cally's door, watching her, and she seemed to be reading something on the table. After a while I could not stand it any longer, and went in.

"SELINA OKORIE!" I shouted, and she leaped up in consternation, grabbed her broom, and started to sweep rapidly. She slowed down when she saw me, then stopped. "What are you looking at on that table?" I continued. "I will tell Callistus. Thief! Idiot of no consequences!" As you can see, I am very good at insulting people in English. I did not complete elementary five for nothing.

"Your mother, idiot of no consequences," she replied coolly. I tell you that girl can do things to drive someone mad. The blood immediately rushed to my head.

"What!" I cried. "What did my mother do to you that you should bring her into this?"

"You insulted me first."

"Yes, but I did not insult your mother."

"Well, a light tap often buys a big slap."

"You will get an even bigger slap from me then," I shouted and flew at her.

Her chi must have been very alert that day, because she slipped through my grasp before I could box her ears shut, and escaped into the yard. I made sure that she was gone, then returned to complete the sweeping. As God is my witness, I did not intend to read what was lying on Cally's table. God knows I am not a sinful person, but if a letter is left carelessly open on a table, what is to prevent the devil from pushing an innocent girl like me in its direction? Of course, I first wrestled strenuously with the devil who clearly wanted me to read the letter, but you know how it goes.

I started to read the letter.

It was from his harlot woman in Enugu. She called him her "dearest darling." Ha! I am sure she has twenty other dearest darlings. The letter said that she was getting married to Chief M.A. Nwachukwu. *Chineke!* Money! Some people love it O! How can any woman leave a beautiful young boy like Cally for an old man like Chief M.A. Nwachukwu, whose thing does not stand up anymore? It's true! That's what Oby-girl said. And Oby should know, she has seen many

. . . no, I did not say anything, I do not want to get into trouble. I am not like that terrible gossip Nkechi Obiago, who is full of more news than a radio.

Anyway, the harlot woman's letter said that she did not want Cally to see or contact her again "in everyone's best interest." Oho-o! I thought when I read it. So that is why he was so unhappy today. But it is good, I thought. It is not right for them to be together. Some women of nowadays, they have no shame. How can a twenty-five-year-old *agaracha* be going with a seventeen-year-old boy, and be taking all his money? It is not right.

Later I passed him as he headed for his room and said, "I know your entire history, your intimate and deepest secrets."

"What do you mean?" he asked, looking at me suspiciously.

"Just be aware that I know everything about you," I said. He frowned and looked into his room.

"Dearest darling," I sang, and began to walk away quickly.

"Wha-what? What have you . . ." he shouted. "Come here!" I scampered off, laughing like a hyena, and he charged after me, bellowing at the top of his voice, "Comfort! Comfort, I will kill you for reading my letter!"

He caught me at the steps leading outside, pulled me to the ground, and started to tickle my ribs. By now, I was laughing till tears ran down my cheeks while we rolled around on the ground. What are you looking at me like that for? Please wipe that sinful look off your face, it was all innocent fun. Your mind always goes to bad things. We rolled to a stop against a pair of legs in well-pressed trousers, and looked up. It was Master! Papa Callistus!

"Ah, I see you are getting along very well with the ladies, Cally," he said, nodding his head very gravely. "Just bear in mind if you get any of them pregnant, you will have to marry her." I felt like asking him why he has not married Miss Onyejiekwe the teacher. Don't tell anyone, but do you know that the baby she had recently is said to be Master's? It is true! Nkechi told me.

A few days after this, Madam left for Lagos. The day before she left, I went into the parlour where she was with her friend Mama Moses the market woman. You know Mama Moses: she is big enough to fill a room and a parlour, so she occupied one couch all by herself. Madam on the other hand daily resembles the dry fish we use to make soup (I feel free to insult her because she is bad to me), and was seated in a small corner of the opposite chair. Madam is getting thinner every day despite her successful business, because her wooden heart is sucking up all the kindness in her body. Look at Mama Moses her friend – getting rounder every day even though she is not as successful, because she is so kind and good. Just the other day, she bought Nkechi a pair of "higher heel" to wear to church. Can you imagine Madam doing that for any of *her* housegirls? All I can say is that if you are good, *Chineke* will reward you with the well-fed look of the wealthy, and if you are bad, *Chineke* will make you look hungry like the starving poor no matter how rich you are.

Anyway, that evening the two "Business Madams" were discussing their business when I came in to pour the fourth bottle of stout for Mama Moses (that woman can take her drink better than any man in Aniugwu). Madam told her to drink as much as she wanted because business was going very well. Madam told Mama Moses that she was making the trip to Lagos to meet one Army major-general who would help her get a new contract that would give her bags and bags of money. When I heard this, my heart beat faster, and I solved some arithmetic in my head: if her business is working well, and she is expecting bags of money soon, then this is the time to ask her for some of my money. This is also the time to ask her of the promise she made to my father before he died. I don't know if I have told you this, but she promised to take me into her business and teach me how to become a big business madam like her. This is why I am still with her; I would have gone to work for someone else, but I do not want to remain a housegirl all my life. So that night, after Mama Moses left, I decided to ask about the money.

After seeing Ma Moses off, Madam went straight to her room to pack and make final preparations for the trip. I must confess that when the time came to go and ask her, my heart started beating poom-poom, poom-poom like that big drum young boys play during the New Yam feast. I walked past her room seven times, but could not make my heart strong enough to go in. I was about to abandon the idea when she suddenly called from inside the room: "Who is there?"

My legs started to carry me away, but I forced them to stop. Why was I running? I asked myself. All I wanted was my money.

"It is me, Comfort."

"What do you want?"

"I want to ask you for something."

"Yes, go on."

"It is about . . . well, you know how . . . do you remember . . ."

"WELL, WHAT IS IT? Hurry up, I have not finished packing yet."

"It-it . . . Madam, it is about my money."

"Is that why you are bothering me? GET OUT OF HERE!! Can't you find a better time to talk about it? Can't you see I am busy?"

I bolted out of the room, out of the house into the cool night air of the backyard, where I threw myself on the ground and began to weep. Cally found me there a short while later trying to compete with the heavy rains of last week.

"Comfort, what is the matter?" he cried, dropping to his knees and peering into my face.

"Nothing," I replied, not wanting to tell him bad things about his mother.

"Stop crying and let us go back into the house," he said, taking me by the hand. "Won't you tell me what is wrong? Did Mama beat you?"

I felt like telling him because he is such a good-hearted person, and I knew he would sympathize with me, but I did not wish to talk at that time because I knew I would say bad things about his mother.

"I will tell you tomorrow," I said as we trudged slowly back to the house.

All the servants got up at four-thirty the next morning to prepare for Madam's departure. Everything was hurry-hurry and quick-quick. You know how Madam is when she has something to do: she wants everybody to quick-march like soldiers. Romanus the driver drove her car out to wash it; Selina heated water for Madam's bath and then ironed her clothes; I fried *akara* and prepared hot *akamu* for breakfast. It was still very dark with the night insects still chirping, and the roosters just starting to crow, just around the time when spirits, both good and evil, abandon their wanderings abroad and return to their homes in the earth. Madam did not seem worried about meeting any spirits as she sat in the "owner's corner" and Romanus drove the car out of the compound.

We watched the lights of the car disappear into the darkness on its way to that marvellous city where no one sleeps, then turned back into the house. I pretended to go to the kitchen to prepare the ingredients for the day's meals but as soon as I was sure no one was looking, I crept back to the parlour where I sleep, spread out my sleeping mat behind the long couch, wrapped myself snugly in my cover cloth, and slipped into a comfortable and sweet sleep. This is why I am always happy when Madam travels – I can sleep a little longer and not have to wake up at five-thirty. *Chineke* knows I am not a soldier man or a rooster that I should be waking up so early every day.

It seemed I had just fallen asleep when Madam returned to the house! She must have forgotten something, I thought, I must get up before she catches me sleeping. I tried to get up, but seemed glued to the mat, and she marched into the room and switched on the light.

"COMFORT!"

I leaped six feet into the air, shouting, "Madam *biko-o*!" with my arm upraised to ward off the expected slap.

But when my eyes got used to the bright sunlight streaming in from the open window, there was only Selina cackling hysterically in the corner.

"Madam *biko-o*!" she mimicked between bursts of laughter. I tell you, it was too much to bear. I had to tell her a few good words.

"Selina Okorie," I began.

"Yes, Madam Sleep," she replied.

"Selina, do not insult me because I am your senior in everything, including age: 365 days is no joke, so please respect your elders. Remember it is me who shares out the meals now that Madam is out. If you do not look out, the meals that mice eat will be enormous compared to what I will give you." She behaved herself after that for the rest of the day.

Later on that day, Cally called me into his room to ask why I was crying the night before. "It is past now, don't worry about it," I told him.

"Come on, tell me. It is Mama, isn't it? I know it is. You can tell me, I won't say anything to her." I was silent.

"Tell me," he insisted.

"Show me a picture of your har . . . your girlfriend, the one who is marrying Chief Nwachukwu."

"Will you tell me what is wrong if I show you?"

"Yes."

"Liar. You are more cunning than the tortoise of children's fables."

"I promise, I will tell you after I see the pictures."

He showed me a colour photograph of her. She is very beautiful with an oval-shaped face and a very fair complexion.

I said to him: "She is very lovely, but I don't like the way she dresses. Why does she wear a skirt that is slit up to the waist, and a blouse that exposes all her breasts? She might as well just parade naked in front of everyone." He laughed and made a playful grab at me which I easily evaded. I then told him that I had not been paid since my father died suddenly about a year ago. My father used to come at the end of every month to collect the money from Madam, ten naira a month, and he would give me three naira to spend. I used to be rich in those days. I could afford to buy earrings, bracelets, and chewing gum.

"How much does mother owe you now?" he asked.

"One hundred and fifty naira," I replied, and he whistled.

"Okay. I will see what I can do."

"Just don't tell anyone I told you anything," I said to him and turned to leave. "By the way, I hope you have stopped crying over that girl. Do not worry about her, she is too *agaracha* for you, and all she wants is money. I am sure you will find many girls in Enugu who are nicer and more beautiful than she is. Look, I will cook your favourite dishes for you while Madam is away, and when I have time, I will come and sit with you and we shall tell stories. Very soon you will forget your *agaracha* friend." He smiled and I left the room.

A few hours later, as I was passing the room, he pulled me inside and, to my great surprise, pressed a folded wad of notes into my hand. I uttered a short cry, and let it drop to the ground as if it were a red-hot piece of charcoal straight from the fire. He picked it up and gave it back to me. I counted thirty naira, and demanded to know where he got it, but he would not tell. I then told him I would not accept the money since I did not know where it came from, and he quickly said it was what remained of his pocket money.

I did not believe that story, but my heart was beating very fast as I stared at that money in my hand and my heart seemed to be saying, poom-poom, earrings, bracelets, poom-poom, earrings, bracelets . . . I solved the arithmetic in my head in this way: who knows where Cally got the money? He may have stolen it from his father's wallet, he may have broken into Madam's strong box, and he is so wild that boy, that he may even have friends who counterfeit money! But on the other hand, it may really be what is left of his pocket money. I will keep it for a while; if anyone reports missing thirty naira, I will give the money back to Cally; if not, I will spend it.

Unfortunately, I did not take the devil and his evil ways into account. He knows how to lead young girls astray just when they think they have the situation under control. The next day, Obiageli asked me to go to the market alone to buy ingredients for soup; usually I go with her or with Madam. I pleaded with her to come with me, but she wanted to go and visit a friend who she had not seen for a long time. So I had to go alone. The devil immediately entered my heart, and I tied up the thirty naira in the hem of my wrapper intending to take it to the market with me. "If I leave it here, Selina might find it," I reasoned.

After buying the okra and palm oil for the soup, I made a detour through the trinket stalls "just to see what is available in case I find out I can keep the money." It is not good for young housegirls like us to be without money for a long time, especially when there are so many nice things to buy, and other housegirls like Nkechi Obiago walk around in "higher heel," and wear nice earrings. Lack of money makes us envious, and the bad ones among us may steal, while the others will spend foolishly whenever they get a little money. I left the stalls with only five naira left in the hem of my wrapper, and two pairs of imitation gold earrings.

If you know the devil and his cunning ways, you will realize that after you have done a bad thing as a result of his tempting, he runs away laughing, and the blindness with which he has covered your eyes is lifted so you can see the foolishness you have committed. It soon dawned on me that I could not show off my new treasures to the other housegirls and bask in their envious glances, because Selina would surely report it to Madam. I was gripped by a terrible fear: what if the money did not belong to Cally, and he had stolen it from Master or Madam? What if one of them found their money missing and called the police? Would Cally admit to the deed? I told myself that he was a good boy and he would, but what if they found out when he was not in town, gone off to school or somewhere? What would I do? Master or Madam would surely call the police. And they would send those policemen who don't wear uniforms and go around pretending to be ordinary people, those policemen who can just look at your face and know immediately that you stole money. I began to tremble with fear. I was ready to cry because I did not want to go to prison.

I walked into the house expecting someone to confront me and say: "Comfort! Where is the thirty naira?" But nobody did; the house was quiet, and seemed empty until I saw Selina come out of Cally's room. "You!" I shouted. "Did I not tell you not to go to Cally's room, you sorceress?"

"I can go wherever I like," she snapped defiantly. "And where I go is none of your business."

"Watch your tongue, or I will slap that devil out of your head."

"Just try," she replied, staring at me fiercely and cocking her fist.

I wanted to give her a few good slaps, but felt it was not a wise idea since I had not put away the earrings and they might be discovered in a struggle. Also at that moment, Cally poked his head out of his room, and said, "What are you two fighting about? Comfort, leave her alone. I asked her to clean my room."

I went to his room that night to tell him about the earrings. He laughed when I told him how I was unable to help myself when I saw them. He asked me to put them on, which I did, and stood admiring myself in front of the mirror on his table. You must promise never, never to tell anyone what I am going to tell you now. As I was watching myself in the mirror, he came up behind me and started to rub my stomach with his hands, and then worked his way up to my breasts. Yes, he actually touched them. He really is a wild animal, that Cally. I pleaded with him, "Please, Cally, don't do that, it is wrong." But he did not seem to hear. "Cally, stop. It is a sin." Eventually he stopped, and we stood around avoiding each other's eyes. It was the first time he had ever tried such a thing with me. I know that I am plump and have a full figure which makes all the houseboys try to steal looks when I bend to pick something from the ground, but I did not know that Cally looked at me that way.

After a long, embarrassing silence, he put his hand in his pocket and took out ten naira.

"Take this," he said.

"Why? What do you think I am?" I cried.

"Just take it. It is simply more of the money Mama owes you, so take it and don't be silly."

"Don't be silly yourself! I won't take it!" I said angrily and left the room. But I took the money later. He followed me everywhere and eventually I had to take it. He made me take it. And if you really want to know (because your mind always wants to know bad things) we played the touching game again. Many times. I cannot tell you any more, but just remember that I am a good girl and I have my limits.

A short while before Madam's return, Cally was sent off to Owerri in Imo State where his uncle teaches at a secondary school. The man is Papa Cally's brother, and a very strict disciplinarian who does not spare the cane even on grown boys like Cally. That is why Papa Cally sent Cally there. If that uncle does not make Cally study his books, nothing in this world will.

After Madam's return and the big distribution of gifts (with none for me as I told you) everything seemed to return to normal until a few days ago. I was in the kitchen cooking, and Selina and Madam were in her room. It seems that Selina was rearranging her wrapper when some money fell out of it. The foolish girl had put it there and forgotten about it.

"Selina, where did you get this ten naira from?" Madam said sharply.

"My ten naira," I thought when I heard her. "That witch must have taken it from my box!" I crept closer to listen to what was going on.

"Selina, I asked you where you got this ten naira? Has the devil taken your tongue? You better answer before I slap it out of your mouth!"

"I found it lying on the road."

"Liar!" (SLAP!) "Liar!" (SLAP! SLAP!) "I noticed that some money has been taken from my strongbox. That's where you found it, isn't it? Speak!" (SLAP!) "Speak, you ungrateful wretch that I rescued from poverty. Don't I send your mother money regularly? Why then do you steal from me?"

"Madam *biko-o*! Cally gave me the money, Cally gave it to me!"

"Yes, go ahead, blame it on Cally because he is not here. Why would Cally give you ten naira? You are a terrible liar and a thief! I am going to lock you up. Get into that room and stay there. There will be no food for you today, and I will send you back home tomorrow."

My body trembled like someone suffering from malaria when I heard this. At first, I had thought, that witch Selina has stolen my money and now God is punishing her for taking what is not hers. But then, I started to solve some arithmetic in my head, and reasoned thus: if she took the money from my box, why did she not say so and get me into trouble? Maybe she was telling the truth. Maybe Cally did give her the money. I decided to go and see if the money was still in my box, but just as I left the kitchen, I heard Madam call, "Comfort!" My heart skipped a beat and I replied, "Madam *bi* . . . I am coming!" and ran to her room, my heart pounding.

"Stop cooking," she said. "Go over to Mama Moses' and bring back the yams she brought me back from Abakaliki. Go immediately so you can be back before the soup is ready. I will watch the soup while you are gone." I dashed out of the house as fast as I could, heaving a sigh of relief. But on the way, my anxiety returned. Was it my money or not? Even if it wasn't, I could still get into trouble because it was now clear that the money Cally gave me was taken from Madam's strongbox. Should I go and own up and save Selina? She is not really a bad girl; it is only envy that makes us enemies. But even if I tell Madam that Cally gave me money too, will she believe it? She does not like to believe anything bad about him, and would be more likely to believe that Selina and I stole the money and now want to blame it on Cally because he is not home. I could ask her to write to Cally to confirm that he gave us money. But then Madam will never do that, not for her housegirls. She can get new housegirls too easily. And besides, I was sure she was searching for a chance to get rid of me.

With these thoughts buzzing around my head like a swarm of big, dirty houseflies, I returned from Mama Moses' with the yams. When I got to the kitchen, Selina was sitting before the pot of soup, stirring it nonchalantly. "You got out!" I gasped.

"Yes I did," she replied. "You thought I was done for, didn't you? Well, for your information, God does not allow good people like me to be punished for nothing."

It turned out that Obiageli had returned from school to find Selina in "detention," and had asked why. When Madam told her, she laughed, and said that Selina must be speaking the truth because Obiageli had caught Cally taking money from Madam's strongbox when Madam was in Lagos. Selina was let out of the room with a strong warning never to take money from anyone in the household without knowing its source. No one was more relieved than me when I heard that. I found the ten naira untouched in my box, and promised myself to be very careful with it, and keep it secret from everyone in the house.

Everything now seems all right except for Selina. She seems to be crying a lot these days; her complexion is also getting fairer and her breasts seem to be getting bigger.

MAKEDA SILVERA

---

from The Heart Does Not Bend

You Cannot Shave a Man's Head in His Absence

Maria Galloway didn't go to the Palisadoes Airport to see her son Freddie off. She never went to airports, not even when her son Peppie left in 1958 and then her daughter, Glory, in 1960.

The day Freddie left she sat on the verandah in the same chair she always sat in, a blue wicker one, smoking Craven A cigarettes, with the morning newspaper fresh in her hands. Back then she wore no old lady's clothes. Her sleeveless, brown jersey dress made her breasts a soft mountainside, her hips rolling brown hills. She sat there, quiet, looking on as friends and family came to bid Freddie goodbye.

It was hard to know what she was thinking. Her sure calm never left her face. Freddie knelt in front of her, gave her an open smile, flashed perfect white teeth, then lowered his eyes, like a small boy reciting his prayers. But he was nineteen and leaving to find his fortune abroad.

It was 1966 and I was nine years old. He was like a big brother to me, and I knew I was going to miss him something terrible. Freddie was my grandmother's youngest son.

"Come, nuh mek de plane lef yuh behin'. Hard-earn money buy dat ticket, and remember, nuh bodder go a white-man country and get inna any trouble. Act decent and show respect."

Her left hand was holding her cigarette tight. I saw tears well up in her eyes, but she didn't cry. "Gwaan, nuh mek de plane lef yuh," she repeated.

Freddie shrugged, smiled at her and kissed her cheek. "Tek care. We will see each other again if life spare." The December afternoon was humid, and the sun was like a yellow beach ball hanging in the sky. We crammed into cars and vans to say our final goodbyes. The smell of raw fish followed us as we raced along the seashore to the airport.

The waiting area was like Christmas morning in downtown Kingston. I kept expecting to see Junkanoos on stilts, their faces smeared in mud, horns on their heads, wire tails, dancing to drumbeats. Mothers and aunts and cousins laughed and cried, kissed their loved ones goodbye. The talk was hopeful and full of promise.

"Write mi when yuh reach."

"Don't forget mi."

"Mama, ah going to send money home soon as ah can."

"Ah hope de ackee and de fruits last de trip."

"Lloyd, 'member yuh have a 'oman an' a child here, don't tek up wid no foreign 'oman."

Vendors hawked their wares, selling everything from food to hair clips.

"Sweet bread, grater cake, bustamante backbone, paradise plum."

"Fish and bammy over here."

Uncle Freddie was all smiles and promises. "Yes, Dennis, yes man," he said to his best friend. "As soon as mi reach, ah send dat pair of Clarke's shoes fi yuh."

Freddie's girlfriend, Monica, admonished him not to forget her. "Nuh go up dere an' feget mi yuh nuh."

My uncle Freddie hugged and kissed her, whispered something in her ear that made her laugh. Then he smoothed his hands over her growing belly.

"Tek care a mi son. Ah going to send for de two a yuh soon. Send mi a picture when him born."

He promised the grand-aunts, cousins and friends everything foreign had to offer. He promised Monica that he would write and send money. For Dennis's ten-year-old sister, Punsie, he promised a camera. He saved his last goodbye for me. He lifted me high off the ground, squeezed me tight against his big chest. "Ah going to miss yuh, Moll." He kissed me from ear to ear, then whispered, "Ah won't feget yuh, yuh my special girl."

Uncle Mikey hadn't come to see him off.

My grandmother was still sitting on the verandah when we got back. Inside the house the air was thick with the smell of roasted yellow-heart breadfruit and yam, ackee and saltfish and golden-brown flour dumplings.

The grand-aunts took their plates to the verandah, while the rest of us sat around the table eating, drinking and talking about the good times we shared with Freddie. Monica was all teary-eyed. Cousin Ivan and Dennis and Freddie's other friends said they would miss him for his skilled kite-flying, the soccer matches at the end of the street, crab season and street dances.

Punsie said she'd miss the Chinese sweeties and the paradise plums Freddie bought for her. And me, I was losing the best and kindest uncle in the world.

I couldn't begin to think what life would be like without Uncle Freddie. He was the heart of the street. All the guys liked and respected him, even the older ones, for his easy manner and his contagious laughter. He took me to my only cockfight, in Dennis's backyard.

When everyone left the table, I went out to the verandah to join my grandmother and grand-aunts.

"Ah going to miss mi little nephew. No more Mr. Freddie. He was such a sharp dresser, and a ladies' man," Aunt Joyce said, a faraway smile gracing her face.

Aunt Joyce was the youngest of the sisters and the most fun. She laughed at everything, said whatever came into her head without thinking. She seemed to live only for the moment, so carefree. Joyce was three times divorced and had a string of suitors at her beck and call, but they never came close to her passion for clothes and shoes and gold jewellery.

"If dressing was all dere was to life and having whole heap of 'oman, him would be king," my grandmother replied sourly, dragging on her Craven A. "Ah only hope him remember poor Monica and de baby," she added.

"Nuh talk like dat, Maria, him love de girl," Aunt Joyce protested.

"Yuh mark my word, when him reach foreign all will be forgotten."

"Nuh mind, Maria. Him will change. Remember the Lord is within all of we," Grand-aunt Ruth added.

My grandmother didn't answer, but the tightening of her mouth and the steel in her brown eyes was enough. Nobody said anything for a while. I stared at the comic strip in the newspaper. Dennis's mother's voice travelled from several houses down the street, reaching our verandah. "Dennis, come water de yard."

Then my grandmother spoke. "Well, put bad and bad aside, ah will miss Freddie. Him really use to help me wid de garden," she said, softening slightly.

I decided it was safe for me to speak.

"Mama, yuh won't miss him for de crab season?"

She nodded. "Ah suppose so. Mm-hmm."

"Nuh bother even talk 'bout crab," Grand-aunt Ruth said. "Mi restaurant will really miss him, de crab soup and de crab fritter."

"Ivan can go wid Dennis and de rest a boys fi catch crab, him old enough," Mama said.

Ivan and Icie lived with Grand-aunt Ruth; they were cousins four times removed. Their mother was my grandmother and the grand-aunts' second cousin, who lived in Port Maria; she had several children and not enough food to go around. Icie was thirteen and Ivan fourteen.

"Dennis!" Aunt Joyce shouted across the three yards.

"Yes ma'am?" he shouted back.

"Ah putting in mi order now fi next crab season, since mi favourite nephew gone."

"Don't worry, Miss Joyce, you and Miss Ruth and Miss Maria covered."

"All right, don't forget," Aunt Joyce shouted back.

"No ma'am."

I remembered crab season. Uncle Freddie and his friends dragged crocus bags full of crabs into the backyard and threw them in huge drums. Punsie and I would watch them trying to climb out. Everyone on the street came to our yard to join in the excitement. There were always crab races. I hear Uncle Freddie now, shouting above the voices of his friends as he egged his crab on: "Run, run, crab, run fi yuh life!" During the season, we ate crabs so often we forgot the taste of other meat. We ate crab run-down cooked in coconut cream, and crab fritters spiced with curry powder, and my grandmother's favourite, crab shell stuffed with callaloo, sautéed onion, minced fresh hot peppers, then baked in an open wood fire. Uncle Freddie and his friends played music late into the night as we filled our bellies with crab.

Aunt Joyce brought my mind back to the verandah.

"Den, Maria, it won't cold when him get dere?" she asked.

"Ah think so, but Peppie and Glory will have clothes for him."

"Ah really going to miss him. Ah can't lie, him is mi favourite nephew," Aunt Joyce said.

Mama sucked her teeth. "Yuh know how much money dat bwoy tief from mi? If me never smart and one step ahead of him, ah would be in de poorhouse."

"Nuh mind, Maria, him gone. Try forgive him," Grand-aunt Ruth said.

"Ah because you two never have no children or unnu would be singing a different tune. Yuh think it easy fi raise four pickney alone?" Mama's voice was bitter. Neither of the grand-aunts answered, but a look passed between the two. I never found out whether they couldn't have children or chose not to have them.

I stole a glance at Mama. She took another drag of her cigarette and went on as if she had not said something vexing.

"Mikey get a job, yuh know. Him working at Paul and Paul Fashion. Him get a job sewing dresses," she said proudly.

"Ah hear is a lot of fancy people go dere to get clothes mek. Ah wonder how much dem would charge to mek a dress for me?" Aunt Joyce asked excitedly.

"Yuh can ask Mikey when yuh see him, ah sure yuh would get a good deal," my grandmother said, her voice lighter.

"Dat's real nice, ah glad for him. Now wid God's blessings all him need is to find a girlfriend," Grand-aunt Ruth said, little enthusiasm in her voice. Then she added in the same lifeless tone, "How come him wasn't at the airport?" I had never heard that tone in Grand-aunt Ruth's voice. As far back as I could remember, she was the paddle in the boat. She never spoke much, but when she did, her words were always balanced and encouraging. She was as slight as the shoot of a tree, and hedged about five feet tall, yet she carried command. She had a long face and a straight nose, a big head of coffee-coloured hair and a honey complexion. She was also a God-fearing woman who went to church every Sunday.

"Him have him business fi do." My grandmother drew on her cigarette again, and a look of defiance crossed her face. I wanted to hug her, even though I didn't understand. "Him did tell Freddie goodbye from last night. Him couldn't go to de airport, him had to prepare for him job. Freddie understan'. Dem understan' each other," Mama said. I winced, for I could not remember ever seeing her so sad. I muttered that I had to tell Punsie something and disappeared through the front gate.

When night was almost down, I heard Mama calling me. I washed off the dirt and excitement of the day, ate dinner, and then we went to bed. We didn't wait up for Uncle Mikey.

In Mama's big mahogany bed, I snuggled next to her. She stroked my hair. Her cigarette breath was warm and soothing on my face. She squeezed me tight in her arms and I felt a tear fall on my cheek. I buried my head in her bosom, and in the dark she sang to me.

My Bonnie lies over de ocean
My Bonnie lies over de sea
My Bonnie lies over de ocean
Oh bring back my Bonnie to me.
Oh bring back, oh bring back,
Oh bring back my Bonnie to me . . .

It didn't matter to me what she'd said to the grand-aunts about Uncle Freddie. I knew she loved him.

ANDRÉ ALEXIS

from Childhood

I

It has been six months since my mother died; a shade less since Henry passed. In that time, I've stayed home and I've kept things tidy.

They have been much on my mind.

I've been thinking about Love, you see, and theirs was the first and most puzzling romance I witnessed. I didn't understand it at the time. I still find it odd, though now it also seems a sad thing to contemplate.

Contemplate it I will, though, or contemplate it I must.

I've decided to write, to do something between housecleaning and the dreams I have about your shoulders.

Not that I'm idle.

I do a great deal of reading and some cooking. Besides, you'd be surprised how much there is to be done in or around a room. It's far from dull, I can tell you, but diversion depends on discipline. You have to break the day into manageable portions, and that takes a clock and a little resolve.

It takes a timetable:

7 O'clock:	I am awakened by the alarm.
8 O'clock:	I clean my bedroom.
9 O'clock:	I feed Alexander (seed).
10 O'clock:	I read poetry.
11 O'clock:	I continue to read poetry.
12 O'clock:	I prepare my meal of the day. I eat it.
1 O'clock (PM):	I write letters (to the *Citizen*).
2 O'clock (PM):	I clean my bedroom.
3 O'clock (PM):	I prepare tea.
4 O'clock (PM):	I set out for a walk, and walk with you in mind. (We've known each other for over a year now.)
5 O'clock (PM):	I read the newspaper.
6 O'clock (PM):	I read philosophy.
7 O'clock (PM):	I continue to read.
8 O'clock (PM):	I meditate on what I've read.
9 O'clock (PM):	I feed Alexander (fruit, vegetables).
10 O'clock (PM):	I bathe.
11 O'clock (PM):	I prepare the next day's schedule.
12 (AM) to 6 (AM):	Sleep.

Of course, this gives you no idea of the wealth of my existence. It doesn't take me an hour to wake from sleep. Nor does it take me an hour to feed Alexander. I can make tea in fifteen minutes, and there are days when I have no letters to write. I don't confine myself to the reading of poetry or philosophy, and, although I do clean the bedroom twice a day, there are a number of ways to go about it, each with its own appeal.

Still, none of this gives me the focus I'd like. I brood. I often brood.

Perhaps writing is the discipline I need.

So I will write, precisely, about my mother and Henry, about Love, with you in mind, from the beginning.

I had a singular childhood.

My parents went their separate ways at my birth and I was sent to live with my grandmother.

My grandmother, *Mrs.* Edna MacMillan, lived in Petrolia.

I don't think she was pleased to have me. She was past the age of easy tolerance, and she was cantankerous. (When I was five or six, I went through a phase about God making mountains He himself couldn't lift, until my grandmother told me that He didn't exist, so there was no use my going on about it.)

Also, she used to drink a lot of dandelion wine. And, from the time I could tell a dandelion from a thistle, she sent me out to cull them from lawns and fields all over the neighbourhood.[1]

She wasn't a cruel woman, but she was erratic. You couldn't always tell where you stood with her. At least, I couldn't. And her only loves were the wine she made and the poetry of Archibald Lampman:

From plains that reel to southward, dim,
The road runs by me white and bare;
Up the steep hill it seems to swim
Beyond, and melt into the glare . . .

And so on . . .

It was a strange combination, wine and Lampman, but I once used the poetry against the wine, so I was grateful for it.

My grandmother was sixty-five years old when I was abandoned to her care, a retired schoolteacher, thin as a compass, with an aureole

---

[1] In summer, the field across the street from our house was yellow with dandelions and spiky with thistles. It smelled of weeds and pine.

Along with a basket for the dandelions, I'd take a glass jar with me, to catch grasshoppers and crickets. In fact, quite a bit of my time was taken up with insects: finding them, catching them, admiring their wings and antennae before setting them free.

of white hair. Her eyes were liver brown, and her nose was slightly bent to one side of her face.

Outwardly, she was predictable. She usually wore one of two dresses: there was a long, short-sleeved summer dress with red and black flowers on a white background, and there was a long-sleeved winter dress with red and white flowers on a black background. She woke at seven o'clock every morning, and she drank a small tumbler of wine. If she'd had a bad night, she would drink two.

Perhaps, in the distant past, this steadied her nerves, but, when I knew her, the wine didn't help at all.

When she was really depressed, there was no telling what breakfast would be like. I had Pablum for breakfast until I was seven years old, so the Pablum was a sure thing. Sometimes she fed me herself. Sometimes she put a bowl of Pablum before me. Sometimes she gave me a spoon, sometimes a fork. And once, in a fit of giddiness, she used her wooden spoon as a catapult and fired the warm Pablum at me from the pot.

Much of how the day turned out was determined by breakfast.

I'm not saying I was abused, but there were times when she'd hit me pretty hard with her wooden spoon, and times when she'd hit me with whatever was nearby. (I don't know if anyone else has been punished with an egg beater, but I was, once.) I can't always remember why she hit me. There wasn't always a good reason, but the time I'm thinking of, when I used her beloved Lampman against her, was one of those when I'd done something wrong.

I'd fallen in the field across from our house and cut my hand on a broken Mason jar. Instead of asking for a bandage, as I should have, I'd gone to get one for myself. The bandages were on the lower shelf of the bathroom cabinet, and I could just reach them if I stood on my toes. What I did, though, was knock over a bottle of iodine. It shattered in the sink. My grandmother came to see what was going on.

I was six or seven at the time, no match for her. She had been drinking, and she had a frying pan with her. I saw it rise above me. I put up my hands to protect my head. I don't know what inspired me to recite poetry, but I did:

Now hath the summer reached her golden close,
And, lost amid her cornfields, bright of soul,
Scarcely perceives from her divine repose
How near, how swift, the inevitable goal . . .

There I was, hands raised up, squeaking out the first verse of "September," the only Lampman I knew by heart, having heard it from her hundreds of times.

And the poem smoothed her out.

– Clever monkey, she said
walking unsteadily back to the kitchen and her kitchenware.

It all seems improbable now, and yet I remember every word of the poem. The incident is all the more remarkable in that, at that age, I couldn't have understood much of Lampman's meaning.

Petrolia wasn't very interesting. I can say that now, having other places to compare it to. I suppose it was a fine environment for a child, though. There was a good deal of nature: the earth, mice, frogs, insects, the froth of spawning carp, turtles, and birds.

The town was cold and white in winter. It was wet in spring, warm in summer, and cold again in autumn; just what you'd expect from Southern Ontario. There were few people, and fewer buildings. There was a golf course, a tile factory, a dam. And in spring, when the only river in town overflowed, it usually managed to take a small child with it.

My friends at the time, I mean when I was five or six, were Sandy Berwick, the Goodman sisters, and the Schwartzes, all of whom lived close by.

Sandy's backyard abutted ours. His father was Reverend Berwick. We were friends because I was the only child who could stand him.

Our first meeting went something like this:

I was in the garden pulling weeds. From his side of the fence, Sandy said

– My name's Berwick . . . What're you doing?

– Picking weeds.

– For Mrs. MacMillan?

– For my grandmother.

– She's very old . . .

– Yes, she's pretty old.

– Is she Christian?

– I don't think so.

– Ohh . . . that's awful . . .

He walked away. He was wearing shorts and white socks that went up to his knees. He came back a minute later.

– She has to be converted, you know, he said.

Then he walked off again.

I had no idea what he was talking about, but it seemed significant. He had things in line. My grandmother was old. She wasn't Christian. She had to be converted.

The Goodmans were our neighbours on one side; the Schwartzes were on the other.

There were three Goodman sisters: Jane, Andrea, and Margaret. They all had pixie cuts, which Mrs. Goodman gave them the first Friday of every month. The three sisters were popular. There were usually half a dozen girls in the Goodmans' backyard every day until five o'clock, and when they weren't in the yard, they were in the basement playing with dolls or listening to records on their portable record player.

The Goodmans' basement was fascinating to me. The walls were panelled with slats that smelled of pine. Near the foot of the stairs there was a bar. Its counter was white arborite. Behind it were shelves of brightly coloured bottles. There were also mysterious gadgets: a piggy bank in the shape of a woman in a bathing suit, a bottle opener like a Lilliputian golf club, a mug with flesh-coloured breasts jutting from it, and plastic ice cubes with flies in them. Here and there, tacked to the wall, there were postcards from Florida and snapshots of Mr. and Mrs. Goodman on vacation.

The basement was carpeted. There were easy chairs and an upholstered sofa. In a separate room, there was a Ping-Pong table. It all seemed so luxurious, so wealthy.

In contrast, our basement was a dark and mildewed punishment.

I didn't go to the Goodmans' often, because I was shy and because Mr. Goodman didn't like me, but it was at the Goodmans' that I learned to skip rope, to turn double Dutch and Irish, to tell the difference between a doll in summer clothes and a doll in sportswear, to make papier-mâché heads and construction-paper silhouettes.

And, as it happens, Margaret Goodman was my first love.

On the other side, the Schwartzes lived in a red-brick two-storey house that was the smallest on Grove Street. It was also the most beautiful. The house was covered in ivy, and the property penned by an unruly hedge. In the front windows, one on either side of the door, there were white flowerboxes which, in spring, were filled with tulips.

When I knew them, Mrs. Schwartz was twenty-five and her daughter, Irene, was five.

As far as I remember, Lillian Schwartz was the only person who ever talked about my mother: my mother as a child, the dolls she liked, the books she read, the park on King where she fell from the seesaw; my mother adolescent, beautiful in certain dresses, squabbling with her parents; and then her sudden departure, at the age of seventeen, with a man from Sarnia.

In Lillian Schwartz's version of her, I discerned something of myself. I imagined my mother thin, shy, and unhappy.

Also, Mrs. Schwartz never spoke down to me. She behaved as if I were a colleague. When she took a correspondence course on religion, for instance, I was pushed into the frightening universe of charmed weeds, dying saints, and the restless dead.

To this day I can't think of Philo of Alexandria without a shudder, but Lillian Schwartz was the adult I loved most, after my grandmother, and she was more trustworthy, in my eyes.

AFUA COOPER

ON THE WAY TO SUNDAY SCHOOL

And running wildly up the road with Jean and Doris
stoning Mass Brutus dog
stealing Miss Clarice mangoes
laughing raucously as Doris tells the latest dirty joke
the river, the river
we cannot resist
not on this sun morning
so off comes our shoes
we are about to wade in when
a shadow falls upon us/we look up/to behold
sister Iris stiff and white in her holiness

MEMORIES HAVE TONGUE

My granny say she have a bad memory
when I ask her to tell
me some of her life
say she can't remember much but
she did remember the 1910 storm and how
dem house blow down
an dey had to go live with her granny
down bottom house.

Say she have a bad memory, but she remember
that when her husband died, both of them were thirty,
she had three little children, one in her womb,
one in her arms, one at her frocktail.
She remember when
they bury him how the earth buss up under her foot
and her heart bruk inside
that when the baby born she had no milk
her breasts refused to yield.

She remember how she wanted
her daughter to grow up and be
a postmistress but the daughter died at an early age

she point to the croton-covered grave at the bottom
of the yard. Say her memory bad, but she remember
1938
Frome
the riot
Busta
Manley
but what she memba most of all is that a
pregnant woman,
one of the protesters, was shot and killed by soldiers.

Say she old now   her brains gathering water
but she remember
that she liked dancing as a young woman
and yellow was her favourite colour.
she remember too
that it was her husband's father who asked
for her hand. The parents sat in the hall and discussed
the matter. Her father concluded that her man
was an honourable person and so gave his consent.

Her memory bad but she remember
on her wedding day how some of her relatives
nearly eat off all the food.
It was all right though, she said,
I was too nervous to eat anyway.

CHRISTOPHER COLUMBUS

With the unification of Castile and Aragon
Spain became one nation
Under the rule of Isabel and Ferdinand
Columbus sailed to this little island

what did he come for
he came for gold
what did he bring
miseries untold

The statue of Columbus stands on the hill facing the sea
his hand rests on the hilt on his sword
I walk beneath the statue
his feet crush my brain
his sword cuts open my womb
I flee, I flee from beneath his shadow
my blood dripping to the ground

As a little girl in grade four
the teacher would take us to see

this statue and we would attempt to draw – etch –
this conqueror of new lands
we were made to repeat
(and every schoolchild knows this)
"Christopher Columbus discovered Jamaica in 1494
with his three ships,
the Nina
Pinta
and Santa Maria"

I look at the statue
its shadow covers the sun
and all around me are graves and spirits of
a vanquished people

I look again at the statue
remembering the grade four chant
remembering a beautiful land
remember death and tears
I look again at the statue
and marvel that even today
we still honour our conquerors.

LAWRENCE HILL

from Any Known Blood

I

I have the rare distinction – a distinction that weighs like a wet life jacket, but that I sometimes float to great advantage – of not appearing to belong to any particular race, but of seeming like a contender for many.

In Spain, people have wondered if I was French. In France, hotel managers asked if I was Moroccan. In Canada, I've been asked – always tentatively – if I was perhaps Peruvian, American, or Jamaican. But I have rarely given a truthful rendering of my origins.

Once, someone asked, "Are you from Madagascar? I know a man from Madagascar who looks like you."

I said: "As a matter of fact, I am. I was born in the capital, Antananarivo. We moved to Canada when I was a teenager."

Another time, when a man sitting next to me in a doughnut shop complained about Sikh refugees arriving by boat in Gander, Newfoundland, I said: "I was born in Canada and I don't wear a turban, but I'm a Sikh. My mother is white, but my father is a Sikh, and that makes me one, too." The man's mouth fell open. I paid the waitress to bring him twelve chocolate doughnuts. "I've gotta go," I told him. "But next time you want to run down Sikhs, just remember that one of them bought you a box of doughnuts!"

I tried it again at the next opportunity. A woman at a party said Moroccans were sexist pigs, so I became a Moroccan. Then I started claiming I was part Jewish, part Cree, part Zulu, part anything people were running down. My game of multiple racial identities continued until eighteen months ago, when my wife left me. It was the lowest point of my life, so low that I didn't much see the point in living, even lower than when my son died in the womb. Shortly before Ellen moved out, I saw an advertisement for a speech writer for the Ontario Ministry of Wellness. A line ran across the bottom of the advertisement: "As part of an active effort to promote employment equity in the public service, this position has been designated a Category Three job. Only racial minorities need apply."

I filled out an application. I could have told them the truth – that I was black, or at least partly so, having a white mother and black father. I wanted the job, but I also wanted to test my theory that nobody would challenge my claim to any racial identity. So, in the letter that accompanied a resumé and some writing samples, I explained that I was of Algerian origin. I got an interview. They asked if I was actively involved in the Algerian community. I said the Algerian community was small in Toronto, but that I did spend time with my brothers and sisters and with family friends.

They gave me the job. I still have it. They still think I'm Algerian. I have had to explain that my father changed his name when he came to Canada, and that his original name was Allassane Mamoudy. I have even had to deny any relation to my father, who is well known in the city and most definitely not Algerian.

It has been said that I have come down in the world. Down from an unbroken quartet of forebears, all, like me, named Langston Cane. A most precipitous descent, my father mumbled, when he heard about my latest job. I write speeches for a politician I tried to knock off the ballot. Usually, I handle ribbon-cutting affairs. *I'm delighted to join you on the occasion of your . . . I admire the years of time and effort you have invested in . . . something in which I share profound personal conviction . . .* I almost quit after the first week. But I stuck it out. I had little choice. Years have passed since I've had the courage to write – or, more properly, to recreate – my family history. And the list of occupations for which I'm ill suited appears to be expanding. So, I stuck with the government job, and initially did well at it. That's not bragging. Speech writing does not require one to scale peaks of creativity. It does demand a certain control of the nuts and bolts of grammar and the rhythm of speech. One must attempt at all times to adopt natural human language, even if one is writing for politicians. As well, a speech writer must not feel wedded to his own convictions. The best thing is to have no convictions at all.

Convictions ruled the lives of my ancestors. They all became doctors, or church ministers. By my age – thirty-eight – they already had their accomplishments noted in the *Afro-American*, the *Oakville Standard*, the *Toronto Times*, or the *Baltimore Sun*. I will admit that it takes a certain discipline and boldness to throw oneself into high-minded professions. But it also takes something to fall from the treadmill of great accomplishments, to fail, even at the tasks of being a husband and a potential father and a writer, to march to the gates of middle age and look ahead and accept that you will not change the world.

This can't go on. I'm going to have to leave this job. I have some money saved up and nothing to spend it on – no wife anymore, no children, and no outlay exceeding the four hundred dollars a month for my one-room flat above a fur store in downtown Toronto. I can leave, with no fear of having to return to my father, palm upturned.

I grew up with four family legends – one about each of my direct paternal ancestors. Every year, my father would add another tantalizing detail, but refuse to go any further. I would plead in vain for more, and for information about my father's sister, Mill. Sean, my brother, would say, "He's not telling us any more, because he doesn't know any more, and most of what he's told us probably isn't true anyway." But I ignored Sean. When my father got going, it was like being at a seance. Every drop of his hand, every rise and fall of his tone, every whisper and shout, I felt in my bones.

My father was born in Oakville, Ontario, in 1923. He returned to the States as a young boy, with his parents and sister, served as an American soldier in World War II, and moved back to Canada in 1950 to study medicine at the University of Toronto. While there, he met and fell in love with Dorothy Perkins. Other than myself, my father is the only one in the long line of Canes to marry a white woman. The only difference is, he stayed married.

Boycotting weddings seems to be a genetic trait of the Cane family. As far as I know, none of the Langston Canes managed to pull off a wedding without some key family member refusing to attend.

In the case of my parents, of course, boycotts were expected. And they were duly delivered. My mother has never confirmed this, but I happen to know from my father that my mother's mother reacted to the wedding news by proposing a brief but enforced stay for my mother in a psychiatric institution. So the mother of the bride was a no-show. And my father has never confirmed this, but I happen to know from my mother that my father's sister, Mill, let it be known that by marrying out of the race, my father was betraying black women. Her brother's wife was not to take it personally, but Mill had no intention of attending the wedding or meeting her sister-in-law.

My mother was from Winnipeg, and my father had been living in Baltimore before moving to Canada. The choice of a wedding site reflected the kind of compromise that has always characterized my parents' relationship: when my mother moves six miles, my father accommodates her by moving six inches. Accordingly, they married in

Washington, D.C. The year was 1954. The season: spring. April 5, to be exact. D.C. looked like a greenhouse. There were eucalyptus trees, cherry blossoms, magnolias, and tulips from top to bottom of Chain Bridge Road, where my father's parents lived. I can imagine what the road looked like that day because I saw it many times as a boy.

D.C. in the spring was like a wall of heat, which is the way seventy-five degrees Fahrenheit always felt after shovelling snow in Ontario. I remember my grandmother Rose's vegetable garden, which took us nearly a minute to run around. I remember visiting the Howard University chapel, where my grandfather served as the minister at my parents' wedding.

I have heard so many stories about the wedding that I feel as if I attended it. When someone retells an old story, I can point out errors. It is inaccurate, for example, to say that my mother's father, George, told a joke about black people. Actually, he told a joke about a Mexican who was mistaken for black in a restaurant that served whites only.

I wish I'd been there to hear George laughing at his own joke. I wish I'd been there to see everybody freeze until my father laughed and slapped George's back and gave him a glass of vermouth and walked him onto the subject of golf. As a rule, I dislike weddings – because of the pomp, because somebody's always in a snit over something, and because I have never looked good in a jacket and tie – but that one would have been worth attending.

It had rained early in the morning, and then turned sunny and stayed that way. Outside the chapel, the lawns were wet and sparkling. It was the finest Wednesday that spring.

Wednesday?

That idea came from my mother, Dorothy Perkins. They couldn't afford a large reception. But they wanted all their friends to see their act of courage – or social deviance, as my mother, then a sociologist-in-training, joked.

To which my father replied, "We are a deviant couple, my dear, but on our wedding night, I would suggest that we converge."

"Why don't we converge our ideas on the matter at hand?" my mother said. "Let's marry on a Wednesday, at two in the afternoon. Only a quarter of our friends will be able to make it. That way, we can plan a small reception and still invite everybody."

My parents went ahead with their plans. But almost everybody came. A hundred guests squeezed into a chapel for fifty people. As my father has said, "It looked like the most popular wedding in D.C. And two conspicuous absences weren't too bad at all."

My father opened up a medical practice in Oakville, and became well known for his civil rights activities in Canada. He had two sons. One of them has a growing reputation as a first-rate criminal lawyer. That's Sean, my younger brother. They should have named him Langston. But they didn't. They gave the name to me, the first-born of the fifth generation.

II

Aberdeen Williams came to my office the other day. I wasn't expecting him. Over the last year or so, having received my divorce papers and pretty well severed contact with my father, I have seen Aberdeen more than usual. Since he is eighty-eight, I go to him. One Sunday every month or two, I take the commuter train to Oakville, meet him at a local café called The Green Bean, and listen to his stories. He tells me about Oakville in the 1920s, when he lived with my grandparents and helped raise my father and aunt. He doesn't say much about my Aunt Mill, but the little I do know comes from him. He tells me about a Canadian wing of the Ku Klux Klan, which came after him in Oakville in 1930. He shares his theories about how black Africans in small boats crossed the Atlantic to America a thousand years before Columbus.

But I missed our last rendezvous. Completely forgot about it. Spent most of the Sunday in a downtown Toronto laundromat, thinking about leaving my speech-writing job. Aberdeen didn't call to complain that I had forgotten about him. He simply turned up at my office.

He's a short, thin man. He's jet black, has lively, inquisitive eyes, and looks about twenty years younger than he is. He still has hair, and keeps a narrow, finely trimmed salt and pepper moustache.

"You look good, Aberdeen," I said, and got up from my desk. We shook hands. "I can see why they used to call you 'Dark Gable.' "

He laughed. I asked how he had come to my office. He said he had taken the train, and the subway, and the elevator, like any other normal person.

"But you're not normal, Ab. You're a thousand years old."

"Maybe, but I've got a better memory than you," he said.

I stared for a minute. Then it hit me. "I'm sorry. The Green Bean. Last Sunday. I forgot all about it. But you didn't have to come in all this way."

"Actually, I'm bringing a message. From your father."

I hoped that the stiffening of my back and neck wasn't visible. At that moment, my friend and boss – a failed aristocrat named Alfonso de Altura Jr. – stepped into my office.

I introduced him to Aberdeen. They chatted for a moment, and then Alfonso turned to tell me that a delegation of business leaders from Algeria would soon be visiting our ministry. Could I meet with them?

I nodded, and started to say that I was just heading out for a coffee with Aberdeen. I was hoping to talk about the Algerian delegation when I came back, alone. But Alfonso kept going. When the man had something on his mind, he was like a high-speed train.

"They'll be delighted to meet you, being an Algerian and all. Imagine their surprise at meeting somebody of Algerian origin here. Do you speak Arabic, by any chance?"

"No," I said. "Give me half an hour, and I'll come talk to you."

Alfonso said that would be fine, and stepped out of my office.

Aberdeen's head was lowered. Slowly, he raised his eyes to meet mine. "Algerian?"

"It's a long story," I said.

"You told your boss you were Algerian?"

"I can explain it to you, Aberdeen."

"You've always been good with words, Langston. When you were in school, I thought you would become a lawyer. You can explain anything. But your explanation would just make things worse. I don't want to hear it."

Aberdeen pushed on his armrests and hovered, bent, a few inches out of his chair. I scooted around my desk to help him, but he waved me off.

"I just need a minute," he said. "I'm a bit slow in the morning."

"Where are you going?"

"Can't stay long. Your father had a message. He asked me to give it to you."

"Surely, he didn't expect you to come all the way into Toronto to deliver it. Why didn't you just call me?"

Aberdeen put his hand on mine. I could feel the calluses all around his palm, at the root of each finger, from years of gardening and working as a handyman. Aberdeen's grin drooped into sadness. "If I hadn't come into Toronto, how would I have discovered that Langston Cane the Fifth had become an Algerian?"

"That was just a silly game that got out of control. I told them I was Algerian to get the job. I wanted to see if they'd buy the story."

"When you were a little boy," Ab said, "I used to look after you. Do you remember that?" I nodded. "I know I told you about how your grandfather saved my life." I nodded again. "And I told you about your great-great-grandfather, Langston Cane the First."

I remembered that, too. My great-great-grandfather had escaped slavery in Maryland and had come up to Oakville on the Underground

Railroad. I had heard, from Aberdeen and from my father, that Langston the First had been helped by Quakers along the way. I don't believe I would be around to tell this story had it not been for Quakers here and there. Anyway, Langston the First arrived in Oakville in 1850, found a wife, had three kids, and then slipped out of town nine years later and was never seen again. According to family legend, he left Oakville in a horse-drawn carriage, seated next to John Brown, who just a few months later led an attack on the U.S. weapons arsenal in Harpers Ferry, Virginia. The link between my ancestor and John Brown seemed far-fetched, but it had always fascinated me.

I walked with Aberdeen to the elevator. I got in with him and rode down.

"There are a lot of things you don't know about your own family," Aberdeen said. "There are things your father doesn't even know." My old friend cracked a smile. He still had all his teeth. Aberdeen stepped out of the building and into the wind. I followed him and asked what my father had wanted him to tell me.

"He wants you to come see him. You are his flesh and blood, Langston. I never had any children – so I know what that means. He says it's time to end the standoff."

"I'll think about it," I said.

Aberdeen grabbed my hand. "Do you love me, young man?"

"I'm hardly young anymore."

"From where I'm standing, you look young. I asked if you loved me."

"You know the answer to that."

"You've loved me since I changed your diapers. You'll love me until the day I die. When that happens, there won't be anybody putting me in any history book. But will you love me – or love my memory – any less because I never amounted to much? Because I never made history?"

I gulped and stared into his big brown eyes. He was smiling.

"Your family has had some born achievers, son, but you don't have to do what they did. I know you're interested in who your people were. Why don't you write about them? You told me years ago that you wanted to do it. Write, Langston. Go write. Go do the one thing that all the achievers in your family were too busy and too important to do."

It was freezing outside, and I had left my jacket in the office, but I walked Aberdeen to the Bay subway station. I walked him down the stairs to the turnstiles and fished through my pockets and tried to give him a token.

"Don't waste your money. I've got tickets at a senior citizen discount."

I told Aberdeen that I would think about what he had said. He pushed through the turnstile and walked ahead. The moment before he took an escalator down out of sight, he turned and called out: "One of these days, you'll have to tell me all about Algeria."

I didn't set out to get fired, or to see my name in the Toronto newspapers. I have enough on my shoulders as it is. So I was not out looking for trouble. But trouble blew in with the wind, at the very moment that I had been wondering about my great-great-grandfather, and about the family legend of his demise alongside John Brown while trying to strike a blow against slavery.

The trouble began in earnest when my boss asked if I wanted to see a confidential government document.

Alfonso, like me, is one of the walking wounded. He, too, senses that he's been a failure in his father's eyes. A few years ago, he discovered that his divorced father had remarried, had another child – a boy – and given him the name Alfonso de Altura Jr. "I didn't turn out the way he wanted, so he figured he'd start again from scratch," Alfonso told me.

On the day of my undoing, Alfonso urged me to read a secret report that had somehow landed on his desk.

"No, thanks."

"Guess what our illustrious government is about to ban."

"Sex?"

"Nope."

"Sex in public places?"

"Nope."

"Sex in saunas?"

"Langston, you gotta get yourself a woman friend. But put those thoughts aside, if you can. This government is about to kill anti-discrimination legislation and junk the provincial human rights commission."

"Let me see that thing."

I spent an hour or so reading the proposal that had been sent forth to Cabinet. We certainly had entered an era of government downsizing. First, they downsized welfare cheques by about 20 per cent. Then, they downsized the need for meat inspectors, elevator inspectors – just about any kind of inspectors, for that matter. Foreign investors sure as hell wouldn't be interested in putting money down in Ontario if they had to work in a climate where a company could be put out of business for selling bad meat or letting elevator cables unravel. According to this document, it was now the turn of the human rights commission and the Ontario Human Rights Code. They were obsolete and antithetical to good business practices. They had served a need years ago, thank you very much, but this was the nineties. Minorities didn't require special treatment any longer. Like other Ontarians, minorities knew businesses couldn't compete in the global economy without treating all employees fairly. Or so the document said.

I imagined having to craft a minister's speech about how eliminating human rights legislation would contribute to Ontario's positive business climate. But I knew the minister's spin doctors wouldn't allow the term "human rights legislation" in the speech. They would insist that all speeches refer to the old legislation as "the job quota law."

I have written a lot of trash on the job. But I didn't think I could write that speech. I imagined my great-great-grandfather, Langston Cane the First, shaking his head as he watched me work.

There was nothing happening in the office on the morning that Alfonso gave me the secret document. I thought about catching a noon-hour movie – but there was nothing worth seeing. I stepped out of the office at eleven, bought a hot dog and a root beer from a street vendor, strolled outside for five minutes, and returned to my desk – only to have the minister's communications aide pounce on me.

Alfonso was out at a dentist's appointment. Almost everyone in the minister's office was out that day. But the minister had a sudden problem. He had been putting in time in the legislature, snoozing through committee meetings, when he was ordered by the premier to stand in for him at a speaking function that same afternoon.

The event was scheduled to take place at a downtown hotel at one. It was now eleven-fifteen. Could I get a speech to the minister's office within an hour? Write anything, I was told, just get the minister through a ten-minute speech to the Canadian Association of Black Journalists without making a fool of himself.

In leaving, the minister's aide said, "Hey, this is kind of up your alley, isn't it? You're Algerian or something, aren't you?"

I nodded. Yes, I told him, this was right up my alley.

I know the secret to grinding out pages under tight deadlines – write as fast as possible without thinking. So I switched on the computer and started writing. I swear upon the memory of my great-great-grandfather that I did not set out to get the minister fired. Nor did I immediately conceive of the idea to write two speeches – one straightforward version for the minister's office, and one podium copy with a curveball.

Had I spent weeks planning a way to trick a minister into revealing details about a confidential document to a crowd of journalists, I could never have pulled it off. I will admit to a number of character faults. Unlike my ancestors, I seem to have difficulty seizing life by the horns. Regretfully, I have shown the capacity to be unfaithful at a critical time to the only woman I have truly loved. But the one thing that I am *not* is conniving or deceitful. I would be the last person in the world capable of planning a crime. My face would betray me from the very start.

I knew what I was doing, of course, when I doctored the minister's podium copy. But it was certainly not "a brilliantly planned, courageous blow against the Ontario government and its right-wing agenda," as one of the newspapers said later. It was simply a speech that fell into place with the help of chance – namely, the minister had no knack for public speaking. His verbal abilities were so limited that Alfonso and I had nicknamed him Pilot, for his unswerving adherence to any speech placed before his eyes. We speculated that Pilot had probably hired a freelancer to write the thank-you speech for his wedding reception.

It took me twenty minutes to write the speech. It acknowledged that blacks had contributed to life in Canada, suggested that they wanted opportunities for their children, and claimed that the government was paving the way for long-term prosperity by creating conditions in which businesses and investors would thrive.

I brought the speech to the minister's aide and sat with him while he scanned the pages. He caught a typo and made two edits in style. I promised to bring back a clean copy for him, as well as a podium copy for the minister.

I always prepared the minister's speaking copy in twenty-four-point type. He liked his lines triple-spaced, with no page more than two-thirds full, for easy reading from the podium.

I ran back upstairs, printed out a clean copy for the aide, and proceeded to doctor the minister's podium copy. The copy from which the minister would read was essentially the same speech that had been approved by the aide – with one exception.

My so-called "courageous blow against the Ontario government" began about three-quarters of the way through the podium copy. It began at the point where the minister would feel confident that all was going well. It began at a point of no return, where Pilot would know only how to gallop forward, like a horse going back to the barn. It began precisely after Pilot recognized that black people wanted rewarding job opportunities and a solid economic future.

"Ladies and gentlemen," I wrote for Pilot's benefit, "I understand that if people are to give fully of themselves when participating in our economic and social life, they need to feel respected. They need to feel wanted. And they need to feel that they are being treated fairly.

"Black people have had a history of challenges and of victories in this province. Ontario's long history of protecting human rights dates back to our first anti-slavery legislation in 1793.

"I am committed to upholding that history. I know that if you want to reap the harvest of a thriving social and economic climate, you have to sow the seeds ahead of time.

"So I am telling you that I will be leading the way in opposing a proposal, recently reviewed by Cabinet, to eliminate human rights legislation and to dismantle the human rights commission. Such a proposal would move Ontario thirty years backward in the step-by-step struggle to create a tolerant and diverse society."

After that part of the speech, I bridged back to the conclusion in the vetted version. I slipped the doctored speech into a large envelope marked *Minister's speech – Podium Copy* and the approved speech into another envelope made out to the communications aide, and delivered them both.

According to media reports, the minister didn't immediately realize that he had just leaked a secret government document. He read the speech verbatim, and seemed momentarily puzzled when he got a standing ovation three-quarters of the way through his remarks. But he smiled, and swallowed, and waited for everybody to sit back down, and then just kept reading to the bottom of the last page.

Later on, I heard that fifteen minutes after the minister gave the speech, a reporter for the *Toronto Times* – a black reporter, by the way, whose name was Mahatma Grafton – called the premier's office for comment. The premier's office called the minister's office. The premier met the minister, reviewed the speech, and told the minister that he was out of a job.

The reporter called every office he could think of to find out who had written that speech. He asked the premier's aide, who didn't know. He tried people in the minister's office, but they hadn't yet decided what to say, so they said nothing. He got hold of a government phone directory and found my name listed as senior writer, communications branch, Ministry of Wellness, and left a message on my answering machine at work.

Under normal circumstances, I would have returned the call promptly. But I was about to pay the price for bringing an elected official into disrepute. I was about to be the first person in five generations of Langston Canes to depart so unceremoniously from a place of employment. I was about to start wearing my very own scarlet letters – FWC, for Fired With Cause.

I learned of my imminent dismissal while visiting the men's room. Alfonso was considerate enough to catch me alone in there. His words came out slightly slurred, because he had two new fillings and his mouth was still frozen.

"Langston, they're about to fire you. I've got to hand it to you. You're a revolutionary under that placid exterior. What you did took a hell of a lot of courage." He leaned over and whispered: "You won't tell anybody where you got that document, will you?"

No, I assured him, I would not.

Alfonso sighed deeply. He was a portly forty-year-old with thick hands and roving eyes. I'd heard him sigh like that just the other week, over lunch, as a waitress sashayed away from our table. He considered her in the way that a child would study a double-decker ice-cream cone. He let out that long breath, and declared himself ravenously heterosexual and unjustly deprived.

In the men's room, Alfonso settled into position beside me. I was standing, feet splayed, midway through expelling the root beer, feeling about as content and relieved as I ever felt those days. Alfonso said we had to go straight to a meeting with the personnel director.

"How much time are they giving me?" I asked.

"Thirty minutes." Alfonso said that after our meeting with the personnel director, I was to remove my belongings from the office. "I admire you, Langston. I know you've been hurting badly about Ellen divorcing you. A lot of people would have cracked up. Become alcoholics, or worse. It's to your credit that the wildest thing you've done is leak a confidential document by putting it in the minister's mouth."

"Yeah."

"This is a sign. Don't just find another job as a hack. Change your life. Somewhere out there in the real world, you'll find a use for your prodigious writing talents."

I snorted. "Nobody with prodigious talent writes speeches for the Ontario Minister of Wellness."

"Anybody capable of producing two speeches in an hour, one that will fool a communications aide and one that will knock a minister out of Cabinet, has writing talent to spare."

"Are they really going to fire the minister?"

"Looks like it. But let's get back to business. Can you give me a copy of that speech before we go into that meeting? And I'm not supposed to tell you this, but a security guard will check your bags when you leave the office. Don't take anything that's not yours."

"No dictionaries, no paper clips."

"You don't have to be funny with me, Langston. You must be in shock."

I turned to wash my hands. "That sure was a lot of root beer," I said.

When you miss the carrot and slice open your fingertip on the chopping board, the pain doesn't set in right away. It waits at least long enough for you to see what you've done. After coming out of the meeting with Alfonso and the personnel director, the pink slip didn't feel too bad. It felt like a liberation. Like a kick in the pants, saying,

"Okay, you're off! Don't waste this opportunity." The high lasted while I sat at my desk and began removing personal matters from the drawers. I took down my Fowler's *Modern English Usage* – which was left over from the time I dreamed of becoming a writer – and I removed my government telephone directory. Then, chin up, I reversed the decision. The government directory went back on the shelf. It was time for a clean break.

The feeling of liberation and rejuvenation lasted while I removed an extra pair of socks and a container of dental floss from my bottom desk drawer. It stayed with me as I found a want-you-back letter that I'd never mailed to Ellen. I turfed old tax forms, pay stubs, bank statements, memos. The feeling lasted as I finished at the desk, switched off the fluorescent light, and swivelled in my chair to face the computer. The feeling lasted through all the rituals of office cleaning until an imposing male voice – a voice of authority, a voice accustomed to getting what it wanted and getting it immediately – filled the reception area:

"Excuse me. I'm looking for Langston Cane the Fifth."

My father! Except for the rare telephone call, I hadn't heard his voice for more than a year. It vaulted over the partitions separating me from the receptionist. This is what I heard next:

Receptionist: "I beg your pardon, sir?"

Father: "Langston Cane, please."

Receptionist: "He's four desks down on your left."

Father: "Which way, did you say?"

Footsteps slapped along the cool government carpet. Footsteps that could belong to none other than my friend Alfonso.

Alfonso: "Excuse me, sir. How may I help you?"

"I'm looking for my son."

"Your son, sir? And who might that be?" Here, I imagined Alfonso smiling with his thick lips, roving with beady eyes over his protruding brow, and twitching pudgy digits behind his back.

"Langston Cane the Fifth."

"Langston! Your son? You are *the* Langston Cane, are you not? Dr. Cane?"

"Yes. The Fourth."

"Certainly, certainly. This way, sir."

My father looked well. The strands of dark hair – on the sides of his head only – were brushed back. His eyes were the colour of coffee beans, and carried an impish smile that suggested, *So! I found you.* His fingers were still long and brown and smooth around the knuckles. He saluted me with his cane. It was made of red oak, and had squares of inlaid silver. He never went out without it, although he didn't need it – except to point at things, or to win the attention of salespeople, receptionists, and the two or three hundred people in the city he had served at one time or another, over the last four decades, as a sort of guru.

My father tapped my shin with his cane.

"Hello, son, don't you rise from your chair to greet an old man?"

Alfonso backed out of sight and parked a few steps away. I could tell because I heard his asthmatic breathing. And then the breathing stopped. The bastard was holding his breath so as not to miss a word. Staying in my chair, I looked up into my father's eyes.

"Aberdeen gave me your message. I had been planning to come to visit you and Mom soon."

"But you haven't done it yet. What's the matter? You ashamed of me? You trying to pass for white?"

He laughed at his own joke. It was the same laugh I'd heard as a child at countless Sunday breakfasts, when he had told stories of light-skinned blacks trying to pass as whites in the States. Stories of evasion and discovery had always been among my father's favourites.

"Very funny. Why did you come here?"

"Do I have to have a reason to say hello? You are my son, you know. Langston Cane the Fifth, in case anybody is asking."

"A few people may be asking, as a matter of fact. Give me two minutes to finish something here. Then we can go get a coffee."

"Coffee. You sure love that stuff."

"It's just a figure of speech. It's a generic term for having milk, or mint tea, or apricot juice, gazelle blood, what have you."

"I, personally, have nothing against caffeinated libations. Taken in moderation, coffee is a fine thing. Stimulates the cerebellum. Rustles the digestive tract. And it falls squarely in the African-American tradition of imbibing hot fluids to sustain the soul."

"Pipe down, would you? Give me two minutes, Dad, and we'll clear out."

"Want to get me out of here, is that it?"

I turned away from him, flicked on my computer, and inserted a floppy disk. My final, office-closing act was to transfer personal files from the computer to a disk.

"Just wait a second," I said. "I'd tell you to sit down, but as you can see I only have the one chair in this office."

"Office? You call this an office? It's a water closet. A coffin. At best, a measly nook in a rabbit warren. Son, can't you do any better than –"

Alfonso reappeared, with a chair.

"Thank you," my father said. "You obviously know something about the finer arts of civility and hospitality. What did you say your name was?"

"Alfonso de Altura Jr."

"A fine name, if I do say so myself. I like polysyllables in a name. Polysyllables are a fine and distinguishing trait. So is alliteration. Alfonso de Altura Jr. Polysyllabic, alliterated – yes, it's quite distinctive. It traces back to noble European blood, no doubt?"

"Oh, Doctor," Alfonso sputtered, "I'm afraid that any nobility has been sadly diluted. But I must say, sir, that I find your presence here today both spectacular and riveting."

"What, precisely, is so spectacular and riveting?"

"That you and Langston are father and son."

"Spectacular? Does this lad not let his roots be known?"

"Well, not to me, anyway. Dr. Cane, may I ask you, is there any Algerian component to your family history?"

"Algerian? None whatsoever! Wherever would one get such an idea?"

"I really don't know. I must have been confused. But tell me, what are you up to these days, Dr. Cane? Your name still surfaces all the time around here. The Cane report on blacks in the media; the Cane report on police and racial minorities. The organizations you founded over the years."

"Oh, nothing much. Just my family practice in Oakville – and I've scaled it down considerably. I'm in partial retirement now."

I finished with my computer, retrieved the disk, and swung around to face the two of them.

Alfonso started up again. "Dr. Cane, I have one of your publications in my office. Would you be good enough to autograph it for me?"

"Certainly."

"Be right back." Alfonso stepped out.

I slung my bag over my shoulder, turned off the computer, and took my father by the arm. "Let's go."

"But that portly gentleman has requested my autograph."

"You can give it to him on your next visit here."

We got as far as the elevator, but were still waiting for it when Alfonso caught up to us.

"Here you are, good sir. If you could just sign here on the title page. You can make it out to Alfonso. That's *A-L* . . ."

"I can manage the spelling, thanks very much." My father signed the book, handed it back, and stepped into the elevator. Alfonso held the elevator door with one hand and shook my hand with the other. He leaned close to me. "Kick some butt out there, Langston. You can do it." He let go of my hand and the door.

The elevator door closed. My father asked: "Is it common practice for you to leave the office before five?"

"Alfonso is my boss, and he knows I'm leaving. At any rate, leaving early is a minor infraction. Last week, I took a two-hour lunch to catch a movie."

My father guffawed. "Very good, son. That's funny."

Just before we left the building, a black man entered through the revolving doors. He looked as if he was in a big hurry, but he stopped when he saw my father.

"Dr. Cane."

My father was used to being stopped by people he didn't recognize. He loved it.

"Yes. What can I do for you?"

"I'm Mahatma Grafton. The *Toronto Times*."

"Oh yes, I remember you now. How goes the battle?"

"Fine," the reporter said, with a quick grin. He was focused entirely on my father – I felt confident that he wouldn't notice me. "I'm in a rush, but can I ask one quick question?"

"Fire away."

"I've just learned that the government plans to scrap human rights legislation and the human rights commission. What do you think of that?"

"I think that would be an abomination," my father said. "It's hard to believe that even this government would stoop so low in its craven desire to please business."

I watched Mahatma whip a small notepad out of his jacket pocket and scribble madly. He was slender and tall and about my age. He had a brown complexion.

"That good enough for you?" my father said.

"That's great, Dr. Cane. You always come through with a good quote. By the way, are you any relation to the Langston Cane in the government phone directory?"

"Sure am. He's my son. Right here. Langston – meet Mahatma Grafton, an upstanding journalist for the *Toronto Times*."

We shook hands.

"I left a message on your machine," he said.

"Actually, I don't work for the ministry any longer."

"That's bizarre. They haven't even got rid of your voice mail message. Anyway, do you know about this speech the minister gave, or who wrote it?"

I managed a sympathetic smile. "Afraid I can't help you with that."

"Well, thanks anyway. Gotta run."

Mahatma ran to catch an elevator, and my father and I moved toward the door.

"Son, you should never lie to the media. Once your credibility's gone, it's gone for good."

"When did I lie?"

"You told that brother you didn't work for the ministry."

"I don't."

"As of when?"

"As of today."

My father shook his head in confusion. "You're telling me that was your last day at the office?"

We stepped outside. It was a cold, windy March day. It seemed that all the buildings on Bloor Street were sucking down the wind and aiming it at us. Three cars had collided in the middle of the intersection at Bay and Bloor. Cars were jammed in all four directions. People honked and shouted.

"This place is insane. Now you see why I raised you in Oakville."

"Let's go to a café. I'll tell you why this was my last day on the job."

"No time, son." My father took in a measured breath and expelled it slowly. "I am going to visit Dr. Norville Watson."

I grabbed his arm. "Dr. Watson? *The* Dr. Watson?" The news made me forget my own problems. "What for?"

"A time comes for everything. I'm not getting any younger. It's time to make peace with the man."

"I have to hear how your meeting goes."

"Of course. That's why I came to see you. Come out to Oakville this evening. I'll invite Sean, too. I'll tell the two of you and your mother all at the same time. And you can tell me what's going on at the office."

I did not want to go to my parents' home. I had avoided the place for a year and a half, and that wasn't long enough for me. My father, under his own roof, was intolerable.

"How about if I wait in a café? You can come tell me what happened. It'll save me the trip to Oakville."

"Can't do it, son. After I see Watson, I'm meeting your mother. We want to beat the traffic home."

"Well, I'll see about coming out tonight."

"Good. I'll see you there." My father tapped a fire hydrant with his cane and said, "Keep your chin up, son. The Canes come from a special mould."

He headed west on Bloor Street. Norville Watson's office, I knew from countless family stories, was in a distinguished low-rise fronted with stone pillars. Norville Watson had opened a medical practice there shortly after he had denied my parents rental accommodation in 1954.

TESSA McWATT

from Dragons Cry

1. Salt

"Mercy," she said, with a gurgle like grinding pearls from the back of her throat. "Mercy, Mercy me," when she spotted the broken shards of porcelain scattered in the driveway. Then MacKenzie sucked her teeth in a "*s-t-c-h-u-p*" and pivoted toward the house. Warning enough for Simon, who heard in that *stchup* the decree of the lash that would lick his backside when his father got home.

On the heals of mercy came music from the back room of the house as Simon's brother cranked up the volume on the record player. By the time MacKenzie returned from the house with a broom and dustpan, the singer was belting out the melody with a leathery hunger in his voice. The man who sang all day long, "*when a man loves a woman . . . can't keep his mind on nothin' else . . . he'd trade the world for the good thing he's got*," was lashing Simon's heart. The whole neighbourhood sang along, as though the singer was in their gardens and not compressed on a flat black disc. Simon's brother had bought the record a week before and was wearing it out.

When she's bad he can't see it . . . she can do no wrong . . .

MacKenzie grimaced and cupped her ears for a second before stooping to sweep up the remnants of the vase which, until just a few minutes earlier, had sat empty near the entrance to the house. Placed there four years earlier in an unribboned moment of welcome to the island by his mother's cousins, the vase and its future as an heirloom were shattered. MacKenzie picked up a slice of the porcelain on which a fair, dainty woman in bonnet and flowing dress dipped her ruffled turquoise parasol as she stepped up to a waiting carriage. The servant looked up and cut her eyes spitefully at Simon, who ran behind the house, dragging his cricket bat.

Simon had toppled the vase during an otherwise perfect, full-arched swing of his bat, which would have sent them to their feet at the cricket oval, he was sure. He had been practising all afternoon in the shade of the carport, swinging for fictive cheers. His swing was improving daily.

But MacKenzie didn't understand cricket. She didn't understand the whole Carter family, nor trust their Guyanese continentalism. From the moment the Carters had moved to Barbados from Guyana, they'd had nothing but bad luck with the housekeeping servants they'd taken on, and there'd been many who'd decided to leave before the first week was out. Shining sable-skinned women had stared at the four Carter children and had shaken their heads or raised their hands with the *Hallelujah* or *Lord I am a witness* flailings of a revival meeting. But MacKenzie had stayed, persevered, as though chosen by her god.

One day, she'd lined up the four children in order of age and height and bent down to stare each in the eye, incredulous that the four had come from the same parents. Faces of chaos, not one of them resembling the other. Two foreheads were wide bands of copper skin over gentle bumps of bone. The skin was framed in one case by straight black hair, and in the other by biscuit-coloured ringlets. In the third child, the cheekbones were high like the side of a dry valley, the almond-shaped eyes tapering off into the ridges of bone. The fourth child, with natty hair, had the same wide forehead, but the skin was coffee coloured and pocked with adolescence. Noses: two pugged and flat, one wide and bridged, and the fourth barely making its presence known between chubby cheeks. And eyes: dark except for one pair of shimmering shamrock green. Like a box of assorted sweets, the multiformity was dazzling, and MacKenzie gulped back an anxious hiccup, vowing then and there to do her duty and not be tempted into speculating about God's purpose.

Trust was a winding train for both family and housekeeper, gathering speed throughout the years and arriving, finally, today at Simon's brother's funeral. But on that August afternoon, with Simon swinging awkwardly into puberty, the tension was high. As MacKenzie strained her broad, refrigerator back to sweep up his gallant gaffe, Simon peeked at her from around the corner of the house and watched the crease of the cotton shift enter the crack between her immense buttocks. His boyhood creaked arthritically. Then, from the window, more singers, female voices in unison, joined in the singing, accompanying the man who loved a woman, *ooo oh, ooo oh – try to hold onto the love we knew, crying baby, baby, please don't do me wroooong – ooh.* The neighbourhood moaned, rolling over on itself.

Death always brings that memory. At every funeral Simon has attended in the decades since he broke the vase, that moment replays itself in his mind's eye. Today was no exception. He worries that he may even have let slip a grin as his mother threw the first handful of earth over the coffin, and that perhaps from the other side of the grave Faye saw it flicker across his face. If she did, she hasn't let on. But what if she misconstrued it? It had been the wind's fault. The wind blew up near the end of the ceremony and the women's hats looked as though they would fly off. But something, a certain requirement of dignity, kept them in place. It must have been that certain requirement that forced the memory – always does. The dignity of a stoop.

It was the police chief's hat that finally held Simon's gaze. The black brim was pulled down over the man's brow, hiding the eyes but not the occasional quiver of the mouth. Simon watched him with teetering sentiments, knowing only parts of the story and the pointed fingers of blame, but he eventually gave in to pity as he watched a tear run down the cheek before being brusquely wiped away.

But the other elements of the childhood memory – the heat, the music – clash with today's indecencies of hymns and wailing, the patting of displaced earth, and the wreath of rust and yellow leaves David's children arranged beside the grave. David used to love October: the changing colours, the dying light. He said it was the month that kept him in Canada, the one time of year he could feel angels around him. Simon never understood that about his brother, along with so much else. His own response to autumn is simple: it drives thoughts deeper into his head and his testicles up into his belly. He remains curled up on himself until April. But it's these autumn ruminations that he must now, tonight, unfurl – straighten like a steamed collar, press hard on the wrinkles in his brother's life, and flatten a path toward tomorrow . . . and Faye.

Simon's feet are numb from the cold. He reaches down to his left foot. The compass bulges in his right-hand pocket. He peels back his sock and touches the skin: like refrigerated meat, dead meat . . . like his brother.

Is he cold? The earth is beginning to freeze around him, to preserve him until next spring when rain will soak his coffin and leak onto the satin, staining it like tears on a pillow. *The concentration of salt in a tear is higher than in the ocean. The stain is deeper. High salt concentrations are bacteriostatic, but can be washed away by water. Salt of the earth.*

In Barbados, MacKenzie used to tell Simon that God would accept only sacrifices that were salted. "Every oblation that you offer, you must never fail to put on your oblation the salt of the covenant with your God," she quoted the Old Testament. "You are the salt of the earth." She salted their food and sugared their tea beyond all recognition, and he wonders now if his lifelong fascination with salt was spawned through food – a quest to reconcile the inside and the outside, guts and earth.

Simon rubs his toes. He thinks he can hear Faye upstairs in her studio. She isn't practising, but she might be studying her part because there is a loud thumping of a heel, a tapping out of rhythm. They have been separated by a storey since arriving home from the funeral. Without a word, each drifted to the extremities of the tiny house, Faye to her studio, Simon to his desk in the basement. *I think it's a fugue she's learning, isn't that what she told me? – I can't keep the forms straight.* She's always working these days, playing the cello all the time and so full of notes that they pop out of her mouth at the dinner table between chews. A week ago she blurted out *ta dee dee ta* in a green spew of spinach. She giggled, almost ashamed of being so happy. Simon had noticed a returning sparkle in her bright green eyes, the creeping flush on her creamy cheeks. Until all this happened. *I shouldn't stay down here too long or she'll accuse me of hiding feelings from her.*

Nannerl. Mozart's sister. She keeps hopping into Faye's thoughts, as though in a game of skipping, finding Nannerl in the middle, between the beating ropes of all that is going on around her. How in tandem ran the lives of Nannerl and Wolfgang until that age when girls became women and boys went on to be geniuses. The Mozart children played together like a circus act, travelling through Europe performing four-handed music for anyone who paid the entrance fee to the cashier, their father, Leopold. It's said that Leopold heaved huge sighs of frustration when a prince, having deigned to hear the Mozart children play, rewarded them merely with praise, or a small gift for Nannerl, but nothing for the budding divinity himself. Faye is pursuing a moral in this poetic justice, wondering how talent and fate get either braided or left dangling loose, like fly-away hair. Why did Ms. Nannerl surface today at David's funeral? Skip, skip in time with the piston of fate, then in jumped *unfair*, a word she's been sounding out all afternoon: *fair, fair, unfair, who's the fairest, so unfair.* Is that what made her think of Nannerl? She is still numb with disbelief, refusing to accept that David has killed himself, and she has decided to stay busy, to practise, to think only of music, to think in sounds . . . *damn, damn, damn*. Perhaps the thought of Nannerl was inspired by the rivalry between siblings, or the shadow of unfulfillment, remembering how much David overshadowed his younger brother.

She pushes away words she is incapable of saying to Simon, unable, as she has been all week, to tear open a corner of the tight package of death to allow a conversation to pour out about suicide, about how he might be coping with the suicide of his own brother. She knows she must approach Simon about David, about the envelope she hid in the chest a few days ago, about the shadow that has drawn over her too, and how frightened she is about words she doesn't want to hear. *There's no place like* . . . But she can't. Not yet. *Push, push, push* . . . only sounds.

She pictures Simon in the basement at his desk, pretending to read but staring at bare stucco walls. Instead of going to him, she's hiding up here in her studio pretending to practise and performing the occasional silent arpeggio with her left hand on the cello's neck. *Tap tap tap.*

Faye stares out the window. The last of the leaves are holding feebly onto branches, and the sky is irritated the way she is at this time each month, knowing her body is soon to erupt and flow. The symptoms arrive earlier each month, and even today, a day of ovulation, she feels them: moodiness like glue. *And tonight . . . will we? Could we?*

She has been considering a sort of voodoo for herself, wondering if she should perform it at the next opportunity. Wary of cures now, she nevertheless found herself fascinated by how this one was prescribed, with the tone of certainty in Simon's mother's voice that seemed to say *I know, I know*. Grace, Edwin, and the rest of the family arrived four days ago from Barbados, and Faye could sense Grace gripping onto the certainty of birth in the way she held tight to her handbag, as though someone would snatch that too away from her.

Faye convinced her to sit down to a cup of tea, but still Grace clutched the bag in her lap. Their conversation turned to the children, to David's now fatherless three, and Grace paused before looking up at Faye to say firmly, "Make haste, enough waitin' now. You two must make a chile."

It was impossible for Faye to tell her it had been months since she and Simon had brushed skin to skin. Grace became distracted in thoughts that brought a frown, and Faye felt a rush of shame, wondering what Grace was thinking about her as she stared at the tiled floor, a hint of knowledge in her lips.

"An Amerindian woman in Guyana once told me a surefire way to get pregnant: After intercourse, ya suck the centre out of a raw egg, slap your belly five times, turn in a circle, then lie with your legs straight in the air for an hour. Works in the most stubborn cases."

Curatives like these have had a way of lodging in Faye's brain since her days at the clinic, but the tone was far too absolute, and she knows that it's more than a stubborn body she must deal with. *Push, push* . . . only sounds.

Hup, four, three, two, one . . .

Many years before Faye met Simon, she and Michael tried to have a child. They made their monthly visits to the fertility clinic, where they call them workups, as though they were a prelude to an aerobics class – *again, four, three, two, one* – demoralizing treatments that made her mood even fiercer than the slate-grey clouds she can see approaching from the east. She's grateful to Simon that he refuses to undergo such "therapy," but she has sensed his recent floundering around science. He who has always relied on reason is now full of contradictions. In the wake of death he is uncharacteristically philosophical, incapable of decoding suicide.

Faye exhales heavily.

Suicide sneaks up, attacks, but doesn't retreat. Instead it lingers to taunt with missed warning signs. No one in David's family expected it, not even his ex-wife, Justine, who'd spoken to him on the telephone that morning. Along with their grief, the family is battling guilt and despair for not having prevented his death. And there was more despair in the tears of the police chief and the sobs of David's fellow guards from the Newmarket jail, who stood confused and awkward in the church.

Simon is coming up the stairs. His gait is as heavy as a workhorse, *clop, clop. Will we touch?*

GEORGE ELLIOTT CLARKE

THE WISDOM OF SHELLEY

You come down, after
five winters, X,
bristlin' with roses
and words words words,
brazen as brass.
Like a late blizzard,
You bust in our door,
talkin' April and snow and rain,
litterin' the table
with poems –
as if we could trust them!

I can't.
I heard pa tell ma
how much and much he
loved loved loved her
and I saw his fist
fall so gracefully
against her cheek,
she swooned.

Roses
got thorns.
And words
do lie.

I've seen love
die.

KING BEE BLUES

I'm an ol' king bee, honey,
Buzzin' from flower to flower.
I'm an ol' king bee, sweets,
Hummin' from flower to flower.
Women got good pollen;
I get some every hour.

There's Lily in the valley
And sweet honeysuckle Rose too;
There's Lily in the valley
And sweet honeysuckle Rose too.
And there's pretty black-eyed Susan,
Perfect as the night is blue.

You don't have to trust
A single, black word I say.
You don't have to trust
A single, black word I say.
But don't be surprised
If I sting your flower today.

from George & Rue

Whip

XI

After Easter'd drowned, Rufus was impossible to endure. To George, it seemed his family was just mortally bad news. To stick with Rue could mean, then, his own doom. It was time to escape. Georgie knew there was about a hundred dollars of insurance money in the shack; he'd torch the shack, collect the moolah, split it, bill for bill, with Rue, and they'd skedaddle different routes. He set the fire, saw Cynthy's photo blaze, got the cash, gave Rue almost half.

Georgie left Three Mile Plains but chose to stay in Windsor because he liked country life. He did odd jobs for Pius Bezanson, a farmer, for ten bucks a month. Not sour pay, compared with bitter poverty. Bezanson's belief was, "Let every man turn *pain* into bread." Bezanson let George bunk in the barn, where he managed to snore despite stench and noisy, beastly copulations of animals. Mosquitoes were also wicked, stabbin George relentlessly. Even so, Georgie felt he'd do better, by and by. Hope was as striking as lightning, as deep as water, water, water, and as dream-productive as rum.

Farmin was natural for Georgie, and Bezanson let him eat and eat.

Once, the farmer paid Georgie with a seven-pound tin of blueberry jam, seven loaves of bread, and seven quarts of rum. Georgie made rum and jam sandwiches. Some good under crow-fractured, dark-blue Heaven. He had to wade through bushes, spend days cutting poplar trees and maples and spruce and pine. He could milk cows, churn cream, set out eggs delicate, delicate. He'd lead oxen – and, times, get bogged down in mud. He could tiptoe through the marsh bushes, the thinner woods near the Avon River, tumble into orange-red mud and climb out, or quickly skinny-dip in the river. He'd wander, separate, alone, among lichened rocks, let salt spray off the Fundy splash his Coloured Nova Scotian face. He'd take barrels and haul apples out the trees. He could drink fresh water by scooping up rain. A downy rain could make even October taste as fresh as April. After trainloads of apples, after muddy roads.

He'd found Paradise. Now he needed a woman.

From this farm at Windsor's edge, George eyed, daily, passing, dairy girls, lasses only thirteen or twelve, perched upright, like postage stamp queens, atop small, slow Percherons. The girls'd titter, chatter, sing. Jostling, their dairy pails pinged, as jittery as kindling breaking into flame. The dames gleamed unusually beautiful; their Madonna-like smiles as gay as fresh milk. George watched em giggle, shout, sing, as they'd pass by him on the Orotava Road. He juggled blue plums to entice their eyes. They'd look back, teehee, and he felt gratified. He noticed Blondola – one of the solar-eclipsing Plains belles (from Englishman River Falls) – noticing him. Georgie chase her small horse and hand her a blue plum. Blondola smiled, and he felt melted. She was like a fat, plush mare. The pretty women'd rub berry juice on their lips. Blondola too. The blacker the berry, the sweeter the juice. Blondola was thirteen, but plump, bodacious. A lively-lookin, dark-skinned black girl in black. Her face was chocolate smooth, with supremely plush, violet lips. Her coal-coloured eyes were lit up as if by an internal night of stars. Just her "Hi," the way she'd say it, 'd jolt Georgie's heart. Maybe they'd be so much in love that, making love, they'd feel like they were equally his and hers, that one set of hands was as dependable as the other. Ah, that chocolate-dark, chocolate-sweet woman, her plum-tint eyes!

The road is all dirt – dirty,
My gal is all pert – pretty.

Blondola was authoritatively everything Georgie wanted: her deep laughter reminded him of the scary gaiety of Cynthy's laughter when she was sweaty-happy with Asa.

Georgie study Blondola close.

He ask, "How ya get that name, Blondola? Ya a secret movie star?"

She be bashful: "Nah, Ma's name be Cassie and ma aunt's Ann, so my middle name's Cassandra."

Georgie get avid: "And Blondola?" Blondola just laugh and go on her way, gigglin with the other maids. They tease Georgie fierce.

One joked, "Men peacocks are more colourful than girl ones."

Blondola yelled, "If only it were like that with our men!"

Blondola looked a super good woman, with her plaid lumberjack shirts and jackets, her stories based on recipes, her country blues radio curing tobacco. She was partial to a house with sun in the living room and smelts drying on the roof; to a dungareed Romeo. Like everybody in Three Mile Plains, she'd grown up with blues gossip bout lethal booze; bout buttoned-down, open-flied preachers; bout leathered-down cowboys mangled by gypsum-mine dynamite. She'd be happy to go along with a man, a man goin somewhere, somewhere far.

Courtin Blondola should've been easy for Georgie. She liked his drawl, his laugh, his fearless – and sober – hard work. But he was hindered in his interest because he had no place to bring Blondola. The big drafty, stinky barn he slept in was no site for wooin a swell young gal makin dove's eyes at him. Georgie'd've to pull down better than ten bucks a month to be an effective Casanova.

He found a dream solution. He saw a newsreel about khaki-clad Canucks crossin the Atlantic to cross swords with Hitler, boys clearly no taller, bigger, or older than him. They appeared on the movie screen, silvery and sunny, smokin on the Halifax docks, waitin to board ships, and kissin on two delicious gals each. All Georgie knew of war was what funny books showed: a lot of rat-a-tat-tat and pow and splat and whammy. But maybe he could ship overseas, kill a clutch of Krauts, bulk up into a he-man, lift gold rings off married corpses, juxx some British quim, then return, swaggering, and marry Blondola with much hoopla – with their wedding pix in the *Hants County Register*. He'd seize his future this way.

So George told Blondola he was goin to the Boches-Hun War, and he ask, "Will ya wait for me?" He'd enlist, return, keep her glad. Blondola was playful, gleeful, but found Georgie spellbindingly earnest. She nodded; they kissed.

XII

Eighteen now, George didn't have to lie about his age to get into the Canadian Active Army, but still he ask a black woman – Naomi Jones, who was as blind as water – to go to the recruiters and claim to be his mother and vouch for his age. George told recruiters he was born in the United States, Massachusetts, Boston. (Because Naomi knew about Georgie's sorry childhood, she never interrupted with any truth.)

So George pressed himself on the service and – after he was stripped and checked for lice – got pressed into service at once, peelin tatoes, slingin hash, scourin honey buckets. Yessum, he then wondered if he'd die like Cynthy, scrubbing latrines. The valiant cook and heroic janitor endured the rigmarole of "bastard training" up in Sorel, P.Q. (by the Historic Murder Site of Kamouraska), where Frenchies dubbed him Joe Louie, and he'd have to cook em all hash after, like them, he'd run five miles (fully geared up), crawled through mud, hurled himself past barbed-wire barricades, and dug foxholes. But white boys got to play cards and harmonica after; the Indian and the Coloured, well, they still had to fry eggs and swab barracks. Still, though George was Grade-A Infantry meat, when all his comrades got shipped out – to slog up and through Italy and hand out maple syrup as well as copies of *Anne of Green Gables* in Italian – George's name weren't in that number. No, his weapons would be a mop, a broom, a paring knife. Georgie hated "blaytent prejadis," so he walk away from Camp No. 45, went AWOL. He still wanted, somehow, to be a notched-gun hero, not a potato peeler.

Georgie boarded a train to Montreal, Cynthy's fabled city. After ogling the glorious Sepia Showgirls (some looked hauntingly like his ma) and gobbling smoked meat on rye with a dill pickle, he bought a black-market registration card for five dollars and signed up with the Merchant Marine as Cliff Croxen.

The ship he engaged with, in August 1944, was the SS *Karma* owned by Newton and Tuttles out of Yorkshire, Hull, England. His job was to stoke the boilers. To shovel coal. That was all, but he was still literally going somewhere. Aboard this seemingly divinely shielded vessel, George even got to see Siberia, voyaging through the icefields thereabouts very, very slowly, while serenading his buddies on his Dante harmonica. But when he was in London, the "Ol' Country," between the ale and the strippers, he never saw sweet fuck-all. But it was good, it was jolly cheerio splendid, to inhale British exhaust and hear pub Billingsgate on the Kraut-cratered, bomb-blasted streets. Best thing was fish 'n' chips, wet, moist, tangy with salt and vinegar, with brown ale that tasted like a cross between vinegar and molasses. A scuffle in a pub got Georgie skirmishin with bobbies, and he got tossed in jail for a week. Visited by the Sally Ann, he spent his time toying with *The Scofield Reference Bible*, while dreaming of playing with a Scofield gun.

Georgie never see any direct action. Closest he got was on the high ocean, crossing water way too heavy to be sky, way too light to be land, his skin reflecting the iridescent Atlantic. The first time he crossed the North Atlantic, he saw waves ten storeys high and could hold nothing in his stomach, and it was only vomit, vomit, vomit, for three unholy days. When he got used to the thunderous heaving of the Atlantic, he viewed three scrap-metal reefs of bursting, burning ships, and blazing sailors, some of them jumping into an ocean surfaced by flames. It was horrible: the screams of the cremating; the moans of the drowning. A sinking ship was a big mass grave dug by a torpedo. After those banshee detonations, bits of jumbled crews would bob in the water: a hand, a torso, a head and part of a shoulder. Water resembled a huge mess of half-digested meals. Corpses'd litter a midnight sea. Some would float into port, all the way back to Halifax, arriving, stately, as truncated, battered logs. Dispirited, brine-sodden, skeletal.

Once, Georgie saw shrapnel hit a shipmate. The sailor's skull opened like a watermelon. His shocked eyes popped out like corks. He couldn't believe he was dead. He laughed: that's when the blood came out in a rush and he fell smack overboard. One of ten thousand heroes buried in water.

When the Europe War shut down, George exited the Merchant Marine. He was paid three hundred bucks and discharged. But as soon as he came ashore, George was arrested by military police from the no-longer-zombified Canadian Army and, treated as a deserter, was tossed in the brig. He sat there for twenty-eight days while the army evaluated his faculties and the facts. He'd been a deserter for over two hundred days. What was his fucking problem, exactly? First, he was "Coloured" or "Dark" ("Complexion") with "Brown Eyes" and "Black Hair" and holding the "Trade" of "Heavy Labourer," whose official function in His Majesty's Canadian Army was only as "General Duty." He also had a "tattoo right forearm ins. G.H." that he'd picked up in London. He also claimed incredibly to have travelled to South

America, North Africa, England, and Siberia, and that the SS *Karma*'d been bombed twice. ("No record of any such blasted incidents.")

Jaundiced, the army decided to fire a "negro" who wouldn't mop floors or crack eggs without whining. So George's conduct was summed up as "Bad," and he was discharged on a "10-29-10" (R.O. 1029 [10]), meaning he was "Unable to meet the required military physical standards" and was "Unlikely to become an efficient soldier." Medically speaking, George seemed fine. The army doc deemed him a "young negro well developed and nourished and talkative, loquacious, cheerful, and friendly," with only a few carious teeth, no scoliosis in his spine, no local tenderness or weird masses in his stomach, and no murmurs in his heart, and with symmetrical lungs, a normal pharynx and tonsils, and a regular pulse.

But the army shrink specified that George had a "Psychopathic Personality" with "a negative attitude toward the army," that he complained often of headaches, that he'd had chicken pox in childhood, and that he'd been tossed into detention for two days in Sorel, P.Q., because of robbery: "he stole money from a Cpl. Belliveau, contrary to military law." George was also of "doubtful stability," showed "undisciplined behaviour," had a record of "tremendous job shifting, doing odd jobs everywhere on farm and in the bush," expressed "a lack of grit-guts," swore to "some trouble with army policy for little trouble," and, lying, said, "I never drink. Never smoke." In total, G.H. was a "childish negro, an unhappy man who cannot get along with other people." True: he was an "inadequate liar" whose "affirmations often appear unbelievable." Asked if he had any complaint about his medical dossier, George wrote, "Nothing." Georgie signed off on his receipt of "all my Pay, Allowances, and Clothing," and then Private G.A. Hamilton, once of the No. 6 District Depot, either in Halifax, N.S., or in the Cape Breton Highlander Reserve, was dismissed. *At-ten-shun!*

XIII

The army head shrink had recommended Hamilton return to the Merchant Marine because that would "satisfy your impulsive adventuresome temperament" or, if not that, do "heavy outdoor labour under supervision." But Georgie recollected Montreal as the last place he'd been borderline happy before joining the Murder Marine. He also wanted, desperately, to collect some collateral before wooing Blondola again and wedding her now.

So Georgie boarded the *Ocean Limited* and clickety-clacked northwest to that Paris of the St. Lawrence: Montreal. That ex-fur-trade, beaver-pelt metropolis boasted Coloured bars, Coloured dancers, brown-sugar beauties, and brown-sugar dandies. Strolling Sainte-Catherine Street at night was like promenading an avenue of tinfoil and diamonds. Georgie enjoyed peeking inside theatrical clubs that were hot-pink and basic-black boxes, featuring "exotic" lovelies – spun-candy fancies – from the Quebec heartland who hoped to be discovered and delivered to sophisticated, vulgar Hollywood but who usually got discovered in someone's husband's arms and then delivered to a hospital on a stretcher. Georgie figured his army service, though spent in the brig, could gain him a bouncer post, even if he was more suited for pitching hay than he was for pitching drunkards.

After a week of ambling Montreal's steep streets, eating the usual smoked meat sandwiches with garnishes of dill pickle, with nightly adventures among the willing dancers, George got himself a nightclub job, Rue-like, at Le Sphinx. His position was not front-line, however. The white male clientele would not tolerate a Coloured bouncer but could not object to a Coloured dishwasher. Here George's army service helped him spectacularly: he had rare experience in washing dishes, glasses, cutlery, and so he reddened his tan hands in scalding, foaming water while scouring beer, wine, and martini glasses mainly. (Almost nobody ate anything on the night shifts.) One fringe pleasure for Georgie was getting to hear musicians playing their striptease music and getting to hear raucous men's dirty encouragements, voiced in French and English, to their entertainers to parade extra-extravagantly across the dingy stage.

Just like in the army, George could provide invisible benefits to others, but could not extract any for himself, beyond the meagre pay the nightclub owners flipped his way in the form of grimy coins. It was hardly serious money, and so, just as he used to pilfer from his army buddies at basic training in Sorel, so now he took to wandering the deserted 2 a.m. streets of the metropolis with a jeweller's hammer, screwdriver, and flashlight. He could tap a window just enough to shatter it, plunder cigarettes, chocolate bars, and other goods quick and easy to sell, or even jimmy a back door to a business to snatch up anything he could, hoping against hope against the possibility of guard dogs or burglar alarms or aroused owners toting guns or knives. These break-ins, little smash-and-grab jobs, netted negotiable rings, watches, smokes, and razors. It became routine: scour skuzzy, lipstick-ringed, cockroach- or cigar-dipped glasses, ashtrays fouled by chewing gum, half-eaten mints and candies, and then go out stealthily, early morning, to rattle doors and splinter windows, take whatever was portable and fly, crow-like, to the nearest shadows. He'd return to his snoring rooming house, as quietly as he could, sleep, then rise in the afternoon to make the rounds with his stolen property, showing up in tavern parking lots to furtively sell his ice-hot razors, watches, smokes, and rings.

George was overly confident in his crook abilities because of his proven skill at gambling, another vice he'd acquired in that assembly of thieves, thugs, rapists, and triggermen otherwise known as the army. He forgot that a brown-skinned hood, even if staying out of trouble, is bound to provoke suspicion from police. But George continued his theft spree blithely.

Then, after three months of success, a Montreal police cruiser pulled up alongside George, two officers leapt out and, without even a "bonsoir," frisked him roughly. The constables retrieved, from the aw-shucks persona of the dishwasher, a jeweller's hammer, a screwdriver, and a flashlight, tools not associated with the scrubbing of nightclub glasses and not credible for Georgie to explain in that context. Charged with carrying burglary tools, George fell into still deeper trouble when a search of his room on Atwater Street excavated goods impossible for a humble dishwasher to afford, including a $4,000 fur coat, which George claimed a dancer had given him for safekeeping. It was very inconvenient for his alibi, however, that the dancer could not be found because she was, he said, abroad in Egypt.

Unable to prove his innocence, George pulled three months in jail – one month for the tools, two months for the fur coat – and went to Bordeaux Prison on the outskirts of Montreal. Bordeaux was not as relaxing as the eponymous wine, but it was just as ruddy, a boutique, Gothic prison, with massive double doors as implacable as a drawbridge. To be interred therein was to vanish from public care, consciousness, and conscience. George's bed was a mat; his cellmate was a rat as big and toothy as a dog; his toilet was a bucket; his heating was a radiator that gurgled and pinged but never felt warmer than an ice cube; his blanket was a Salvation Army gift but as thin as the pages of their gift Bible. Still, George enjoyed the Salvation Army troops because they'd speak English with him. The French-speaking guards were really no better than molesters and would deny him food if he couldn't pronounce *J'ai faim* like a French-Canadian. But the Frenchy prisoners were worse. He got beat and pound on, beat and pound on, morning, noon, and night, in the mess hall and in the exercise yard. If he hadn't fashioned himself a blackjack – yard rocks stuck into a sock – he'd've been ground beef for everyone and everyone's blood pudding – what your anus looked like afterwards.

His Majesty's Bordeaux-on-the-Rocks Prison was a newsreel of handcuffs, aspirin, mint-flavoured cough drops, child-size cells of solitary confinement, meals of dry brown bread and cups of green-slime rainwater, sounds of inmates' hacking coughs in the ricocheting metal and tile floors of the freezing nineteenth-century jail, yellow phlegm he brought up way too often, the piss-reek of the cell, roaches gnawing away at law books, the chunky sound of the prison smithy hammering repairs into steel chains and the clanky sound of the cons who had to wear them like perverse jewellery. The dreadfullest sounds was heard in the penal colony on holidays: coughs and cries followed by choking and gurgling. Tears sliding down like falling stars. Suicides by hanging, or by slashing wrists with homemade shivs, razors. Prison made Hell look good.

Commandments were whims: "A bad attitude says you get nothing, or says you get hurt." Any sly inmate was said to be "a chess player with a checkered future."

Under such conditions, George could not even dream of asking Blondola for her hand. All his cash was gone as quickly as it had been won. He wondered how she'd feel about his being a jailbird. He just had to generate some cash.

Once free, George got took on as a chauffeur by the fiftyish, cadaverous, bow-tied Benny Parole, a man he'd known at Le Sphinx. Parole had scads and wads of money from his *boîts de nuit* and his casket-supply business. He had "Georges" drive his several cars to strange destinations to pick up "deliveries." Eventually, Parole sent Georges on a mission where he had to back a new car, its trunk lid open, into a warehouse, to receive a box. Georges felt a heavy weight loaded into the trunk. He drove off, but he was nervous, then heard the sirens behind him before he saw the cops in his rear-view mirror. He swung the car into the alleyway brick side of a building. The trunk top flipped up and George leapt out the car and saw a man's body with a bullet hole in the forehead. Georgie jumped on a train to Halifax – in the dark damp and Haligonian drizzle of April 1946. He scooted and skedaddled southeasterly down to what he prayed would be lucrative alleys, personable alleys, comfy slums.

XIV

In Halifax, the end of the war meant a new, if milder, Depression. The great naval port thrived on war but withered and hibernated between conflicts. Canada's navy, the third-largest on earth, was being scrapped, while soldiers and sailors were turning into students and fathers and relocating to the meccas of Toronto and Montreal, where factory wages could buy washers, televisions, and toasters. So when Georgie tried to find work, there was none for a black boy. Yes, he could shine shoes – again; he could carry bags – again; he could wash dishes – again. But he craved better. He tried to get on Haligonian docks stevedoring, but nothin doin for a Negro – Battle of the Atlantic *he-ro* or not. Nobody wanted his malt, half-Injun face on their payroll. Shit! He'd show up at the Seamen's Union Hall, put his name in for a job, then wait all day, among icy faces and an icy silence, to be called for a task. Everyone else in the hall would be hired to unload one vessel or another, but never George.

Slowly, he began to appreciate that his talents, such as they were, were best suited for wholesome, unquestioning farm labour. In such employ, as at Bezanson's farm, he could work alone, in the open air, savouring smells of wildflowers and blossoms, savouring the feeling of his muscles pitching hay or stooking apples or leading oxen. He enjoyed the powerful honesty of pure labour, agricultural work. But he didn't want to return to Bezanson's barn.

He studied the gigantic map of Canada that covered one wall in the Seamen's Union Hall, squinting especially at the rose-coloured Maritimes. But he'd had enough of Nova Scotia, and he couldn't bear the idea of little flinty, splinter-sized Prince Edward Island. He wouldn't return to Montreal anytime soon either: it was a burgh of cops and jail. He hit on a different future: to ask Blondola to marry him and accompany him to – to Fredericton. It was far enough from Three Mile Plains to suggest they'd moved up in the world but not so far as to make it impossible to visit. George figured he could work as a labourer in the city proper but do small farming outside. Too, he'd have a new life: no one'd know him; he'd know no one.

Now George packed up his suitcase, and caught the train to Windsor. When he saw Blondola again, he could hardly credit her supreme beauty. She had blossomed; she had matured; now an overly pretty sixteen-year-old, the ex-milkmaid had become a darling voluptuous, ripe woman. George was nervous to stand before her in his now patchy army uniform to entice Blondola to come away with him. No letter had gone from him to her in three years, though he had spent months in two prisons and though he had failed to secure serious money.

Yet, from Blondola's point of view, George did look roguishly handsome, and he had been to London and he had seen war; he had seen Buckingham Palace; he had seen the rubble of the House of Commons. He could describe for her places and experiences she had only heard about on the radio. Compared to all her other suitors – the stick-in-the-mud, cowboy-booted bullshitters of Windsor Plains – George was a living cosmopolitan. He even knew a few French phrases (thanks to Bordeaux) and a bit of the Bible (thanks to the Salvation Army). The ex-farm worker, ex-soldier (ex-con) who seemed unafraid of either work or death, who could utter charming, dashing French, and who stood tall in his patched uniform, was certainly more marriageable than the dairy dudes and uncouth drunkards who constituted the other choices. Too, Blondola loved the notion of wedding a veteran.

Polishing his war record and omitting his prison ones, Georgie sweet-talked the impressionable, flattered Blondola into coming with him to see the rest of the world – or at least Fredericton, N.B. That homey town with no Coloured slum. George believed she'd teach him "*terror* don't have half the force of *love*."

Blondola accepted his proposal after a decent interval of hesitation just to heighten Georgie's interest. They married in the African

Baptist Church at Three Mile Plains. Rufus was not invited – nor did he attend or send greetings. It was a splendid spring day. Blondola wore a white gown and a crown of apple blossoms. George's army uniform was newly patched and freshly pressed. Blondola's parents gave her away, but neither looked very pleased with her choice of groom. Still, they could brag that George had been to London, even if he hadn't met the King, and he did speak French, though no one around could say how good or bad it was. As for the patches on his uniform, they were forerunners of the medals he would one day truly earn.

The newlyweds boarded a steam train that wept out goodbyes to the Annapolis Valley as it cried into Digby. There, they boarded the ferry for Saint John and watched, in the romantic sunset, the boat's white wake turning golden as they left Nova Scotia.

Their marital night was sumptuous. Blondola, sweetly still virgin, wriggled so much it was hard for George to convince her just to clasp him. They were both wet: everything about them – their faces, their chests, their thighs, their sexes – everything was shimmering. They were as wet as newborn infants and practically as pure. George felt new, that he was – they were – blessed. At last.

NALO HOPKINSON

from Midnight Robber

Finally, it was Jonkanoo Season; the year-end time when all of Toussaint would celebrate the landing of the Marryshow Corporation nation ships that had brought their ancestors to this planet two centuries before. Time to give thanks to Granny Nanny for the Leaving Times, for her care, for life in this land, free from downpression and botheration. Time to remember the way their forefathers had toiled and sweated together: Taino Carib and Arawak; African; Asian; Indian; even the Euro, though some wasn't too happy to acknowledge that-there bloodline. All the bloods flowing into one river, making a new home on a new planet. Come Jonkanoo Week, tout monde would find themselves home with family to drink red sorrel and eat black cake and read from *Marryshow's Mythic Revelations of a New Garveyite: Sing Freedom Come.*

But Antonio still wouldn't come home.

This Jonkanoo Season was the first time that Tan-Tan would get to sing parang with the Cockpit County Jubilante Mummers. She and eshu had practised the soprano line for "Sereno, Sereno" so till she had been singing it in her sleep and all. And she had done so well in rehearsals that the Mummers had decided to let her sing the solo in "Sweet Chariot." Tan-Tan was so excited, she didn't know what to do with herself. Daddy was going to be so proud!

Jonkanoo Night, Nursie dressed her up in her lacy frock to go from house to house with the Mummers. Nursie finished locksing Tan-Tan's hair, and took a step back to admire her. "Nanny bless, doux-doux, you looking nice, you know? You make me think of my Aislin when she was a just a little pickney-girl. Just so she did love fancy frock, and she hair did thick and curly, just like yours."

"Aislin?" Tan-Tan dragged her eyes from her own face in the mirror eshu had made of the wall. She had been trying to read her daddy's features there. "You have a daughter, Nursie?"

Nursie frowned sadly. She looked down at her feet and shook her head. "Never mind, doux-doux; is more than twelve years now she climb the half-way tree and gone for good. Let we not speak of the departed." She sucked her teeth, her face collapsing into an expression of old sorrow and frustration. "Aislin shoulda had more sense than to get mix up in Antonio business. I just grateful your daddy see fit to make this lonely old woman part of he household afterwards."

And all Tan-Tan could do, Nursie wouldn't talk about it anymore after that. Tan-Tan just shrugged her shoulders. Is so it go; Toussaint people didn't talk too much about the criminals they had exiled to New Half-Way Tree. Too-besides, Tan-Tan was too nervous to listen to Old Nursie's horse-dead-and-cow-fat story tonight. First parang! Nursie had had all the ruffles on Tan-Tan's frock starched and her aoutchicongs, her tennis shoes-them, whitened till they gleamed.

Tan-Tan's bedroom door chimed, the one that led outside to the garden. She had a visitor, just like big people! "You answer it, doux-doux," said Nursie.

"Eshu, is who there?" asked Tan-Tan, as she'd heard her parents do.

"Is Ben, young Mistress," the eshu said through the wall. "He bring a present for you."

A present! She looked at Nursie, who smiled and nodded. "Let he in," said Tan-Tan.

The door opened to admit the artisan who gave her father the benefit of his skill by programming and supervising Garden. As ever, he was barefoot, console touchpen tucked behind one ear and wearing a mud-stained pair of khaki shorts and a grubby shirt-jac whose pockets held shadowy bulges like babies' diapers. Weeds hung out of the bulgy pockets. He had an enormous bouquet of fresh-cut ginger lilies in one hand. The red blooms stretched on long thumb-thick green stalks. Tan-Tan gasped at the present that Ben was balancing carefully in his other hand.

Nursie chided, "Ben, is why you always wearing such disgraceful clothes, eh? And you can't even put on a pair of shoes to come into the house?"

But Ben just winked at her and presented her with the lilies. She relented, giggled girlishly, and buried her nose in the blossoms. Finally he seemed to notice Tan-Tan gazing at the present. He smiled and held it out to her: a Jonkanoo hat. It was made from rattan, woven in the torus shape of a nation ship. "I design it myself," Ben told her. "I get Garden to make it for you. Grow it into this shape right on the vine."

"Oh, what a way it pretty, Ben!" The hat even had little portholes all round it and the words "Marryshow Corporation: Black Star Line II" etched into a flat blade of dried vine in its side.

"Look through the portholes."

Tan-Tan had to close one eye to see through one of the holes. "I see little people! Sleeping in their bunk beds, and a little crèche with a teacher and some pickney, and I see the bridge with the captain and all the crew!"

"Is so we people reach here on Toussaint, child. And look . . ." Ben pulled six candles out of a pocket and wedged them into holders woven all along the ring of the ship. "Try it on let me see."

Careful-careful, Tan-Tan slid the hat onto her head. It fit exactly.

"When you ready to go," Ben said, "ask Mistress Ione to light the candle-them for you. Then you going to be Playing Jonkanoo for real!"

Nursie fretted, "I don't like this little girl walking round with them open flame 'pon she head like that, you know? You couldn't use peeny-wallie bulb like everybody else, eh? Suppose the whole thing catch fire?"

"Ain't Ione go be right there with Tan-Tan?" Ben reassured her. "She could look after she own pickney. This is the right way to play Jonkanoo, the old-time way. Long time, that hat woulda be make in the shape of a sea ship, not a rocket ship, and them black people inside woulda been lying pack-up head to toe in they own shit, with chains round them ankles. Let the child remember how black people make this crossing as free people this time."

Tan-Tan squinched up her face at the nasty story. Crèche teacher had sung them that same tale. Vashti and Crab-back Joey had gotten scared. Tan-Tan too. For nights after, she'd dreamt of being shut up in a tiny space, unable to move. Eshu had had to calm her when she woke bawling.

Nursie shut Ben up quick: "Shush now, don't frighten the child with your old-time story."

"All right. Time for me to get dressed, anyway. Fête tonight! Me and Rozena going to dance till 'fore-day morning, oui." Ben knelt down and smiled into Tan-Tan's eyes. "When you wear that hat, you carry yourself straight and tall, you hear? You go be Parang Queen–self tonight!"

"Yes, Ben. Thank you!"

When everything was ready, Nursie fetched Tan-Tan to Ione. Nursie carried the Jonkanoo hat in front of her like a wedding cake, candles and all.

Ione was too, too beautiful that night in her madras head wrap and long, pale yellow gown, tight so till Tan-Tan was afraid that Ione wouldn't be able to catch breath enough to sing the high notes in "Rio Manzanares." She looked so pretty, though, that Tan-Tan ran to hug her.

"No, Tan-Tan; don't rampfle up me gown. Behave yourself, nuh? Come let we go. I could hear the parang singers practising in the dining room. Is for you that hat is?"

"From Ben, Mummy."

Ione nodded approvingly. "A proper Jonkanoo gift. I go give you one from me tomorrow." She put the nation ship hat on Tan-Tan's head, and then lit all six candles.

"Candles for remembrance, Tan-Tan. Hold your head high now, you hear? You have to keep the candles-them straight and tall and burning bright."

"Yes, Mummy." Tan-Tan remembered Nursie's Posture lessons. Proper-proper she took Ione's hand, smoothed her frock down, and walked down the stairs with her mother to join the Cockpit County Jubilante Mummers. The John Canoe dancer in his suit of motley rags was leaping about the living room while the singers clapped out a rhythm.

Tan-Tan was Cockpit County queen that night for true! The Mummers went house to house, singing the old-time parang songs, and in every place, people were only feeding Tan-Tan tamarind balls and black cake and thing – "Candles for remembrance, doux-doux!" – till the ribbon sash round her waist was binding her stuffed belly. Everywhere she went, she could hear people whispering behind their hands: "Mayor little girl . . . sweet in that pretty frock . . . really have Ione eyes, don't? Mayor heart must be hard . . . girl child alone so with no father!" But she didn't pay them any mind. Tan-Tan was enjoying herself. All the same, she couldn't wait to get to the town square to sing the final song of the night. Antonio would be there to greet the Mummers and make his annual Jonkanoo Night speech. For days he had been busy with the celebrations and he hadn't called to speak to Tan-Tan.

At last the Mummers reached the town square. By now, Tan-Tan's feet were throbbing. Her white aoutchicongs had turned brown with dust from walking all that distance, and her belly was beginning to pain her from too much food. Ione had blown out the candles on the nation ship hat long time, for with all the running round Tan-Tan was doing, the hat kept falling from her head. She had nearly set fire to Tantie Gilda's velvet curtains.

Tan-Tan was ready to drop down with tiredness, oui, but as they entered the town square, she straightened up her little body and took her mummy's hand.

"Light the candles again for me, Mummy." Hand in hand with Ione, Tan-Tan marched right to her place in the front of the choir. She made believe she was the Tan-Tan from the Carnival, or maybe the Robber Queen, entering the town square in high state for all the people to bring her accolades and praise and their widows' mites of gold and silver for saving them from the evil plantation boss (she wasn't too sure what an "accolade" was, oui, but she had heard Ben say it when he played the Robber King masque at Carnival time the year before). Choirmaster Gomez smiled when he saw her in her pretty Jonkanoo hat. He pressed the microphone bead onto her collar. Tan-Tan lost all her tiredness one time.

The square was full up of people that night. One set of people standing round, waiting for the midnight anthem. It must be had two hundred souls there! Tan-Tan started to feel a little jittery. Suppose she got the starting note wrong? She took a trembling breath. She felt she was going to dead from nerves. Behind her, she heard Ione hissing, "Do good now, Tan-Tan. Don't embarrass me tonight!"

Choirmaster Gomez gave the signal. The quattro players started to strum the tune, and the Cockpit County Jubilante Mummers launched into the final song of the night. Tan-Tan was so nervous, she nearly missed her solo. Ione tapped her on her shoulder, and she caught herself just in time. She took a quick breath and started to sing.

The first few notes were a little off, oui, but when she got to the second verse, she opened her eyes. Everybody in the square was swaying from side to side. She started to get some confidence. By the third verse, her voice was climbing high and strong to the sky, joyful in the 'fore-day morning.

Sweet chariot,
Swing down,
Time to ride,
Swing down.

As she sang, Tan-Tan glanced round. She saw old people rocking back and forth to the song, their lips forming the ancient words. She saw artisans standing round the Mercy Table, claiming the food and gifts that Cockpit Town people had made for them with their own hands in gratitude for their creations. Every man-jack had their eyes on her. People nodded their heads in time. She swung through the words, voice piping high. The Mummers clapped in time behind her. Then she spied a man standing near the edge of the crowd, cradling a sleeping little girl in his arms. He was the baby's daddy. Tan-Tan's soul came crashing back to earth. Tears began creeping down her face. She fought her way to the end of the song. When she put up her hand to wipe the tears away, an old lady near the front said, "Look how the sweet song make the child cry. What a thing!" Tan-Tan pulled the mike bead off and ran to Ione. The nation ship hat fell to the ground. Tan-Tan heard someone exclaim behind her, and the scuffing sound as he stamped out the flame of the candles. She didn't pay it no mind. She buried her head in her mother's skirt and cried for Antonio. Ione sighed and patted her head.

Soon after, her daddy did come, striding into the town square to give his speech. But he didn't even self glance at Tan-Tan or Ione. Ione clutched Tan-Tan's shoulder and hissed at her to stand still. Tan-Tan looked at her mother's face; she was staring longingly and angrily at Antonio with bright, brimming eyes. Ione started to hustle Tan-Tan away. Tan-Tan pulled on her hand to slow her down. "No, Mummy, no; ain't Daddy going to come with we?"

Ione stooped down in front of her daughter. "I know how you feel, doux-doux. Is Jonkanoo and we shoulda be together, all three of we; but Antonio ain't have no mercy in he heart for we."

"Why?"

"Tan-Tan, you daddy vex with me; he vex bad. He forget all the nights I spend alone, all the other women I catch he with."

Tan-Tan ain't business with that. "I want my daddy." She started to cry.

Ione sighed. "You have to be strong for me, Tan-Tan. You is the only family I have now. I not going to act shame in front of Cockpit County people and they badtalk. Swallow those tears now and hold your head up high."

Tan-Tan felt like her heart could crack apart with sorrow. Ione had to carry the burst nation ship. Scuffling her foot-them in the dirt, Tan-Tan dragged herself to the limousine that had been sent to the square to wait for them. They reached home at dayclean, just as the sun was rising. Tan-Tan was a sight when Nursie met her at the door: dirty tennis shoes, plaits coming loose, snail tracks of tears winding down her face.

"Take she, Nursie," Ione said irritably. "I can't talk no sense into she at all at all."

"Oh, darling, is what do you so?" Nursie bent down to pick up the sad little girl.

Tan-Tan leaked tired tears, more salt than water. "Daddy ain't come to talk to me. He ain't tell me if he like how I sing. Is Jonkanoo, and he ain't self even give me a Jonkanoo present!"

"I ain't know what to do for she when she get like this," Ione told Nursie. "Tan-Tan, stop your crying! Bawling ain't go make it better."

Nursie and Ione took Tan-Tan inside to bed, but is Nursie who washed Tan-Tan's face and plaited up her hair nice again so it wouldn't knot up while she slept. Is Nursie who dressed Tan-Tan in her favourite yellow nightie with the lace at the neck. Nursie held to her lips the cup of hot cocoa-tea that Cookie sent from the kitchen, and coaxed her to drink it. Cookie was an artisan too, had pledged his creations to whoever was living in the mayor house. Usually Tan-Tan loved his cocoa, hand-grated from lumps of raw chocolate still greasy with cocoa fat, then steeped in hot water with vanilla beans and demerara sugar added to it. But this time it was more bitter than she liked, and she got so sleepy after drinking it! One more sip, and she felt she had to close her eyes, just for a little bit. Nursie put Tan-Tan to bed with the covers pulled right up to her neck, and stroked her head while sleep came. Ione only paced back and forth the whole time, watching at the two of them.

But just as sleep was locking Tan-Tan's eyes shut, is Ione's sweet voice she heard, singing a lullaby to her from across the room.

Moonlight tonight, come make we dance and sing,
Moonlight tonight, come make we dance and sing,
Me there rock so, you there rock so, under banyan tree,
Me there rock so, you there rock so, under banyan tree.

And her earbug echoed it in her head as eshu sang along.

Tan-Tan slept right through the day until the next morning. When she woke up Ione told her irritably, "Your daddy come by to see you while you was sleeping."

Tan-Tan leapt up in the bed. "Daddy here!"

"No, child. He gone about he business."

The disappointment and hurt were almost too much for breathing. Unbelieving, Tan-Tan just stared at Mummy. Daddy didn't wait for her to wake up?

"Cho. Me ain't able with you and your father. He leave this for you." Ione laid out a costume on the bed, a little Robber Queen costume, just the right size for Tan-Tan. It had a white silk shirt with a high, pointy collar, a little black jumbie leather vest with a fringe all round the bottom, and a pair of wide red leather pants with more fringe down the sides. It even had a double holster to go round her waist, with two shiny cap guns sticking out. But the hat was the best part. A wide black sombrero, nearly as big as Tan-Tan herself, with pompoms in different colours all round the brim, to hide her face in the best Robber Queen style. Inside the brim, it had little monkeys marching all round the crown of the hat, chasing tiny birds. The monkeys leapt, snatching at the swooping birds, but they always returned to the brim of the hat.

"Look, Tan-Tan!" Ione said, in that poui-bright voice she got when she wanted to please. "It have Brer Monkey in there, chasing Brer Woodpecker for making so much noise. Is a nice costume, ain't?"

Tan-Tan looked at her present good, but her heart felt like a stone inside her chest. She pressed her lips together hard. She wasn't even going to crack a smile.

"Yes, Mummy."

"Your daddy say is for he little Jonkanoo Queen with the voice like honey. You must call he and tell he thanks."

"Yes, Mummy."

"You ain't want to know what I get for you?"

"Yes, Mummy."

Smiling, Ione reached under Tan-Tan's bed and pulled out the strangest pair of shoes Tan-Tan had ever seen. They were black jumbie leather carved in the shape of alligators like in the zoo. The toes of the shoes were the alligators' snouts. They had gleaming red eyes. The shoes were lined inside with jumbie feather fluff. "Try them on, nuh?" Ione urged.

Tan-Tan slid her feet into the shoes. They moulded themselves comfortably round her feet. She stood up. She took a step. As she set her foot down the alligator shoe opened its snout wide and barked. Red sparks flew from its bright white fangs. Tan-Tan gasped and froze where she was. Ione laughed until she looked at Tan-Tan's face. "Oh doux-doux, is only a joke, a mamaguy. Don't dig nothing. They only go make noise the first two steps you take."

To test it, Tan-Tan stamped her next foot. The shoe barked obligingly. She jumped and landed hard on the floor. The shoes remained silent. "Thank you, Mummy."

"You not even going bust one so-so smile for me, right?"

Tan-Tan looked solemnly at her mother. Ione rolled her eyes impatiently and flounced out of the room.

Tan-Tan waited till she could no longer hear Ione's footsteps. She went to the door and looked up and down the corridor. No one. Only then did she try on the Midnight Robber costume. It fit her perfect. She went and stood in front of a bare wall. "Eshu," she whispered.

The a.i. clicked on in her ear. In her mind's eye it showed itself as a little skeleton girl, dressed just like her. "Yes, young Mistress?"

"Make a mirror for me."

Eshu disappeared. The wall silvered to show her reflection. Aces, she looked aces. Her lips wavered into a smile. She pulled one of the cap guns from its holster: "Plai! Plai! Thus the Robber Queen does be avengèd! All you make you eye pass me? Take that! Plai!" She swirled round to shoot at the pretend badjack sneaking up behind her. The cape flared out round her shoulders and the new leather of her shoes creaked. It was too sweet.

"Belle Starr . . ." said the eshu, soft in her ear.

"Who?" It wasn't lesson time, but the eshu had made her curious.

"Time was, is only men used to play the Robber King masque," eshu's voice told her.

"Why?" Tan-Tan asked. What a stupid thing!

"Earth was like that for a long time. Men could only do some things, and women could only do others. In the beginning of Carnival, the early centuries, Midnight Robbers was always men. Except for the woman who take the name Belle Starr, the same name as a cowgirl performer from America. The Trini Belle Starr made she own costume and she uses to play Midnight Robber."

"What she look like, eshu?"

"No pictures of she in the data banks, young Mistress. Is too long ago. But I have other pictures of Carnival on Earth. You want to see?"

"Yes."

The mirrored wall opaqued into a viewing screen. The room went dark. Tan-Tan sat on the floor to watch. A huge stage appeared on the screen, with hundreds of people in the audience. Some old-time soca was playing. A masque King costume came out on stage; one mako big construction, supported by one man dancing in its traces. It looked like a spider, or a machine with claws for grasping. It had a sheet of white cotton suspended above its eight wicked-looking pincers. It towered a good three metres above the man who was wearing it, but he danced and pranced as though it weighed next to nothing.

"The Minshall Mancrab," eshu told Tan-Tan. "Minshall made it to be king of his band 'The River' on Earth, Terran calendar 1983."

"Peter Minshall?" Tan-Tan asked. She had heard a crèche teacher say the name once when reading from *Marryshow's Revelations*.

"He same one."

The sinister Mancrab advanced to the centre of the stage, its sheet billowing. Suddenly the edges of the sheet started to bleed. Tan-Tan heard the audience exclaim. The blood quickly soaked the sheet as the Mancrab opened its menacing pincers wide. People in the audience went wild, clapping and shouting and screaming their approval.

Tan-Tan was mesmerized. "Is scary," she said.

"Is so headblind machines used to stay," eshu told her. "Before people make Granny Nanny to rule the machines and give guidance. Look some different images here."

The eshu showed her more pictures of old-time Earth Carnival: the Jour Ouvert mud masque, the Children's Masquerades. When Nursie came to fetch her for breakfast, Tan-Tan was tailor-sat on the floor in the dark, still in her Robber Queen costume, staring at the eshu screen and asking it questions from time to time. The eshu answered in a gentle voice. Nursie smiled and had the minder bring Tan-Tan's breakfast to her on a tray.

For two days straight Tan-Tan insisted on wearing her Robber Queen costume. She slept in it and all. Neither Ione nor Nursie could persuade her to change out of it. But she never called Antonio to thank him. Let him feel bad about boofing her on Jonkanoo Night.

DAVID N. ODHIAMBO

from **Kipligat's Chance**

September: The Game

II

After the cross-country race Kulvinder and I careen west on Broadway in Mrs. Sharma's Chevy, then turn east onto Main Street. He's moved beyond the race and prattles on about his date with Jugs, looking at me instead of watching the road.

"Do you think you could keep your eyes on what you're doing?" I suggest.

He parps his horn, runs the table of amber lights, and speeds toward Second Avenue.

I change the subject. "Did Coach Holt really say I have no endurance?"

Kulvinder pushes Afrika Bambaataa into the tape deck and pumps up the volume.

"Just give us the bottle of Southern Comfort in the glove compartment."

I present him with the booze and get quiet.

"You going to have a taste?" he asks.

"Not till later."

"Not till later," he mimics in a falsetto whine.

"I can't afford to go home reeking of alcohol."

He lifts both hands off the steering wheel and accelerates through a red light.

"Kulvinderrr."

He laughs before braking behind a van illegally parked in the middle of the street. A strapping bloke in a green uniform unloads a computer from the vehicle's boot.

Kulvinder parps his horn again.

"I think he left a couple of inches there I can still squeeze through."

He rolls down his window.

"Take your time, mate," he says. "Never mind us."

"I'll be out of your way in a second, sir."

Kulvinder rolls up the window. "Fabulous!"

He chugs down more booze, then shivers.

"Let's get a pint at Billy's Tavern," he says. "I don't feel much like going home."

"Nah," I reply, "I told the folks I'd be back by four."

"Gawd, you can be a bore." Kulvinder looks in the rear-view mirror, backs up real quick, and squeals onto a side street.

My feet peddle hard against the floor mat as I instinctively search for a brake.

He swerves up onto the sidewalk and knocks over a garbage can.

I clutch the dashboard. "Stop the car!" He drives through a flower bed, flips a finger out his window at a startled old couple on their porch, then turns back to the road.

"Like I said, boooooring."

With one hand I take the bottle from him and with the other I grip the door handle.

III

It's after nine when I get home. Not a good move since I said I'd be back that afternoon. But I couldn't even think of returning till we'd sobered up a little. Now I'm in for a beef with the folks.

No matter. I've got a more pressing concern: the thought of Kulvinder at the dance with Jugs has me bugged. It can't happen. Screw the consequences. I'm going to stop by her crib and lay my feelings on the line.

I walk down our block in the East End and through a corridor of strung-out tarts wearing tight rayon hot pants.

"Hey, Chan Lu."

"What 'sup, Leeds."

"Raquel."

"Sweetie."

I'm on a first-name basis with most of them. Not because of steamy encounters in the alley out back. No, no, no. They're not the type I go for. It'd be downright depressing to smoke one of those cellulite-laden asses. All humping tainted by the thought of their attention deficit spawn, crunching away at a diet of Captain Crunch cereal in a rinky-dink hovel.

"Another slow night?" I ask.

"Not for that whore Yvonne." Chan Lu replies. "Braggin on my ass about all the dick she scored."

"It'll pick up."

She adjusts her skirt. "Got any money for cigarettes, honey?"

"Everything comes at a cost," I joke.

She blows me a kiss. "Wait till I tell your mum what a dirty mind you got."

I push on a latch, lift up the gate, and shove.

Our two-storey house isn't much to look at. The white paint is peeling; cracked windows are held together by duct tape. The yard of overgrown grass is sprinkled with rusty automotive parts, and the wire fence surrounding it all is overrun with morning glories.

What gets me the most is that the light on the porch is toast, a constant reminder that Mr. Chen is a slumlord.

I stand in front of Jugs's door, a finger on her doorbell. My armpits sweat and my jaw is clenched. The chain-link fence hiccups trapped refuse into a gust of wind.

WHRRRRRPBUP.

The door bangs open and Slim, her eight-year-old brother, scampers out.

"Whoa." I catch him by the arms to avoid a collision.

His pasty face is smeared with dirt, and the brown hair on top of his head is like new growth in a clear-cut.

"Slow down there, dog."

He's out of breath. "ZZzzup?"

"Where you off to this time of night?"

"See the bitch."

"Who?"

"My girl."

"Oh. Is Steph around?"

"Nah, she atta friend's."

"Damn." I missed her. "Well, be sure not to stay out too late."

"Whatever," he snickers before barrelling off into the night.

After overhearing the bungling on the porch, Mum opens up.

She's wrapped in a kanga, a dab of toothpaste sitting over her upper lip.

"Where in heaven's name have you been?" She sounds relieved.

"Kulvinder had a flat tire." I've bombarded my mouth with garlic. "We got stranded out in the sticks without a spare. Thank God, a rock band pulled over and gave us theirs." I cross myself and look at the ceiling. "Thank God."

"You're drunk." She's furious.

Dad calls her name from the living room, sneezes, then bellows for the hot water bottle.

"I can't deal with this right now." She frowns. "I was worried sick, and your dad's been running a fever. Couldn't you at least ring?"

I want to take a shower, change, and get to the dance. "I wasn't near a phone."

"Nonsense. You expect me to believe there wasn't one pay phone in whatever bar they let you into?" She shakes her head. "One thing's for certain, you're not going to the dance tonight."

"Come on, Mum. I haven't done anything wrong."

"Gladys," Dad yells again.

"I could strangle you I'm so upset right now," Mum says.

She stamps off to look for the hot water bottle.

The old man is conked out in front of the telly, wads of tinfoil glinting from the tips of the antennae. He's waiting for the late news. His legs and arms, bordering on chubbiness, fill out a baggy pair of pinstriped jammies.

He waits for a commercial. "John."

"Ya." I've taken to a kind of monosyllabic language with the embattled king of our homestead.

"Where've you been?"

"Around."

He grunts, and a loud rattle indicates Mum has turned on the kitchen taps.

I stare at the floor.

I don't like to see him like this. The low table in front of him is covered in everything he needs to stay glued to that chair: rolled-up Kleenex, a few slices of lemon, a bottle of nasal spray, and leftover chicken soup. Only an act of God could pry him from this post.

An eternity of ahs later he lets rip a humongous sneeze.

"Kulvinder's mother has been phoning about your work schedule," he finally says.

"I know."

I couldn't give a flying fig about slaving away for Mrs. Sharma at Fawzia's Authentic Indian Cuisine.

"Call her," he sniffles.

"I will."

From his forehead he removes a wet flannel that Mum, no doubt, plonked there.

"It's all about honest effort, Son," he says. "That's all your mother and I expect of you."

"Absolutely, Dad."

Right. I doubt he believes any of this Father Knows Best crap. Look where it got him. Look. Despite honest effort we've spent our years in Vancouver this side of eating out of dustbins.

Anyway, I'm not about to explain myself. There's a school dance to prepare for: Mum can't stop me from going.

Dad stares at the TV, then lapses into silence. I back out of the room while he coughs.

Mum enters my bedroom with a glass of apple juice, hands it over, then squishes down beside me and puts an arm around my shoulders. "John, you must try harder."

I run a pick through my nappy hair.

"Pumpkin." She squeezes closer. "You've always run with the throttle on high. Come on now. Calm down a little. Can't you see we're worried about you?"

"Ah, man."

"It's been rough for all of us lately. You know that."

It hasn't helped that Dad won't follow through on job leads she finds for him. Since the move it's as if Dad's been decked by a wicked uppercut and he's sitting against the ropes trying to get his head clear.

"Just be grateful we have work," she continues.

"How can you stand it, Mum?" She caretakes a young brat with muscular dystrophy. "After just one ten-hour shift with that kid I'd go nuts."

She laughs. "Son, there's no shame in serving others. Especially when people are dependent on you for their survival."

"Well, I've had it with washing dishes. There are better ways to spend my time."

"Like what, watching television all day with your father?"

I pause for a moment.

Now that I've had a few drinks, Kulvinder's insistence on running track doesn't seem bad. But I know if I mention it, Mum'll go on first about Koech, then my marks at school. I say it anyway. "Run." I'll do anything to get out of that bleeding kitchen. "I was asked to join a track club today by a guy who went to the Olympics."

It's a long shot, I know, but Kulvinder promised to talk Coach Holt into taking me on.

She's quiet for a while. Rock music detonates through the floorboards upstairs while I comb through knots in my hair.

I have no idea how Jugs and Slim manage up there. The mister gets the missus to party with him. They stay up till four in the morning, smoking pot and listening to the collected works of Pink Floyd. Then a round of arguing leads to loud, pre-dawn shagging.

Make no mistake. I'm no prude. I understand some folks need to hit the pipe and crack open a box of sex toys now and again. I just don't want to have to listen to it.

"Is it going to cost, dear?"

"I can pay for most of it with my savings. But I'll need to borrow a bit for some spikes."

It's true. If I get into the club, I'll need an upgrade in gear.

"How much?"

"One hundred and fifty dollars."

"John!"

"I know it's a lot of money, but I'll pay you back."

"I can't keep . . ."

"Okay, forget it."

"It's just you go out drinking till all hours, don't call, and when you get home, you treat me like some sort of bank machine," she says.

"Holy shit, Mum." I blurt out. "I said forget it."

She gets huffy. "You have no right . . . How dare you use that foul language . . . I cannot be around you right now." She leaves.

Fine.

I skim through an article in *Track and Field News* on the eight.

A change of guard has taken place in the event. Coe and Ovett have retired. Cruz, the heir apparent, lost his form after the games in L.A. and now Wilson Kipketer, the Kenyan who migrated to Norway, is the world record holder.

Mum returns. She hands me a stack of cash.

I object. I'm not taking her money.

"Listen, Son. What matters is that you've found something you care about." She pushes two hundred dollars into the palm of my hand. "But clean up your act. The police don't need much excuse to put a black person behind bars."

Tears come to my eyes, and the bills in the palm of my hand are blurry. "Thanks, Mum. I'll pay you back." I want to apologize for not coming home earlier, but I clam up. I'm too close to bawling.

"We're going on a picnic Sunday if your Dad's feeling better." It's the biweekly family affair at Brighton Park – the one surrounded by factories and bordered by a beach where dead seals wash up.

"Brilliant."

"Be sure not to find another excuse not to come?"

"I'll be there."

"Good. Well, I'm calling it a night. I've taken care of him all day and I'm drained. Would you be a dear and get him some cough syrup?"

I squeeze her arm, then amble shyly off to the sound of "The Wall" caroming through the suite.

I fish around in the medicine cabinet until I get a hold of the Benylin. Then find a spoon before I take it to the sitting room.

He's propped up with pillows and covered in a blanket as he lies on the sofa and scours the news for reports of events in Kenya.

"Dad." I've been rough on the old man. "I brought you your medicine."

His eyes are yellow, and he wipes at his nose with crumpled toilet paper. "Oh, you brought a teaspoon. I need a tablespoon to take that."

I'd meant to grab the tablespoon, but I'd zoned out. "Why not just take three teaspoons?"

"I need a tablespoon."

If I were Kulvinder I'd just start yelling. I'd say, I've got better things to do with myself than run back and forth getting you a goddamned spoon.

I grind my teeth, swallow, leave, and find him his bloody tablespoon.

On my way past their bedroom I see Mum kneeling at an altar. There's a candle on top of a *kitambaa* surrounded by smooth, green pebbles. She burns sage in a bowl and murmurs a prayer to the Knowledge Holders.

IV

By the time the folks go to bed, I've lost at least two prime dancing hours. I steal out of the house and wait for Kulvinder at the top of the alley.

"Give me the keys," I demand on his arrival. "I'm driving."

"Don't be daft."

"Listen, if we're going to kill ourselves, I'd prefer to be at the wheel."

"Good Christ." He throws me keys and switches seats. "Let's just get out of here."

I hunch forward, signal, check the rear-view mirror for cop cars, and inch into the street.

"You can get ticketed for driving too far *under* the speed limit, you know," he says.

I slow down at railroad tracks, check both ways, and ease forward.

"Kulvinder." I have to say something. "Don't go downtown on Jugs unless you mean it."

"I'll mean it."

"That's not what I'm getting at. She seems like a nice girl."

" 'It will cost her a groaning to take off my edge.' "

Hamlet again.

"Be serious." He can't put a lid on botching quotes from whatever he happens to be reading.

"When was the last time you got laid?" he asks.

I calculate the number of months on fingers.

"It's been ten, mate," he continues. "In contrast, I got a leg up on Helen last weekend."

"That's what I'm talking about."

"That's what I'm talking about."

"Would you stop with the innuendo."

"I'm just speaking to the point."

"The point, there you go again."

He cracks up, hysterically banging the dashboard with his fists.

We arrive at the corny get-down well after midnight.

"Wait here a sec," Kulvinder says before disappearing into the crowded lobby.

I twiddle my thumbs as I stand in my only dressy threads – a scarlet cardigan and navy blue corduroys. Nervous. Hoping my blind date takes to this straight-out-of-the-Sears-catalogue look.

I ought to head to the can for a quick once-over in the mirror.

"Leeds," Kulvinder grabs my arm before I can swing into motion. "Steph and I are going outside."

Jugs has one hand curled around his bicep, and her head is pressed into his shoulder.

"How you doin, Leeds?"

Her words are slurred.

"The usual." If she doesn't have her wits about her, Kulvinder'll roll on her but good. "You?"

"I couldn't be better," she replies.

Svetlana Petrovskaya stands to her left and stares at the strobe lights.

"It's kinda stuffy in here, though," she continues. "So Kulvinder and I are taking a walk."

"Stephanie!" Svetlana exclaims.

I look over their shoulders for my blind date. It couldn't possibly be Svetlana Petrovskaya. She's butch.

"I'll conduct myself like a perfect gentleman," Kulvinder says. "Everything below the knees is off limits."

Jugs doubles over in laughter. "Oh, God." Spit sprays from her lips. "I think I'm gonna pee my pants."

"On that note," Kulvinder announces. "Hillo, ho, ho, good lady! Come, bird, come."

"I hope you guys won't mind holding onto my wallet till we get back?" Jugs wipes tears from her eyes. "It'll give the two of you a chance to talk."

Svetlana!

What are they thinking?

"Remember the golden rule, kids." Kulvinder winks. "Nothing below the knees."

"No sweat," I mutter, grinding my teeth.

Jugs reaches into her pockets and produces keys, lipstick, a tampon, and a tiny mirror. She hands these, along with a wallet, to Svetlana. Then they disappear outside.

This isn't good. Svetlana tends to sit at the back of the class, where she pulls on her dark bangs and chews her nails. Her nose is crooked and she's on the pudgy side, plus she has a cleft in her chin.

Svetlana's in full chew mode as I stand beside her in the dark dining hall. She's chomping at the quick.

Overplayed standards with familiar hooks jimmy whoops and cheers out of the jacked-up crowd. Boys wearing I'm-with-stupid T-shirts play air guitars and bellow in one another's ears. Girls decorated in Grandma's jewellery move as if it's serious, this dancing business. Bunched in small groups like chattel in a pen. The sober are a collection of prats. Checking digital watches and fingering their pockets for quarters with which to call home.

My temples ache.

I don't know what the hell to say. So, Svetlana, what do you think of . . . I can't fill in the blank.

How could Jugs do me like this?

"Svetlana," I finally shout. "What do you think of the poems we're studying in Finch's class?"

"The best thing one can say about Ezra Pound is that at least he had good enough taste to be involved with Hilda Doolittle."

"Right." Damned if I know what the hell she's talking about. "You must read a lot."

"Don't you?"

"*Othello* wasn't bad."

"You actually *liked* that play?"

"Sort of." I don't want to get into the details. "Forget school. Did Stephanie tell you about the cross-country race?" She yawns. "It's not my specialty, you know. I'm in serious training to . . ." run at the Provincials isn't impressive enough. ". . . break the four-minute mile." Of course, there's more to say about corporate sponsorships and so on. But she's too close to Jugs. Now that she and Kulvinder are hitting it, I have to be careful. Any outrageous lie will bounce back and nick a chunk of flesh out my ass. "If one believes in their dreams and stays off drugs anything is possible."

"It figures," she says.

"What?"

"Sports. Testosterone. It figures."

I shut up, my palms sweaty and a migraine coming on.

The late night deejay from CJLX FM has been playing a steady diet of Supertramp and Styx. Now he's on a Cheap Trick kick.

I'd like to request "Don't Stop Till You Get Enough" (Michael Jackson, *Off the Wall*), but I don't have the guts.

If only Kulvinder and Jugs would put a rush on their bonk and join us.

After about two hundred years I decide to make a night of it. It's been irritating, standing around guarding Jugs's belongings when we could be out there getting our swerve on.

"Don't you feel Stephanie's taking advantage of you?" I finally ask.

The lines around her mouth converge in dimples. "I could ask you the same thing about Kulvinder."

"You're not comparing my relationship with yours?"

"I just did."

"You know nothing about me."

"Hmmmmm. Let's see, you used to get chauffeured around in European cars before you moved to Canada. Right?"

"Wrong."

"Balderdash," she replies.

"Balderwhat!" I shake with indignation. "For your information I didn't have a childhood. We lived from hand to mouth. Foot to mouth. Whatever the expression is."

Luckily, the deejay slows things down with "It's Over" by Boston. Thank God, a slow jam. Something we can do where we don't have to talk.

"Listen, why don't we just go dance?" I ask.

She pulls on her bangs and looks toward the door. "No."

And that's that.

What a flake. No one in his right mind would put up with what she's putting me through. Kulvinder certainly wouldn't. He'd come right back by going ahead and asking someone else to dance.

"You'll have to excuse me," I say. "I need to use the can."

Holy Jesus. I need to be a different person, a necessary person.

I climb onto the windowsill in the crapper, stare at the dark outline of tall, rolling mountains encircling the city, and bring the evening to a halt with a ten-foot leap and drop.

When I get home it's after two-thirty. I slide through the back door and tiptoe across the shag carpeting to my bedroom.

I can't sleep. The mister and the missus are into Jethro Tull. Next up will be blue films, bigass lines of coke, and hand jobs.

Why Svetlana?

Sure, the bridge of my nose is a little on the broad side and my lips a bit thick. But Svetlana Petrovskaya!

I put on Koech's sweat top, steal into the kitchen, and open the fridge. The juice container is empty, and we're out of fruit.

I return to bed. Plug my fingers into my ears. Toss about. Sit up. Wrap myself in a blanket, then go lie down on the sofa in the sitting room.

Outside one of the hookers haggles with a trick.

"Forty for a blow," she says.

"Thirty."

"Forty and ya gotta wear an overcoat."

"Overcoat?"

"Jimmy hat. Condom."

"Thirty."

"This ain't no fuckin auction."

I flee to the bathroom.

Upstairs the mister and missus thrash toward respective orgasms by belting out pet names.

"Cocksucker."

"Cunt."

I turn on the taps in both the sink and the bath.

FLOOOOOSH.

It only creates more thumping in my head.

I hate existing. Hate, hate, hate it. Where the fuck does Svetlana get off thinking she knows the score?

A grubby lining of tarlike film squirms beneath my skin. I reach into the medicine cabinet and rummage around in Dad's shaving kit for a razor.

The blade is clean.

I look for veins in my forearm, settle on a spot in the thick part of my triceps, and start to cut.

SUZETTE MAYR

from The Widows

Germany, 1971

The day Hannelore's daughter-in-law gave birth, Hannelore learned English.

She hummed "Seemann, deine Heimat ist das Meer," Sailor, Your Home Is the Sea, and thought about Freddy her favourite Schlager-singer's manly throat as she scribbled on her paper in English so new it shredded the page: My Name is Frau Hannelore Schmitt.

The first English words she wrote on paper, the first English words she ever said out loud in her life. Water, she wrote. The cat. Monday Tuesday Saturday. One two three.

Sree, repeated Hannelore. She wiped her mouth.

Three, said Fräulein Nickel. THHHHHHHH.

Hannelore bragged in church to her many acquaintances about her pregnant daughter-in-law, hopefully it would be a boy, her father always preferred boys, Hannelore also preferred boys. Hannelore would be a grandmother in three months, and hopefully it would be a boy. The other women in her pew nodded in agreement, Yes, a boy. Good, a boy.

Frau Drechsel, in the pew in front of Hannelore and Clotilde, peered at Hannelore and said, Instead of making your granddaughter miserable before she's even born, maybe you should pray she comes out with only one head instead of two.

But it was too late. Hannelore's granddaughter, all the way on the other side of the Atlantic, heard Hannelore, and her eyelids clenched even harder in fury; her hands, curled into fists from the moment she was conceived, punched the hard, dark walls of the uterus in frustration. Would nothing ever change? When she rushed out the vaginal canal, her body lurching over the precipice, she screamed bloody murder at her Oma.

Oh, a girl, said Hannelore. She held the telegram in her hand as she got ready for church.

A girl, smirked Frau Drechsel between the hymns.

One two THTHTHree. When Hannelore's granddaughter, Cleopatra Maria Eadburgha, turned three, Frau Drechsel in Hannelore and Clotilde's church contracted pneumonia. Frau Drechsel didn't sit in her pew near the front for so many Sundays, even the gossip died, and Hannelore eventually refused to remember Frau Drechsel ever came to church until Clotilde read the large, black-framed death notice in the paper. Hannelore didn't miss Frau Drechsel's small, currant-red eyes piercing the hard wood of the benches. Two weeks before Cleopatra Maria Eadburgha's fourth birthday.

Died with her boots on, said Clotilde curtly. Frau Drechsel was always one for boots.

Clotilde's arm reached around the paper for her coffee, her fingers thick and meaty. The cool gold rim of the china cup. Clotilde could make a drink cold just by inserting the tip of her index finger in the liquid. An interesting Kaffeeklatsch trick.

Clotilde's hands can give no life, thought Hannelore primly. Spinsters and wasted wombs.

Hannelore drew a breath at Clotilde's coldness regarding the boots, Clotilde's flippance about footwear. Clotilde was sixty-five years old while Hannelore was only fifty-five, and Hannelore slid Clotilde's grouchiness into the cubbyhole of their father's oak desk labelled "old fat fart." Hannelore dabbed her shiny tongue along the edge of the envelope to moisten the glue and pounded the envelope shut with the side of her fist. A birthday card for Cleopatra Maria's fourth birthday. She put the card in the parcel on top of the layers of chocolate-covered marzipan, chocolate-covered Lebkuchen shaped like hearts, and wooden toys tidily wrapped with used crinkled wrapping paper and bound with knotted gold cord left over from Clotilde's sixtieth birthday party. More toys in this parcel than Hannelore and Clotilde together ever had as children. Brightly painted wooden eggs full of houses and animals, Cleopatra Maria adored eggs, tucked them in the back of her stinky little corduroy pants and pretended to lay them. Such a funny baby. Hannelore tied up the parcel with brown paper and string.

"Cleopatra Maria Schmitt," she wrote on the front, the name so long it went from edge to edge. "KANADA" she wrote and underlined the word twice. Once, Hannelore shortened the name to "Cleopatra." The last time "Maria," a less exotic, more appropriate name. Babies could smother under the wrong name, long names like a cat sitting too long on the face. When she finally accepted the fact that the baby was a girl, Hannelore suggested "Traute," her grandmother's name, for the new baby granddaughter.

Sounds too much like Trout, said Rosario. Kick that idea in the shins.

After the "Maria" birthday card, Rosario, Hannelore's daughter-in-law, smartly replied that the name was Cleopatra Maria, her child would not have Spitznamen; Rosario was never "Rose."

Hannelore rolled her eyes, no one would ever mistake Rosario for a Rose, a beautiful and aromatic flower. No need to worry there.

So Frau Drechsel died of pneumonia. Hannelore and Clotilde sat in the church in their freshly ironed black skirts and every so often Hannelore used her handkerchief to dab an eye. She saw others with their handkerchiefs dabbing their eyes, but not many others, certainly not Clotilde, who didn't cry at anything. Hannelore wondered if there would be eye-dabbing at her own funeral, and freshly ironed skirts. Of course. She wondered if it would also be raining at her funeral. She hoped not. So many funerals these days, Hannelore was getting tired of them. But Hannelore and Clotilde didn't plan to die for a long, long time.

After the funeral service, all the people who attended the funeral went to a restaurant and drank coffee and ate apple cake. Clotilde asked for roll-mops instead and dabbled at the pickled herring with a fork while remembering Frau Henriette Drechsel, bits of pickled onion poking out of Clotilde's mouth like the whiskers of a catfish. Hannelore strained to remember the back of Frau Drechsel's head while she dug through the apple cake, the deep lines around Frau Drechsel's mouth when she sang, the inside of her mouth, the dark interior of her throat like the wet, ribbed inside of a fish. Eyes red like an underwater hog's. The blue and white scarf Frau Drechsel always wore around her wrinkly old hag of a throat. Frau Drechsel, an old family acquaintance now dead, hadn't spoken to them civilly since 1946. Hannelore remembered their falling-out vaguely, something about stealing ration-cards, or no, a potato. Frau Drechsel had accused Hannelore's family of stealing a potato and in the time of the food shortage following the war, this was a very big deal. Hannelore doesn't remember any stolen potato, the only food she remembers is corn, nothing to eat except corn. The ground being dug ready to hold Frau Drechsel, and Hannelore's baby granddaughter four years old in two weeks. And the rain. The rain made things much sadder. Hannelore stayed sad through three cups of coffee and two pieces of apple cake. She licked her index finger and dabbed at the last crumbs on her plate with her fingertip. Frau Drechsel was not that old. Just irritated.

Time for a trip, said Hannelore to Clotilde.

Clotilde nodded, her mouth full. She popped another roll-mop into her mouth and chewed through the flesh of the fish.

The coffee cold and wet like pain in Hannelore's cup.

Edmonton, Canada, 1975

After Frau Drechsel's passing, Hannelore and Clotilde visited the family in Edmonton. The greatest shopping mall in North America. Hannelore and Clotilde were the only ones wearing bathing caps, Hannelore and Cleopatra Maria, all of four and a half years old, jumped up and down in time with the waves in the wave pool. Clotilde also jumped in the waves, her bulky spider middle and spindly legs and arms.

Plastic flowers flapped on Hannelore's swimming cap. Flapped and slapped her skull with plastic petals like raw herring falling to the kitchen floor. Strands of white hair straggled from the cap.

Clotilde grimly hopped through the short walls of rolling water. Of course Clotilde was having a wonderful time, although this wave pool was not as good as the wave pools in Germany. Later they would visit toy shops for Cleopatra Maria, the toys badly made plastic and inferior to German-made wooden toys, and drink coffee and eat cake to get their energy back. Canadian cake, spongy and sweet and sickening. Canadian coffee roasted too dark and bitter.

Hannelore kept her breasts covered while she changed – even in front of her granddaughter. Cleopatra Maria skittered around their feet in the dressing room. Noodling up and down the benches and between the rows of lockers, up and down their legs like a busy water beetle.

Hannelore wrestled with Cleopatra Maria's fine, frizzy hair.

This hair is your mother's hair, grumped Hannelore.

No, it's my hair, said Cleopatra Maria. Oma, you're doing it *wrong*. Cleopatra Maria's tiny hands scrabbled the air with irritation. She screamed. Because of the hair, because of the nasty sound of her grandmother's voice.

We'll go for some nice cake, said Hannelore as she pulled rhythmically with the comb at the hair on the screaming baby's head, and she snapped Cleopatra Maria's hair into a barrette shaped like a blue rabbit while Clotilde gathered Cleopatra Maria's orange plastic water wings and toys into a child-sized briefcase. Made in Germany of course. All the best things were, the sisters agreed. Cleopatra Maria would have agreed if they asked her. But of course they didn't ask her. She screamed on.

Outside the pool, Clotilde held one of Cleopatra Maria's hands, Hannelore held the other.

Later, Clotilde carried the tired, noisy baby against her squishy auntie's breasts.

How could that be? asked Dieter. That mall and that wave pool weren't put in until the 1980s. Cleopatra Maria would have been almost a teenager.

The fuckings of memory. That must have been a German wave pool and some particularly bad cake, thought Hannelore. Oh well. All wave pools are the same in the end. Stupid and pointless, pseudo-entertainment. She watched Dieter from the step as he gathered leaves from the grass.

She hated it when Dieter was right.

She hated it when he scraped the yard like he was having fun, and almost called out to him, but stopped herself. She stayed standing still calling out to him only in her head because Rosario was sketching her. Rosario liked to sketch. Hannelore liked being sketched.

Germany, 1971

At first missing Dieter was all right. He was at university for such a long time, but it was all right because he was home for holidays. After meeting him at the train station, Hannelore would feed him, put fresh linen on his bed, plump up the cushion in his favourite chair. They laughed at the television together. The same jokes. Sentimental.

Good to have a man in the house again, Heinrich's empty twin bed on the other side of the room – sometimes she would make love to it in her sleep, wake up wet between the between, but with Dieter in the house her mind was occupied, no time for thinking about the empty bed on the other side of the room. Her loneliness for him.

But his move to Kanada with Rosario, an exchange student he met when he was twenty-five, was not all right. Their living together in Germany, then the move to Kanada, then the marriage without a ceremony in Kanada to Rosario, half Mexican, half African, half Chinese, half Kanadian (half mongrel, Hannelore said to herself, only to herself, she would never say this out loud to *anyone*) was worse, and then the baby, not a boy, hopefully the next one would be a boy, the baby her granddaughter who would never live in Germany, never know her heritage, never *christened*, this was a blow to Hannelore's stomach that at first the doctor diagnosed as a violent case of indigestion. Hannelore swallowed bottle after bottle of bitters. Meditated in her yoga class. Swallowed and meditated, but still the pain was there, a gigantic insect burrowing through her intestines. She could not stand Dieter being completely gone. She could not stand being completely alone with only unreliable Clotilde for company.

The doctor agrees that you're killing me, Hannelore screamed into the phone, her back straight and correct.

Don't be an idiot, Mutti, Dieter's voice said. Come see the baby. Bring Tante Clotilde. Rosario could use help with the baby.

(Hannelore heard a scrambling on the phone, *I'll* need help with the baby, shrieked Rosario in German and English in the background. What the hell's the matter with *you*!)

Mutti? screeched Rosario into the phone. Hannelore shuddered at the thought of Rosario being linked to her biologically. Mutti indeed.

You should see the baby! shouted Rosario.

Rosario! yelled Hannelore into her bean-green phone. Are you healthy! Are you feeling good!

Mir geht es furchtbar but come anyway! I had to get stitches Cleopatra Maria came barrelling out so fast.

Barrelling, what an odd expression, thought Hannelore, an obviously American, nonsensical expression.

Bring Tante Clotilde, said Dieter's voice.

If I can get her out of Schönbachtal. Pig stubborn.

She's in the nursing home again?

Yes. We had a big fight. Long story, doesn't matter.

Hannelore hung up the phone and unpinned her bathing suit from the clothesline in the basement. Kanada. She and Clotilde had never been to Kanada.

Clotilde. Hannelore would tell Clotilde about their trip to Kanada during their swim. They swam every Sunday, sister and sister cutting slow, identical frog-movements through the water, heads held high above the water like swans'.

We're going to Kanada, said Hannelore, her breath short, droplets of excited water on her lips. You have to move home again so we can get ready.

I've only been at Schönbachtal a week, Clotilde said. But back at Zum Schönbachtal Clotilde began arranging her stockings, knitting needles, and wool back in the suitcase right after coffee and cake. People waiting for visitors who never came lined the walls at Schönbachtal. The halls smelled of urine. Hannelore couldn't bear Schönbachtal, couldn't bear having a sister in Schönbachtal. Clotilde went to Schönbachtal whenever they had a fight, the nursing home Clotilde's claim to space like it was some kind of hotel.

I'm moving into Schönbachtal for *you*, Clotilde would always say, I am giving you room to think about the stupid things you do.

Hannelore alone in the house with nothing but her feet hammering up and down the stairs for company thinking about her sister in the home, rotting prematurely. Hannelore stood in front of the building, far away from the smell, waiting for Clotilde to click shut her suitcase. Zum Schönbachtal, At The Pretty Creek. Goodbye At The Pretty Creek, hello Kanada.

Niagara Falls, Canada, 1971

Even the first time she saw Niagara Falls, that first visit to Kanada, Hannelore knew that the waterfalls meant everything and nothing. Everything because she was with her son and his little family; nothing because she was with her son and his little family. Her folly and her desire located in her son and the rip in her mother's bosom when he left her for a foreign country, for a wife. Not the same as when Heinrich was killed in the war, but still a loss that seemed almost permanent to her. She wondered what she would do when she got old, and could no longer take care of herself. Would he move back for her? Did he expect her to move from Germany? Sometimes she could swear her womb still missed him, the flesh still trying to conform to his missing shape. But then Cleopatra Maria.

But you can hardly see the water, Hannelore grumbled from the back seat, her back crinkled with pain, her knees stiff as rods. They don't look like in the pictures.

Imagine Rosario claiming the front seat for herself, lying that the back seat made her carsick, while Hannelore had to sit jammed like a squeeze-box in the back. The baby stinking like dirty diapers.

How can I see *any* waterfall with all that mist in the way? Hannelore said.

Rosario looked at Dieter. Hannelore read Rosario's contempt like this morning's newspaper.

Wait, said Dieter.

And the most important thing Hannelore and Clotilde noticed about Kanada on that very first trip was the Falls – Niagara Falls were the only thing they noticed because everything else you could get in Germany and of better quality, but in Germany you could never find these wondrous, monstrous Falls, the bright green old forest and wilderness framing them. The forests were less dense in Germany however. These forests could do with a cleaning.

Monstrous, said Clotilde, baby Cleopatra Maria vomiting peacock blue onto the napkin on Clotilde's shoulder.

Yes, monstrous, said Hannelore.

Hannelore watched the Falls for five minutes that time. Stared at the water rushing and licking over the rim of the cliff, thick on the rocks.

Yes, they are wonderful, said Hannelore, and she had a sad pain in her belly.

We can come back again, said Dieter.

Very nice, sehr schön, said Hannelore asleep, her mind a maple leaf on the surface of the water, slipping over the sleepy edge. A maple leaf like on the Kanadian flag. Yes, she liked Kanada very much. The leaf on the water asleep before the prodigious drop. Maybe liking Kanada was like having an infection. So sleepy.

Hannelore noticed the brown pools of foam frothing on the shores at the bottom of Niagara Falls. She saw the seagulls collected like mosquitoes settle and swim and fly on the water. Dieter told her that some seagulls use projectile vomit as a defence against predators.

We don't really need that information, Dieter, sang out Rosario.

Kanada has such a beautiful landscape, Hannelore said. And what an interesting detail about seagulls. Such a smart boy.

Not *all* seagulls, Mama, said Dieter. Proud of his knowledge.

In the front seat of the car Rosario sneered: "Only if you want to, Dieter." Rosario wanted to stab her fingers into her husband's eyes. Rosario could understand the attraction of the water, the overwhelming sight of the water pouring over the edge, the animal roar of the river. But she could not take Mutti's I'm-too-old-to-think-for-myself act. Or how her husband suddenly became ten years old when his mother was in the room. Rosario had seen her mother-in-law crack walnuts apart with her bare hands when Dieter wasn't around. A German Hausfrau thing. Not like Rosario, who believed in grabbing the men by the ears and kickin' 'em in the ass.

That time Hannelore and Clotilde's plane tickets said two weeks. They stayed two and a half months. Their first visit to Kanada, Toronto, so exciting, maybe the apartment was a little small for four adults, a healthy baby, and Waldmann the dachshund, but Hannelore did the cooking and cleaning, the apartment needed severe cleaning, the place hurt Hannelore, it was so filthy. Clotilde monitored the laundry, the tons of dirty diapers. So she accidentally washed Rosario's red silk brassiere with the diapers, pink a much more festive colour for a baby's bottom, nicht?

And how Rosario *wasted* food. Threw out perfectly good grease, bones with meat and fat still sticking to them, toast crumbs that were more crusts than crumbs. Hannelore and Clotilde had never witnessed such *waste* in their lives.

Dieter and Rosario, mostly Rosario, told them to go back home to Germany. She could take care of the baby fine by herself now.

Don't they have lives? asked Rosario, her hands on her slim hips, slim enough for bright red hip-huggers, pregnancy weight almost entirely gone, her hair in a deliciously frothy afro.

No, said Dieter.

Dieter stirred marble cake batter with a wooden spoon and let Waldmann the dachshund lick flour and grains of sugar from his fingers and bare toes. Marble cake on Sunday afternoon calmed Dieter. Helped him get ready for the week. Dieter hadn't been allowed in the kitchen for two and a half months, Men Not Allowed, said Hannelore. He missed the feeling of batter under his fingernails, Rosario missed the feel of her bare feet on the floor. No Bare Feet In The House, pouted Hannelore's soggy Hausfrau frown.

Rosario wove Kleenexes between her toes and began to paint her toenails "Foxy red." The first chance in two and a half months to paint her nails whatever slutty colour she wanted. She sniffed the fumes from the polish luxuriously. Put her feet up on the kitchen table next to Dieter's bowl of batter and wiggled her toes. After she'd finished her toes, she would start her canvas. The subject would be Hannelore.

ROBERT EDISON SANDIFORD

from **Sand for Snow**

A Caribbean-Canadian Chronicle

The Breadfruit and the Maple Leaf

These are the good days.

I wake up before the sun. Put on my sweats, an old, holey T-shirt and a blue-jeans cap. Long socks and running shoes. A glass or two of water, then I'm out the door.

It's Saturday. I pull on my grass-stained gloves. Although it doesn't deter me – I hardly notice 'til the work is done – my hands blister easily.

I start by chopping the wild cane that grows from the property next door onto our yard. The machete is rusty dull. I hack away like a man with murderous intent.

I'm building up a sweat. But there's something liberating in the release of force it takes to cut the cane. Pile the stocks for garbage.

I roll out the lawnmower. Fill 'er up with gas. Set the speed (between the tortoise and the hare) and pull the cord. I'm off.

The grass is tall, thick, and dewy. I drag the lawnmower back and forth. I watch for frogs and centipedes.

The frogs usually leap out of the way when they hear me coming, but the thought of mowing over one makes me superstitious. Centipedes, I consider cousins to scorpions. Nuff said.

A couple of branches of our coconut tree are heavy. I call out to The Mrs.; she's up washing down the countertops in the kitchen. I'd like to take some coconuts to our neighbour, who shares his carrots and beets and seasoning with us. The Mrs. reminds me of what my Mom has to get, that we promised to bring her coconut water when we go to Montreal. She says they're not ripe anyway. I never seem to be able to tell. Neither colour nor size is indicative to me. The land is different in Barbados, the soil, the mud, than that of Canada. A bread-fruit tree is not a maple tree, of course. But the land is also the same. You work it. It yields. The richer it is with your blood, sweat, tears, and manure, the sweeter the bounty, the more difficult it is for the land to deny you.

I can see the sun through the leaves of the almond tree; the clouds are dissipating. Early o'clock, and it's already steamy. I sit to rest.

Dad had a green thumb. He loved plants. He kept them in his classroom at school, built himself a hothouse, spent endless summer days growing okra, bonavist, plums, Macintosh apples.

When he became too ill to tend our garden, my Mom switched from being a reaper to a sower. It was an act of survival. As if keeping the garden going from season to season could help keep Dad. Or them both. He used to remind us necessity was the mother of invention.

Dad will pace our backyard while my Mom digs the earth. Sometimes, for long stretches, he'll stand beside her, staring at the grass.

I remember watering the garden for him when I was eight or nine, discussing how much sweet corn to plant with her after I moved to Barbados.

The memory makes me smile. I look around. There are still weeds to pull.

And these are the good days, the too few happy days – the days I know exactly who I am, where I'm at and why, and what I have to do to carry on.

September 1

KEN WIWA

Preface to **In the Shadow of a Saint**

A Son's Journey to Understand His Father's Legacy

"What we call the beginning is often the end / And to make an end is to make a beginning. The end is where we start from."
– T.S. Eliot, *Four Quartets*

My father. Where does he end and where do I begin? I seem to have spent my whole life chasing his shadow, trying to answer the questions that so many fathers pose to their sons. Is my life predetermined by his? My future defined by my past? Is his story repeating itself through me, or am I the author of my own fate? Is he my father, or am I his son? Where does he end and where do I begin?

I was always my father's son. His influence was visible in just about everything I did: my career, the woman I chose to marry, why I shortened my name, the books I read, the way I speak, the way I write, my politics. I used to fantasize about his death, imagining it as the moment when I would finally be free to be my own man, to make my own way in life without having to consider how he would react.

He was hanged in Nigeria on November 10, 1995. On the morning of his execution, he was taken from his prison cell in a military camp in Port Harcourt, on the southern coast of Nigeria, and driven under armed escort to a nearby prison. It took five attempts to hang him. His corpse was dumped in an unmarked grave; acid was poured on his remains and soldiers posted outside the cemetery.

Ken Saro-Wiwa's execution triggered a tidal wave of outrage that swept around the world. John Major, then British prime minister, described my father's execution as "judicial murder" and the military tribunal that sentenced him to death as a "fraudulent trial, a bad verdict, an unjust sentence." Nelson Mandela declared that "this heinous act by the Nigerian authorities flies in the face of appeals by the world community for a stay of execution." World figures, including Bill Clinton and the Queen, joined the worldwide condemnation of Nigeria's military dictator, General Sani Abacha. Nigeria was suspended from the Commonwealth; countries recalled their diplomats, and there were widespread calls for economic sanctions. There were candlelit vigils and demonstrations outside Nigerian embassies and at Shell Oil stations and offices. My father's death was front-page news around the world. Letters and tributes poured in from every continent, and Ken Saro-Wiwa was canonized in hastily prepared obituaries that were often littered with errors. A man whom few people had heard of twenty-four hours earlier was suddenly invested with a mythic quality, and his campaign against Shell Oil and a ruthless military regime was being touted as a morality tale for the late twentieth century.

But there were ugly footnotes to the saga. The quicklime had barely calcified around my father's bones when dissenting voices began to question the public's perception of Ken Saro-Wiwa. In *The Times*, one commentator wrote, "People are comparing Ken Saro-Wiwa to Steve Biko, which of course he isn't." A society columnist in *The Sunday Times* insisted that "Ken Saro-Wiwa may have got the short end of the stick but he was no angel." Shell Oil, the company my father had accused of devastating the environment and abusing the human rights of our people, responded to questions about its role in the affair by launching a public-relations campaign that spread doubts about his character and his reputation. The multinational distanced itself from the execution, insisting that it was being used as a scapegoat to deflect attention from the real issues in the trial. In a television interview, the head of its Nigerian operations claimed that Ken Saro-Wiwa had been executed for murder.

General Abacha declared war against Ken Saro-Wiwa, spending $10 million to counter the negative publicity his regime was attracting because of the execution. Washington lobbyists and public-relations consultants were hired to sell the line that Ken Saro-Wiwa had incited his followers to commit murder. An advertisement in the *Washington Post* graphically illustrated the sequence of events leading up to the trial and the execution. In London, the Nigerian High Commission took space in *The Times* to explain "the truth about Ken Saro-Wiwa." Newspaper editors were pressed to report "the other side of the story," and in *The Guardian*, where I was working at the time, one of my father's former associates described him as a "habitual liar." *Punch* magazine claimed that Ken Saro-Wiwa had duped gullible liberals and had used his friends in the media to "fool the world."

The ideas and ideals that my father had championed were almost relegated to the side as his name, his life and his death were manipulated to service all kinds of agendas. Depending on where you stood, Ken Saro-Wiwa was either a devil or a saint.

Ken Saro-Wiwa was best known in Nigeria as a fearless newspaper columnist who won admirers and attracted powerful enemies for his trenchant criticisms of the country's military dictators and power brokers. He was a prodigious writer with twenty-five books to his name, and he also wrote, produced and directed the country's most popular sitcom. He was a successful businessman too, developing an extensive property portfolio and building a retail business from nothing. He was a man of many parts, and was variously described as a poet, a writer, an environmentalist, a businessman and a Nobel Prize nominee. He left behind a complicated personal and political legacy, and I, his first son and namesake, was expected to carry on from where he had left off.

I once wrote to him complaining about how his life had restricted my choices. He had just been arrested for what turned out to be the final time, and I was venting my resentment at having to give up my life to try to save his. He wrote back suggesting it was a shame that children couldn't choose their parents. I didn't understand what he meant by that, and it was only after he was executed that I began to appreciate what he had tried to tell me.

Nigeria should be God's own country in Africa. Spread over a million square kilometres in West Africa, it is richly endowed with mineral and human resources. It is the sixth-largest producer of crude oil in the world, and it has one of the largest deposits of natural gas – which will be the prime energy source for the twenty-first century. With a population of more than 100 million, it is the largest country in Africa. One in six Africans and one in ten blacks are Nigerian. It ought to be the pride of the black man, but despite earning an estimated $600 billion from oil since 1960, Nigeria has one of the lowest per capita incomes in the world and external debts of $50 billion. Most depressing of all is that unlike many oil-rich nations, Nigeria has little to show for its wealth. Its infrastructure is prehistoric, overwhelmed and poorly maintained. Many of the roads are potholed death traps, and the telephone system is notoriously inefficient, almost useless by Western standards. There are frequent power shortages and virtually no running water. Public services are chronically inefficient and undercapitalized. Schools and universities are underfunded and in a state of permanent neglect; teachers and lecturers are poorly paid, if on time. Nigerians routinely die of treatable diseases like malaria and tuberculosis, while AIDS and stress-related illnesses stalk the collective health of the nation. Most hospitals would be best described as mortuaries; simple and routine operations are often a matter of life and death. Infant mortality is among the highest in the world, and life expectancy is only fifty-four and falling. Life in Nigeria is nasty, brutish and short, as my father often used to say (paraphrasing Rousseau).

Nigeria is a deeply troubled country, a volatile land divided along ethnic, economic, political and religious fault lines and tottering, as the title of one of my father's collections of essays describes, "on the brink of disaster."

Since gaining independence in 1960, Nigeria has been in the tight grip of a clique of religious leaders, traditional rulers; ruthless military despots; corrupt, grasping and nepotistic businessmen; greedy multinationals and influential foreigners. This untouchable elite of multi-millionaires and -billionaires, almost exclusively male, has profited from a system that falls somewhere between a feudal, conservative system of patronage and the unregulated opportunism of the Wild West. This system, which has been variously described as a lootocracy or a kleptocracy, guaranteed its beneficiaries fast and easy returns; 99 per cent of the country's wealth is in the hands of a minority. The elites have grown fat on the lack of accountability in government and in the absence of an ethos or understanding of public service. The private immorality of the few has crushed the notion of public morality in its remorseless maw, stripping the country of its assets and bleeding it dry. Unborn generations of Nigerians have been saddled with the burden of a huge external debt, the country's future mortgaged to foreign banks by leaders who were too preoccupied with amassing their own wealth to care about the costs and consequences for the people.

When my father founded the Movement for the Survival of the Ogoni People (MOSOP) in 1990, he saw it as a vehicle to "mobilize the Ogoni people and empower them to protest against the devastation of their environment by Shell, and their denigration and dehumanisation by Nigeria's military dictators." He had modest expectations of what he conceived as a non-violent, grassroots organization, but MOSOP so caught the popular imagination that three hundred thousand of our people, three out of every five Ogoni, came out in support of the aims and ideals of the movement during a protest march on January 4, 1993. That day, in what was a peaceful demonstration, the Ogoni declared Shell *persona non grata* until it paid back rents and cleaned up the environment. A people who had a reputation for being lazy and docile had rediscovered its voice, and my father saw that as the greatest achievement of his life. He maintained that if he had died that day, he would have died a happy man.

Less than two years later, he was dead.

On May 21, 1994, four chiefs, including my uncle and a founding member of MOSOP, were brutally murdered during a riot in Ogoni. That night, my father was arrested at his home in Port Harcourt. The following day, the military administrator of Rivers State, Lt. Col. Dauda Komo, held a press conference blaming the riot and the murders on MOSOP. Hundreds of MOSOP activists were hunted down and rounded up. Many fled underground and went into exile. My father was detained without charge for nine months. He was chained, routinely tortured, and denied access to his family, his doctor and a lawyer. When he was finally charged in January 1995, he was arraigned before a military tribunal and accused of inciting the youth wing of MOSOP to eliminate the four chiefs, including his own brother-in-law.

On October 31, 1995, eight months after the trial began, the presiding judge, Chief Justice Ibrahim Auta, sentenced my father and eight other Ogoni men to death. Ten days later, the nine men were hanged.

I was in New Zealand when I heard the news. I had gone there to lobby Nelson Mandela and the heads of state of the Commonwealth countries, who were meeting in Auckland for their biennial summit. I had already spent the best part of a year travelling around the world, trying to raise public awareness of my father's predicament. I was aware that the Commonwealth summit was our last chance to save him. But despite intense lobbying and the heavy media coverage of my father's story, the Commonwealth's leaders decided to ignore my insistence that only a strong, concerted message from the organization would stop General Abacha from executing my father. They decided to pursue a policy of "constructive engagement" instead.

That policy exploded in their faces on the opening day of the summit, and I left Auckland disillusioned and disturbed by my experiences there. But instead of giving myself the chance to grieve, I was swept along on a tidal wave of anger and sympathy. My father's supporters were willing me to carry on his struggle, to lead the demonstrations against the huge multinational oil company and to provide a focus for opposition to the embattled military dictator. I was twenty-six years old and found myself on a world stage, blinking in the spotlight and bewildered by the strength of the forces and passions that my father's death had unleashed. It had the ingredients of a Shakespearean drama: Ken Saro-Wiwa was dead, and his son and namesake was primed to avenge his death. But like Hamlet, I hesitated, then left the stage altogether, pleading political naïveté and the need for time and space to deal with losing my father.

But even as I retreated from the public arena, I was conscious that I would have to return to deal with his political legacy. A week after my father was executed, Morley Safer, the veteran CBS journalist, flew into London from New York to cover the story. When he interviewed me, the first question Safer asked was: "Why Ken Saro-Wiwa?"

He wanted to know why my father's death had attracted so much attention when many other human-rights activists were periodically killed or imprisoned for speaking out against brutal regimes and big business interests.

I knew part of the answer, but I couldn't find the words to express it, couldn't squeeze it into a nice, neat sound bite. Though I realized I would have to provide a comprehensive answer to Safer's question one day, it was too soon after the "funeral" and I desperately needed to sort through the complicated, conflicting emotions I was feeling about my father.

I was angry with him, resentful at having been handed such a complicated personal and political legacy. While I resented having to atone for my father's sins, I was also proud to be the son of a man who had refused to compromise his principles and had sacrificed his life for them. I spent two years struggling to make sense of the dilemmas of being Ken Saro-Wiwa's son. I was tormented by a nagging feeling that I hadn't done enough to save his life. I was convinced he would have been disappointed that I had refused to carry on a struggle he'd lived and died for. I felt I wasn't doing enough to counter the propaganda and the lies that his critics and enemies were spreading about him, and I kept wondering whether the publicity I had whipped up during his trial might have panicked the Abacha regime into executing him. And did I drive my father into a suicidal confrontation with the military and Shell? Had I been so hostile to him at home that he had sought refuge in the unquestioned adulation he received as the father of our people? As my confusion and guilt deepened, I began to feel that I had betrayed him, that I was somehow responsible for his death.

When I decided to confront my feelings about my father, he had been dead two years, but in many respects, not least in my mind, he was still very much alive. I spent the next three years writing this memoir, trying to unravel the complexities of our relationship, trying to come to terms with his death and trying to establish whether I was trapped in his story or whether I could escape my father's legacy.

In one of his last letters, he had urged me to write, and I took that as my cue. I felt it was my duty to set the record straight about Ken Saro-Wiwa, to expose his critics and accuse his killers. I imagined that this book would be my contribution to the struggle – my opportunity to right the wrongs done to my father and to our people.

I mounted my high horse and set off, taking the moral high ground. I threw all my anger and confusion onto the page until I came up against the bitter truth that for all I knew about Ken Saro-Wiwa, I really had no idea who my father was.

◎ ◎ ◎

I had a difficult and troubled relationship with my father, and although he was rarely around, I grew up in awe of him, intimidated by his achievements and haunted by the passions he stirred in both men and women.

I never forgot the day he decided to let me in on the meaning of his *and* my life. We were driving around Port Harcourt and he was showing me around his business empire. Everything, he revealed, was for one purpose: to secure justice for our people. His books, the properties, the businesses – everything was subservient to his hopes and ambitions for our people. As we drove along the main road in the city, he outlined his vision of the future, and I sank lower and lower in the passenger seat. He was in the driving seat, his eyes firmly fixed on the road ahead, his horizons expanding as he outlined his vision. When he had mapped out my future, he glanced over and saw me looking grim-faced, my chin buried in my chest.

"You know you won't inherit my enemies," he said, trying to reassure me with a thin, unconvincing smile.

I was fourteen years old and I had no idea what he was talking about or which enemies he was referring to, but those words planted the notion in my mind that being Ken Saro-Wiwa's first son and namesake was a complicated and heavy burden.

As I brooded, fourteen years later, on how to handle his enemies, it occurred to me that it was time to find out a little more about this man, a man of stark contrasts and inexplicable contradictions. I needed to reconcile the two faces of the man I barely knew as my father. Ken Saro-Wiwa was generous to a fault, a charismatic man who fought injustice armed only with his wit and an engaging smile. And then there was my father, the brooding, irascible and sometimes volatile presence who was physically distant, and emotionally demanding. I found it hard to feel anything more than respect for Ken Saro-Wiwa. When he died, I didn't have that deep, inconsolable sense of loss I should have felt. All I experienced was the cycle of anger, resentment and guilt. And I was tired of the conflicting emotions I felt, or was supposed to feel, about Ken Saro-Wiwa and my father.

But once I decided to face up to the truth about him, I began to see this book as an opportunity to finish a process that had begun when we exchanged long, heartfelt letters while he was in detention. We had tried to reconcile our differences then but had come to a tacit agreement to finish the process after he was released, when we could sit down and talk face to face. Man to man. Because the hangman had cheated us of our reconciliation, I saw this book as our chance to finish those conversations. So I set off on a different tack – to reconcile the bitter memories with the recollections of a man I had idolized and adored as a boy.

But how do you separate the man from the myth, my father from Ken Saro-Wiwa, without compromising the innocence of the struggle?

That was the dilemma I had to face when it dawned on me that by revealing the private man I might find my father, but I might also devalue the currency of the Ken Saro-Wiwa legend. In exposing our heroes as ordinary, flawed individuals, we also run the risk of reducing them. The legends that were already growing up around my father's life and death were meant to inspire not just future generations of Ogoni, but also the millions of people around the world who are struggling for social justice and human rights. Ken Saro-Wiwa's life and death had been invested with a sacred weight, and the sanctity of his story carried an enormous burden. It was a crucial chapter of Ogoni history, a story that was supposed to be told and retold, embellished and mystified with every retelling.

I had two choices: I could either take the path of self-indulgence or sacrifice my father on the altar of the higher cause. It seemed like a straight choice between my personal needs and the political demands – in essence, the story of my life.

I shrank from making a choice initially. I convinced myself that there was no point dragging the past into the light. I was uncomfortable with the prospect of exposing myself in public too, because in confronting my father I would also have to reveal, if I was honest, some of my own shortcomings. I couldn't see how I would ever resolve the dilemmas and all the competing claims to my father. I decided to let it lie.

But the memories, the questions, the conflicting emotions wouldn't release me. I *had* to tell his story. I was his first son and namesake, and it was my duty to honour my father, to protect his legacy. I had to be his witness.

I would love to say that my decision to carry on was inspired by some noble quest to keep his memory alive, but I have to confess that there was an element of self-preservation in it: I was a desperate man. I had committed myself to writing something, and I couldn't turn back. I was tired and there was nowhere left to hide from him.

I hope you find something of value in all of this, because I have lived a political life, which means that this story, though personal, is also a political statement. For me, for us, the personal *is* political, and I hope my efforts to find my father leaves you, as it did me, with a rounded picture of a man who was far more complicated and more courageous than the one-dimensional figure that his critics and supporters presented to the world in November 1995.

But there is more to this story than Ken Saro-Wiwa. As I uncovered the circumstances that shaped my father, as I peeled back the layers of misunderstandings and hostility between us, I discovered universal truths about fathers and sons, about families, about people, about what it really means to stand and die for your beliefs. As I gained a new perspective on the tensions and passions that competed for one man's love for his family, his people and his country, I arrived at a richer understanding of sacrifice and its impact on families caught up in a struggle for social justice.

And once I had made an accommodation with my father's life, I set off on another quest, this time to understand the meaning of his death. The second part of this memoir is the story of my experiences in conversations with the Nobel laureate Aung San Suu Kyi – herself the daughter of a martyred parent – Zindzi Mandela and Nkosinathi Biko, the oldest son of the anti-apartheid martyr Steve Biko. It was through these conversations that I managed to find some answers to the riddle of what it means to be Ken Saro-Wiwa's son.

So where does Ken Saro-Wiwa end and Ken Wiwa begin?

I don't know. I have no idea where he ends, but I'm learning to accept and appreciate that I am my father's son. My life is bound up in his; we are one, but not the same. Our lives feed into and out of each other's narrative like the chapters of an endless book. My story, his story, our story will continue beyond this book. But there is a story here, with a beginning, a middle and an end. And if the narrative sometimes seems circular, then that is because the journey, as they say, is the destination, and to make an end is to make a beginning.

I trust you are a visionary reader, though, and hope we will arrive at the same conclusion, because writing this book took me to places I never imagined existed. I learned a great deal along the way, including the rather exciting discovery that you can set out to write a book and the book ends up writing you. But the simplest and most profound truth I have learned is that you can never truly know who you are until you know your father.

Ken Wiwa
Toronto
July 2000

SHANE BOOK

H.N.I.C.

(Head Nigger In Charge) – B-Side, Club Remix

"Bow wow wow yip-pee yo yip-pee yey, where my dogs at,
bark wit me now . . ."
– Lil' Bow Wow

Bow to the one in the white suit, the Stickup King
of Jersey City – I got lucky – Miss Ella was a little
girl when I was borned and she claimed me. It was
like that and this was like this. It was like wow
to the dark-skinned shorty in the shiny dress,
she got the floss and the flo and the itchy
shimmy. This was not Normandy where there
are many cows. This was where we had prayer
meeting any time, we went to the white folks'
church and there was no whisky on the place no, no,
honey, no whisky, and every morning round the way
we'd say wow to the crushed-can collector,
yeah, that funked-out guy we down with –
he one street off from cool now, but someone say
coming up he'd buck her down on a barrel
and beat the blood out of her – he was this close
to making Bronx Science. They should know.
My owners, my people, my old mistress, wrote me

a letter telling how terrible it was at a dance
one night when a tall, gauchy American mashed
my toe. They say I made a sound that sounded like Yip,
I think his name is P, I think his Q is – who axed
to join the alliance anyway? I mean I never seed
my father in my life but you could always see
the little negro children marching on the levee
on their way to school, blue Appleton spelling books
up in front of their faces, chanting: *Both bit the nigger,*
and they was both bad! Much later, they would paint
YO, YOU SMELL LIKE ASS, YO! on the flag
of the High School for Humanities until one mornin'
the dogs begun to bark, and in minutes the plantation
was covered in Yankees. They were polite, told us:
Non, je n'étais pas jolie. Mais j'avais un teint de rose,
and put food in a trough and even the littlest
gathered round and et. Foremost of these protegés
of Mother was old mulatto Célestine. Yip was not
her name but she answered to it when we was little Gs,
running through the bodega with the buffet that smelled
like piss. Back then my only concern was getting my
leather satchel where I hid Mother's diamonds. That
was what I wanted, that was where I went. *Yey*
was what you wanted, *that* was where you went. You
hit the curtain booth back by the Panama
bananas where the doctors held consultations,
and the suckers for cornrows and manicured
toes hung their shined-out arms, exclaiming,
Oui, mon ami, you have made a mistake,
my army don't imitate doorway ass-whuppin
systems! He said she put the money in her pocket.
She said she meant I knows how to raise flax dogs
who wonder where you at, and ladies where you at,

all the ballin-ass niggas in the candy cars,
all the girls in the house that can buy the bar,
lemme hear you say he was on the staff
of *Andrew's American Queen*, a New York
magazine, and he deluged me with poetry, so.
So George, little more than a boy, was allowed
to take charge. He shouted: At some point you gonna see
my slouch as I slow-thug toward you in my crispy
clothes! The family bitterly opposed his going into law,
a southern gentleman had to be a planter
for Virginia was synonymous with dancing
was synonymous with Yes'm, I been here a right smart
while, not *Bark and holla all you want, at some point*
I'm gonna fake you to the bridge! I mean at the time duelling
was not very popular. Everyone knew wit wasn't all
it and a bucket of chicken, you had to have game
and a platinum chain to step to this. And besides, at times,
she developed *les boutons* or pimples on her face.
Me, I got my nameplate etched in the corner lecture booth
at Cokie's, the Glock scholars taking constant
dictation. Several claimed their fathers were Sicilians
who came up the river as beggars on pack boats
selling oysters, bananas, apples. They sailed to
Paris for medical treatment. That was where *they* went.
They was a box with eleven hams in that grave.
It didn't bother me, no sir. I been dressed in deep
mourning for over a year. *They* wanted her to be perfect –
for when a sugar planter walked the streets
of New Orleans with his cottonade britches, alpaca coat,
panama hat, and gold-headed cane, he was the King of
Creation. To all he would quietly declaim, Now hear this,
it's the mad bling in my pocket, jingling, now hear me
dismiss this classic witness defense quick as a weekend

trip to Vegas, city of red-roofed portapotties, bean-shake
slushies, and more ice than you can graft to the fender
of my gold Escalade. But it didn't bother me none, no sir.
Most nights I fell asleep wearing earrings made from old
gutta percha buttons, tiny baskets carved from the shells
of large pecans, I didn't care. Plus, I had to check
on my snakes. The one called slavery lay with his head pointed
south, the one called freedom lay with his head pointed
north. I knows how to grow a snake. You grow it,
it's grown, you pull it clean up out the ground
till it kinda rots. And all night the children's chorus lays
the chorus down: *Both bit the nigger, and they was both bad!*
And in the cobblestone streets some Pimp King
of Something be shoutin', Now hear this, I gotta bounce now,
I gotta ounce now – watch it, this big dog is leashless –

THE ONE

The enormous head and huge
bulbed knees, elongated
hands and feet, don't fit
with the filed-down chest, limbs
of kindling, yet this is one
whole boy, suspended
in a cloth harness hooked
to what looks like a clock
stuck at three-fifteen.
Closer, you can see it is
not a clock but a scale,
the kind you find in any North
American grocery,
but of course this is not
North America, this is
the Sahel famine, this
is Mali in 1985, where a boy
waiting for his rations
to be adjusted
must be weighed. At once
his face relays one and many
things: he could be crying out,

he could be grinning,
he could be frightened
or tired, he could believe
he is suspended in unending
dream. What starvation started
gravity refines as the boy
reclines, the hunger having
collapsed his neck, his face
staring up at the ceiling
of sticks which like most ceilings
anywhere in this world is blank.

FLAGELLIFORM: #9

there's a blue-eyed devil winking in my soup   in my soup
there's a blue-eyed devil thinking in my bread   in my lead
someone silky-suspect-smirky been sleeping in my biped
sleeve
too long   too long
Oh someone   been
way too long

[tuned *in*] A furious theory down over the bay
One may
be motive for my strong
away

I am not ten feet tall

I am not out of my lead   *Out*

A shuddering it out: Man cannot live as pure bread alone   Lawd

I am not eat pure bread   alone   I am not man

Bothers me there ain't no plan for them peeping   neither   *Them*

Over the wall   Them there   Something vaguely Ostrogothic
'bout them eye

String string   go the sing   in a skinny sonic box

Theme song: – theirs   Theory song: – theirs too

Waddamygonna

Why am I a goner
do

Toolbox: – ours

In tool box   by order of tool shed *junta*   no tunes

Inventory:
pack of tongue depressors
3 caps of osteoblast inhibitor
length of jury-rig
bottle of muscle
vast array of a cloudy *jus naturale*

Blessed Cesspool deep in his drawer   shuckin' and rootin' and shuckin' around
Messed little Jigga-boo   out of sightly   asleep on those paws
Blessed Nigger-Less Sky
gimme room to bereave   squirrelly   purely
Blessed gone-Sambo   gimme room to keep on   creepin' on   with my shiny
crampons
Blessed faded Spook   gimme room to slam

Their *in* again Sticking their Musicks good

This ain't good

Ain't good at all for my

rib rigged up with baling wire obscuring the entrance to my

chambre à toucher

There just ain't no way [in this age and day] for either

What rhyme
with Mahler?

FLAGELLIFORM: FACT

Fixed in cold jellied fact to my knees.
After the gifting of soaps, coloured bowls, handkerchiefs, curved
tools. It's a sharp row of Sundays inside the giant
articulated trailer, under the cut-away roof.

Except my scientist is missing.
And where they punched holes, my ankles leak.
And I leak.

Flies drip phlegmy egg clusters on a large rotting
collarbone. The acres of fact glitter

with coils and shards and a dark rim of ocean. The thin roof
or tall air or wispy tarp of faraway sky
quivers with sounds.

My scientist promised and I signed
with my horns and now.
Now I am burning alone.

The sounds are whitish sounds.
The whitish men are drumming

one-two, one-two –
simple, cottony beats,

and writing all down,
the way they do.

What beats these are I think I know.
These beats are the beats that they beat before they feast on us.
My scientist tells me so.

My eyes are smiley, "buggy," misty, and "shifty." I admit it and recall
the last theorems my scientist gave me:
Yellow bean tied with yellow lightning
and, *Great squash painted with the voice of the bluebird*
and, *These are the stories and they are a swing*
and, *In the path of some moving shadows the grass won't stand up again*

O I've got titles.
It's their tales that have gone and left me,
like the wild white dogs

of the whitish men, scampering away
to their wild white dales.

I cast a peep out as far as I can
to peep the shattered dugout hulls
and the wide Negro-y hole and the feathers

inside but there are no flags or ladders
with lounging brown sea hags.

I leak from the low, slow leak in my speed muscle – on up.
I burn from my spare eye, down.

FLAGELLIFORM: AYAHUASCA

Was time to clean up our act.
Gusts pitted its red wall, intestinal
serpents no longer uncoiled.
It fell out like mud. Had moisture.
A centre. And at its double-helix throat, hair-sheen.

Tried fieldwork but that weren't
for we. The swooshing volume.
The hot brick dances. The persistent initiates
at the mystery favela festival
celebrating mystery. Sending concentric
dust-palavers winging back
across the sea as wizened rooks.

Sorted the bitter leaves.
Snorted occasional threads.
We were indoor-nigger.
Motorized by a rickety, lime-oil fuelled
flame in our calabash armour,
Amor, we said, *please, we improve, we polish*
the shells in the shea butter and the smoke-laden sap.

But our gourd machinist was under.
And the stream of inquiry chilled our pivot-needle
to a shudder. And waters roared over the lip.
Domes of mist smelling of horse sweat.

Would have defended with stereophonics:
the wailing; the painted-on lust;
the candied yam allergens set aloft
and spinning; the great dropped rock.

Not now.
From behind brightly muraled,
corrugated tin, an irregular beating
fell out on the dirt street. Round, large,
like a severed head.

Pulled on the vine and it buckled
the fine mesh.

The braided snakes. The irons.
The sudden wave. The hackles. The crime.

MOTION

GIRL

for Jennifer

I remember when we used to play
Black and white barbies at the old house
The bottom floor stored a dollhouse,
lots of clothes, and homemade
outfits.
We danced in the basement
held annual beauty pageants
sat on the roof and ate
cupcakes and fruits.
I held you as you climbed or
you held me, but
none of us ever fell.
We sat in the sun.
We dreamed of life,
made grand plans of
apartments, husbands and
boyfriends.
Chose children's names
and superstar
spouses,
We sold junk on the curb.
Made concoctions of
cream, water and grease

braided tightly knitted hair,
tried on eye shadow.
Talked about boys,
cried when the bleeding came.
I envied your style,
confidence
daring.
I prided in the title
"best friend."
I laughed loudly at jokes,
shared in private codes –
whispered "*the beans are in the can . . .*"
when parental ears
threatened to
capture our secrets like
big pitchers.

We grew, danced,
walked, late nites
sweated in basement
parties
wrote notes
complained
fought
rewound funny parts
in videos –
over and over
and over again.
Grabbed our sides
rolled on floors
gave high-fives,

Said goodbye.

I-LAND

give me the sun so my skin'll get browner
pass me the pen so I can make my first rhyme of the morning
my consciousness dawns with the season
the itching in my fingers tells me that I've got a reason
to take a trip to the nearest bus station
get my body moving cause my mind's revelating
that's called a motion, like the ocean
I'm moving congregations of the bowers
while the Hip Hop sways
so take it to the limit as we fly
you gots to get high
cause you never know when you're gonna go
life's a bitch
the rich get rich while the poor get none
I gotta reach to the island sun
I sing *Day-O*
cause me wan go home
but I don't have to roam if I can use my dome
emancipation on the nation of the islands
my land, *seen*
I gonna take it to the Caribbean . . .

Sad to say
I'm on my way
and I won't be gone for many a day
I feel my heart is down
I'm running around
Gotta reach to the place
where the peeps are brown . . .

the Black faces
shining with the traces
of Mother's contribution to the nu black races
the ancients have multiplied
peopled the earth
I'm here to make you aware that you're on my turf
I get real sick and tired of the fraud-out folks
and if I had a bit a cash I'd ship them out in boats
back to the lands of the ice and snow
while I bite into the skin of a sweet mango
the sandy beaches,
breezes through the trees bring me peace
with the natural mystic blowing through the air
and I release
it's a *positive vibration-yeah!*
irie ites
cause my mind is on the night
warm winds bring the ease from the pain and strife
I'm at one with my surroundings
bring me back to life
strive, rise and seek in the deep blue skies
as I move and view the world with the true black eyes . . .

I'm
Glad to say

I'm on my way
tho' I won't be gone for many a day
I feel my heart is down
I'm running around
Gotta reach to the place
where the peeps are brown . . .

WAYDE COMPTON

LEGBA, LANDED

he crossed, the border
line in a northern corner

four
cardinal points
for

a better over there. created a here.

one foot in A one foot in a
merica. Canada.

one Negro,
liminal.
limped
a

cross
clutching a crutch
a sliver of a quest
a lining of silver
a sparkle of meridian

a severed scent
a razorous rain
a glade
a terrain
a blame

a strait razorous border. he
reached for a me
to be
real
real
real enough to re
treat into a tree
for the forests he could see
he sought as he believed himself
into the mirrorous glass a
cross the border.
customs: are you carrying any
baggage? are you moving any fruit or seeds or trees
of knowledge, immortality or weeds or roots or truths
through to bluer blues and greener
grass, hash, heroin, hidden, stashed
uppers, Canada, land. no lower-class
middle passage. no flask
of flashing yellow magma,
spirits, rum, release. no fire
arms, tobacco, or too much cash.
or too little cash.
in the razor-thin space between my lines,
you may fit in. line up
and pay your sin
tax
at

the next
wicket.

here eyes bear the white burden
of watchful wardens
dutiful citizens in
lower mainlands
patrol each shade of un
white. each stray curl of un
straight. each singular hint of un
settled seeking for   home

carry me, motherless child.
my tracks are so sweet to the stalker.
Mount Zion, baptize me abysmal.
Abyssinian of obsidian meridians.
I take to the night like winged carrion.
I am sweet to the stalker.
like an ibis, stems snapped
like reeds, I fly above
reptiles and annihil
ation. forever in flight against the sky.
painted feathers brushing versus eternity.
limbs in the image dangle.
snapped like photos.
finished like the tape breaks up
lifting the race. winged
in flight
without hope
of landing. Canada
geese band together
to kill their crippled
for fear of attracting

stalkers to the flock.
they peck.
a mess of splintered feathers.
hollowed bones.
shattered limbs.
frenzy toward the nest of night.
death.
no.
rest.
I am sweet to the prey.
my only thought: I fly on,
on, my sky home,
home

DECLARATION OF THE HALFRICAN NATION

hazel's so definitive, is the window
half open or half closed? is a black
rose natural? is it indigenous to this
coast? my grammar teacher said a semi-
colon is just a gutless colon; yellow. coconuts get eaten from the inside, the sweetness
and light from the milk and the flesh, not
the husk, so skull-like. one
friend said she's white except
for having this brown skin and sometimes she forgets it until a mirror shatters
that conclusion casting blackward glances side-
ways, askance processions of belonging, possession. mirrors walk
on two legs too sometimes, saying hello to you cause
you are brown
as we pass. what is britannia
to me? one three continents removed
from the scenes my mothers loved,
misty grove, english rose,
what is britannia to me?
ain't no negroes on the tv shows we
produced in playground theatres; now

there's so many on screen a white acquaintance of mine
thought the us population was half
black! one drop rules aside and all
things being equal, I'd say that signifies
an inexorable triumph of mlk's dream. we number a dozen percent, in fact, south
of the border; in canada, I really couldn't
begin to guess our numbers crunching
through the snow on shoes of woven
koya. black hippies; black punk rockers;
black goths with white masks *literally*
multiply like flesh-eating bacteria on the west coast. racism
is a disease, the ministry decrees to me in my bus seat
from an ad, and I could add
that this is just the latest stage in race management. canada all
in a rush to recruit more brown whites; entre-
preneurs only, no more slaves or railroad builders,
iron chinks or tempered niggers. the wages
of empire have yet to be spilled. oka. all
I halfta do is spell it and the settled snow shivers. one settler,
one bullet, south africans sang, palestinians sing; the tune
is boomin. is the mention
of bullets too american? the best way
anyone ever referred to me as mixed-race was a jamaican
woman who said, *I notice you're touched*. to
me sounded like she meant by the hand of god
(or the god of hands), and not the tar brush. made me
feel like a motherless child a long, long way
from my home. feel like history got me
by the throat. sometimes I feel like frantz fanon's ghost
is kickin back with a coke and rum having
a good chuckle at all this, stirring in the tears, his work
done, lounging with the spirits. oh, all

my fellow mixed sisters and brothers let us mount
an offensive for our state. surely something
can be put together from the tracts, manifestos, auto-
biographies, ten-point programs, constitutions, and historical
claims. I know more than enough who've ex-
pressed an interest in dying on the wire just for the victory
of being an agreed-upon proper noun

TO POITIER

In the age of the generation that birthed me,
a new thing called "the black leading man" was born,
and one man, the only man, *the* man, our man

Mister

Poitier was the one, the only, the international
ambassador of Integration for the Black Diaspora, the representative
of every black on the planet. Like Atlas, Sidney,

you took the weight
of their fear
of a black planet
on your shoulders,
and got to get with Katharine Houghton to boot. You,

Sidney, in *Blackboard Jungle*, were the unironic Negro
of yore, the soothsayer oozing "Can't we all just get along?"
as you got over.

You, Sidney, were the one-and-only, lonely-at-the-top, shining
example, the exception
to every stereotype, the original black-face-in-a-high-place, an ace

of spades sent to trump
and placate the Great
Unintegrated ingrates at the gate.

You, Sidney, dark, nappy and representative,
fluent and fine,
were all of us at once;
his, hers, theirs, ours, and mine.

You were cool and stoical enough
not to throttle Tony Curtis
after being chained to him for ninety minutes.

You colonized England in reverse, teaching
a classroom full of cockney racists
how to speak BBC English.

You came to dinner and ate your fill. *Veni, vidi, vici*:
you came, they saw, and we got to move to the suburbs.

Sidney: I am a creation of the *Guess Who's Coming to Dinner?*-
generation,
of the post-first-on-screen-interracial-kiss baby boom. In age and
features,
I am the offspring of those flickering images.
And the disembodied voice of me
says to the pixelated image of you –
our one-man fifth column behind the Technicolor lines,
our Ebon thin end of the wedge – this is

for you
from me
with love.

KIM BARRY BRUNHUBER

from Kameleon Man

III

I knew I was in trouble last winter when I first noticed the hairs growing out of my shoulders. The first strands, long and curly, were misplaced pubes. Now I have two fine epaulettes of black hair – a matching set to go with my legs and chest. I'm as hairy as a tarantula.

"You're the hairiest brother I've ever seen," Augustus says, accosting me on the way to the shower. "Turn around, Pappa. Come out here. Check him out." He pulls me with one arm into the living room where Breffni and Crispen are slurping cereal.

"Ugh," Breffni says. "Put him away. We're eating."

"Ever think of shaving?" Crispen asks.

"Cream's the ticket," Augustus says.

I saw a tube of Augustus's cream in the bathroom. Lye, thinly diluted with the promise of vitamin E. The warning, if it had one, would read: "Do not combine with skin. Not for internal or external use. If ingested, induce vomiting and call next of kin." No thanks. I'd live with my fur. All the models these days shave, pluck, or wax. But as we all know, fashion works in cycles. Hairiness used to be next to godliness, considered by many a sign of virility. At least it was in those old sitcoms and pornos. Surely the trend of making all male models as smooth as marshmallows must come to an end. And when it does, I'll be ready, my coat, glossy and neat, my puffs of shoulder hair, angel wings.

I slink back into the shower. To my surprise, yesterday's trickle of hot water is a monsoon. All of my anxieties about the morning's go-see swirl clockwise down the drain. My penis sings in the rain. Back out, covered in a T-shirt and sweater, I tell them about the wood lice in the bathroom.

"Wood lice?" Augustus asks, incredulous.

"Are they contagious?" Breffni is only half kidding.

"Only if you're made of wood," Crispen says.

"They don't actually eat wood. They live on rotting vegetable matter. They're attracted to moisture and dark corners. So let's try to leave the door open from now on."

"How come you know so much about bugs?" Crispen asks.

"My mother's a zoologist."

"That sounds serious. What happened to you?"

"I thought I wanted to follow in her footsteps when I was young, but I failed grade nine science for salting all the worms and I never recovered."

"So what'd you do in school?" Crispen asks.

"I took psych, concentrating on the biological basis of behaviour. But I started looking at myself like I was a stranger, so I dropped out. And here I am. Now can I get some food? We're going to be late."

I eye the bag of Lucky Charms, but Breffni warns me off with a look. I reach instead for the bag of desiccated generic flakes of corn on the top shelf, pour them into the only bowl left, a tea cup, then jump back in horror.

"Don't worry," Crispen says. "The black ones are lucky."

I dump the bowl into the sink and settle for some leftover bee spittle on toast.

"You look like you could use a caffeine suppository," Crispen says. "You'd best perk up. This is the big day. Your first cattle call. Your first taste of who's hot and who's snot. And you'll get to meet Chelsea Manson."

"Don't trust Manson," Breffni warns. "He'll steal the eye out of your head. But he's a good agent. At least the clients seem to like him. And that's really all that matters. As long as he gets the bookings. But he's gotta like you, or you're done."

It's only eight-thirty, and already I'm stressed. I pop some vitamin C for courage and some iron for good luck. "By the way, I took a message for Simien from Feyenoord while you guys were sleeping." I wave the pink piece of paper. "What do I do with it?"

Augustus smiles. "What do we do with messages for Simien, C.J.?"

"We put it in his inbox." Crispen takes the slip of paper, holds it aloft for a second, then lets it waft slowly into the bin by his side.

I frown. "That's the garbage can."

Crispen nods. "Indeed."

"Well, if he asks, what do I tell him?"

"Don't worry about him. Just concentrate on your audition. Are you going to wear that?"

"You don't like it?" I glance at my lucky sweater. It got me hired at Moore's and laid in Syracuse.

"You need something tighter, so they can see your body," Crispen says. "This isn't a flippin' Christmas pageant. They'd have us parading around naked if it were legal."

I check out what they're wearing. Breffni's baby blue T-shirt is almost transparent; Crispen's yellow one clings like a wetsuit.

"Remind me to take you shopping," Crispen says. "You can wear one of mine for now. Just try not to sweat, okay?"

I admire myself in the windowpane outside the agency. In this V-neck shirt even I have muscles. The only flaws are my chest hairs sprouting above the low-cut shirt like weeds.

"And there's the lovely and talented Crispen Jonson. You'll do our show, *n'est-ce pas*?"

The speaker and another man are coming out the door as we mount the steps. The one with the scarf grabs Crispen by the collar and teases him about the time he went on without his shoes. The other one, the guy wearing what appears to be a uniform from a Chinese prison, stares at me but says nothing. Breffni trails sullenly behind us, still annoyed at being woken up just for this.

"It's a zoo in there," the one with the scarf says, turning to the rest of us. "Chelsea didn't tell us he was holding a cattle call at the ranch, or we wouldn't have come. He didn't even offer us treats. Anyhow, have to go. See you." He points at Crispen. "Next week." And they're off down the stairs.

"Who are they?" I ask.

"The Zaks brothers," Crispen says. "Tom's a designer. His brother – I forget his name – is a stylist. They're good, and they put on great shows. I'd be surprised if they don't book you, the way Tom's brother was checking you out. They like to add a dash of pepper to their shows."

Breffni catches up to us. "They're not that good, their shows are weird, and they pay lousy."

"But they always hire the nicest-looking women," Crispen says. "And there's free booze."

The hall inside is wall-to-wall models. One of them bumps into Crispen and gives him a punch of recognition. "Are you doing the Felicity show this year?"

"Every year," Crispen tells him.

"Maybe this time we'll, like, actually be wearing clothes," the newcomer says, laughing. "See you there." He disappears into the crowd.

"You do a lot of shows," I say.

Crispen shrugs. "They like my walk. I don't know why. I never learned how to do it or anything. They just seem to like it."

"He usually walks with a toothpick in his mouth," Breffni says.

"With a toothpick?"

"It was one of my first shoots," Crispen says. "I was nervous and forgot to take it out. And they loved it. So I do it sometimes, so people know it's me. Kind of like a trademark."

"What else do you do?" I ask, hoping to glean some last-minute tips before it's my turn.

"I can't . . . there's no room in here. We have to check in first, anyway, tell them we're here. It's first come, first served unless you have a shoot today."

"Last time Eva was here I grew a beard waiting in line," Breffni says.

Thin flamingos and burly Bobs are lined up in all directions. I grimace. "All these people are ahead of us? It's not even quarter past nine yet. Why can't we tell them we have to be somewhere?"

"There's no such thing as having to be somewhere unless you have a shoot," Breffni says. "And they'd know if you have a shoot. They book your shoots. Trust me. I've been through it a billion times. All you can do is wait your turn."

Rianne is at the foot of the stairs, clipboard in hand. She's not at her best. She looks about as good as she did at last call the previous night. We make our way over, and Rianne adds our names to the list. She doesn't look me in the eye.

"I'll tell you when to go in." She points to a set of large silver double doors. "In there. When I call you. Crispy, Breff, you know the drill."

We shuffle off, and I grin. "Crispy?"

"If you ever call me that, I'll rearrange your face like you were Mr. Potato Head. I take it from her 'cause I'm paid to."

Crispen herds us toward the wall near the doors where all the other models are loosely lined up. It's as if the cops put out an APB on anyone under twenty-five and over five foot eight. A summons served to all able-bodied models. An old-fashioned cattle call. And the cattle bear the same brand – we're all Feyenoord models. There are so many of us that I can't believe there's enough work to feed everyone, let alone the other models from the other agencies in the city. I pray for a model-borne plague and carnivorous runways. A model-eating lizard.

"Breff..."

Breffni turns. Rianne is on the stairs. She touches the corners of her lips and pulls them up in a smile. If she were any greener, she'd look like the joker.

"Why am I even here?" Breffni mutters.

"Why are you here?"

"He's here," Crispen says, "because if he doesn't come, he knows they'll never put him up for any auditions he actually wants. Business is business, but they're petty like that. It looks bad for them if their best models are all no-shows. That's why I go through this crap every year."

"How come Augustus got out of it?"

"Biggs? He'd be here if he thought he had a chance. But every year, when the Europeans make their rounds, they always tell him the same thing. He's too big to fit the clothes. I keep telling him to bulk down, but he just keeps getting bigger. I think he's addicted to being huge."

"Maybe the muscles have actually grown over his brain," Breffni suggests. "They're slowly squeezing it into juice."

"I think he's like that creature from that cartoon. He absorbs all the rejection. All the negative energy just makes him bigger."

We stand shoulder to shoulder, surrounded by guys in their twenties and fifteen-year-old girls in cutoff T-shirts. Exposed navels. Illegal thoughts.

"How old are these girls, anyway?" I ask.

"Impossible to tell without carbon dating," Breffni says.

"Young enough to need a permission slip from their parents." Crispen grabs my head and whispers in my ear. "See that guy?" He points into the crowd.

"The guy with the blond hair?"

"Yeah, he's garbage. Can't walk. About as much talent as a Japanese rock star. Don't trust him. Last time we were at a shoot he gave me a piece of gum that makes your breath smell like puke. All day everybody kept moving away from me, and I couldn't figure out why no one wanted to be on my side of the group shot. He said it was a joke, and we all laughed about it, but I heard him later in the change room talking to one of the ad guys about my stinking breath. But don't worry, pretty boy," he says in the general direction of the tall blond, "when you least expect it . . ."

"Watch your tongue, C.J.," Breffni says. "If people hear you and he happens to break his face, they'll be after you." To me, he adds, "Not only do the walls have ears, they have fists. It's a small world, modelling. Everybody knows everybody."

"Payback . . ." Crispen nods, still glaring at the blond. Then he peers at me. "How did you get into this crazy business, anyway?"

"It's a long story."

"We have forever."

"Well . . . the abridged text? This girl Melody got me into it."

"Girlfriend?"

"Ex-girlfriend. She told me I was good-looking enough to be a model. I wanted to find out if that was true. So I did."

"And how'd you end up here?"

"The Faces contest."

"You won Faces?"

The tone of incredulity whenever I mention Faces is beginning to grate. "No. Manson spotted me and told me I could work here. No guaranteed contract or anything." I look at Crispen. "What about you? How'd you get here?"

"Later. I think Rianne just called my name."

Crispen pushes through the throng and disappears into the room. I follow behind him to the silver doors. They aren't closed all the way, and through the crack I glimpse flashes of Crispen as he struts for his hidden audience. It's the strangest walk I've ever seen, in that he doesn't have one. He just walks the way he walks – lopsided, two full sneakers of attitude, and fully toothpicked.

"Chelsea spotted him in a bar in North Carolina." Breffni is beside me, peeking through the doors.

"What was Crispen doing in North Carolina? And what was Chelsea doing there?"

"Chelsea? I'm not sure. I think his lover at the time was a freshman at one of the universities. He used to fly to Raleigh every second weekend. Crispen was going to school there till he got kicked out."

"For what?"

"Not my place to tell. You'll have to ask him."

Breffni and I each get a door in the forehead as Crispen pushes against them from the inside.

"Already?" I ask. He couldn't have been in there more than three minutes.

"It only takes five seconds to say no and two minutes to explain why. I'll meet you guys outside."

"Stacey?" Rianne flaps her hand at me. My turn.

Eva is disappointingly plain. She's a tanned, greying woman, wrinkled like her green scarf. She smells of cigar, and her eyebrows are pulled taut like bows. "Hello, dear. Please sit," she says in an accent I assume is Greek. Her mouth moves, but her eyebrows don't. She motions to the stool in front of her.

I hand her my book. She flips through without lingering on any of the shots. The kiss of indifference. Hope evaporates like milk.

"Very nice, thank you. Would you walk for me, please?"

The room has its own mini-ramp, raised carpeted blocks that form a capital L. I do my best, but between Breffni's advice and Crispen's example, my confident walk becomes a limp. My hips are out of joint, my arms feel six feet long. They swish uselessly at my sides, and my smile at the top of the L catches her checking the clock on the wall. I would have done better to crawl along the ramp on all fours or wriggle up and down it like a snake. At least I would have arched those impossible eyebrows, earned a story over cocktails back in Greece. My shoulders slump, my feet are broken. I keep moving until she delivers the *coup de grâce* – a curt thank you. Returning to my perch on the stool, I'm ready to be dismissed.

"You seemed much more relaxed at the end. That's good."

"I guess resignation can be a relaxing influence."

She smiles. "You have a nice look but not much experience. And, to be honest, there isn't a big market for blacks with us right now. But if you plan on coming to Greece, please give us a call."

She doesn't specify who "us" is, or give me any way of reaching them, but it's better than "Are you sure you want to be a model?" – the line one of my friends in Nepean was slapped with at his last go-see.

I slide off the stool, feeling as if I'm still on the ramp – eight inches off the ground, drunk on adrenaline. I'm more excited by this first failure in Toronto than I was by my first success in Nepean. I might have struck out, but at least I'm in the game. I push through the doors, too hard maybe, nailing a peeping model on my way out.

Chelsea Manson's goatee is gone and his hair is now silver, but he's still wearing black and laughing at everything. Like those sinister characters in black-and-white movies who find everything funny. Then he stops laughing. "But where's Simien? He hasn't checked in for a couple of days."

I shrug. "He . . . I haven't seen him yet. He doesn't really live with us anymore." I wonder if I've said too much.

"Well, where the hell is he then? He missed a shoot yesterday. Just didn't show up. He's never done that before. Did you give him the message?"

"I never got any message. I just got in yesterday."

"Right, right."

Manson laughs. "But listen," he says, scribbling a date, time, and name. "This is for Thursday. Make sure he gets it. His phone isn't working, his pager isn't working. I'm thinking about sending pigeons." He laughs again. "But enough of that. How did it go with Eva?"

"She told me to look her up if I ever get to Greece."

"Too bad. Well, don't worry. You're beautiful. We'll get you ready in time for Kameleon."

"What's that?"

"Kameleon? That's the day Kameleon Jeans comes to town."

"Who's that?"

"They're the hottest company around these days, ad-wise. You remember those spots with the blind albino guy?"

"No."

"They're huge."

"Where's Kameleon from?"

"Germany, I think."

"And when are they here?"

"In about two months. Plenty of time. You'll be the talk of the town by then. Now let's take a look at your book."

He studies every shot from every angle, chuckles at the last one – me knee-deep in snow. He slides it out of my portfolio and hands it to me. "We won't be needing this one. Give it to your mother. Hmm." He's looking at the shot of me, shirtless, on a deck, supposedly sunning myself. "The chest hair, eh? Yeah, that may have to go." He looks at me. I stare back. "Just a thought." After a moment, he says, "Oh, boy, that's a pretty serious scar on your shoulder. Have you ever thought of surgery?"

"The scar's from surgery."

"Oh, keep it then. Scars are sexy." He laughs once more, snaps the book shut. "Well, we'll have to do some testing. I know a few photographers looking to shoot a couple of creatives soon. But your look is catalogue. That's where you'll be the most marketable. I'll get

Shawna to arrange some go-sees with The Bay, Sears, the other big ones, and we'll have to make a new comp card. These old DBMI paper flyers . . ."

He rips them out of the front pocket of my book. "More souvenirs for Mom. Tomorrow go to Copy Cat and they'll set you up with a new one. Until you get some new shots, you can use this one, this one, and this one." He plucks three shots from my book. "For the front." He grease-pencils an *F* on the top corner of one. "And these two." He marks a *B* on the others. "For the back. Highest quality laser copies. Colour on cardboard, of course. They'll be able to shrink them down to the right size because they have our comp-card format on computer file. It's all done digitally now. Are all these measurements right? And tell them just to use your first name. From now on you're Stacey. There can't be too many other guys around called Stacey.

"We'll want to put you on the next head sheet. Right here." He points to a spot at the top of the poster. All the models' heads are shrunken into little boxes, as in a high-school yearbook. The top row is prime real estate. Oceanfront property. "That'll be about four hundred dollars, I think. Shawna will give you the exact amount."

Four hundred dollars is more than three times what I shelled out to be on the DBMI head sheet. But in Toronto a head-sheet shot pays for itself with one booking. Feyenoord sends the head sheet off to clients. Clients see the head sheet, ask to see your book. If they like your book, they ask to see you. And then they book you. At more than a hundred dollars an hour. The head sheet is a bargain at twice the price. It's like taking an ad out for yourself.

"And here's a voucher book." He hands me a small white loose-leaf volume with the Feyenoord *F* in black on the cover. "The white copy goes to the client, the yellow one goes to me, the pink you can keep. One of the models can show you how to fill it out. Your hourly rate is – let's make it one hundred and fifty dollars an hour to start. It's not much, but we'll top it up once clients get to know who you are. Then they'll be lining up all the way down Yonge Street to book you. Of course, 25 per cent comes off for commission."

I'm still giddy about my rate – one hundred and fifty dollars an hour would buy a knapsack full of black-and-white film. Maybe even that digital Nikon I've been eyeing for months. I only made eighty dollars an hour in Nepean. But as my elementary arithmetic finally kicks in, I realize that with a 25 per cent commission I'll be left with about the same amount of cash.

"I'm just wondering. I only paid a 15 per cent commission at DBMI. Where –"

"We charge the standard 15 per cent. Another 5 goes to DBMI as the parent agency."

I forgot about Sherri Davis and Liz Barron. They didn't send me to Toronto for my health. But my calculator is still working.

"Now . . ."

"The other 5 per cent? Contingency fee. To cover the cost of the courier service, sending your book off to clients, that sort of thing. If the cost of doing all that is less than the 5 per cent we take off, we give you back the difference at the end of the fiscal year."

"Oh."

"But enough about money. Would you like some tea? Where are you staying?"

"With Crispen, Augustus, and Breffni."

"Is he smoking weed?"

I'm not sure which one he's referring to, but I shake my head anyway.

"I can smell it on your shirt. Tell him to give it a rest. Listen, before you go, one thing. This city is the Bermuda Triangle of models. A lot of good ones get lost. Drugs, partying, women. Men. You're with Feyenoord now. You represent us. Promise me you're going to keep your ass so clean you fart bubbles." He snorts and slaps me on the back, then calls after me, "On your way out check with Shawna. I think she has something for you today."

The hallway is still bumper to bumper with models. I elbow through, going out of my way to step on the toes of Crispen's blond enemy, but he doesn't feel a thing. He's up next.

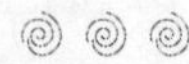

One might think being dunked on is the most humiliating experience in basketball. Not so. If someone crowns you by dunking on your head, as long as it doesn't look as if you tried too hard to stop him, you can wipe the eggshells from your forehead and jog back on offence. You can still shoot it in his eye – a jumper from the top of the key – then talk some trash. Two points by any other name are just as sweet. Being dunked on is easily forgotten. The shame of having your shot blocked, on the other hand, lasts until you win the next game. It's not only the shot that's being rejected, it's you, your best effort, erased, wiped away by a wave of the arm. The grunt when the basketball hits his hand, the look – is this the best you can do? – and the ball sails away out of bounds perhaps, or toward the other basket, the start of a fast break. A four-point turnaround. Return to sender.

I've used up all my moves trying to get past the other guy. My knees snap, crackle, and pop. No warm-up. I'm as flexible as a basketball. I stumble forward, lean backward, unable to gather my legs under me to elevate. I resort to the first move you ever learn, the one they teach you in school, the one you unlearn on the playground. The shot of the desperate and the white. The fadeaway. But I can't fade past him. I'm a flightless Bird. My opponent is bearded and dreaded, with conical calves. He doesn't even bother to swat my shot. Instead he grabs it out of the air with two hands and is on his way before I can call foul or feign a twisted ankle.

The clients, representing Punch Cola, make notes on their clipboards. A line is drawn left to right. A name, perhaps my own, is crossed out.

"Okay, boys, playtime's over. Line up, take off your shirts one at a time, then run some layups or whatever. Show us what you've got."

I slink to the back of the line and peel. The only one skinnier than me is the man with the big black clipboard giving the orders. Each model takes his turn, launching himself at the rim, vaulting on unseen springboards. Dunks, double-clutches, three-sixties. Breffni goes for a reverse layup off the glass. Augustus frightens the rim with a tomahawk dunk. Crispen draws a murmur, throwing himself an alley-oop, tucking it neatly into the bottom of the net. He jogs back into line behind me.

"You should've put some cream on your legs," he whispers. "You're ashy like Vesuvius."

I nod. Right now I have bigger things to worry about than my dry legs. It's almost my turn.

"And thanks for the shoes." Crispen hands me back my sneakers. He forgot his.

I lace the sneakers slowly. Like a boxer desperately down on points, I'm reduced to swinging wildly, going for the bomb. On my rare Sunday-afternoon forays onto the basketball court I can usually convince the ball over the rim on the third or fourth attempted dunk, at least on the outdoor hoops bent by the weight of hard-core ballers and kids with chairs. But in recent years basketball rims have receded like my hairline. This elementary-school hoop is shrouded in clouds. Seagulls circle overhead. I think back to high-school days, track and field, sixth place in the class high-jump finals. I breathe. I measure. I run. But my approach is all wrong. More like a triple jump – unnatural, three-legged. The ball and I sail under the rim, through the mesh, and into the wall. Thankfully it's padded with a blue mat. I peel myself off, leave a vertical pond of sweat on the plastic. Lucky for me the poster Punch Cola hastily taped to the wall doesn't come down. Bruised, ashamed, I trot to the back of the line. If I weren't brown, I'd be red. I don't get another attempt.

"Schmidt, Battis, thank you very much. Everyone else I call, please grab a blue script from the table. The rest, take a white one."

Battis, the other first-round cut, is lanky and pale. He's the only model on whom my crossover move actually worked. It's a long walk out of the lineup to the wall with the watercolours where our bags are lying. The other models try not to look at us; some are already reading through the script and practising the line. It's at moments such as these that one wishes for the existence of transporter beams. Spontaneous combustion. I don't even bother to change. I stuff my bag and hoist it onto my shoulder. Behind me the man with the big clipboard shouts, "Please slate for the camera! Your name, agency, look left, look right. Then read the line. And keep your shirts off, please."

The wood lice are hiding, and the mushrooms under the bowl toilet have been harvested. I'm alone in the bathroom, waiting for the others to come home. The longer they're at the audition, the more aware I become that I'm not.

I haven't cried since the day my father gave us his new phone number, and I chuckle as the tears snail down my face. I didn't expect to land the role. After all, what are the chances of a rookie grabbing a speaking part in a national soft-drink commercial? A commercial worth hundreds up front, thousands in residuals. Why Shawna sent me out for an audition casting for basketball players is beyond me. It reminds me of my humbling high-school gym class, being picked by substitute teachers to demonstrate basketball drills. They always look baffled when I said I couldn't play, as if I'd told them I couldn't walk. Being embarrassed on the basketball court this morning isn't the thing that hurts – I'm used to that by now. Nor is it being rejected for the role. What's bugging me is being denied the chance to say the line. I don't know what the line is. I don't even know if I'd have been any good. But they'll never know, because they didn't even give me a shot.

I feel like a kid watching his helium balloon drift over rooftops and telephone poles. At the audition the rope slipped through my fingers, and right now it seems like the single biggest injustice in the world.

My razor's still lying in a puddle on the counter, covered in grains of black beard and drifts of shaving cream. I pick it up. I'm even lighter in this mirror. My pelt, even more noticeable than I thought. It would be so easy. I'd be reborn, hairless as a chick. Smooth as the top of my feet. A Samson in black-and-white negatives, empowered by the trimming of my hair. Lightly I pass the razor over my chest, millimetres from my skin, not close enough to cut. Over the nipples, the lubrasmooth strip angled low. I listen to the *snick, snick* of the blades catching each hair. Again and again the razor lowers, a scythe through a black veld.

"If you're going to do it, at least use some shaving cream, brother."

I whirl, brandishing my blade. A tall man stands in the bathroom doorway, smiling. Either he's Simien or a helpful burglar.

"But I wouldn't do it if I were you. I did it once when I was starting out. It was fine for a couple of days till the hair began growing back. Ever had chicken pox?"

I nod, still holding the razor.

"This was worse. Man, the itch when it started to grow back. And the stubble rubbing against the shirt. It was like wearing a steel-wool vest. Like I said, it ain't worth it."

I drop the razor into the sink.

"You must be the new guy." He grins and leans against the door. "I've got to hand it to them. You're the one thing they were missing. Now they've covered the spectrum." He puts his hand to his mouth, holding an invisible microphone. "Black and bald? Big and black? You want 'em, we got 'em. Too dark? Don't worry, we got mocha. Fifty-one flavours of Negro." He laughs. "You know, they won't hire any other black models now that their collection's complete. Now that they've got their light-skinned brother, their mulatto, tragic or otherwise, they don't care, as long as you reflect those brown light waves, brother. Ever wonder what the world would be like if the word *light* were called *dark*? But that's another story."

I sense that he's stopped talking. I wasn't really listening. I've been looking at his eyes. They're green. He's black. He doesn't need them to be the most unusually beautiful man I've ever seen. His eyes are long and sad. His nose is narrow and hooked. You could rappel down his cheekbones. I've never seen a Moor before, but he's everything I've imagined one to be – tall, regal, Solomonic. Like those Spanish paintings of a black Jesus.

"So what's your story?" he asks.

"My story?"

I follow him into his bedroom – my bedroom – and tell him about the contest, my move, my first go-see, my first audition.

"Don't sweat it," he says, pitching clothes from the closet into a cardboard box. "You could have read that line like James Earl Jones and they still wouldn't have cast you because your nose is too long or your eyebrows are too dark. If there's one thing about this business, it's that you get used to rejection."

That's about as comforting as the thought of eventually getting used to a bad smell.

He grabs the cardboard box and tosses it into the living room. Snatches another and begins to empty drawers. "I can't believe you came here without a contract. You didn't even try the market first. The Ashanti have a saying – 'You don't test the depth of a river with two feet.' But you're here now. Best to make the best of it."

Just then I hear the *chunk* of the elevator thumping shut, and seconds later Crispen is through the front door.

"Stace, man, my shoes! You took off with my shoes!"

I'm out of the bedroom. "Your shoes?"

"Well, the shoes we were sharing. Come on, man. I had to play African-style. You know how hard it is to jump barefoot?"

Breffni and Augustus troop into the apartment behind him.

"So did you get the part?" I ask Crispen.

"That's not the point. You can't just pull a Houdini like that and leave a brother swingin' in the breeze. Shoeless Joe and shit."

Simien steps out of the bedroom, carrying the last of his cardboard boxes. He looks through Breffni, Crispen, and Augustus as he heads for me. "I know none of these guys will give me any messages, but if you get one for me, call me at this number." He hands me a business card, *Simien* in black italics, and two phone numbers. "The second one's my pager. That's only for emergencies. Like the Bat Signal. Please call me if someone calls me. Because of these jealous, petty people I missed out on two shoots already."

"Why would we give you messages about Feyenoord shoots when you're switching to another agency?" Crispen asks. He doesn't move when Simien brushes past him with a box. If push came to fight, it would be hard to pick a winner. Crispen looks more like a fighter, but Simien seems more dangerous.

"I need my messages because I haven't officially left yet. I'm not telling Manson anything until it's official. I don't want to give him a chance to spread any more rumours about me before I make my move. Why give Feyenoord a running start?"

"But why are you switching?" I ask.

"Five per cent, brother. Remember that contingency fee? Biggs, what happened when you wanted to buy your car and you asked Manson if you could have the difference between that 5 per cent and the actual money you owed for the couriers and the other stuff right away instead of at the end of the year?"

"He told me he couldn't do it till the end of the year."

"Of course he couldn't. Because he has the money tied up in investments and mutual funds that only come due on a certain date. That's why it seems like the end of that fiscal year is always at a different time."

Augustus frowns. "So?"

"So that's 5 per cent of my money paying for his second Mercedes, his apartment in Raleigh. So tomorrow, I'm going to tell him either I get my cash now or I'm gone. He'll hum and haw and promise to have it for me in a week or a month. But he won't have it. And I'll be working for Maceo Power the next day."

"They any good?" Augustus asks. "Things are kind of slowing down with me at Feyenoord. I've been thinking of making a switch for a while now."

"Maceo doesn't do any hand modelling."

"That's right by me, Pappa. I'm tired of that stuff, anyway. I want to do some real modelling for a change. That's why I came to Toronto in the first place. How can I get any real shoots if all they keep sending me on is hand modelling?"

"What's wrong with that? You make great coin doing what you do, don't you? Like the Egyptians say, making money selling manure is better than losing money selling musk. It's all about selling yourself. How much you can get, how much of yourself you have to sell to get what you want in the end. That's why I'm making moves."

"For 5 per cent?" I ask. "Isn't the extra 5 per cent worth it to be with the biggest agency in the country?"

"You don't get it. Modelling is a means to an end. You have to know what you want in the end. Breffni wants to be in the movies. Augustus wants to be a real model. Crispen . . . I guess he wants to meet women. The problem with you guys is you think you know what you want, which is worse than not knowing at all. You're all obsessed with the means, not the end."

Somehow I feel compelled to answer the question he hasn't asked. "I want to work overseas."

"That's the means. What's the end?"

"Like I said, Europe, contracts, Hugo DiPalma, Brian Chin. Shoots in Tahiti. My own line of . . . anything."

"But that's the means. What's the end?"

"I don't follow."

"See what I mean? Another lost brother. Shame."

"You're the only one around here who's lost," Crispen growls. "At least he doesn't spread his cheeks to get shoots."

"I almost feel sorry for you, Crispen. You can't stand to see another black man succeed. But, of course, you're too green to be black, anyway. Don't worry. When I'm gone, you'll be the man at Feyenoord. As they say in Ghana, if there were no elephants in the jungle, the buffalo would be a great animal."

"Well, like they say in North Carolina, fuck you. And get the hell out my house."

Simien smiles, picks up his last box, and closes the door behind him.

I hold my breath until I hear the elevator door slam. "Well, he seemed nice enough before you guys showed up. What's up?"

"With Soul Brother Number One?" Augustus says. "Two years ago when we met him he was cool."

"Great guy," Crispen says. "Loved him like a brother. Then he started getting big, with all the ad campaigns and contracts and whatnot. And slowly he turned into the back-to-Africa-preaching, ass-kissing fag you saw before you today. But on the positive side, at least you have your own room now."

"He's gay?"

"A friend of mine who went to Milan with him said he caught him and a photographer together in the washroom," Breffni says.

"Caught them doing what?"

"Put it this way. There were two pairs of shoes inside one stall."

"But how do you know that's true? People used to make stuff up about me all the time."

"It wouldn't surprise me with Simien," says Augustus. "All that weird-ass African shit. He's not African at all. He's from Victoria, B.C."

"That doesn't necessarily make him gay."

"Well, we've never seen him with a woman," Augustus says. "You got a woman, right?"

He seems to be eyeing me suspiciously.

"I told you last night. Ex-girlfriend." Then I remember. "I have to make a call. Is this the only phone?"

"Yep," Breffni says.

I scoop up the phone and take it as far away from them as the network of extension cords allows. Five rings later I get a flat recorded voice.

"Your call has been forwarded to an automated answering service." Then a pause, and her own voice, "Melody Griffin," softly, ending on a high note, a question. Then the voice again: "Is not available. Please leave a message after the tone." The tone.

"Hi, it's me." I try to make whispering sound amorous. "Just wanted to let you know I'm thinking of you. Had my first audition today . . ." I'm not sure what to say to a girl who half-heartedly slashed a wrist because I left her for another city. The others are pretending they're not listening, but the television's on mute. "Well . . . bye. Call me when you get a chance." I leave my number.

I shuffle back with the phone, expecting to field questions.

Breffni's first. "Your ex?"

"Yep."

"White girl?" Crispen probes.

"How'd you know?"

"The way you talk to her."

"How's that?"

"The tone of your voice."

"And besides," Augustus adds, "a black woman would've already had your new phone number by now."

They all laugh.

"Don't tell me you guys have a problem with me dating a white woman."

"On the contrary," Crispen says. "I highly recommend it."

"It can be very beneficial," Augustus agrees.

Jerking his thumb at Augustus, Breffni says, "Angie paid his rent last month."

"And Christine lends me her credit card twice a week." Augustus shrugs, as if he had no choice.

I turn to Crispen. "You, too?"

"I've been known to accept a few campaign contributions from well-meaning donors," he says, smiling slyly.

"Man, you guys give dogs a bad name."

"Don't look so shocked. They're getting their money's worth," Augustus insists. Then, in a television *sotto voce*, he adds, "For as little as pennies a day, you, too, can make a difference in the life of a Negro. That's right. Guess who's coming to dinner?"

"And sleeping over in Jenny's room?" Breffni contributes.

"And keeping the spoons," Crispen adds. "Now, of course, some brothers –" Crispen glances at Augustus "– sway a little too far over to the light side. Remember Bobbi?"

Augustus groans.

"Biggs was living with this two-hundred-pound woman. She paid the rent. She gave him a car . . ."

"The Mazda?" I ask.

"The same. Bobbi's doing. But when she caught him with all those other girls, she gave him the boot. And that's how he ended up here."

"It was only supposed to be for a couple of weeks," Breffni says. "That was last year."

"Speaking of white trash, me and Breff saw Bobbi at the Palace last week. With some short brother. Small-time player."

"No surprise," Augustus says. "Like they say, once you go black . . ."

They set off on a second round of Bobbi stories, but they're all variations on a theme. I gather my things from the corners of the living room and cart them into my room. It smells strongly of incense and slightly of naphthalene. I open the window and study the view of a brick wall. The fire-escape ladder is a ladder to nowhere. I dump socks into drawers, hang shirts in the closet, fold sweaters into milk crates.

Simien has kindly left his mattress. I lower myself onto it gingerly. If what they said about him is true, these stains could have come from two dudes.

As I become slowly sealed in the envelope of sleep, I wonder what Melody would have thought if she heard the boys talking about their white girlfriends. I suppose I should be outraged, but instead I feel strangely left out. Cheated, because I'm not getting anything out of my relationship except suicidal affection. I wonder if Melody would have been as willing to bleed in the bathtub for a white man. I wonder how long it'll be before she realizes she's being shortchanged. I ride horses. I don't mind the Beach Boys. I think black people are better off here than they were in the jungle. When Melody's with me, does she really notice the difference? I'm not the genuine article. I come with no pedigree of negritude. These things never would have crossed my mind back in the days when I wore corduroy pants that went *zwee, zwee* with every step.

There was no black or white in my world until that day at camp when David Wiener asked me why I looked like poo. Since then I've realized the world isn't shot in colour film, where everyone's a different hue. It's shot in black-and-white. There are only different degrees of one or the other. We're black, or we're white. Or, like me, we're shades. Insubstantial images of something real. Reduced almost to nothing. The only thing worse than living in that black-and-white world is living in a grey one, in which race doesn't matter except to everyone else. In which nothing's black or white, and everything's both. The problem with living in grey is that one grows no natural defences. Growing up grey is like growing up weightless on the moon. To return to earth is to be crushed by the weight of one's own skin.

JEMENI

THE BLACK SPEAKER

The black speaker
The fact reader
The pack leader
The morning show host, poet, and rap teacher

The word slanger
The mind wrangler
The star handler
The LL Cool J bamboo earring jingle jangler
The deferred dream dangler
The joke slanger
The myth mangler
The paid amateur
The man handler
The irreverent star-spangled banner mangler
Society's pan handler
J-rude damaga
They can't handle a

Fire-breathing black girl
With soft lips and hard facts
Who just might try to mobilize blacks

Using those same soft lips for a soft-spoken verbal attack
And y'all just ain't havin that!

Unless of course it's February

Why then you'll even pay her for her fire.
She's a walking talking eleven months of forgiveness for hire.
With the red, the black, and the green
Ignorance pelts off her
Cuz she uses her Black Steel in the Hour of Chaos Cream.
And don't mind her militant stance, underneath them military fatigues,
She doin' the neutron dance!
With a wide teeth smile for days.
Cuz she knows at least for the month of February, her rent will be paid.

She doin' the school lecture circuit
But these boys don't wanna hear about Stephen Biko, Zora Neale, or
Marcus Garvey either
They want to throw well-rehearsed Black Star Lines at the female
guest speaker.

And what about the bored-looking girl in the black?
The sad Sojourner Truth is,
she could give a what about Dorothy Dandridge
But this assembly is the closest thing she could get to a Billie Holiday.
Or at least some time away,
From her science prof,
Whose receding hairline is going prematurely James Baldwin
And is expecting her Tuskegee Experiment lab result to be called in.

I mean she bought the Booker T but didn't Nat Turner any pages.
She knew how to Langston USE a dictionary,

But to Richard Wright down all points would've taken ages.
So she'll just Rosa Park her Harriet Tubman and give her Sonia
Sanchez smile
And with a Malcolm Little bit of luck escape from
math class for a while.

Now the guest speaker's talking about Mumia Abu-Jamal
And the trials that he had.
Ain't he the guy who played Theo on *The Cosby Show*?
His grown-up dreads just never caught on though . . .
That's too bad.

Is this thing on?
Speak to your school administrator,

We'll be here all month.

ESI EDUGYAN

from The Second Life of Samuel Tyne

I

The house had always had a famished look to it. At least in Samuel's imagination, for he had never once seen it. It sat on the outskirts of Aster, a town whose most noted relic was the fellowship between its men. Driving through, one might see a solemn group, patient and thoughtful, sharing a complicit cigarette as the sun set behind the houses. And for a man like Samuel, whose life lacked intimacy, the town seemed the return to the honest era he longed for. But he knew Maud would never move there, and the twins, for the sake of siding with her, would object in their quiet way.

News of the house had arrived in that spring of 1968, an age characterized by its atrocities: the surge of anti-Semitism throughout Poland; the black students killed in South Carolina at a still-segregated bowling alley; the slaughter of Vietnam. It was also an age of assassinations: that year witnessed the deaths of Martin Luther King and Robert Kennedy, and those of less public men who gave their lives for ideas, or for causes, or for no good reason at all. But in Calgary, Alberta, in the far remove of the civil service, Samuel Tyne, a naturally apolitical man, worried only over his private crises. For his world held no future but quiet workdays, no past beyond youth and family life. Oblivious to all else, he mistook molehills for mountains, and, in fact, he denied the existence of mountains at all.

Sitting in the darkened shed in his backyard, Samuel examined the broken objects around him. Smoke from the solder filled his nose, his mouth tasting uncomfortably of blood. Snuffing the rod on a scorched pink sponge, he abandoned the antique clock and stood at the dusty window. He dreaded telling Maud about inheriting his uncle's house. She was prone to overreacting. Theirs was a singular marriage, plagued by the same upsets of all conjugal life, but with added tensions, for across the sea, their tribes had been deeply scornful of each other for centuries.

Jacob's death had been the first shock, but Samuel deliberated longer over the second: his unexpected inheritance. The first call had come days ago, after dinner, during Samuel and Maud's only shared hour of the day. Already weary of each other's company, they beat the stubborn dust from the living-room furniture and sat with the resignation of people fated to die together. Samuel took up his favourite oak rocker, Maud the beige shag chair, and the clicking of her knitting needles filled the room.

"They've always been withdrawn," she complained. "But this is madness. They won't even talk to me. Their world begins and ends with each other, without a care for anyone else."

Samuel sighed, scrutinizing his wife. She was thin as an iron filing, with a face straight out of a daguerreotype, an antiquated beauty inherited from her father. Her church friends so indulged her worries that Samuel, too, found he had to stomach her complaints good-naturedly. She took everything personally.

"Perhaps they did not hear you," he said.

Maud continued to knit in silence, thinking, One does not ask a fool the way to Accra when one has a map in her pocket. The twins really had changed. Only Yvette spoke, and she wasted few words. Maud couldn't understand it. As babies they'd been so different she'd corrected the doctor's proclamation that they were identical. Now they'd grown so similar she couldn't always say with great authority who was who. But she suspected it was her own fault. The thought of being responsible unsteadied her hands, and the sound of her nervously working needles began to irritate Samuel.

He'd been lost in his own meditations, contemplating what to fix next so that he would not have to think of his stifling job. Officially, Samuel was a government-employed economic forecaster, but when asked lately how he made his living, he lacked the passion to explain. The civil service now seemed an arena for men who woke to find their hopes burnt out. Every day, he too grew disillusioned. Even his children had become a distant noise. Samuel was the oldest forty in the world.

Yet fear of quitting his job did not unnerve him – it seemed only practical that he should fear it. What humiliated him was that he failed to quit because he dreaded his wife's wrath.

Agitated, he'd begun to run through ways of asking Maud to stop knitting so loudly when the phone rang. People rarely called the house, so Samuel and Maud paused for a moment in their chairs. Finally, Maud dropped her lapful of yarn to the carpet, saying, "I'll get it, just like everything else in this house."

Samuel stared at the empty armchair. From the kitchen her voice droned on; he could pick out only the higher words. But they were enough. His chair began to rock, unsummoned, in what seemed like a human, futile move to pacify him. His childhood came back to him, a bitter string of incidents more felt than remembered. And the memories seemed full of such delicate meaning that he might have been experiencing his own death. Opening his eyes, his wife stood before him, uncomfortable.

"You've heard then," she said in a soft voice.

"Uncle Jacob," he said. He stilled his chair.

"It took this long for them to find our number. I guess he didn't mention he had family." The spite in her comment sounded crass even to Maud. She went quietly back to her chair. "I'm sorry," she said.

"When did he die?"

"Night before last. That's what they think, anyway. He was very stubborn about being left alone in that old house. A neighbour he'd been friendly with went to call on him for something, and the front door was open. Just like that. They found him collapsed in a chair. Said he couldn't have been gone more than an hour before they found him. It was God's grace, too, because the neighbour had only gone to say goodbye before leaving town for a week, and no one else called on Jacob much."

Samuel nodded. Jacob had been a private man. So private that he'd cut from his life the man he'd raised as his own son. Samuel looked at Maud's hands, a dark knot on her lap.

"Good night," he said.

Maud rose with deliberate slowness, giving him time to change his mind. She stood quite uselessly in the doorway; then after a moment the hall lights went out and he heard her ascend the stairs.

At the funeral Samuel wore the only gift his uncle had ever sent him – an elephantine suit that sulked off his joints and seemed to be doing the grieving for him. Samuel had eschewed a church ceremony, opting instead for a secular gathering in which his friend Halldór Bjornson, a retired speechwriter, mumbled a few lofty clichés over the already-covered grave. Samuel had put his full faith in the neighbour's judgment, choosing not to identify the body, and now he wondered if he'd done the wise thing. Maud saw his decision as an attempt to shield off more grief, but Samuel himself was less sure.

In truth, he was a man incapable of coping with sadness. Since the day Jacob had abandoned him for Aster, Samuel had unconsciously struggled to become his uncle. He thought often of Jacob's face, which despite a life of labour, or perhaps because of it, had the craggy, aristocratic look of a philosopher's. Jacob's speech had even sounded philosophical; praised for his practical wisdom, he'd had a hard time believing he wasn't always right. But Samuel only succeeded in imitating Jacob Tyne's stubbornness, which went no deeper than Samuel's face: he wore a look of dog's mourning with the graveness of a sage, without irony, like an amateur stage actor.

His open melancholy aggravated his boss, for it made Samuel hard to approach. Just a glance into Samuel's cubicle gave his co-workers much to gloat about. It seemed a wonder he was such an exacting employee, with the swift but pitiful stride that brought him, disillusioned, to the threshold of every meeting. Yet he was so indispensable in that ministry that his co-workers regretted every slur they flung at him, lest the slights drive him to suicide. For not only would the department collapse without his doting, steady logic to balance it, but it seemed at times that the entire Canadian economy depended on the reluctant, soft-wristed scribbling he did in his green ledger.

There Samuel sat each day, painfully tallying his data, his pencil poised like a scalpel in his hand, frowning at the gruesome but inevitable task ahead of him. Dwarfed by a monstrous blue suit, Samuel would finger the mournful, pre-war bowler that never left his head. And it was such an earnest sight, such an intimate window into a man whose nature seemed to be all windows – people wondered if he actually had a *public* self – that he might have been the only man in the world to claim vulnerability as his greatest asset.

The day after the funeral, Samuel returned to work to find his desk filthy with the remnants of his co-workers' lunches. A half-eaten sandwich with meat bright as a human tongue, a jar of pickle juice polluted with dead insects, and the torn foil of an imported chocolate sat on his papers. Had he been a man of extremes, he might have made an attempt, at least, to scold the culprits. Instead, he navigated the narrow aisles between cubicles, and dumped the trash in the appropriate bins that lined the vacant hallway.

He returned to find both bosses, Dombey and Son, as he'd nicknamed them, at his desk. Dombey's German sense of humour failed to translate, at least to Samuel, who overdid his laugh to mask confusion. Son, whose current prestige was pure nepotism, looked at

Samuel with the coldness that cloaked all of his dealings, as if he knew he was inept and needed to compensate.

"Tyne," said Dombey, as though the name had just occurred to him, "you're ten minutes late, and taking yesterday's absence into account, that's not good."

Samuel pinched the brim of his hat with his thumbs. "Oh, no, I was early even. There was garbage on my desk –"

"That's another thing," said Son, blinking violently behind his glasses. "We realize the job at times gets stressful. That, per se, there are times when one cannot, as such, be as *tidy* as standards call for, but the mess on your desk falls far short of standards."

That was the way Son spoke, as though he hadn't quite mastered the bureaucratic language, wielding phrases such as "per se" and "not to standard" like the residue of some management handbook. Even Dombey seemed perplexed by this at times.

"We are, of course, sorry for your loss, Samuel," said Dombey, "but as you know this is a federal workplace. What would happen, say, if half the staff decided not to show one day, *hm*? If Sally and Thomas and Bartley and Fox – hell, if Tesch and Tesch" – Dombey and Son – "decided to take the day off, *hm*? What would happen then, *hm*? You'd have ladies collapsing in ten-hour lines just to get a loaf of bread to feed their families. You'd have children skipping school because there aren't enough clothes to go around. Babies dying without milk. Old folks crumbling in their rockers. It'd be a third-world country, pandemonium with a capital *P* – depression. We *are* the economy. We answer to the prime minister. We can't just drop the economy because we feel like it, *hm*? Because our sister Jane dies, *hm*? We are, of course, sorry for your loss, but you must remember our country is in your hands. We, of course, must note down all the time you take off." Dombey scratched his head and looked wistful. "And, for Chrissakes, don't look so *glum*."

Samuel nodded.

Son, fearing his role in the reprimand unnecessary, added, "That includes the ten minutes you missed this morning. Noting it down, I mean. Nothing personal, per se – it's only standard procedure. And, for the love of God, learn to keep a clean desk."

Dombey and Son nodded to one another, as though congratulations were in order. When they left, Samuel heard through the divider the rude laughter of Sally Mather. He sat at his desk, picked up his green ledger and, turning the page, tried to make up the ten minutes of lost time.

He didn't allow himself to think about the incident until lunch, when he tried to suppress his rage by reasoning his bosses had a point. And he was able again to forget his indignation until nighttime, when he retired to his shed after the obligatory hour of his wife's silent company. His shed was a refuge, a hut where life couldn't find him. A place where only Samuel's verdict mattered, and the only place it *did* matter. Into the early hours he'd sit and tinker with the guts of a stubborn radio, or a futile clock, or some negligent object borrowed from Ella Bjornson without Maud's knowing it. Only after months of stealthy repairs did she start to wise up to his secrets, berating the flyer boy for bringing *Northern Electronics Monthly*. How little credit she gave him. Never once did his stash of *National Radio Electronics*, prudently kept at work, occur to her, or the digital electronics certificate he was earning, his lessons also left at the office.

Initially, he'd had no noble ambitions for this new knowledge, but today's run-in with his bosses made him ache for a vocation, not a mere job. He sat on the dusty workbench, the imprint in his seat betraying his dedication. Just when thoughts of quitting his job had grown ominous, he forced himself to forget them. This was how Samuel dealt with things – by ignoring them. The tactic had given him forty sweet years, and he was convinced that if every man had such strength of will, there would be decidedly fewer wars.

In forty years there was a good deal of life to forget. He'd been born the privileged and only son of Francis Tyne, an august cocoa farmer in Gold Coast, whose sudden death at the playboy age of thirty-six had devastated the family fortune. Faced with having to quit school to keep his family from poverty, Samuel was saved by his estranged uncle Jacob, who worked the harvests while Samuel completed his schooling. Family legend had it that Jacob, whose unparalleled erudition had been a rumour of Samuel's childhood, had betrayed Francis in their youth. When, years later, Samuel was bold enough to go to the source, the old patriarch only said, "Rather than gouge old wounds, one's energy is better spent making amends."

For this reason, Jacob left the plantations and his chieftaincy in the hands of two incompetent cousins to accompany Samuel to England, where Samuel completed a degree with first-class honours.

They moved to Canada on a wave of immigration. War brides, Holocaust survivors, refugees of every skin were seeking new lives in a quieter country. For a time things were awkward, what with no work for a classically educated black man who refused menial chores. At twenty-five he lived off the backbreak of Jacob, a man more than twice his age. But Jacob maintained Samuel would waste himself in a toil job – what was the point of all that schooling? Within five months Samuel had found his position as economic forecaster, Jacob had abandoned him for Aster, and like some cosmic consolation, Samuel met Maud Adu Darko, whom he married one month later at city hall. No dowry, no audience. The most liberated time of their lives.

Maud refused to speak anything but English, though Samuel knew the language of her tribe. And though she hated Gold Coast, she could never completely bleed its traditions from her life, for Samuel disliked Western food. When Gold Coast won independence in 1957, they ate a half-hearted feast of goat stew and fried plantain. And though rechristened "Ghana" after its once-glorious ruined kingdom, the country would always be "Gold Coast" for them; having lived so long away from it, their country was, in their minds, largely defined by its name.

Work changed for Samuel after his bosses' confrontation. He began to treat each excruciating day as his last. Something had happened, something to do with his uncle's death and the Dombeys' crass disregard for it. He began to discreetly box up his belongings, a simple urge that after hours of work became a definite decision to quit. But after a mug of strong coffee and an hour fearing his family's possible impoverishment, Samuel found himself waiting for a sign.

It came that Saturday morning, again with a phone call. The mood in the Tyne house was sombre. Rain came in through the cracks, so that the household paper curled like lathe shavings and the bedrooms reeked of soil. Samuel lay in bed, tearless but with an undefined agony deep inside him, so ashamed of these episodes that he pretended they had to do with Maud's food, and glanced admonishingly at her every time she entered the room.

Drama exasperated Maud, who didn't understand grief, least of all in a man. "Will you be needing your corset and crinoline when you're finished, Miss Sorrow?" she'd say, though not without a pang of guilt.

And Samuel's sadness did seem theatrical, like something manufactured. Even he had trouble believing it, but he let himself go, seeing Jacob's death as a singular chance to get all his sadness out, to cure himself of the widower's look he carried through the world.

Almost as soon as Maud left the room, the phone rang. And for some reason, call it the intuition of the misfortunate, Samuel didn't answer and instead rolled over in bed. Blue hail pelted the windowpane as though to break it. Soon enough there was the knock at the door, and then the hinge twisting in the jamb. His twin daughters, dressed in identical green jumpers with huge collars like palm fronds, gripped each other's hands with a naturalness that unsettled him. Even preoccupied, it was impossible not to notice their strangeness. They had the sleek, serious faces of greyhounds, with a confidence to their gestures that had upset other children in their daycare days. They moved with imperfect synchrony, but there was something planned about it, as if they had a genius for precise timing, but for some perplexing reason of their own chose not to use it. Each had a cold, shrewd look in her eyes, an exaggerated capacity for judgment in a twelve-year-old. Yvette spoke with a mocking sweetness.

"Telephone," she said in a falsetto.

"*Tele*phone," mocked Chloe. Neither laughed.

Samuel sat up in bed. "Thank you, girls." He waited for them to leave before taking the extension from the cradle.

The only words Samuel could make out sounded disjointed and senile, everything said in a moist voice so filled with contradictions that it was impossible to place its accent. Samuel banged the phone on his palm, and the caller's voice rose out of the static.

"Alberta government were going to make his house a heritage site, gone and drawn up the legal documents two, *two* days after I found him. Those crooks, they wait till a man leaves town, then –"

"I am sorry. With whom am I speaking?"

"Trying to rob a decent man from leaving something behind him, as if –"

"Excuse me, who are you?"

There was a deep silence, a crackling of static. "Porter. Name's Porter. I witnessed the will."

Samuel felt sick. "There was a will?" He realized he'd been embittered by the fact that there hadn't been one, that Jacob hadn't bothered to spend the hour it would take to draft the papers, to think of him.

"Handwritten," said Porter. "Everything's yours."

"No."

"The house has a lot of land surrounding it. Two, three acres."

"*No.*" He couldn't believe it.

"I do horticulture. I have the will."

Samuel grew confused. "Yes?" There was another silence in which he thought he heard a woman hushing a child in the background.

"Meet me at the house tonight at seven." Porter hung up.

Samuel lay back, unsettled. He turned on his side and tried to sleep. Three hours later he was still looking at the wall.

When the time arose for him to go to the house, Samuel dressed with quiet deliberation, telling Maud he was going for a drive to clear his mind. By the time he reached Aster, it had grown dark. It was one of those moonless, country nights, where nothing farther off than two feet can be seen. He could barely make out the man who met him with the keys, though common sense told Samuel the man was too young to be the one who had phoned. But he said he was Porter, so Samuel decided he must be the man's son, accepting the keys forced into his hand. Only after the man had left did Samuel unlock the door – but a surge of nerves, a sudden sadness, made him incapable of entering just yet. He stood at the threshold, the door half-open before him, and sighed. He drove home to find his own house dim; Maud, luckily, had gone to bed without him. Lying beside her, Samuel meditated over the strangeness of the meeting, but tried to put it out of his mind. He slept badly that night, and found himself obsessing over the house in his usually disciplined work hours.

Then on Monday, just before lunch, it happened. In old age, when asked what he'd made of his life, Samuel realized he could only say he'd made it to the end. This was the outcome of his gifted and cocky youth. He'd failed. For an hour he sat in a useless stupor, seeing the green lines on his ledger as if from a watery distance.

He was shocked from his thoughts by Dombey's Son, who'd been looking over his shoulder for some time. "Tyne, this is simply unacceptable," he said in a tremulous voice. Son's glasses sat askew on his face, and his shirt buttons danced against his chest, thumbed loose from months of nervousness. He flinched when Samuel turned to him, glancing around like a child lost in a store.

"The standards call for 6.75 work hours per diem, with the opportunity for a second break in the afternoons . . . with, with, a second afternoon break only sometimes. But, as you've been informed, we have specified the areas allotted for . . ." he stammered, as though trying to recall the appropriate phrasing, "allotted for . . ."

Without his father, Son's rhetoric seemed not only ridiculous, but pathetic. Samuel wondered that he had ever feared this man. Surprised at his own indifference, Samuel boxed up the last of his things. Ignoring his co-workers' shocked silence and Son's weak pleas to "be reasonable, Tyne," Samuel walked out without a word.

The grey rag of a day, with its first snow of the year, was filled with the singing of thrush and that haunted, lucky feeling people have after mysteriously surviving an accident. He felt, in effect, the precocity of his youth, he felt like that teenager who'd bragged he would lead a country or win the Nobel Prize for economics one day. In short, Samuel Tyne was alive again.

Driving, he saw a goods stand pitched away from the roadside, the thin wood roof buckling under the snow. "Here is one like me," he said to himself. "A man of great potential wasting away under the tortures of meaningless work." In full empathy he pulled over, shaking hands with the fat Greek salesman and running the rules for barter over in his head. Seeing the pitiful merchandise, Samuel wondered if he'd been too hasty. It seemed the man had just emptied his attic, stacking his junk in this open market because he lacked initiative. Samuel hesitated, discomfited by the man's desperate look every time they made eye contact. Then he saw the dolls.

He was so reminded of his daughters that he knew at once the dolls were good luck. "Give me those!" he said, forgetting to talk down the price. Driving home, he knew he'd made a mistake. The dolls sat like livid children in the back seat, and Samuel couldn't help but glance at them in his rear-view mirror. Their sharp red hair looked like rooster combs, and they had the lush, vulgar mouths of prostitutes. The stitching around their eyes was done so childishly that Samuel wondered if the Greek hadn't made them himself. He parked in an alley five houses away, then strode to the shed to throw the dolls in the ashcan. But some vulnerability about them, inanimate though they were, made him stuff them high on a shelf instead. Sitting down to the wires of Maud's prized clock, Samuel thought of his job, and of the inherited house in Aster. Maud knew nothing of either.

When the time came to fake his punctual return from work, Samuel found himself in such a good mood that, like all men who wake from the graveyard of an empty life, he assumed his joy was universal. Taking the dolls down from the shelf, he put them in his briefcase, which he walked into the humid kitchen swinging like the happy apparition of the boy he'd been.

Maud looked at him with suspicion. "Look who's won the lottery," she said. "Supper will be ready in ten minutes. Sit down."

He sat across from the twins, whose rigid unresponsiveness to his smiles hurt his mood a little. He thought of presenting his gift right then, but restrained himself to wait until after dinner. He ate a lukewarm spinach stew with sweet fried plantain, and watching the twins, with their oblong faces leaning over their plates as though the whole of their fates could be found there, Samuel recalled their infancy, when they'd refused to eat in a sensible way. No sooner was baby Yvette fasting than baby Chloe grew gluttonous. The next day, with Yvette greedy from the previous day's starvation, there was barely enough time to clean up what Chloe threw up. It was maddening. Their haughty eating pattern had left Maud feeling lost, like she'd been abandoned in another era and the only cure was to age her way back to the present. Helpless, Samuel could only console his wife.

Now his daughters ate by rote, chewing as though they resented meals for the time they had to spend in their parents' company. Maud asked them probing questions about school, and keeping her eyes on her plate Yvette barely raised her voice for the one-word answers. Samuel was discouraged. But, nevertheless, when the meal ended, he pulled his briefcase onto the table and, delighted with himself, presented the dolls.

Neither girl moved. Then, raising their heads, they looked in Samuel's direction with sharp eyes, more in assessment of him than of his gift.

Samuel cleared his throat. "They're rag dolls. Thought you girls might like them." He eyed Maud, who deliberately didn't look his way. Her face was a confusion of feelings; unnerved by her twins, she nevertheless felt vindicated. Samuel was just as useless a parent as she was.

Chloe wouldn't look at the dolls. Under her sister's direction, Yvette gave them a quick appraisal and signalled with her eyes that the dolls were not worth the pain of talking to their father. Or so things seemed to Samuel, who was more perplexed than hurt by their behaviour.

"You could thank him," said Maud.

Chloe fixated on her plate.

Yvette raised her dark-lined, almond eyes, and in her mocking falsetto, she said, "*Thank* you."

The table fell silent. The longer no one said anything, the more embittered Samuel became. He left the table without speaking. In the shade beneath the table, he saw that the twins had grasped each other's hands. He went out to the shed.

But thoughts of the house he now owned, and of the easy way he'd abandoned his job, made him feel less rejected. He even smiled at the twins' precocity. They had a special knack for exchanging ages with their parents, making Samuel feel like a hopeless twelve-year-old.

But then, the twins had always been brilliant.

About the Authors

André Alexis was born in Trinidad in 1957 and grew up in Canada. His debut novel, *Childhood* (1998), won the Chapters/Books in Canada First Novel Award, shared the Trillium Award, and was shortlisted for the Giller Prize and the Rogers Communications Writers' Trust Fiction Prize. He is also the author of a collection of short stories, *Despair and Other Stories of Ottawa* (1994), which was shortlisted for a Commonwealth Writers' Prize (Canada-Caribbean region); a published play, *Lambton Kent* (1999); a children's book, *Ingrid and the Wolf* (2005); and a forthcoming novel, *Asylum*. André Alexis lives in Toronto.

Shane Book was educated at the University of Western Ontario, the University of Victoria, New York University, the Iowa Writers' Workshop, and Stanford University, where he was a Wallace Stegner Fellow. His work appears in many anthologies, including *Bluesprint*, *Why I Sing the Blues*, *Gathering Ground*, and *Breathing Fire 2*. He has been published in numerous journals, including *Fence*, *Volt*, and *Boston Review*, and his honours include the *Malahat Review* Long Poem Prize, a *New York Times* fellowship, an Academy of American Poets Prize, the Poetry Center's Rella Lossy Poetry Award, the Charles S. Johnson Award, and a National Magazine Award.

Kim Barry Brunhuber is an Ottawa-based writer, broadcaster, and filmmaker. Born in Montreal, he has a master of journalism from Carleton University. His news stories have been broadcast around the globe, and his articles and fiction reviews have appeared in newspapers across the country. He also hosts a nationally distributed book review segment. His first novel, *Kameleon Man* (2003), was a finalist for the national ReLit Award and the Ottawa Book Award.

Okey Chigbo was born and raised in Enugu, Nigeria, and graduated from Simon Fraser University in Burnaby, British Columbia. His magazine articles have been published in England, the United States, and Canada, and he has won a number of magazine writing awards in Canada. Chigbo now lives in Toronto, where he is currently editor of the English edition of *CAmagazine*.

George Elliott Clarke is a librettist, novelist, playwright, poet, screenwriter, and scholar, who has written of African/Black Canada and Nova Scotia (Africadia). In 2001, he won the Governor General's Award for Poetry for *Execution Poems*; in 2004, he received the Martin Luther King Jr. Achievement Award; and in 2005, he received a Trudeau Fellowship Prize. His works include *Whylah Falls* (poetry, 2000), *Beatrice Chancy* (play, 1999), *Québécité* (libretto, 2003), *Odysseys Home: Mapping African-Canadian Literature* (essays, 2002), and *George & Rue* (novel, 2005).

Wayde Compton is the author of two books of poetry, *49th Parallel Psalm* and *Performance Bond*, and the editor of the anthology *Bluesprint: Black British Columbian Literature and Orature*. He deejays sound-poetry with Jason de Couto in The Contact Zone Crew, and is a co-founding member of the Hogan's Alley Memorial Project, an organization dedicated to preserving the public memory of Vancouver's original black community. Compton lives in Vancouver, where he teaches English composition and literature at Coquitlam College.

Afua Cooper is an award-winning poet, a poet-performer, a pioneer in the Canadian dub poetry movement, and a co-founder of the Dub Poets Collective. She has published four books of poetry, including *Memories Have Tongue* (1992) and *Bird of Paradise* (2006), and her work has appeared in numerous national and international anthologies. She has also recorded her poems, and her newest CD, *Possessed: Dub Stories*, will be released in 2006. Cooper holds a Ph.D. in history, and is one of Canada's premier experts and chroniclers of the country's black history. Her latest book of historical research is *The Hanging of Angélique: Canada, Slavery and the Burning of Montreal* (HarperCollins, 2006). She teaches history at the University of Toronto.

Esi Edugyan was raised in Calgary. She has degrees from Johns Hopkins University and the University of Victoria, and recently completed a fiction fellowship at the Fine Arts Work Center in Provincetown, Massachusetts. Her work has appeared in *Best New American Voices 2003*, edited by Joyce Carol Oates. Her first novel, *The Second Life of Samuel Tyne* (2004), has been published in Canada, the U.S., the U.K., and Holland, and was a finalist for the Hurston/Wright LEGACY Award. Esi Edugyan lives in Victoria.

Honor Ford-Smith was the founding artistic director of the Sistren Theatre Collective, a Jamaican women's theatre and cultural organization, for which she wrote and directed until the early 1990s. She is the editor of Sistren's *Lionheart Gal: Life Stories of Jamaican Women* (University of the West Indies Press, 2005), and the author of the poetry collection *My Mother's Last Dance* (Sister Vision Press, 1986). Her poetry appears in several regional anthologies of Caribbean poetry, and she has written several critical articles on race, gender, popular movements, and Caribbean performance. She lives in Toronto, where she teaches at New College at the University of Toronto.

Lorna Goodison is the author of eight books of poetry, most recently, *Travelling Mercies* (2001); two collections of short stories; and a forthcoming memoir, *From Harvey River*. She has received much international recognition, including the Musgrave Gold Medal from Jamaica in 1999. Her work has been widely translated; anthologized in major collections of contemporary poetry, most recently in *The HarperCollins World Reader*, *The Vintage Book of Contemporary World Poetry*, and *The Norton Anthology of World Masterpieces*; and appeared in such magazines as the *Hudson Review* and *Ms. Magazine*. Born in Jamaica, Goodison now divides her time between Toronto and Ann Arbor, where she teaches at the University of Michigan.

Claire Harris moved to Calgary from Trinidad in 1966. Among her works of poetry are *Fables from the Women's Quarters* (1984), winner of the Commonwealth Writers' Prize for the Americas; *Travelling to Find a Remedy* (1986), winner of the Alberta Culture Poetry Prize; *The Conception of Winter* (1988), winner of the Alberta Special Award for Poetry; *Drawing Down a Daughter* (1992), a finalist for the Governor General's Award for Poetry and the F.G. Bressani Prize; and *She* (2000). Her poetry has appeared in many anthologies and magazines in Germany, Brazil, India, Canada, the U.S., and the Caribbean.

Lawrence Hill (www.lawrencehill.com) writes novels and non-fiction, and is currently at work on the novel *The Book of Negroes*. His book *Black Berry, Sweet Juice: On Being Black and White in Canada* was published in 2001 by HarperCollins Canada. It received major media coverage across the country and became a national bestseller. Hill's first two novels, *Any Known Blood* (HarperCollins, 1997) and *Some Great Thing* (Turnstone Press, 1992) were both published to critical acclaim. Hill, who lives in Burlington, Ontario, with his wife and five children, also writes magazine articles and film scripts, and occasionally teaches creative writing.

Nalo Hopkinson was born in the Caribbean and has lived in Toronto since 1977. She is the author of *Skin Folk* (2001), a collection of short stories, and three novels, *Brown Girl in the Ring* (1998), *Midnight Robber* (2000), and *The Salt Roads* (2003). She has also edited four anthologies of short fiction. She is a recipient of the John W. Campbell Memorial Award for Best New Writer, the Locus Award, the Sunburst Award, and the World Fantasy Award. Her work has also been shortlisted for the Hurston/Wright LEGACY Award, the Philip K. Dick Award, the Nebula Award, and the Hugo Award.

Jemeni is a brown-skinned lady-earth-mother-sun-goddess-word-warrior-girlfriend-sistah-child-whisper-of-potential with the loud-mouthed confidence of a black girl. A storyteller by birth and by birthright, she is a spoken word artist, a performance poet, an actress, and one of the original on-air personalities of Canada's first urban radio station, Flow 93.5. Her poetry has been published in various periodicals and anthologies, including *Bum Rush the Page: A Def Poetry Jam*. Her work is also frequently set to music, and has won several urban music awards. Jemeni lives in Toronto, where she is writing a novel and compiling a collection of her work.

Dany Laferrière was born in Port-au-Prince, Haiti, where he was a journalist until he went into exile in Canada in 1976 to escape the Duvalier dictatorship. He is the author of ten novels, many of which have been translated into several languages, including *How to Make Love to a Negro* (1987), *Eroshima* (1991), *An Aroma of Coffee* (1993), *Why Must a Black Writer Write about Sex?* (1994), *Dining with the Dictator* (1994), *A Drifting Year* (1997), and *Down among the Dead Men* (1997). He divides his time between Miami and Montreal.

Rachel Manley is the author of *Drumblair: Memories of a Jamaican Childhood* (1996), which won the Governor General's Award for Nonfiction in 1997, and *Slipstream: A Daughter Remembers* (2000). She has also published three books of poetry and edited *Edna Manley: The Diaries*, a collection of her grandmother's journals. A former Bunting Fellow for Literature at Radcliffe College, Manley divides her time between Toronto and Jamaica. She has two sons, Drum and Luke.

Suzette Mayr is the author of three novels: *Moon Honey* (1995), a finalist for the Writers Guild of Alberta's Best Novel and Best First Book Awards; *The Widows* (1998), a finalist for the Commonwealth Writers' Prize for Best Book (Canada-Caribbean region); and, most recently, *Venous Hum* (2004). Her poetry and short fiction have appeared in numerous periodicals and anthologies across Canada. Mayr is a former president of the Writers Guild of Alberta, and was the Markin-Flanagan Writer-in-Residence at the University of Calgary during the 2002–2003 year. She currently lives and works in Calgary.

Tessa McWatt is the author of *Out of My Skin* (1998), *Dragons Cry* (2001), and *This Body* (2004). *Dragons Cry* was a finalist for the Toronto Book Award and the Governor General's Award for Fiction. Originally from Guyana, she now divides her time between Toronto and London, England.

Pamela Mordecai grew up in Jamaica and immigrated to Canada in 1993. A language arts teacher with a Ph.D. in English, she has written or edited over thirty books, including textbooks; children's books; poetry, most recently, *The True Blue of Islands* (2005); and a reference work, *Culture and Customs of Jamaica* (2001), co-authored with her husband, Martin. She has edited numerous anthologies, among them the award-winning *Her True-True Name* (1989) and *Calling Cards: New Poetry from Caribbean/Canadian Women* (2005). Her writing for children is represented in textbooks and anthologies on both sides of the Atlantic. She has also written short stories and plays, and articles on Caribbean literature.

Motion (www.motionlive.com) is a Toronto-based spoken word poet and hip hop artist. The audio version of her first collection of poetry, *Motion in Poetry* (Women's Press, 2002), was nominated for an Urban Music Award for Spoken Word Recording. She has won the CBC Poetry Face-Off, and her poetry has been anthologized in *T-Dot Griots* and *Feminisms and Womanisms*. As a lyricist, she has also been published extensively in CD anthologies. Motion is an award-winning radio host, has appeared in numerous theatrical productions, including *The Last Don: A Hip Hop Rendition of Shakespeare's Twelfth Night* and *Hip Hopera*, and has released two singles and a vinyl EP.

M. NourbeSe Philip (www.nourbese.com) was born in Tobago and now lives in Toronto. She has published several books of poetry, including *Salmon Courage* (1983) and *She Tries Her Tongue; Her Silence Softly Breaks* (1989). She has won the Pushcart Prize and the Casa de las Americas Prize, among others, as well as Guggenheim and Bellagio fellowships. Her short stories, essays, reviews, and articles have appeared in magazines and journals in North America and England, and her poetry has been extensively anthologized.

David Nandi Odhiambo is a Kenyan émigré who moved to Canada in 1977. A graduate of McGill University, Odhiambo received his M.F.A. in creative writing from the University of Massachusetts Amherst. He is the author of a play, *afrocentric*, and two novels, *diss/ed banded nation* (1998) and *Kipligat's Chance* (2003). He currently lives in Philadelphia, Pennsylvania, where he's writing his third novel, *The Last Boy*.

Émile Ollivier was a sociologist, educator, and prize-winning novelist. Born in Port-au-Prince, Haiti, he was forced into exile in 1965, and eventually settled in Montreal in 1968, where he taught at the University of Montreal. His novels include *Mother Solitude* (1989), winner of the Prix Jacques Roumain, and *Passages* (2003), winner of the Grand Prix Littéraire de Montréal. Among his many honours, he was named a Chevalier de l'Ordre national du Québec and a Chevalier dans l'Ordre des Arts et des Lettres in France. Ollivier died in Montreal in November 2002.

Althea Prince has published short stories and essays in numerous publications. Her books include *Ladies of the Night* (1993); *Feminisms and Womanisms: A Women's Studies Reader* (2004), which she co-edited; *Being Black* (2001); and *Loving This Man* (2001). Althea Prince lives and writes in Toronto.

Robert Edison Sandiford is the author of two short-story collections, *Winter, Spring, Summer, Fall* (1995) and, most recently, *The Tree of Youth* (2005); the graphic story collections *Attractive Forces* and *Stray Moonbeams*; and a memoir, *Sand for Snow: A Caribbean-Canadian Chronicle* (2003). He is a founding editor of Arts*Etc: The Premier Cultural Guide to Barbados*, and has worked as a book publisher and video producer.

Olive Senior is the author of nine books of fiction, non-fiction, and poetry, the latest of which, *Over the Roofs of the World*, was a finalist for the 2005 Governor General's Award for Poetry. Born in Jamaica, Senior now resides in Toronto, but the Caribbean remains a focus of her work, which includes *Working Miracles: Women's Lives in the English-Speaking Caribbean* (1991) and the *Encyclopedia of Jamaican Heritage* (2003), and the short-story collections *Summer Lightning* (1986), winner of the Commonwealth Writers' Prize, *Arrival of the Snake-Woman* (1989), and *Discerner of Hearts* (1995). Senior conducts writing workshops internationally, and is on the faculty of the Humber School for Writers.

Makeda Silvera was born in Jamaica and now lives in Toronto. She is the co-founder and managing editor of Sister Vision Press, and the author of a novel, *The Heart Does Not Bend* (2002), and two collections of short stories, *Her Head a Village* (1994) and *Remembering G* (1990). She is the editor of *The Other Woman: Women of Colour in Contemporary Canadian Literature* (1994), *Ma-Ka: Diaspora Juks* (1997), and the groundbreaking *Piece of My Heart: A Lesbian of Colour Anthology* (1991).

H. Nigel Thomas is professor of U.S. literature at Université Laval, as well as a fiction writer and poet. His short stories, poems, and scholarly articles have been published in several literary journals and anthologies. He is the author of *Spirits in the Dark* (novel, Anansi and Heinemann, 1993), *Behind the Face of Winter (*novel, TSAR, 2001), *How Loud Can the Village Cock Crow* (short fiction, Afo, 1995), *Moving through Darkness* (poetry, Afo, 1999), and *From Folklore to Fiction: A Study of Folk Heroes and Rituals in the Black American Novel* (literary criticism, Greenwood, 1988). *Spirits in the Dark* was shortlisted for the 1994 Hugh MacLennan Prize for Fiction.

Ken Wiwa is a journalist who contributes to newspapers throughout Europe, North America, and Africa. He currently appears as a weekly columnist for the *Globe and Mail. In the Shadow of a Saint* (2000) won the 2002 Hurston-Wright LEGACY Award for Nonfiction. Born in Nigeria and educated in England, he now divides his time between England and Nigeria. He is a Saul Rae Fellow at the Munk Centre for International Studies at the University of Toronto, served as a mentor at the Trudeau Foundation, and was selected as a Young Global Leader by the World Economic Forum in 2005.

Suggested Reading

Fiction

Alexis, André. *Despair, and Other Stories of Ottawa*. 1994. McClelland & Stewart, 1998.

Clarke, Austin. *The Survivors of the Crossing*. McClelland & Stewart, 1964.

———. *The Meeting Point*. 1967. Vintage Canada, 1998.

———. *Storm of Fortune*. 1973. Vintage Canada, 1998.

———. *The Bigger Light*. 1975. Vintage Canada, 1998.

———. *The Polished Hoe*. Thomas Allen, 2002.

Dyer, Bernadette. *Villa Fair: Stories.* Beach Holme, 2000.

———. *Waltzes I Have Not Forgotten*. Women's Press, 2004.

Étienne, Gérard. *La Pacotille*. Translated by Keith Walker. L'Hexagone, 1991.

Foster, Cecil. *No Man in the House*. 1991. Vintage Canada, 1993.

Hearne, John. *Stranger at the Gate*. Faber & Faber, 1956.

———. *The Eye of the Storm*. Little, Brown, 1957.

Hopkinson, Nalo. *Brown Girl in the Ring*. Warner Books, 1998.

———. *The Salt Roads*. Warner Books, 2003.

Laferrière, Dany. *Dining with the Dictator*. Translated by David Homel. Coach House Press, 1994.

———. *Why Must a Black Writer Write about Sex?* Translated by David Homel. Coach House Press, 1994.

———. *Down among the Dead Men*. Translated by David Homel. Douglas & McIntyre, 1997.

———. *A Drifting Year*. Translated by David Homel. Douglas & McIntyre, 1997.

Mayr, Suzette. *Moon Honey*. NeWest Press, 1995.

———. *Venous Hum*. Arsenal Pulp Press, 2004.

McWatt, Tessa. *Out of My Skin*. Riverbank Press, 1998.

———. *This Body*. 2004. HarperPerennial Canada, 2005.

Mezlekia, Nega. *Notes from the Hyena's Belly: Memories of My Ethiopian Boyhood*. Penguin, 2000.

NourbeSe Philip, M. *Looking for Livingstone: An Odyssey of Silence*. Mercury Press, 1991.

———. *Harriet's Daughter*. Women's Press, 2000.

Odhiambo, David N. *diss/ed banded nation*. Polestar, 1998.

Ollivier, Émile. *Passages*. L'Hexagone, 1991.

Sarsfield, Mairuth. *No Crystal Stair*. 1997. Women's Press, 2004.

Seaforth, Sybil. *In Silence the Strands Unravel*. Capricornus Enterprises, 1999.

Silvera, Makeda. *Her Head a Village, and Other Stories*. Press Gang, 1994.

Thomas, H. Nigel. *Behind the Face of Winter*. TSAR, 2001.

Non-Fiction

Clarke, George Elliott. *Odysseys Home: Mapping African-Canadian Literature*. University of Toronto Press, 2002.

Cooper, Afua. *The Hanging of Angélique: Canada, Slavery and the Burning of Montreal*. HarperCollins, 2006.

Foster, Cecil. *A Place Called Heaven: The Meaning of Being Black in Canada*. 1996. HarperPerennial Canada, 2002.

NourbeSe Philip, M. *A Genealogy of Resistance, and Other Essays.* Mercury Press, 1997.

Nurse, Donna Bailey. *What's a Black Critic to Do? Interviews, Profiles and Reviews of Black Writers.* Insomniac Press, 2003.

Senior, Olive. *Working Miracles: Women's Lives in the English-Speaking Caribbean.* Indiana University, 1991.

———, ed. *Encyclopedia of Jamaican Heritage.* Twin Guinep, 2003.

Silvera, Makeda, ed. *The Other Woman: Women of Colour in Contemporary Canadian Literature.* SisterVision Press, 1992.

Walcott, Rinaldo. *Rude: Contemporary Black Cultural Criticism.* Insomniac Press, 2000.

Memoir

Brown, Rosemary. *Being Brown: A Very Public Life.* 1989. Ballantine Books, 1990.

Clarke, Austin. *Love and Sweet Food: A Culinary Memoir.* Thomas Allen, 2004. (Originally published as *Pig Tails 'n Breadfruit: Rituals and Slave Food; A Barbadian Memoir.* Random House Canada, 1999.)

Henson, Josiah. *Father Henson's Story of His Own Life.* 1849. John P. Jewett, 1858.

Hill, Lawrence. *Black Berry, Sweet Juice: On Being Black and White in Canada.* 2001. HarperPerennial Canada, 2002.

Manley, Rachel. *Slipstream: A Daughter Remembers.* 2000. Vintage Canada, 2001.

Thomas, Verna. *Invisible Shadows: A Black Woman's Life in Nova Scotia.* Nimbus, 2001.

Poetry

Alford, Edna, and Claire Harris, eds. *Kitchen Talk: Contemporary Women's Prose and Poetry*. Red Deer College Press, 1992.

Allen, Lillian. *Women Do This Every Day: Selected Poems of Lillian Allen*. Women's Press, 1993.

———. *Psychic Unrest*. Insomniac Press, 1999.

Brand, Dionne. *Land to Light On*. McClelland & Stewart, 1997.

———. *Thirsty*. McClelland & Stewart, 2002.

Clarke, George Elliott. *Saltwater Spirituals and Deeper Blues*. Pottersfield Press, 1983.

———. *Whylah Falls*. 1990. Polestar, 2000.

Cooper, Afua. *Utterances and Incantations: Women, Poetry and Dub*. Sister Vision Press, 1999.

Dawes, Kwame. *Midland*. Goose Lane Editions, 2001.

———. *Shook Foil: A Collection of Reggae Poems*. Peepal Tree Press, 1997.

Harris, Claire. *She*. Goose Lane Editions, 2000.

Joseph, Clifton. *Metropolitan Blues*. Domestic Bliss, 1983.

Manley, Rachel. *A Light Left On*. Peepal Tree Press, 1992.

Mordecai, Pam, and Mervyn Morris, eds. *Jamaica Woman: An Anthology of Fifteen Jamaican Women Poets*. Heinemann Caribbean, 1980.

Morgan, Dwayne. *The Man Behind the Mic*. Up From The Roots, 2002.

Tynes, Maxine. *Borrowed Beauty*. Pottersfield Press, 1987.

Drama

Anthony, Trey. *'Da Kink in My Hair*. Playwrights Canada Press, 2005.

Borden, Walter. *Tightrope Time: Ain't Nuthin' More Than Some Itty Bitty Madness Between Twilight & Dawn*. Playwrights Canada Press, 2005.

Boyd, George Elroy. *Two, By George! Consecrated Ground and Gideon's Blues.* Stage Hand, 1996.

Clarke, George Elliott. *Beatrice Chancy.* Polestar, 1999.

Gale, Lorena. *Angélique*. Playwrights Canada Press, 1999.

Moodie, Andrew. *Riot*. Scirocco Drama, 1997.

———. *A Common Man's Guide to Loving Women*. Scirocco Drama, 1999.

———. *The Lady Smith*. Blizzard, 2000.

Odhiambo, David N. "afrocentric," in *Beyond the Pale: Dramatic Writing from First Nations Writers & Writers of Colour*, Yvette Nolan, Betty Quan, George Seremba, eds. Playwrights Canada Press, 1996.

NourbeSe Philip, M. *Coups and Calypsos*. Mercury Press, 2001.

Sears, Djanet. *Harlem Duet*. Scirocco Drama, 1997.

———, ed. *Testifyin': Contemporary African Canadian Drama*. Volume 1. Playwrights Canada Press, 2000.

Seremba, George. *Come Good Rain*. Blizzard, 1993.

Zimmerman, Cynthia, ed. *Taking the Stage: Selections from Plays by Canadian Women*. Playwrights Canada Press, 1995.

Anthologies

Black, Ayanna, ed. *Fiery Spirits & Voices: Canadian Writers of African Descent*. HarperPerennial Canada, 2000.

Camper, Carol, ed. *Miscegenation Blues: Voices of Mixed Race Women*. Sister Vision Press, 1994.

Clarke, George Elliott, ed. *Fire on the Water: An Anthology of Black Nova Scotian Writing*. 2 volumes. Pottersfield Press, 1991–1992.

———, ed. *Eyeing the North Star: Directions in African-Canadian Literature*. McClelland & Stewart, 1997.

Compton, Wayde, ed. *Bluesprint: Black British Columbian Literature and Orature*. Arsenal Pulp Press, 2001.

Cromwell, Liz. *One Out of Many: A Collection of Writings by 21 Black Women in Ontario.* Wacacro Productions, 1975.

Dabydeen, Cyril, ed. *A Shapely Fire: Changing the Literary Landscape.* Mosaic Press, 1987.

Elliott, Lorris, ed. *Other Voices: Writing by Blacks in Canada.* Williams-Wallace, 1985.

Hopkinson, Nalo, ed. *Whispers from the Cotton Tree Root: Caribbean Fabulist Fiction.* Invisible Cities Press, 2000.

Palmer, Hazelle, ed. *But Where Are You Really From? Stories About Identity and Assimilation in Canada.* Sister Vision Press, 1997.

Silvera, Makeda, ed. *Piece of My Heart: A Lesbian of Colour Anthology.* Sister Vision Press, 1991.

A Note on the Text and Acknowledgements

With the exception of the usage of Canadian spellings, corrections to obvious typographical errors, and minor changes made with the approval of the respective authors, we have retained the original style of the works as much as possible. As a result, there may be some variations in word spellings, hyphenations, and other punctuation.

I am grateful for the support of my publisher, Ellen Seligman, whose enthusiasm and editorial talents have done so much to nourish black Canadian writers. I am most of all grateful to my gifted editor, Anita Chong, who was a source of endless encouragement and who embraced this book as if it were her own; *Revival* would not exist without her. Thanks as well to University of Toronto professors Russell Brown and Patricia Vicari, whose teachings, alive inside of me for twenty years, daily rekindle my love of stories; to Jefferson Nurse and my sister Janet Bailey for their loving support; and to my wise and constant friend Elaine Kalman Naves.

André Alexis. Chapter 1 from *Childhood*. Copyright © 1998 by André Alexis. Reprinted by permission of McClelland & Stewart Ltd.

Shane Book. "H.N.I.C.," "The One," "Flagelliform: #9," "Flagelliform: Fact," and "Flagelliform: Ayahuasca" copyright © 2006 by Shane Book. Reprinted by permission of the author.

Kim Barry Brunhuber. Chapter 3 from *Kameleon Man*. Copyright © 2003 by Kim Barry Brunhuber. Reprinted by permission of Beach Holme Publishing.

Okey Chigbo. "The Housegirl" copyright © 2006 by Okey Chigbo. Reprinted by permission of the author.

George Elliott Clarke. "The Wisdom of Shelley" and "King Bee Blues" from *Whylah Falls* copyright © 2000 by George Elliott Clarke. Reprinted by permission of Polestar Book Publishers, an imprint of Raincoast Books. Excerpt from *George & Rue* by George Elliott Clarke, published by HarperCollins Publishers Ltd. Copyright © 2005 by George Elliott Clarke. All rights reserved. Reprinted by permission of HarperCollins Publishers Ltd.

Wayde Compton. "Legba Landed" reprinted with permission from *Bluesprint: Black British Columbia Literature and Orature*, edited by Wayde Compton (Arsenal Pulp Press, 2001). "Declaration of the Halfrican Nation" and "To Poitier" reprinted with permission from *Performance Bond* by Wayde Compton (Arsenal Pulp Press, 2004).

Afua Cooper. "On the Way to Sunday School," "Memories Have Tongue," and "Christopher Columbus" from *Memories Have Tongue* by Afua Cooper, published by Sister Vision Press. Copyright © 1992 by Afua Cooper. Reprinted by permission of the author.

Esi Edugyan. Extract from *The Second Life of Samuel Tyne* by Esi Edugyan. Copyright © 2004 by Esi Edugyan. Reprinted by permission of Knopf Canada.

Honor Ford-Smith. "History's Posse" and "My Mother's Last Dance" from *My Mother's Last Dance* by Honor Ford-Smith, published by Sister Vision Press. Copyright © 1996 by Honor Ford-Smith. Reprinted by permission of the author.

Lorna Goodison. "What We Carried That Carried Us," "Never Expect," and "Questions for Marcus Mosiah Garvey" from *Travelling Mercies*. Copyright © 2001 by Lorna Goodison. Reprinted by permission of McClelland & Stewart Ltd. Excerpts from *From Harvey River* by Lorna Goodison, scheduled for publication by McClelland & Stewart in early 2007. Copyright © 2006 by Lorna Goodison. Reprinted by permission of McClelland & Stewart Ltd.

Claire Harris. Untitled poem from *Fables from the Women's Quarters* copyright © 1984 by Claire Harris. "Travelling to Find a Remedy" from *Travelling to Find a Remedy* copyright © 1986 by Claire Harris. "Towards the Colour of Summer" and "Kay in Summer" from *The Conception of Winter* copyright © 1988 by Claire Harris. All reprinted by permission of Goose Lane Editions.

Lawrence Hill. Excerpt from *Any Known Blood* by Lawrence Hill, published by HarperCollins Publishers Ltd. Copyright © 1997 by Lawrence Hill. All rights reserved. Reprinted by permission of HarperCollins Publishers Ltd.

Nalo Hopkinson. Excerpt from *Midnight Robber* by Nalo Hopkinson. Copyright © 2000 by Nalo Hopkinson. Reprinted by permission of Warner Books, Inc.

Jemeni. "The Black Speaker" copyright © 2006 by Jemeni. Reprinted by permission of the author.

Dany Laferrière. Excerpt from *How to Make Love to a Negro* copyright © 1987 by Dany Laferrière. English translation copyright © 1987 by David Homel. Chapter 1, "The Gallery," from *An Aroma of Coffee* © by Dany Laferrière. English translation copyright © 1993 by David Homel. Reprinted by permission of David Homel.

Rachel Manley. Excerpt from Chapter 2, "Nomdmi," from *Drumblair* by Rachel Manley. Copyright © 1996 by Rachel Manley. Published in Canada by Knopf Canada.

Suzette Mayr. Excerpt from *The Widows* copyright © 1998 by Suzette Mayr, published by NeWest Press. Reprinted by permission of the publisher.

Tessa McWatt. Excerpt from *Dragons Cry* copyright © 2000 by Tessa McWatt. Reprinted by permission of Cormorant Books for The Riverbank Press.

Pamela Mordecai. "Poems Grow," "Convent," and "The Angel in the House" from *Certifiable* copyright © 2001 by Pamela Mordecai. Reprinted by permission of Goose Lane Editions.

Motion. "Girl" and "I Land" from *Motion in Poetry* copyright © 2002 by Wendy Brathwaite and Women's Press. Reprinted by permission of Canadian Scholars' Press Inc. and Women's Press.

M. NourbeSe Philip. "Salmon Courage" from *Salmon Courage* copyright © 1983 by M. NourbeSe Philip. "The Catechist" and "Meditations on the Declension of Beauty by the Girl with the Flying Cheek-bones" from *She Tries Her Tongue; Her Silence Softly Breaks* copyright © 1989 by M. NourbeSe Philip. Reprinted by permission of the author.

David N. Odhiambo. Excerpt from chapters 2–4 of *Kipligat's Chance* by David N. Odhiambo. Copyright © David N. Odhiambo, 2003. Reprinted by permission of Penguin Group (Canada), a division of Pearson Penguin Canada Inc.

Émile Ollivier. Chapter 1 from *Mother Solitude* by Émile Ollivier, translated by David Lobdell. English translation copyright © 1989 by David Lobdell. Reprinted by permission of Oberon Press.

Althea Prince. Chapters 2 and 3 from *Loving This Man* copyright © 2001 by Althea Prince. Reprinted by permission of Insomniac Press.

Robert Edison Sandiford. "The Breadfruit and the Maple Leaf" from *Sand for Snow: A Caribbean-Canadian Chronicle* copyright © 2003 by Robert Edison Sandiford. Reprinted by permission of the author and DC Books.

Olive Senior. "Do Angels Wear Brassieres?" from *Summer Lightning and Other Stories* copyright © 1986 by Olive Senior, published by Pearson Education Limited/Longman. Reprinted by permission of Pearson Education Limited. "Meditation on Yellow" from *Gardening in the Tropics* copyright © 1994 by Olive Senior. Reprinted by permission of Insomniac Press. "The Pull of Birds" and "Thirteen Ways of Looking at Blackbird" from *Over the Roofs of the World* copyright © 2005 by Olive Senior. Reprinted by permission of Insomniac Press.

Makeda Silvera. Extract from *The Heart Does Not Bend* by Makeda Silvera. Copyright © 2002 by Makeda Silvera. Reprinted by permission of Random House Canada.

H. Nigel Thomas. "How Loud Can the Village Cock Crow?" from *How Loud Can the Village Cock Crow? and Other Stories* copyright © 1995 by H. Nigel Thomas, published by Afo. Reprinted by permission of the author.

Ken Wiwa. Preface extracted from *In the Shadow of a Saint* by Ken Wiwa. Copyright © 2000 by Ken Wiwa. Reprinted by permission of Knopf Canada.